THE STARS ARE ON OUR SIDE

JENNIFER HARTMANN

For you, dear reader.
I wrote this book for you.

AUTHOR'S NOTE

Friends and readers,

I'm so thrilled that you've decided to read Gabe and Tabitha's angsty friends-to-lovers romance. Please know that this book is a <u>follow-up novel</u> to **STILL BEATING** and **LOTUS**. For the best reading experience, it is **highly** recommended that you read those two novels prior to starting this one. Because those books are with a publisher and this one is releasing independently, there was no way to link all three books into a series. *Still Beating* and *Lotus* are true standalones and can be read interchangeably. However, *The Stars Are on Our Side* is a meshing of both books and feature beloved characters and past storylines from those two worlds.

This story is truly a love letter to my readers who have been asking for this story for the past two years. I hope you enjoy the ride. ♡

For a list of triggers, please click here.

"It does not matter how slowly you go as long as you do not stop."
Confucius

PROLOGUE
TABITHA

February

Three months.

That's the time it took for my double wrist fracture to fully heal. It's also said to be the typical duration of a Midwest winter, even though the snowfall and frigid temperatures often stretch till May. It was the span of each trimester during my pregnancy with my daughter, and it's the length of time it took me to journey through the entire *Harry Potter* series.

It's also the time it took for him to lean in and kiss me.

"What do you think they are?"

Shoulder blades to grass blades, we gaze up at the midnight sky sprinkled in starlight as a gust of wind tries to steal my earmuffs. It's cold. February chill turns my nose pink as my breath escapes in little plumes of white.

I twist my head to the left, glancing at Gabe as he readjusts his knit cap. His nose is pink like mine; his cheeks, too.

"The stars?" he wonders, sparing me a quick look.

I nod.

Shrugging, he exhales a breath like a pillowy cloud. "Giant

balls of gas held together by their own gravity, I guess. Pretty wild if you ask me."

Memories invade me, adding to the frost in my bones. I flash back to a dank, mildewed basement and the narrow window across from me, too far away to reach. Stars would glow brightly on the other side of the glass, beckoning me to make a wish.

I always did.

They never listened.

I sigh, closing my eyes and letting my lids slowly flutter back open. "I don't like the stars," I admit. "They scare me."

It's a ridiculous thing to confess, but I feel safe with Gabe. I can tell him anything.

Three months ago, I walked through his front door, finally brave enough to venture out on my first date in nearly two years. I was lonely. Being a single mother is a specific kind of struggle, because it's the most beautiful, rewarding, soul-churning experience I could ever ask for, and yet...it's so *lonely*.

I walked through Gabe's front door, prepared to go on a date with his stepbrother.

But all I saw was him.

Love at first sight isn't a real thing—I know that. But there is certainly a *something* at first sight. A jolt, a magnetic draw, a heartbeat that skips and a world that narrows down, focusing on nothing but the space between you and that other person. It's a moment when intuition overpowers reason and butterflies burst to life inside of you, their delicate wings tickling your heart.

And in the span of these last three months, Gabe and I have become inseparable. I wouldn't call it dating. We haven't even shared our first real kiss. There has been couch-snuggling, hand-holding, and some innocent pecks on the cheeks and lips—but the truth is, I'm still scared. I haven't been brave enough to cross that line, because the last time I opened my heart to another man, that man died.

It wasn't a freak accident.

It wasn't a disease.

He was murdered.

Right in front of me.

Gabe pulls my thoughts away from my past and reaches for my hand. "You don't have to be scared of the stars, Tabs," he tells me softly.

Swallowing, I tilt my head skyward.

I live with a lot of fear. Too much. I'm afraid of men with dark eyes and receding hairlines, of closing my eyes at night, of losing the people I love, of not being a worthy mother...even of the stars.

I'm afraid of the night, of the shadows that dance around darkened corners, and of meaty hands grabbing me and siphoning away the little light I have left.

I'm afraid I'll never find my way back to the person I used to be.

I'm afraid that even if I do, I'll lose her again.

"Do you trust me?"

Gabe's question trips up my heartbeats as I turn to glance at him through the blanket of nightfall. My heart stumbles but my answer doesn't. "Yes."

That single word does something to him. His breath catches and his eyes glaze over. Blinking through a slow nod, he inches closer to me on the grass. "Will you do something for me?"

"Okay," I say. "Sure."

"Close your eyes."

I close my eyes. Darkness coils around me like a lonely ghost.

"Take a deep breath and picture yourself flying."

The familiar trickle of fear worms its way underneath my skin. It punctures my chest. Stings my throat.

I don't like flying.

I don't like the dark.

I don't like the things I see when I close my eyes.

My body stiffens, terror threatening to take me down.

And then I feel his hands on me, gliding up my arms, cradling my face. His breath is warm and soft as it feathers along my jawline. A sense of peace overrides the anxiety when his thumbs lightly graze the skin below my ears. Back and forth. Slow and tender.

"Can you see the stars?" he whispers.

I see them. They betrayed me once, so I squeeze my eyes tighter, wishing I could unsee them.

"They're flying with you. They're right by your side," he tells me. "Just don't look down."

My hands lift to lock around his wrists, using him as my

anchor. I let the feel of him, the warmth of him, fuse with starlight until all I feel is safe.

I let myself fly.

"The stars won't let you fall." Gabe leans over to press a gentle kiss to my hairline. His lips linger as his thumbs dance across my skin, and then he says, "I won't let you fall."

When my lids peel back open, his face is inches above me. Two green eyes skim over my features as his dark-blond hair drapes across his forehead. I raise a hand and brush the bangs away. "Thank you," I say. "That really helps."

He smiles for a beat. He smiles until the beats press on, infusing with something heavier, and that smile starts to fade.

Electricity crackles. A charge flickers between us and heat blossoms in my chest then travels south. My breath hitches as both of my hands slide to his neck and tug him closer.

His eyes flare with implication, with meaning. With want. I watch his throat work, his jaw clench, his gaze dipping to my mouth and holding.

We don't speak.

I say nothing.

I'm terrified that a slew of mismatched words will tumble out of me and the moment will be tainted with my bone-deep fears. All I do is pull him closer until his eyelids flutter and his lips part.

Gabe cups my cheek with one hand, his other braced beside me on the grass.

And then he leans in all the way.

He kisses me.

It's tentative, at first. Featherlight and curious. Our mouths meet and our lips part at the same time, and then his tongue flicks out and grazes my bottom lip. I inhale a sharp gasp, my body arching into him. My grip on his neck tightens until my fingernails are digging into his skin and a groan falls out of us both. Gabe sweeps his tongue against mine, tasting gently, and he does it again as my mouth opens wider and I draw him closer.

He devours me.

Whimpers catch in my throat as our faces angle, his hand in my hair, my earmuffs toppling off my head. We kiss and we kiss, and my leg winds around his hip, his tongue plunging in and out of my mouth as the temperature in the air rises to a scorching degree.

I'm floating.

I'm weightless.

I'm flying.

And then I'm nosediving from ten-thousand feet in the air with my heart in my throat.

The moment Gabe takes my wrists in his hands and lifts them above my head, the scene changes. Darkness creeps into my psyche. The man looming over me morphs into my worst nightmare, laughing in my ear as he violates me with my arms chained behind my back.

My eyes ping open and it's him.

The monster.

The man who ruined me.

My captor.

"You taste so sweet, Kitten," he snarls, inserting his large body between my legs and taking what was never meant for him.

A scream is trapped in the back of my throat.

Cement walls cage me in.

The smell of rot and sewage infiltrates my senses and I writhe and fight and beg.

Matthew.

Matthew watches from a few feet away, chained to his own pole. He can't help me. He can't stop this. And still, I cry out for him.

Matthew.

Please save me.

Matthew, Matthew…MATTHEW!

I inhale a sharp breath when a faraway sound seeps into my ears, wrenching me from chains and monsters and the echo of drippy, dirty pipes.

It's a choking sound.

A sound of absolute horror.

Gabe stares down at me like something inside of him just shriveled up and died.

I freeze.

I gasp.

I blink away the past and career back into the present moment.

The moment when Gabe is holding me,
Cherishing me,
Kissing me beneath the stars…
And I just said another man's name.

CHAPTER 1

GABE

July, five months later

I'm certain one can find dignity in most things, but there is no dignity in unrequited love.

It's fucking painful.

There's no harmony, no beauty, no triumph in it. There is no hard-fought prize to be won. I'd go so far as to say it's a curse—especially in these moments when the sun wraps her up in a golden blanket, spotlighting her perfection like the universe is dangling a carrot in front of me, then yanking it back the moment I move in for a bite.

Maybe not a carrot; carrots are offensive.

She's that all-you-can-eat taco bar spread out by the beach at an all-inclusive resort while a salt breeze kisses your skin and waves crash along the shoreline like your favorite song.

But then a storm rolls in, raining it all out.

You're miserable, drenched, chilled to the bone.

Worst of all, you're still hungry.

That's what one-sided love with your dream girl feels like. More so because she's not just a dream girl that I love from afar—we're friends.

More than friends, really. I'm her almost-everything.

And an almost-everything is a specific kind of torture.

"Cannonball!"

Sydney dives into the swimming pool ass-first, and the

splashback has me pulling my attention away from Tabitha as I swat wet hair off my face. I glance into the pool, the sun sinking behind a cloud. My ride-or-die since childhood shrieks when she catapults herself up from the deep end and shakes water from her hair.

"It's cold, it's cold, it's really freakin' cold!" she chants, skin puckered with goosebumps. "Why is it so cold?"

Her fiancé, Oliver—who also happens to be my stepbrother—floats beside her in a unicorn-shaped innertube, sipping strawberry slush from a wide straw. "The water is only seventy-four degrees," he deadpans. "That is the reason, I would deduce."

She splashes him.

A smile tips my lips while I watch my favorite people enjoy the magic of a midwestern summer afternoon. Sipping my beer, I lift a hand to my brow and squint as a harsh wash of light drags across my vision. My gaze tracks Tabitha as she steps toward the pool and dips her toes into the water. She winces and pulls back, confirming Sydney's claim that it's really freakin' cold.

Chugging the rest of my beer, I discard the empty bottle beside me and stand from the chaise lounge. She glances up when I begin to approach, her smile quick to bloom.

It's not the same smile I witnessed eight months ago when she stepped through my front door and into my life, after arriving for a date with Oliver that went nowhere.

The smile doesn't reach her eyes anymore.

I whip off my sunglasses, revealing that mine still does. "C'mon, Tabs," I call out, my bare feet slapping the pavement as I saunter up to her. "Jump in. I'll give you a push if you want."

"It's freezing," she laughs lightly. She tugs at her high ponytail, black like a raven's wing. "I need to get used to it first."

"Nope, that's way worse. You jump in and suffer for five seconds—everyone knows that."

My chest pangs with double meaning.

I don't think she knows that.

Tabitha steps away from the pool's edge, adjusting the thin strap of her minty, one-piece swimsuit as brown eyes with matching green flecks sweep up to me. "Sunscreen first. Then I'll think about it."

"I got you." I jog the rest of the way over to the covered patio and snatch the tube of sunscreen off one of the glass tabletops.

I'm always stocked with sunscreen now, especially after my neighbors, Sydney and Oliver, installed an inground swimming pool this past May. I don't spend too much time in direct sunlight due to a third-degree burn I suffered seven months ago on Christmas day. The scar covers a good portion of my upper arm, travels up my neck, and fades just before it reaches my jawline. I call it my epic battle wound, but Sydney calls it a love scar.

After all, I got it while saving her from a burning bedroom. Eternal dibs on our Netflix-binge marathons were earned, that's for sure. That, and a lifetime supply of free taco dip.

Tabitha follows me over to the patio, her arms draped across her chest like a hug. I squeeze a large dollop of cream into my palm, keeping my gaze leveled with my task and not on her polka-dotted swimsuit inching into my periphery. When I finally glance up, her focus has zeroed in on my scar.

It's not a revelation, yet she always seems to zone out when her eyes drink in the leathery, raised skin. They glaze over and she retreats. She goes somewhere else.

I never make a big deal about it, often slicing through the brief tension with a distraction or humor. Snatching her by the wrist, I tug her toward me with a playful smile. "Turn around."

She blinks as the fog fades from her eyes and a sheepish smile crests. "Sorry, I spaced."

She's been doing that a lot lately.

Within the eight months I've known her, Tabitha Brighton has wilted. Her resilience gained cracks, and her colorful spirit dimmed to gray.

It started with a kiss, a breath of new life.

It ended with my heart in a coffin.

Clearing her throat, she swivels around and faces the pool, just as Sydney leaps onto Oliver until he topples off the inner-tube, his daiquiri marginally spared. A giggle spills out of Tabitha when Oliver sets the glass along the edge of the pool and Sydney jumps onto his back and links her ankles, their laughter louder than the nineties playlist seeping through the speakers.

Sex and Candy by Marcy Playground plays as I begin to lather her in sunscreen.

Her skin is white as snow but warm to the touch. My hands trail up and down her arms, over her collarbone, down her back, and I swear she shivers, but it could be the chill from the cream.

I'm reminded of a memory from early February when she sat between my legs on the living room floor, my back pressed against the couch. I'd been giving her a massage, my hands eager to explore, my heart racing with the yearning to bend over and kiss that sweet spot right below her ear where a tiny birthmark colored her pale skin. I'd been taking our relationship slow, familiar with her history, knowing the horrors she went through at the hands of a madman.

Knowing she'd been in love before, and that I had a damn lot to live up to.

She made a whimper-like sound that had my blood rushing south when my thumbs kneaded a muscle at the peak of her spine. I'd been bold, trailing my hands down her body and cinching her waist as I dipped my nose to the crown of her head. The moment I breathed her in, my own groan falling out and feathering against her hair, Tabitha went stiff in my arms. She wiggled free of my grip and muttered something about hearing her baby daughter, Hope, crying before disappearing down the hallway.

I never ended up kissing her that night.

Sometimes, I wish I never had at all.

The scent of Banana Boat and jasmine shampoo float over to me, mingling with chlorine when a warm breeze sweeps through. Tabitha leans into me a little, her ponytail tickling my chin, and I try not to read into the gesture. I don't overanalyze the choppy breath that escapes her when my fingers accidentally graze along the side of her breast.

And I absolutely ignore the heated look she sends me when she turns around and murmurs a raspy, "Thank you."

Cloud cover battles with the onslaught of sun rays overhead as her eyes dip, slide up to mine, then return to her flip-flops. She's lost in her own war.

I like to think that I'm a part of that war, but I can't allow myself to mull over it for it too long. I laid down my sword five months ago when the girl I was helplessly falling for surrendered to her dark past—to the ghost of another man—forsaking a future with me.

It was a heart-rending defeat.

But I'm a patient soldier, and I'll wait. I'll wait until she's ready to see me for who I am, instead of as the man who is replacing her long-lost love.

"When you're done copping a feel with your wifey, get your ass in here," Sydney bellows as she bounces in the water. "I want to play chicken."

Wifey.

She has no idea how much that nickname cuts me to the bone. I never let on to the pain, though—I put the familiar mask on and shoot Syd a wink. "One sec."

Oliver frowns, his confusion carrying over to us. "Chicken?" he wonders.

"Yeah, the shoulder game."

"We will acquire poultry for shouldering?"

I bark a laugh as Tabitha takes the sunscreen from my hand and squeezes a portion into her own palm.

My stepbrother is an interesting character. After being sheltered away from society for twenty-two years, he still embodies a new-to-the-world innocence and an articulate dialect that never ceases to make me smile, even on the darker days.

Chuckling softly, Tabitha lifts a hand, an espresso-brown eyebrow arching with question.

I extend both arms. "Feel me up. I'm all yours."

A blush stains her cheekbones as she reaches out, smearing the sun protectant over my scar. Her touch is tender. Searching. My skin heats as her hand skims and her gaze floats over to me with that same kind of searching. I can't prevent a hiss from escaping, from breaching the air and sounding like a carnal sin.

She pulls back, throat bobbing through a swallow. "You should wear a wetsuit or something...so your scar is more protected from the sun. I worry."

It's true she's always worrying about me. While I find comfort in that, I know it's more of a mother's love, paralleling the type of worry she doles out when her sixteen-month-old daughter sticks a small, circular object in her mouth. It's not the kind of love I crave.

It's not the kind of love *he* had.

Tension still crackles between us, and instead of lighting a match, I point at the water to douse the flame that is determined to incinerate me. "We've got two hours before your sitter needs to bolt," I announce, schooling my voice not to break. "That's two hours of belly laughter, music, friends, and a riveting game of chicken, because, apparently, we're fourteen again. Zero parental duties, zero responsibility, and zero frowns. Only sun and fun. Got it?"

The shadows that have been teasing her eyes all day are stolen by a sunbeam that breaks through the clouds.

Sunshine wins.

"Got it," she says, teeth flashing for one glorious second. She shakes her arms at her sides, as if ridding herself of any lingering darkness. "Only fun."

I watch, my grin charmed, as Tabitha marches away, shimmies out of her flip-flops, and pauses at the edge of the pool.

There is no hesitation this time. She shuts her eyes, holds her nose, and dives right in.

And *God…*

How I wish she'd do the same with me.

This was a shit idea.

Tabitha is perched atop my shoulders, her thighs hugging my face to the point where I'm damn grateful for the arctic water soaking through my swim trunks.

Oliver teeters across from me, holding on to his counterpart, as the girls squeal and laugh, their arms engaging in a light-hearted war.

"Oliver! You're going to drop me," Syd shrieks, nearly toppling, her giggles more to blame for her impaired balance than Oliver is.

"Well…" he says, voice strained, grip white-knuckled around her knees. "Perhaps…you should stop squirming so much."

"That's the point of the game!"

My forearms are locked around Tabitha's upper thighs as she crisscrosses her ankles at my chest. Her ponytail came loose two battles back, causing long, dark hair to curtain my face, the dampened ends tickling my skin. Her thighs squeeze, and I hold the groan in the back of my throat. When Sydney gains the upper hand, Tabitha almost tips, catching herself by latching onto my hair with her fist.

The groan cuts loose. I cover it with a cough.

"Sorry!" Tabitha squeaks through a laugh. Her grip loosens. "I didn't mean to—"

She almost slips again, so my hand curls around one of her inner thighs to hold her steady. I feel her tense, my fingers digging into dangerously soft skin. My heart rate jack-knifes.

Regrouping, the girls' hands interlock as they sway precariously back and forth, Sydney laughing so hard Oliver can hardly maintain his grip on her.

I use his moment of weakness to my advantage, swinging Tabitha sharply to the left, in the same direction Syd is slipping. Holding tight, I watch as my girl goes in for the kill and yanks her opponent until Sydney is plummeting into the water with a shrill yelp.

She pops back up, inhaling a giant breath, her light-blonde hair shimmering in the sun. "Dammit."

Oliver sighs. "It appears we've been defeated." He shakes his head with disappointment. "My apologies. I had a neck cramp."

Tabitha raises her arms in the air with victory before I slide her down my back, and we face each other with a high five. When our hands part, she's quick to pounce on me with a hug. Her arms lace around my neck and she buries her face into the curve of my shoulder, her breath warming the icy droplets on my skin. "Thank you," she whispers. "I think I needed that."

My eyes catch with Sydney's over the top of Tabitha's head, and Syd pulses her eyebrows knowingly.

I only recently confided in Sydney that my relationship with Tabitha had taken a turn from romantic to platonic. My best friend had been on cloud nine over the past few months, thinking I'd finally found my match, right at the same time she reconnected with her childhood soulmate.

Everyone was happy, blissful and thriving. It made the confession daunting.

I've been an eternal bachelor all my life. It's not something I'm proud of, but it was easier that way. Emotion has always been difficult for me, making genuine connection an illusive idealism I always thought was limited to movies and fiction books.

Until there was Tabitha.

Interestingly enough, Sydney didn't buy it. She told me

Tabitha just needed time. Patience. She said we were written in the stars, and she was convinced of that, just as she was convinced that the look in Tabitha's eyes went far deeper than platonic every time she glanced my way.

I suppose that gave me a sliver of hope.

The thing is, hope can be a savior, or it can be an executioner. There's no way to know which way the cards will fall. Only time will tell, and time is just as unpredictable as hope.

Tabitha releases me.

Our eyes tangle when she lowers to her feet, and I pretend that I don't see that same glimmer of hope staring back at me.

She pushes an inky strand of hair from her eyes and tucks it behind her ear. Dancing away from me, a tiny smile pulls at her lips. "I'm going to see if Mandy texted me," she says. "I should check on Hope."

I nod, and she moves to the other end of the pool.

When she's out of earshot, Sydney swims toward me and punches me on the shoulder. "God, you two drive me crazy. It's like watching a TV show where the two main characters are clearly in love, but the writers draw that shit out just to torture us. Like Mulder and Scully. Or Buffy and Spike." Her lips twist. "I'm calling you guys 'Spuffy' from now on."

The sound I make is part hum, part huff. Syd is obsessed with all things nineties. "An explosion of no."

"It does seem imminent," Oliver agrees. "The heart is a complicated beast. Sometimes it wants, and sometimes it hurts to want." He inches over to the side of the pool and leans back on his elbows. "If I've learned anything from the human condition in recent months, it's that *want* tends to win out. It's too powerful to remain dormant."

Hope.

Stop giving me fucking hope.

Before I can scoff at them, the song changes and the carefree mood is compromised.

I'm not sure what's happening right away. First thing I notice is that Tabitha goes ramrod still near the edge of the pool. Stiff as a beam.

"Hey. Tabs." My voice clings to a smile as I call out to her, because it doesn't know any better. "You okay over there?"

Sydney is even more oblivious than me, waving her hands in

the air as the music chimes loud over the twitter of songbirds. "Ooh, I love this one."

It's a Radiohead song. *Karma Police*, if I recall.

"Tabs."

She doesn't respond. Her eyes are locked on Sydney's cell phone lying idle on a nearby stool.

Quickly, I wade toward her, abandoning my sunglasses along the side of the pool before I pull myself out. "Tabitha," I repeat, concern slicing at my chest. She's still cloaked in vacancy. A darkness festers in her eyes, almost like her pupils are trying to swallow any trace of rich chocolate and lively green.

Sydney belts lyrics from the pool behind me, swaying back and forth.

"Talk to me." When I reach her, I extend my hand. "Hey…"

She's frozen.

I curl my fingers around her upper arm in a tender hold. "Are you—"

I'm blindsided when she gasps, whips around, and shoves at my chest, forcing me to stumble backward into the water with a resounding splash. I breach the surface quickly, sputtering as I sweep wet bangs from my eyes and scrub a hand over my face, expression steeped in bewilderment.

Her eyes widen to saucers.

All color drains from her cheeks.

She starts trembling, shaking, inching back and away from me, horror lacing the little croaking sound she lets out. "Oh God…I-I'm sorry…"

I'm not sure if I should approach or retreat.

She looks like she's going to be sick.

"I'm so sorry." Her words are a fractured whisper as she spins around, then takes off.

I follow.

I have to follow.

"Tabs!" Deep concern bleeds into my voice and makes my heart gallop with fear as I jump out of the water. I race after her through the grass, toward my house on the left. "Tabitha, wait."

She keeps running. She runs until she collapses near my driveway, head dropping forward as her hands fist the blades of grass.

I skid to a stop and fall to my knees, wasting no time as I pull her into my arms.

Sobs pour out of her.

Anguish rips through her body, causing her to shake desperately as I clutch her.

"Hey, hey, you're okay," I whisper near her ear, kissing her temple. "It was just a moment. A blip. You're fine."

She swings her head back and forth, clinging to my bare shoulders, nails digging into me. "No. I-I can't do this. I-it's getting worse," she sniffles, close to hyperventilating. "God, Gabe…"

I do what I always do when she starts to unravel in my arms, soaking my skin with tears. I cup her face between both hands and stroke my thumbs right beneath her ears, leaning in to whisper, "Shh. Close your eyes."

She obeys. She always obeys.

"You're flying," I say gently, still caressing, still holding onto her. "You're free. You're safe."

She nods, her breathing beginning to steady, her body going lax as her eyelids flutter.

"Don't look down, okay?"

She nods again, inhaling.

Exhaling.

"Don't look down."

The shudders quell, her grip on me easing.

I press a kiss to her hair, then lay my cheek atop her head, my thumbs brushing and grazing until she's calm.

In the beginning, her pain was just a ghost. It would flicker in her eyes every now and then when a long silence lapsed, or when she stared up at the stars for too long.

Now it's become a living thing.

And living things have a pulse, a will, a beating heart. They come with claws and sharp teeth. There's no telling what a living thing might do.

Tabitha leans back, her eyes rimmed red and glistening with tears. She stares at me for a long moment. A breeze rolls through, taking her hair with it, sending the tree branches into a slow dance overhead. Leaves break free from stems and float down, foliage and flower buds landing beside us.

She plucks a pink bud from the grass and caresses it between her fingers.

"I'm going to do it, Gabe," she murmurs, looking up at me, a tear slipping free and pooling at the corner of her mouth. She licks it away, lips parting with a frayed breath. "I'm going to talk to the writer. I want to tell him my story."

I blink.

I didn't think she was going to do it. She said it would be too much, too hard, too triggering.

Skimming my thumb across her cheekbone, I whisper. "Are you sure?"

"I'm sure."

"What if…" Panic rains down on me. It settles in my throat and feels like a noose. It bites at my chest, causing my next words to tinge with acid on my tongue. "What if I lose you?"

The smallest smile strains Tabitha's mouth. "I'm already lost," she says, glancing down at the bud pressed between her thumb and finger. A sprig of new life, waiting to bloom. "I need to go there to come back."

CHAPTER 2

TABITHA

Two glasses of orange juice tumble off my tray in slow motion. I'm less than graceful as I attempt a dramatic balancing act, causing the glasses to leap into the air like it's an Olympic event and shatter onto the kitchen floor at my feet.

"I'll be dockin' your paycheck for that, Brighton," Smithers barks from his perch at the cooktop.

Sighing, I pinch the bridge of my nose with my free hand, glancing at the clock. It's 11:02, which is one minute past the last time I checked, and one minute closer to my interview.

My stomach clenches.

I'm off my game today; it's true.

In less than five hours, I'll be on my way to spill my darkest secrets to a man I don't even know. A stranger. To say I'm rattled would be an understatement.

"Sorry, Smithers." I bend to retrieve the larger pieces of glass, piling them onto my now-empty tray. When I toss an apologetic glance over my shoulder at my boss, he's unapologetically leering at my backside.

I straighten and clear my throat, the clenching of my belly twisting tighter with anxiety, before moving out of his line of sight to retrieve a broom.

Bacon sizzles from a frying pan as a hint of maple wafts underneath my nose, mingling with the scent of our signature sausage gravy. The lunch-hour rush is upon us, but patrons hardly stop in for club sandwiches and soup and salad combos. It's all about the breakfast.

Happy Plates Pancake House sits right on the outskirts of Marengo, Illinois in a village called Clancy. With a population of only two-hundred-and-fifty, it's nearly a ghost town, save for the little restaurant with yellow bricks and a smiling pancake mascot —the only proof of life on most days.

The pancake house is where I spend the majority of my time, working grueling hours just to keep a roof over our heads. Government assistance, state insurance, and a humble two-bedroom house Hope's grandparents purchased for us are the only things keeping me and my baby daughter afloat.

I shouldn't complain.

With my unsavory backstory and a small child that limits my availability, I'm lucky to have a job at all. Most employers took one glance at my resume, strained a smile that reeked of pity, and sent me on my way, never to follow up again.

I'm grateful.

I am.

Smithers has two fresh glasses of juice sitting on the counter for me when I finish cleaning up the mess. I glance at the ticket, smile my thanks, then push through the kitchen door with a steadier grip on my tray.

I make my way toward table number seven, offering wide smiles to some of the regulars, including a middle-aged gentleman and his service dog—a little Bichon Frisé with the cutest corkscrew curls puffed out around its face—along with two elderly ladies who stop in for coffee and cottage cheese with fruit every single morning and tip me far more than what the bill suggests.

I'm mid-grin when my attention jerks to the right and I spot the familiar faces sitting at table seven. "Oh my gosh…" My smile grows, blooming with genuine affection. "What are you two doing here?"

Cora gives me an enthusiastic wave from the booth, while Dean twists around in his seat to greet me with a signature wink.

Cora Lawson and Dean Asher.

Both dear friends. Both survivors of an unspeakable horror…like me.

It's not a noble club to be a part of, but it brought us together, and I'd rather be in it with them than trudge through the aftermath lost and alone.

"Surprise." Cora stretches a smile, teeth flashing white. Golden-blonde hair drapes over both shoulders, the loose curls bouncing when she jumps from the booth to hug me. She's filled out more over the past year, her soft curves molding against my willowy frame. "I know you don't love surprises, but I figured you'd make an exception in this case," she says.

I almost drop the orange juice again when she untangles herself from my one-armed hug. Dean swoops in to snag the glasses off the tray before they plummet for a second time, his reflexes sharper than mine.

My sigh of relief earns me another wink.

"Whoops," I mutter with a self-deprecating chuckle, letting the tray fall to my side. "I already dropped them once in the kitchen."

"I was wondering why you smelled like a creamsicle," Cora notes, wrinkling her nose.

They both glance down at my still-damp pantlegs and soggy sneakers.

"Orange juice and vanilla body mist." I shrug. "I guess it could be worse."

She laughs. "We'll pretend you planned it."

"Well, I'm glad I could be of service," Dean adds, leaning back in the booth, one hand ruffling his mess of dark hair. "I can be useful on occasion."

Cora folds her muted-rose lips between her teeth as she nods slowly. "You did manage to change out the roll of toilet paper this morning—in the correct *over* position."

"Be not afraid of greatness."

"Dean." She gasps. "Did you just Shakespeare me?"

"You can't Shakespeare anyone. It's not a verb."

Another gasp. "Did you just English-teacher me?" Her eyes narrow, but they don't dim. Only love leaks out, strengthening her jaunty smile.

Their hands clasp over the tabletop and I duck my head to look away.

Cora and Dean went through the same traumatic ordeal I did. The difference is, they came out of it together.

I came out alone.

There are moments when the notion sinks me, drenching me in a shot of misplaced envy. Within those moments, I lose myself. I slip farther away from the person I was, from the person I want to be again. It's an awful feeling, looking upon these courageous, loving people and being consumed with dark thoughts.

It's not fair.

Two months ago, I fell apart in Cora's backyard beneath a sky of fireworks when a simple question echoed through the night and sent me into a blinding panic attack. Dean was there to catch me. Cora was there to hold me.

And they were both there to cling to each other, watching helplessly as my pieces came loose.

"Dean heads back to Bloomington tonight," Cora announces, pulling her hand away from Dean's and curling it around her glass of juice. Her eyes flick up to me. "I'm going to come over after your interview. I don't want you to be alone."

The statement brings me back to the restaurant and I shake my head with a weak smile. "That's so sweet of you to offer, but I won't be alone. Gabe will be with me."

She nods, a wash of relief stealing her expression—or maybe it's hope.

Cora was the person I confided in the moment I realized I'd been developing feelings for someone.

Someone new.

Someone…*else.*

She was the person I confided in the moment I broke, too.

"Well, how about a coffee date tomorrow after work? I'm free after four o'clock."

"That sounds great. I'll have Hope with me."

"Even better." She smiles kindly. "I'm a little jealous that my sister sees her more than me. I've considered giving up the whole teaching thing to become Hope's live-in nanny. You'd be fine with that, right? I'm a great roommate. Laundry is my specialty."

A giggle spills out of me. "Do you cook?"

Her gaze skates back to Dean across the table. "On weekends, yes, Dean does cook."

"See?" He winks at her. "Useful."

Cora and Dean are currently in a long-distance relationship due to complicated circumstances, only seeing each other on the weekends until Dean is able to secure a job transfer back to his hometown with Cora.

While they came out of the horror alive, they did not come out unscathed. What should have been a blissful reunion ended up becoming another painful nightmare.

Dean was engaged to Cora's sister, Mandy, at the time.

And that was…complicated.

I'm about to reply but my words are cut short. I flick my head to the right when a patron begins to cough. It's the gurgling kind, phlegmy and lung-rattling.

It's strange the things that trigger me these days. I've become susceptible to insignificant moments.

A string of familiar words. A song. The way the breeze kisses my face when I step outside my front door.

A cough.

I stare at the coughing man as coffee dribbles over the top of his ceramic mug. He's heavyset and balding, wearing a white T-shirt soiled with sweat stains. He clears his throat, regaining his composure, and glances over at me when he senses my zoned-out stare aimed in his direction.

A lecherous grin curls on his lips.

I blanch, a suffocating feeling squeezing my chest, my blood freezing with ice.

He rises from the booth.

Sights set on me.

He hobbles forward and a familiar odor commandeers my senses, curdling my stomach. Gasoline and rot. Something odd, like moldy vegetables. Carrots simmering in a pot of waste.

The man stops right in front of me.

His eyes are dark and beady, swirling with every shade of gray. Leaning in, his foul breath mists my cheek as he whispers, "I've missed you, Kitten."

Stars float behind my eyes as the tray clamors to the vinyl flooring.

Or maybe it's cold cement.

Chains…I think there are chains.

Blood and darkness.

Hopelessness.

No, no, no.

He's dead.

The man is dead and he can't hurt me anymore.

This isn't real, this isn't real…

"Tabitha?"

My name punctures through the thick fog threatening to choke me. I blink, inhaling a sharp breath before my knees buckle, and turn to my left, finding Cora gazing at me with warmth and worry. "What?" I murmur, out of sorts. When I look back at the man, he's still sitting in the booth, sipping his coffee.

He does send me a smile, but it's kind.

A friendly hello.

"Are you okay?" Dean wonders.

More warmth, more worry, more evidence that I am not okay.

I squeeze my eyes shut, shaking my head as if to dislodge the memories. "Sorry. It's been one of those mornings." Bending, I retrieve the fallen tray and pop back up with a smile that takes far too much effort to produce.

Cora and Dean stare back at me, their own smiles long gone.

"I really appreciate you guys coming by," I fluster, combing shaky fingers through my side ponytail. "I need to get back to work, but I'll stop over and take your orders in a few minutes."

Swiveling around, I make a quick escape, running from the dark cloud eager to chase after me.

I need therapy.

That's the main reason I connected with the writer who lives three doors down from Gabe. He writes psychological thriller novels, making him a prime candidate for hearing my story.

For *writing* my story.

Regrettably, my particular state insurance plan doesn't cover therapy.

My checking account doesn't come close to providing the extra funds required to put toward my mental health.

And my severed education and lack of employment history doesn't afford me any decent-paying positions other than being a grocery store clerk or a diner waitress.

In the beginning, my only source of therapy was my pregnancy and the subsequent birth of my daughter, Hope. The knowledge that Hope was a precious piece of him—of *us*—was enough to anchor me for a little while. After all, life as a single mother doesn't leave much room for focusing on anything other than the little human wholly reliant on you.

But she's getting older now.

Walking. Saying a few words. Making tiny friends at daycare. Occupying herself with toys and cartoons.

And I'm...slipping.

There are gaps. Idle lapses. Too many quiet moments.

Don't look down, don't look down.

Keep flying.

Gabe's words flicker through my mind, centering me, as I push through the kitchen door and drink in a calming breath. When the world becomes too loud, and my mind too crowded, he tells me to close my eyes and envision myself flying.

Soaring, weightless, rising above it all.

He gives me wings.

And I realize...

I may not have a licensed doctor, or a comfy armchair, or a quiet office to purge my pain.

But I do have Gabe.

CHAPTER 3

TABITHA

I spin the tungsten ring around my finger as the band reflects a sliver of window light. I'm not sure why I put it on. It's way too big, sliding over my knuckle whenever I drop my hand at my side. Maybe it's a sign. Maybe it's telling me I should tuck it back into the dresser drawer and forget the moment he placed it in my palm.

The drawer is partway open so I peer inside at the clutter, my eyes landing on the old mechanical wristwatch staring up at me. The failing alarm mechanism echoes around me like a cacophony of shrieking cicadas as I zone out. It's still broken, still as unlucky as it's ever been.

Luck.

It's ironic how he believed in good fortune when he had so little of it in the end.

"Are you ready?"

Shaking away the ringing in my ears, I slam the drawer shut and paint a smile on my lips, pivoting toward Mandy as I let the ring slip into my opposite hand. "I think so. I'm not sure how ready I can be, to be honest."

Her trademark white-blonde hair, usually colorless, glints beneath the hall light as she stands outside my bedroom door, the glow tingeing it a shade of yellow. She smiles her Mandy smile. A Mandy smile is all teeth and eye twinkles, cheeks stretched wide, nose crinkled. "Personally, I think it's a terrible idea." Snapping her gum that smells like passion fruit, she swoops a fist into the air, as if to say, "go team!," and harnesses that smile. "But I'm cheering you on. Poms-poms, short skirt, cringey rhymes—the whole shebang."

"Thanks?" I chuckle. "I think."

"I mean, all I can imagine is mind-altering post-traumatic stress rising to the surface and suffocating you until you're no longer a functional member of society. It doesn't sound good." Somehow, the smile sticks. "Not at all."

I blanch a little at the mental image.

Is she right?

Am I setting myself up for greater emotional damage by reliving the very worst thing that ever happened to me? It sounds plausible.

Likely, even.

My chest fills with dread.

Before the notion can sink me, Hope toddles from the main living area, pushing through Mandy's legs and rushing toward me with a shrieky, "Mama!"

Blinking away my nerves, I slip the ring into the front pocket of my jeans and crouch down to welcome a teetering hug. Her dark-brown curls smell like baby powder and lavender, and my eyes mist.

The scent of lavender always does that to me.

"Mama go?" Hope murmurs into the crook of my neck.

Guilt and shame wash over me.

I only just picked her up from the in-home daycare provider an hour ago and now I have to leave again. Mandy is my non-work-related babysitter, always coming to the rescue when I need an hour or two for self-care, or a Netflix-binge with Gabe.

Our friendship is a strange one, as we couldn't be more different. She's a salon manager, always dressed to the nines in the latest fashion trends, makeup perfect, not an eyelash out of place. She smells like freshly blow-dried hair and orange honeysuckles.

I usually smell like spilled milk and goldfish crackers and I'm lucky if I can find a set of unwrinkled clothes that match. While my friendship with her sister, Cora, is steeped in deep connection and mutual strength, my friendship with Mandy is easy and fun. She has no filter, which is an honesty I can appreciate.

It's necessary sometimes.

Graciously, she offered to watch my daughter while I head to

THE STARS ARE ON OUR SIDE   29

my interview with Evan Hart—the fiction writer who agreed to hear my story and weave it into a new novel.

It was my idea. This wasn't a ploy to sensationalize my trauma and make money off of my greatest loss.

I wanted this.

I need this.

He's even going to split the royalties with me, which will help with living expenses immensely.

"I won't be long, Pumpkin," I tell Hope, pressing a kiss to her soft cheek. "Miss Mandy is here to play with you. She'll make you your favorite noodles for dinner, tuck you in, and..." Lifting my eyes to Mandy, I watch her perfectly-shaded eyebrows arc, as if wondering what I'm about to rope her into. "And sing you all the lullabies."

"Yay!" Hope hops up and down like a bunny.

Mandy glares at me from the doorway.

My smile is twice as genuine when I pull myself to a stand, caressing Hope's tufts of soft curls. "She loves the Gummy Bear song."

"You're evil."

"And the Barney song."

"Soulless."

I laugh. Sparing the mirror a final glance, I flick my fingers through my long tresses, noting that my hair never seems to hold a curl anymore.

It doesn't hold its curl in the same way my smile doesn't hold its sparkle.

But I've learned to fake it.

Mandy moves from the doorway to let me pass and I slip into my sandals that are strewn across the hallway, thanks to Hope.

"Those don't match." She follows me to the foyer, which is basically just an owl-printed welcome mat and a coat hanger. "I refuse to let you walk out the door like that."

I glance down at the sandals, realizing she's right.

I never would have noticed.

Looking around for one of the two missing sandals, my cell phone sings from my back pocket as I snatch my purse from a wall hanger. The ringtone is a Bad Omens song—Gabe's favorite band.

Smiling, I answer his call. "Hey, you. I'm just heading out now."

A chatter of noise crackles in the background. Power drills and jackhammering. Gabe is an on-site supervisor for a construction company, having traded in his khakis and desk job as a project manager for a position providing more physical labor; something he craved.

His voice tries to override the construction noise. "Tabs? Can you hear me?"

"Kind of." I'm still on the hunt for the missing sandal as I balance the phone between my ear and shoulder. "How's work?"

"It's work," he says, sounding like he's moving away from the racket. "It's not where I want to be."

"I'll be okay. This is right. It feels like something I need to do."

"I wanted to be there."

Warmth sweeps through me, a soft smile touching my lips. Gabe was supposed to be the one watching Hope today, but a building project ran into complications and he was forced to stay late to clean up the mess. "I know, but don't worry. We can meet up this week and commiserate over greasy pizza and raunchy sitcoms." I add a hint of levity to my tone, as if making up for the incident that transpired yesterday at his stepbrother's pool.

It's only been twenty-four hours since I allowed myself an afternoon of fun and sunshine, only to succumb to the darkness that won't let me be.

I pushed him.

I put my hands on him and shoved him backward into the water, disoriented and terrified, all because I was triggered by a song.

Guilt claws at me, its talons sharp and unforgiving.

Gabe.

The man who's only ever given me patience and stability, who has never *once* made me question my safety or welfare when he's around.

I hurt him.

He'd never admit it, but I saw it in his eyes.

And the twist of insecurity in my gut has me wondering if Gabe didn't *really* need to stay late because of a construction project…maybe he *wanted* to. Maybe it was just an excuse to get out of being near me.

He could be scared of me. Scared of my confused mind, of my loosening grip on reality. Scared of that blurry line that separates the now and the then.

I can't think of anything more tragic than that.

But my anxiety is eased when a smile bleeds into his words. "I do love pizza," he says.

I turn the volume up on my phone to hear him better, so his response makes its way to Mandy's ears. She gives me a triumphant thumbs-up, wiggling her eyebrows as she sucks her bottom lip between her teeth.

I'd call her our resident matchmaker if that title didn't hold an entirely different, painfully insidious, meaning.

Blowing out a breath, I turn away from my meddling friend and pretend I can find a pocket of privacy somewhere in my tiny nine-hundred-square-foot house. "I guess I am a little nervous," I confess to Gabe, still trying to maintain some levity but failing. "It scares me to revisit my past, but…you told me once, there's reward in overcoming the fear."

He's silent for a few beats and I wonder if he's regretting his brush with wisdom. Gabe clears his throat. "Yeah, there is," he replies, his voice rich and deep, laced with grit. "The reward just needs to be worth the uphill battle to reach it."

My heart pounds, wondering if it'll be worth it.

Hoping it'll be worth it.

"Promise me you're coming back," he says, tone pleading. "Swear to me I won't lose you."

I suck in a sharp breath. "I'm coming back."

"*Promise* me, Tabs. It already feels like I lost—" He stops himself short.

My mind reels with bitter memories mixed with sweetness. His lips on mine, how I felt alive again, reborn, and how it all crumbled with a single, shameful word.

He thinks he lost me in that moment, but the truth is, I was never really there at all.

It had all been a ruse. A smokescreen. A veil to conceal my pain.

This is different.

This is taking action, instead of trying to hide.

Tears burn behind my eyes as I nod, drinking in a big breath. "I promise."

I hear him sigh—relief or doubt, I'm not certain.

"Good," he whispers. "Call me as soon as you're done, okay? I'll keep my ringer on."

"I will. Thanks, Gabe."

We end the call and my gaze trails to the open window in the living room, landing on the abandoned sparrow's nest settled among the tree branches. The baby birds gained their wings months ago but the nest still sits empty, waiting for new life.

A little hand tugs at my pearly-white blouse, pulling my attention from the window as I slip the phone into my purse and swing the strap over my shoulder.

Hope stares up at me, her cup of juice dangling from one hand. "Mama come back," she babbles, dark-blue eyes wide and worried.

Blue like his.

Worried like mine.

I lean down to wrap her up in a hug, peppering kisses across her cheek as my heart clenches. I'm doing this for her. I'm doing this so I can finally let go of the things that hold me back from becoming the best mother I can be. A tear tracks down the side of my face, and I say with all the reassurance I can muster, "Mama come back."

"Come here, little munchkin." Mandy ushers Hope away from me, jiggling a plastic baggie filled with puff snacks in her direction. "A night of debauchery awaits. Girlie gossip, prank phone calls to Reid, water spiked with Kool-Aid, and one or two unsavory PG-rated movies are on the agenda."

I giggle, the melancholy dissolving.

She waves me off with a Mandy smile, hauling Hope into her arms while I make my way to the front door. Her diamond engagement ring from Reid glitters in the light from a dated chandelier and I instinctively tap my front pocket, searching for strength.

Waving back, I walk out the door in my mismatched sandals.

CHAPTER 4

GABE

The phone is heavy in my grip as the call disconnects and the screen goes black.

Heavy like my heart.

I swipe the back of my hand across my forehead, my skin glistening with sweat from the summer sun and hours of back-breaking labor as my team tries to get this project back on track.

The timing fucking sucks.

All I want to do is be with Tabitha, hold her hand, quiet her nerves, and protect her restless heart. Instead, I'm stuck in this construction zone that mimics Satan's playground, dealing with equipment breakdowns that are delaying an otherwise uncomplicated project.

It's this damn weather.

The concrete mixer is toast, thanks to the hydraulic system overheating.

"Yo, Mason!"

I glance up to find Darius barreling toward me, pulling a hard hat off his head. The dude calls me Mason because, apparently, I resemble some male model his girlfriend has the hots for named Christopher Mason.

I guess there's a reason I've never been introduced to his girlfriend.

His ebony skin is slick with sweat as the July sun nails him in a harsh wash of light and reflects off his hi-visibility vest. "This fuckin' blows, man. We've been here since the ass crack of dawn."

I nod, sympathizing. "I hear you, but we're stuck here until it's done. We can't afford another delay. We're already over budget."

"Damn," he grumbles. "We deserve a drink after this shit. How about The Oar after we wrap up? It'll probably be last call by then, but fuck it."

"Nah, I can't tonight. Plans."

Honestly, I'm not sure if I have plans, considering I don't know when the hell I'll be off the clock, or if Tabitha will be passed out from exhaustion whenever that may be, but I can't risk not being there for her. She might need me.

The little horned fucker on my shoulder cackles in my ear, sneering at my wishful thinking.

Darius puckers his lips with disappointment. "You know we're due for a cold one soon. When's your next party?"

My last party was three weeks ago on the Fourth of July.

I spent the entirety of it watching Syd and Oliver grope each other on my living room couch after a fairytale-esque engagement beneath the fireworks while jealousy nibbled away at my heart. And then I dragged myself to bed early, sunk with guilt because I couldn't keep my envy in check.

I realize I'm only twenty-eight years old. I'm still young and there's plenty of time for me to settle down and create the picture-perfect family life I crave.

The hard part is, I found the woman I want to create that life with—I just can't have her.

"Not sure." I readjust my hard hat, tipping my chin toward the sun and squinting at a bird family skating across the lone cloud. "I'll take you up on that beer, though. Next weekend good?"

"Right on, brother."

We fist bump, and he saunters away, his vest lighting him up like a sunbeam.

Another one of my co-workers breezes by, and he also bumps me, but it's not the friendly kind. It's an icy shoulder bump that has my work boots stumbling in a patch of unlevel gravel.

I glance up to find him scowling at me, eyeing me up and down as if I personally affronted him somehow.

The interesting thing is, I hardly know the guy's name.

But he knows mine.

Everyone knows my name because I'm the son of a felon.

I share blood with the man who made national news for setting fire to my neighbor's house in an attempt to murder my best friend *and* my stepbrother so he could cover up his sick, twisted secrets.

Yeah...I'm *that* guy.

I'm the son of Travis Wellington and not everyone is as lenient and forgiving as Darius.

Some don't give a shit that I risked my life running into that burning house, pulling two people I love to safety. Some forget that I spent weeks in a burn unit receiving a skin graft.

Some choose to ignore the blatant fact that I'm not *him*.

I'll never be him.

I'd be lying if I said the wary looks, workplace whispers, and snide shoulder bumps don't eat at me sometimes. It fucking sucks. My father is a stone-cold piece of shit and the fact that I'm compared to him, associated with him, *related* to him, is just another bone-deep burn destined to leave a permanent scar.

I'd also be lying if I said I don't wonder if that's who Tabitha sees when she looks at me.

My father.

A man who will destroy her.

A monster.

The sound of a pile driver hammering steel has me jolting in place, reminding me that I'm standing around doing jack shit while my team is sweating their balls off.

I shake away the storm cloud and refocus.

Wiping at the sweat dripping into my eyes, I glance up, then do a double-take when my sights land on an unfamiliar figure looming a few yards away, right at the edge of the jobsite.

He's wearing a dark newsboy cap and is standing stock-still, his hands hidden inside the pockets of his black slacks. It's hotter than two goats in a pepper patch, but the man is wearing a smoky-gray trench coat over his clothes, looking like he's blissfully immune to heatstroke. He kind of resembles one of those cliché *Scooby Doo* villains.

And he's staring right at me.

I frown.

Creepy motherfucker.

My attention redirects to the bird family again, all lined up along the cable wires overhead. I can't help but smile. I can't help but think of her, and thinking of her always makes me smile.

Plucking off one of my cut-resistant gloves, I send Tabitha a quick text.

ME:

Remember…don't look down :)

She reads it right away, then shoots back a little red heart.
I grin.
When I glance back up, the man has vanished.

CHAPTER 5

TABITHA

"Hey! I love your shoes." A young girl whips open the front door, pulling an earbud out of one of her ears. Dirty-blonde hair is tied into two low pigtails as she sends me a megawatt smile. "Dad's just cleaning up the kitchen and putting the spaghetti away. Come on in."

I take a tentative step inside the quaint ranch home, nodding my thanks as I cling to my purse strap. The scent of Italian spices and ripe tomatoes fills my nose. "Thank you. Are you Evan's daughter?"

"Yep, I'm Summer. Don't worry, I'll be in my room, so I won't bug you. Dad told me he's writing a book for you." Her eyes light up like little blue moons. "That's so cool."

I release a halfhearted chuckle. "It's pretty cool, I guess. Are you also his secretary?"

Her nose scrunches up before she lets a giggle spill out. "Totally. I don't exactly have my work permit yet, thanks to being nine, but you won't tell anyone, right?"

"Your secret is safe with me." I zip my lips with an invisible key.

We share another laugh as clattering from the other side of the house pulls my chin up.

"Shit. Hey. Sorry I'm running behind," a male voice says, traveling from the adjoining kitchen. "Unprofessional, I know. I promise I write better than I manage my time."

Evan Hart jogs over to greet me in the little foyer no bigger than mine, extending a hand. I smile and accept the handshake. "No worries. I'm a few minutes early."

I'm not sure how I imagined a published author might look, but I suppose I pictured a crisp button-down, ironed slacks, spectacles perched on the bridge of his nose, and an articulate dialect that would make Oliver seem uneducated.

This man looks like the epitome of single-dad life: messy dark hair, shadows under his eyes, a wrinkled band T-shirt paired with ripped blue jeans, all topped off with a well-loved dish rag draped over one shoulder.

Instantly, I feel right at home in my mismatched sandals and apple-juice-stained blouse.

"You should've worn the fancy pants," Summer notes, eyeing her father's casual dresswear with distaste. "Wrong move."

"Tabitha doesn't care about my fancy pants."

She crosses her arms and puckers her lips. "You look borderline homeless, Dad."

His eyes narrow. "I'm taking a cut of your allowance for that very valid observation."

"Is that open to negotiation?"

"Yes."

"I'll finish cleaning the kitchen for you."

He relents with an easy nod. "Deal."

My eyes ping-pong between them, watching as they high five each other before Summer skips across the living room and disappears into the kitchen.

Evan sends me an apologetic smile. "Sorry. She's nine going on twenty-seven," he chuckles. "Follow me."

I slip out of my sandals and trail Evan down a short hallway that leads to three bedrooms. One is clearly Summer's room, adorned in purple paint and band posters, while another has a closed door—likely Evan's bedroom. The third room appears to be a space mostly used for storage, neatly tidied for our interview and equipped with a small desk, laptop, and two chairs.

As we enter, my eyes land on a tape recorder resting among a notebook and an assortment of pens and highlighters. I glance at the device with a raised eyebrow.

Evan shrugs. "A relic from a bygone era, I know."

"Very retro."

"It's a family heirloom and I always wanted an excuse to use it. Also, I was hoping it would make me look more sophisticated than I actually am…but I guess I just made it less effective by telling you that." He scratches at his shaggy mop of hair, cringing slightly when we're fully inside. "I realize this isn't the classiest set up, but I did clear out the cobwebs and remove the pile of dirty clothes from the corner." He shoots me another smile that oozes both charm and a request for pardon. "I considered doing this at a café or the library or something, but given the nature of the interview, I thought privacy would be best. A more controlled environment. But if you're uncomfortable, I'm adaptable. We can do this wherever."

I shake my head. "No…no, this is perfect. I agree that privacy is best. I'm…" Wringing my hands together, I inhale a shuddery breath. "I'm prone to triggers these days. The less distraction the better."

"I figured as much. Here, take a seat." Evan moves to pull out the cushy rolling chair and points at it. "Did you need anything? Water, coffee?" He pauses, a grin lifting. "I have leftover spaghetti. My daughter says it's excellent. World famous, I'm told."

Taking my place in the chair, I drop my purse to the floor and huff a laugh. "No thanks. I'm okay for now." Glancing around the small space, I take note of a few pillar candles flickering from the wall ledge, adding a warm ambiance. "I appreciate you doing this for me. I'm sure it was an odd request. Sydney told me you wrote psychological thrillers and it got my wheels spinning. I thought maybe it would be therapeutic to finally share my story. And, hopefully, you'll get something out of this experience, too."

Evan nods, gliding over to the other side of the desk and taking a seat across from me in a wooden dining chair. He powers up his laptop and fiddles with the tape recorder. "I won't lie and say I wasn't intrigued when I got your email," he tells me. "But I realize the circumstances are…delicate. I want to be trans-parent with you and let you know that I'm not a doctor or a licensed professional. Take any advice I might offer with a grain of salt—it'll be more me trying to work through ideas and conflicts in my head. While I've done a lot of research on psychopaths, sociopaths, and criminology, I'm far from a guru on the matter."

"I'm not going to sue you. Don't worry."

He lets out a relieved breath. "Much appreciated."

Harnessing my smile, I fold my hands in my lap and circle my thumbs, trying to drown out the erratic beats of my heart. Anxiety weighs heavy inside my chest. Nerves have my knees bobbing up and down, restless and uneasy.

"Let's start with something light," Evan suggests, clicking away on his mouse, his hazel-swirled eyes panning over to me. "Tell me about yourself. Who you are, things you enjoy, a little insight into your past."

Who I am, or...who I was?

Before.

Before evil gouged out my essence with sharp claws and hungry fangs.

I consider the starting point.

Images cloud my mind and I'm taken back to my early life back in Arizona. It was a decent life. A normal life. I'm whisked away to cherry trees and mockingbirds that sang sweet songs, and the scent of lavender in late June as I sat cross-legged in a plum romper, daydreaming of my grandmother's cherry lemonade and citrus cakes.

It was a lifetime ago, but it was still my life.

My trauma isn't my life. It's nothing but an awful piece wedged between a million beautiful pieces.

I reach for those pieces, clinging to their soft edges for strength.

"I grew up in Arizona but moved to Chicago on a scholarship to Edenbrook University. I was a psychology major," I tell him. "The human mind has always fascinated me. How it ticks, how it dreams, how it remembers. Ever since I was a little girl, I wanted to learn more about it."

Evan taps away at his keyboard, attention shared between me and the screen. He nods at me to continue.

"Um...I love chamomile tea and butterflies. I've never once dyed my hair. I hate heights and avoid airplanes at all costs," I ramble, trying to think of interesting facts about myself, deciding that he's probably weaving together a character profile. "I don't like surprises or abrupt changes anymore but I used to be sponta-neous. I loved road trips, once upon a time." I smile weakly. "I'm a cautious person. I always have a back-up plan. Pizza is my favorite food, and summer is my favorite season. I'm a mother. My daughter is my entire world."

He sends me a smile between typing. "That's relatable. Do you have a big family?"

"I don't have any siblings. My parents are separated and Mom now lives in Utah. I tried moving back in with my mother a couple of years ago, but...it was difficult. She didn't know how to deal with me and my father isn't in the picture anymore." I swallow. "So, I came back, and now I live in a little house a bit west of here. My family was never the warm and fuzzy type."

Somehow, that sounds better than saying, "*They just don't care.*"

My mother came out to visit Hope and me once last year during the holidays, and that was it. It was a brief, anxiety-ridden visit, and she spent a good portion of it on her phone, hardly paying us any attention.

That was actually the weekend I spent with Gabe, resulting in our first real date.

As soon as I returned home, my mother left that same day, claiming she had another visit to make in a nearby town. I'm fairly certain that visit was the reason for her venture out to Illinois and we were simply a convenient pitstop along the way.

I haven't spoken to her since and she hasn't made any effort to get in touch. Mom was never the maternal type, and after my father left when I was a preteen, she became even less involved with my life. It used to bother me, but not anymore. Life is too short to waste precious time on people who don't appreciate and value you—family or not.

My daughter deserves better.

"Do you ever get lonely?" Evan continues, jotting down notes. "Do you prefer independence?"

"I have a toddler and a full-time job, so I stay busy. I have a handful of close friends," I explain without truly answering the questions.

"Husband? Boyfriend?"

My heart fumbles.

I can't help but think of Gabe again.

Rich green eyes, fused with emerald and jade.

Shaggy waves of dirty-blond hair painted with highlights from the summer sun.

The way he holds my hand and calls me Tabs, and how he smells like coastal trees and ocean waves. I envision his crooked, playful smile, and how it can turn the sourest day sweet.

The way he listens; the way he truly *listens*.

I'm never a burden or a nuisance.

He listens even when I have nothing to say.

I think of the way his heartbeat picks up speed when I press my cheek to his chest, and the way mine does, too, when his hand cradles the back of my head, fingers braiding through my hair.

Swallowing, I shake my head. "No."

I slip two fingers into my pocket and feel for the metallic band, a tiny weight against my thigh.

Sorrow pinches me.

"Okay," Evan says gently, a soft expression staring back at me. "Now, take me back to the beginning. Tell me about that first day."

That first day.

The day that culminated in the worst two months of my life.

I fly away into the past, to two long years ago, to a day that colors my nightmares with crimson stains and silver chains.

Tortured howls and unspeakable acts.

Horror in its truest form.

Don't look down.

I don't look down, but I do allow myself to look back, because I know, undoubtedly, that looking back is the only way to keep moving forward.

I close my eyes.

Centering myself, I lean back in the chair and imagine that wooden bench on a breezy April evening.

The click of the tape recorder has stuttered words falling out of me.

My lips part.

My breath wavers.

My heart squeezes.

And away we go…

"It all started with a crush."

CHAPTER 6
TABITHA

Two Years Earlier

"Have you seen my car keys?"

I dumped my purse upside down, letting the contents spill out onto one of the outdoor benches. Watermelon lip balm, paper receipts, bobby pins, and loose change littered the wooden seat bench, but my keys were nowhere to be found.

Hmm.

My friend, Corbin, slanted his eyes as he shook his head, eating half of a banana in one bite. His response was muffled as he chewed. "Nah. Why would I?"

"I don't know. They were in my purse. I only left it here for a second."

"Beats me, Brighton. Do you need a ride home after class?"

Nerves raced through me. It didn't make any sense—they were *just here*. "Maybe…I guess." I gnawed on my lip as anxiety lit up my chest. The campus grounds were swarming with students and faculty members, but no one looked suspicious. Everyone was mingling with friends, catching up on school work, or munching on sandwiches in between evening classes.

Did someone take them?

I checked every pocket, peeked underneath the bench, retraced my steps.

I'd only stepped away for a minute to catch up with one of

my classmates. I'd abandoned my purse on the bench beside a lipstick-stained coffee cup and a wrapped granola bar, not giving it a second thought. It wasn't like I had more than two dollar bills in my wallet; not to mention, the purse itself had been purchased off the clearance rack at Target.

And I knew Corbin wouldn't take my keys.

Blowing a loose strand of hair off my face, I plopped down onto the bench and ripped open the granola bar with my teeth. "This terrible day is ending with a bang. I knew I should have spiked my coffee with something stronger."

"Never too late." Corbin, always the enabler, discreetly plucked a miniature bottle of rum from his jacket pocket and waggled his eyebrows at me.

I sighed. "I shouldn't. I have class in twenty minutes."

"The brain-voodoo class. Right." He shrugged, slipping the liquor back into his pocket. "Can't have your common sense compromised when you're trying to make sense of…sense."

"Mmm. Someone should hire you to write up the course descriptions."

"I do have a gift," he agreed with a smirk.

I took a small bite of my oatmeal-raisin snack bar and began to chew. The sun set lower in the sky, tinting the slow-blooming branches a dark lavender and crimson. Normally, I'd whip out my cell phone right about now and take a flurry of pictures of a sunset like this, losing myself to the brilliant colors.

But not tonight.

Tonight, the beauty of nature felt deceptive somehow. Ominous, dangerous. My stomach rolled with warning, and I didn't know why.

It was the keys.

The missing keys had me rattled.

"I gotta bolt, Brighton," Corbin announced, situating a ballcap over his light-blond curls. "I'll text you after my class. Meet me in the parking lot when you're ready—it's the white Corolla with a Phish bumper sticker."

I smiled my thanks, grateful for the ride. "I appreciate it. See you after class."

"Later."

He sauntered away, leaving me alone with my prickling anxiety.

A few minutes passed and Professor Gleason caught my eye as he ate a late meal by himself at a nearby picnic table. My belly fluttered. It was true I wanted to pick his brain in regard to my thesis on the relationship between dream content and waking life experiences, but that wasn't the only reason I was currently working up the nerve to go talk to him.

It wasn't even the primary reason.

His steel-blue eyes found me munching on my granola bar as I tried to remain inconspicuous a few yards away. I failed, of course, and my stolen glances were all too obvious. Inhaling a breath of courage, I stood from the bench, flattened the skirt of my floral-printed dress, and marched over to my psychology professor as he quickly dipped his eyes to his partially eaten sandwich.

"Eating alone?" My tone was teasing, my smile soft. I watched as he straightened at the table, his broad shoulders squaring at the sight of me. The way his gaze panned around the common area for a split second, as if taking careful note of his surroundings, did not go unnoticed.

"Are you looking for an invitation to join me?"

His light tone paralleled my own. It sent a shot of warmth down below and had me fidgeting with the ends of my loose hair. "Just an observation."

"Have a seat." He gestured toward the empty space across from him, the ghost of a smile claiming half of his mouth. "You looked frazzled over there. Lose something?"

Nodding, I inched my way onto the bench and tucked my hair behind my ears. "My keys are missing. Did you see anyone going through my purse while I was talking to Shelley?"

"No, but I only just sat down a few minutes ago. My last class ran late."

"It's so strange," I muttered with disappointment. "Oh well. I'm sure they'll turn up."

His eyes flicked to the table before lifting back to mine. A spark crackled between us and he cleared his throat, like he was casting it away. "How's that thesis coming along?"

I shrugged, trying not to get lost in his heated stare as I rubbed my hands up and down my arms. "Pretty good. I'm digging into the theory that dreams serve as a way for the brain to resolve challenges we might face in our waking lives. For example, if someone is grappling with a difficult decision, a dream could provide insight or guidance into resolving that conflict."

"Do you believe that?"

I blinked. "Do I believe dreams hold that much power over us?"

He nodded.

"I…don't know. Dreams are fascinating and complex. I think there's more to them than what humans can ever realistically uncover." I chewed on my cheek and tilted my head to the side. "I mean, they could be a vivid manifestation of our subconscious, or they could be their own entity. Do dreams themselves have power, or is it simply our own minds *giving* them that power?"

He scrubbed a hand underneath his lightly stubbled chin. He didn't respond to the rhetorical question, but his eyes encouraged me to keep going.

"The most practical scenario is that *we* hold all the answers within ourselves, and dreams only give us a nudge in the right direction," I continued. "But the more compelling alternative is that dreams are a gateway to something else entirely. Something that science and humanity could never fully explain."

My heart kicked up speed at the notion.

Dreams always fascinated me.

Professor Gleason studied me through black-rimmed glasses, his dark eyebrows creasing with thought. Inhaling a slow breath through his nose, he reached for his sandwich with another nod. "The mind is a powerful thing," he agreed before taking a bite. "It can be our greatest weapon."

"For good…and for bad," I added.

"That's right."

I rested my elbow atop the wood table and propped my chin in my hand. A small smile crested, broadening when his own smile stretched to dance with mine.

He dipped his eyes away quickly, glancing around the courtyard again. "Well," he said, brushing crumbs from the tabletop. "I'm looking forward to reading about which direction you're ultimately leaning in."

"I'm looking forward to sharing it with you."

My professor gathered up the remains of his meal and slung a briefcase strap over his shoulder as he stood from the bench.

Hesitating, he sent me a final glance that said more than it probably should have. "I'll see you in class in a bit, Miss Brighton."

"Sounds good. See you soon, Matthew."

I almost choked.

My cheeks burned when the sound of his first name met my ears and hung between us, causing him to fluster.

Totally inappropriate.

He regrouped, sweeping long fingers through neatly styled, gelled-up hair, and pulled his eyes off me. Pivoting away, he paused for another beat, then traipsed off toward the entrance of the building.

I let out a long breath as my forehead dropped to the picnic table.

Having a crush on my psychology professor, ten years my senior, was idiotic at best.

At worst?

It could be lethal.

"SOMEONE GIVE me a breakdown of Maslow's Hierarchy of Needs," Professor Gleason said, removing his dark-framed glasses and cleaning the lenses with the hem of his sweater. "What comes first?"

"Sex," someone blurted from behind me.

Giggles followed and I smiled into the palm of my hand. I loved this class, and it wasn't *just* because my teacher was prime eye candy—though, that did keep me from zoning out on the days I forgot my necessary midday coffee refill.

Adjusting the thin strap of my lilac midi dress, I let my gaze track Professor Gleason as he paced back and forth in front of the white board.

"Mm," he mused. "Reproduction does fall into that category, yes."

"Dude had his priorities straight," the student added.

More laughter rang out, a muddle of disruption. I kept my attention on the professor, my belly coiling with knots when his eyes skated over to me and notably lingered.

My face heated.

"Miss Brighton," he addressed softly. His arms crossed as he leaned back on his desk, head canting to the side, almost quizzically. "Enlighten us?"

I knew the answer. Any entry-level psychology student should have had the order of needs memorized, one through five. But now I was thinking about sex, and my attractive college professor was staring at me with a curious gleam in his eyes, and everything jumbled in my mind and I accidentally pictured him naked.

Clearing my throat, my voice squeaked like a frightened mouse. "Physiological needs. Basic human needs."

"Go on."

"Means for survival. Shelter, food, water."

The professor lifted two fingers, prompting me to proceed onto the second need.

"Safety needs," I continued, fidgeting in my seat and tapping the end of my pen to the desk. "When our basic needs are met, we seek stability. Safety, security, whether it be financial or emotional."

A third finger went up.

"Love," I murmured through a tight swallow. "Intimacy."

"Sex made it to two levels," the student interrupted, snickering behind me. "Nice."

Professor Gleason's eyes remained fixed on me. He didn't pivot, didn't laugh or blink. I sank deeper in my seat, my heart galloping as a tangible tension grew. "Um, esteem needs are fourth. The desire for recognition and respect. Status," I explained. "And number five is self-actualization, ultimately culminating into a sense of purpose."

He gave a thoughtful nod, returning his glasses to the bridge of his nose.

No man has ever looked sexier in glasses. Everyone called him Professor Clark Kent, and I couldn't say I disagreed.

"Correct. Thank you," he said, shifting his attention to the rest of the class as he popped up from the desk. "I have an assignment for all of you."

Collective groans hummed throughout the classroom.

"Our thesis is due this week," the girl next to me griped. "Cruel and unusual punishment if you ask me."

"This is a social sciences course, Mirabelle," he said, tone even. "You're welcome to run your complaint by Mr. Jackson over at the College of Law center."

She snorted a laugh.

I stared down at my desk, my skin itchy.

He called every other student by their first name, but I was only ever *Miss Brighton*.

The professor continued. "I'd like you to think of a situation in which the order of needs may be rearranged, or even inverted. Cultural beliefs, religion, et cetera. The assignment will be due on Wednesday."

When the bell rang, everyone jumped to their feet and chaos ensued. Professor Gleason continued to talk over the tangle of voices, uncaring that everyone was ignoring him.

Everyone except for me.

I hung onto his every word like I always did.

Students scattered, gathering loose papers and bookbags, while I remained seated, slipping my notebook and collection of multicolored highlighters into my own backpack. My gaze skipped over to the wall clock. Corbin was definitely finished with his class by now and likely waiting in his car to give me a ride home.

Stupid keys.

Where could they have gone?

I sent Corbin a quick text, asking if he was ready for me, but it didn't show Read right away, so I pursed my lips and waited.

My dallying became more obvious when a palpable quietness washed over the once-bustling classroom. I realized everyone had departed, save for me and Professor Gleason.

He was scribbling something onto a piece of paper, head down, when he addressed me. "Did you need assistance with something, Miss Brighton?"

I fidgeted in my seat, clearing my throat as I moved to stand. "I, um...no, I guess not. A friend is giving me a ride home since my car keys disappeared. I'm just waiting on him." My teacher continued to write, not glancing up. "I'll wait outside. Sorry if I'm—"

"I can give you a ride."

"I—" His offer registered and I froze. My heart erupted into a stampede of clunky beats, my palms turning clammy. "Oh, that's really nice of you, but I'm sure he'll reply soon."

Professor Gleason popped his head up, setting down his pencil. He stared at me from his desk chair a few feet away. "It's not a problem. I'm heading out now, anyway." Glancing at the open door, he added, "You don't live far, no?"

I shook my head. "It's three miles."

"All right. Text your friend that you have it covered."

Scratching at my collarbone that was newly dappled in bright-pink flush, I swallowed the rock in my throat and nodded. "Okay. Great. Thank you."

I pulled out my cell phone and sent Corbin a follow-up text, alerting him of the change of plans.

Professor Gleason stood from the desk and stuffed things into his briefcase before reaching for his tan double-breasted overcoat. "Ready when you are," he said.

"Right, of course. I'm ready." Squeezing the strap of my purse, I hauled it over my shoulder along with my school bag and followed him out of the classroom. A cloud of masculinity wafted around me as I sidled up beside him and fell in line with his steps. It must have been his aftershave or some type of cologne resembling intoxicating, forbidden sin; something woodsy, like cedar and oak, mingling with spicy notes. My voice cracked when I attempted speech. "You didn't have to do this, but it's very much appreciated. I…" A cough fell out. "Appreciate it."

Oof.

Why was talking hard?

"It's no trouble. I hope you find your keys." He sent me a flat smile as we passed by the dwindling handful of students and staff.

Nothing looked suspicious or amiss.

We were an arm's length apart and I was doing everything in my power to control my body language so it didn't scream, *"Strip me bare and have your way with me, please and thank you."*

This was normal.

Everything was fine.

We exited out the main doors and into the cool spring night. Stars and lamplight brightened the sidewalk leading into the parking lot and my grip tightened on my purse strap as nerves worked their way through me. The lot was close to empty, final classes having ended for the day.

I looked around for Corbin's Corolla, but it was nowhere to be found. A peek at my last missed text confirmed that he'd received my message and headed home.

Professor Gleason guided me toward the farthest section of the lot where a lone black Lincoln Navigator sat idle, the lights blinking to life when he pressed a button on his keychain.

I reached for the door handle.

He intercepted and opened it for me, gaze flaring with the hint of a smile. Our arms brushed, and suddenly, the upper-fifty-degree evening felt like the dead of summer in Death Valley.

I was sweating as I slipped into the cool leather interior.

The door snapped shut beside me before my professor situated himself in the driver's seat and started the engine. He glanced at me, smile still in place. "You seem frazzled again. Is it the keys?"

He knew it wasn't the keys.

I swallowed and braved eye contact. "Something like that."

The corner of his mouth ticked. "Do you like music?"

"Of course." *Who didn't like music?*

Swiping through his music app, he settled on a selection and fiddled with the volume dial. A song came to life, something eerie and enigmatic. I didn't recognize it, but the display in the dash told me it was called *Karma Police* by Radiohead.

I sank deeper in my seat, my lashes fluttering as the music revved my pulse and the scent of leather and spice heated my blood to boiling.

"You like this song?" His voice was rich and deep as he made no move to put the vehicle into drive. We just sat there, chemicals churning between us, unsaid words dangling amid chords and moody lyrics. "I'm a sucker for the older stuff. Radiohead, Porcupine Tree, Nick Cave. Bands with complex and layered instrumentation." He paused, blue eyes glimmering by dashboard light. "Feels like I'm in a dream. This one has always been my favorite."

My chest tightened as our gazes locked. "I do like it. It's different."

"Yeah?" Half of his mouth drew up. "I thought you might be too young to appreciate it."

I swallowed. My tender age of twenty-one was the least of my worries, I decided, as I stared into his stirring navy eyes and fantasized of bare skin and entangled limbs fused with mewls and moans.

He was my teacher.

I was his student.

A tryst wasn't just morally unethical—it was prohibited. Our college institution had a strict policy in effect against teacher-student relationships.

He would lose his job.

I nibbled my lower lip, watching his gaze drop to the gesture. "I'm not young, per se. I'm just younger than you."

Those eyes slid back up to mine. One hand cupped his khaki-clad knee while the other curled around the steering wheel, a tungsten band glinting from his right hand and an old vintage watch encasing his wrist. His knuckles whitened as his grip went tighter around the wheel, almost like he was holding himself back from reaching for me.

That's what I chose to believe, anyway.

"Mmm," he said, more purr than word. His Adam's apple bobbed as he flicked his attention to the windshield. "You do come across as older."

"Your stern lectures are giving me age lines."

A laugh rumbled in his chest, causing my smile to spread, my lip still caught between my teeth. Was I flirting? I might have been flirting.

The mood music was making me bolder, and the way his eyes slowly glided back to mine with a heated hold had me not caring one bit.

"You're bright," he said. "Some might say an ideal student; teachable yet steeped in conviction. You have the ability to turn staunch facts into subjective discussions and breathe new life into old philosophies. Having you in my class can be…" Trailing off, he swallowed his words.

"What?" I whispered.

Wonderful? Fulfilling? Rewarding?

He blinked once, then twice. "Distracting."

My thighs clenched. I hoped the night shadows were enough to veil the deep blush staining my cheekbones as that single word wreaked havoc on my heart.

A beat passed and he cleared his throat, exhaling a breath. "Sorry." He looked away again. "That…wasn't appropriate."

I wetted my dry lips since all of the moisture in my body seemed to have traveled south. "You don't have to apologize."

"I do. It was a mistake to drive you home."

"Is that a staunch fact, or can I broach a subjective discussion?"

Another laugh fell out of him as he shook his head a little. Lifting his chin, he let a smile slip. "I'm open to countering theories."

"Well…I lost my keys and you were being kind. Human decency is never a mistake."

"You already had a ride."

"Corbin may have forgotten. I could have been stranded."

"Ah," he said. "You would have been reliant on Uber. The horror."

I shrugged. "The driver could have been a twisted serial killer moonlighting as a trustful driver for unsuspecting college girls. You may have saved my life."

"Your imagination is certainly a compelling place, Tabitha." He smirked.

The sound of my name on his tongue did something to me. I found myself all out of counter theories as our eyes continued to dangerously tangle, one foot over the ledge of a cliff, the other still firmly planted on solid ground.

Whether or not we free-fell was dependent upon the strength of the wind and the endurance of that firmly-planted foot.

I inhaled a shaky breath, averting my attention to the cell phone sitting between us.

The song ended and I hadn't even noticed. Deciding that I wasn't ready for it to be over, I leaned over to the console where his phone rested, screen-side up, and pressed the back button to restart it.

Before I could retract my hand, he reached out and curled his fingers around my wrist.

I stopped breathing.

Our eyes met, cast in shadow and a trace of moonlight. His features were pinched tight but his grip on my wrist was loosely held indecision.

"Matthew," I murmured.

And then that grip tightened.

Shadow eclipsed the moonglow when he inched closer.

His eyes closed through a low groan, thumb grazing along the back of my knuckles. "You shouldn't say my name like that." Moving closer still, his warm breath beat against my hand as he leaned in and pressed a kiss to the underside of my palm. "It's—"

Tap, tap, tap.

A sharp knocking at the driver's side window had us pulling apart like a spontaneous brushfire had ignited in the space between us.

A glimmer of fear stole his expression for a split second before he ran an agitated hand through his hair, swallowed, and twisted toward the intruder.

I readjusted the strap of my dress that had slipped off my shoulder and tried to stop my hands from shaking.

God, what were we thinking?

In public?

Sitting in the campus parking lot?

Terrified, I peeked my head around the professor and spotted a large man hovering beside us.

Professor Gleason rolled down the window. "Can I help you?"

The stranger flashed us a set of yellowing teeth as he hiked up a pair of ratty blue jeans over his protruding belly. A foul stench seeped into the vehicle. Rotting carrots and rancid body odor. It was an awful combination.

I cowered back in my seat.

"I'm the janitor," the man said, pausing to hack up a lung. A phlegmy cough rattled his chest until he almost doubled over. "Found these keys. They yours by any chance?"

He dangled them outside the open window, attention fixed on me.

For a moment, I was elated.

My keys!

"Oh, wow. Yes, thank you. How did you…" But then confusion set in, because I wasn't sure how he would know that. "How did you know they were mine?"

A gurgling laugh erupted from him. "Good at my job is all." Two dark, beady eyes slanted in my direction. "I'm observant."

My professor turned to me, wariness clouding his eyes. Something didn't feel right. Danger prickled the back of my neck, crawling down my spine like an icy omen.

"You're a teacher here, yeah?" the unfamiliar man wondered, leaning forward into the car on both arms. Then he nodded toward me. "And you're a student?"

Instinctively, I curled my hand around Matthew's bicep.

Matthew scratched at his hair. "Uh, yes. I'm just giving Miss Brighton a ride home."

"That so?"

My heart thumped. "Since you found my keys, I can just drive home myself now," I interjected, reaching over the professor. "Thank you again."

As I moved to snatch the key ring, the stranger yanked it back, just out of reach.

"Eh, eh, eh," he goaded. "Say please."

Oxygen thickened in my lungs.

A shudder raced through me, head to toe.

The man straightened from the window and looked from left to right.

Right to left.

Behind him, then over the hood of the car.

Was he...casing his surroundings?

Queasiness swirled in my gut. I dug my nails into Matthew's arm and whispered, "Let's just go."

He sensed the same thing I was sensing and gave me a quick nod.

But it happened too fast.

One moment, Matthew was moving to roll the window back up.

And in the next, a flash of shiny black metal collided with his temple, and he sagged like a ragdoll, slumping over the console, looking lifeless, while instinct had me lurching forward and reaching for him.

"*Matth*—!"

The stranger snapped his hand out when I was within reach and grabbed me by the hair until it was tangled in his meaty fist. A shriek of terror climbed my throat.

Before I could let it loose, the man yanked me closer and I was staring down the barrel of a pistol.

Time froze. Fear seized me. Disbelief blanketed me with shock.

"Don't make a damn sound, Kitten, or I'll blow this pretty little head right off your shoulders," he snarled through his teeth.

My hand clamped around my mouth as I held in the scream.

Tears blurred my vision.

That song continued to play, a soundtrack to my nightmare.

And then…

The butt of the gun struck me in the forehead and darkness carried me away.

CHAPTER 7

TABITHA

D rip. Drip. Drip.

I heard something.

Tiny whispers dancing along the roof.

I was in my old bedroom, a little girl again, staring up at the ceiling as rain trickled down in intervals of soothing pitter-patters.

I smiled, relaxed and at peace.

And then the sweet sound was replaced by an awful—

Pop, pop, pop!

I lurched into a sitting position.

It was my father; I knew it. He was terrorizing the mocking-birds again.

I flew down the staircase in my plum romper, ribbons of hair trailing behind me as I slid open the patio door and glared at my father. "Daddy, please don't!"

He mumbled through the cigar in his mouth, sparing me a brief glance. "They're damn pests."

Standing in front of our wild cherry tree, my father lit up another handful of firecrackers with the flame from his match. He tossed them underneath the tree and took a long stride back-ward, pleased when the firecrackers burst to life with a jarring round of shrieky pops.

The tiny birds went flying.

Pop, pop, pop!

I covered my ears and squeezed my eyes shut.

I hated when he did that to the poor birds. Their crime had only ever been music.

Rain continued to fall from a leaden-gray sky, not hard, not fast, only a slow-sliding drizzle.

Drip. Drip. Drip.

My head pounded.

It must have been the firecrackers echoing in my eardrums.

Drip. Drip. Drip.

Everything started to blur, sound becoming disjointed, until the only thing that rang loud and clear was the languidly timed drips.

One, two, three, four, just a second and a half apart.

Eyelids fluttering, the images began to fade from my mind, nothing but a dream.

A memory.

I blinked, vision clouded.

Drip. Drip. Drip.

It was dark. I wondered if I was in my bed for one blissful moment before awareness set in, and the feel of cold cement against my cheek replaced the fantasy of warm sheets and a pillowy mattress.

What in the…?

I blinked again, and again, a deep-seated chill thickening my veins with ice. I could hardly see anything, the cloak of blackness blotting out my surroundings. A narrow window across the space, a few feet above me, came into view first. The stars and moon offered a small trace of light.

The pounding in my head came next. Painful, disorienting, relentless. I tried to lift my hands to rub away the hammering, but I was horrified to discover that my hands wouldn't move.

They were locked. Chained. Fettered behind my back as I lay sprawled out on my side on a stone-cold floor, my knees tucked to my chest.

Oh, my God.

Whimpers fell out first, panic inching its way inside of me, but they quickly morphed into petrified shrieks.

I screamed, and I screamed, and I *screamed*.

I rattled my chains, scrambling into a sitting position as sections of crusty hair fell into my eyes.

"Tabitha."

Jerking my head to the left, a shock of pain exploded behind my eyes and traveled down to my toes. I tried to see him through the dark.

The voice was familiar; a shred of relief amid the terrifying nightmare.

"M-Matthew?" My voice was raspy, full of grit and fear. His shadowy outline came into focus, hardly visible, and that relief disintegrated when it appeared that he was also bound and chained. "W-what's happening? Where are we? What…"

Tears fell harder than the raindrops that had comforted me in my dream only moments ago.

"Tabitha," he repeated. "Are you all right?"

He sounded more coherent than I felt.

More lucid.

He'd been privy to our Hell for longer than I had been, and I didn't envy him for that.

My back was supported by nothing but a steely rod, my wrists locked behind it in what I assumed were handcuffs. Dirt and rubble dug into my bare feet as I slid them toward me, knees shaking. "I-I don't know what's happening. Are you chained? Are you hurt?"

His shadow moved from a few feet away. "I'm chained."

"What happened? That man…he…" Terror infiltrated me when I recalled the stranger with dark eyes and a receding hairline brandishing a pistol in front of my face.

He'd knocked me out.

He'd knocked us both out.

And then…he'd taken us.

"Tabitha, listen to me. I'm getting you out of here."

Matthew's voice was level but it cracked with fear. I heard it. I heard the splinter, the fracture, the stark truth telling me that he was just as scared as I was.

I cried.

I buried my face in the valley between my knees, sobbing my heart out.

"I swear to God, I'm getting you out of here," he said, voice filled with more cracks, more truth.

"This isn't real," I croaked, my tears dampening the skirt of my dress. "This can't be real. This can't be happening."

When I lifted my chin, my eyes had adjusted, just marginally.

His features were obscured by shadows, but I could make out the tint of blue in his sweater and the dejected sag of his shoulders that were usually squared with certitude.

His sigh was loud against the quiet backdrop, mingling with that drippy sound. Something was leaking, mimicking what was left of my sanity.

"This is real," he said. "It's real, and the sooner we come to terms with it, the sooner we can find a way out."

"Why is he doing this? What does he *want*?"

This couldn't be real.

It just couldn't be.

These things happened in movies and books. Not even my own nightmares could have fathomed such a thing.

"I don't know." Matthew shifted in place, his chains rattling against the pole. "Once I figure out his motive, I can piece together a plan."

"How?" I cried. "We're trapped. Chained like animals. We have no weapons."

"We do have a weapon."

I sucked in a breath, blinking a dozen times in hopes of seeing him better. "I—"

The sound of a door creaking open snuffed out my next words and all of my muscles locked up, my heart dropping into the pit of my stomach.

A hint of light seeped out from the top of a stone staircase.

We were in a basement.

A cellar.

A dirty, cold prison.

And the man with the jiggling belly and phlegm-drenched cackle stood on the landing of the staircase, staring down at us.

I scuttered to my feet, almost toppling when my wrists caught on the pole. My legs were quivering, my head shrieking with agony. "Please. Please, please, let us go. We won't tell anyone. We won't—"

That awful laugh traveled down to us as the man descended the steps with a pistol dangling from one hand. "My pets have awakened. Goddamn, I love this part."

Matthew rose to a slow stand across from me. "What do you want?"

He asked it so seriously, as if he was expecting a serious answer.

The man barked another laugh. "Can't wait for you to find that out."

My face twisted with more tears. My words were hardly audible through my sobs. "Please. I'm begging you. Don't hurt us. Don't hurt him."

"Keep begging, Kitten. Makes me horny." He grabbed his crotch and gave it a squeeze.

I looked away and closed my eyes, realization dawning.

His intentions for me were clear and my stomach churned.

The man pulled a cell phone out of his pocket and flipped on the flashlight, shining it right at me. I backed away as much as I could, slipping my body around the pole, as if I was able to dodge his reach somehow.

"I have money," Matthew said quickly. "A fair amount of it. I'll give you the name of my bank, my pin number, my credit cards. Take everything. Just leave her alone."

I continued to cower, whimpering with fear.

The man ignored him, attention on me and only me.

He inched closer.

"No. Please, stop this," Matthew continued, voice rising in pitch, in panic. He yanked at his chains, clanking them against the pole. "Don't fucking touch her." *Clank, clank, clank.* "Fuck!"

The stranger stepped up to me, his stomach protruding from the waistband of his jeans and grazing my elbow. Slipping the firearm behind his back, he snatched my chin between dirty fingers and wrenched my face toward him.

The light from the phone nearly blinded me and I slammed my eyelids shut, trying to pull away.

"Pretty little thing…so scared, so pathetic." He sneered at me, reeking of rotting carrots, engine fuel, and landfill waste. "Just the way I like 'em."

I tugged at my restraints, legs almost giving out. "D-don't touch me. Don't come near me."

"Or what?" he goaded. "You'll wiggle too much? I hope you do."

My knee drew up on instinct, gouging him between the legs.

It was a direct hit, but my strength was verging on depleted so he hardly flinched.

I only made him mad.

"Silly bitch." His hand latched onto my throat as he yanked me toward him, spit misting my face. "Can't wait to punish you for that."

I tried to pry myself free but his hold was too tight.

His hand loosened from around my neck and crawled lower, his eyes following, and he groped my chest with a grimy, thick paw. Desperate sobs fell out of me. I tried to unhear the groans he made while he touched me, squeezing and massaging my breast through the thin fabric of my sundress.

"Jesus, just stop." Matthew clapped his chains against the pole, the shrill sound of metal on metal doing nothing to distract the monster. "Leave her alone. Don't touch her. Tell me what you want and I'll do it." More clanks, more growls, more futile pleas. "Tell. Me. What. You. Want."

The man's evil eyes lifted up to mine for a beat before he shoved me backward, my wrists slicing with pain against the cuffs.

A new horror sunk in when I watched him retreat from me and pivot toward Matthew.

"No!" I shouted at his back. "It's me you want. Please…don't hurt him!"

Our captor ignored me and halted toe to toe with Matthew, raising the phone. Matthew flinched back from the brassy light.

"You're her teacher, eh? An esteemed professor," the man mocked.

Matthew growled, pulling at his chains.

"Or…you *were* a professor. Now you're just my dirty dog. My new plaything." He plucked the glasses from Matthew's face, then dropped them to the cement floor. A steel-toed boot lifted up and stomped down on them, crushing the glass beneath its sole. He gurgled an amused laugh before bending over and picking up the wrecked spectacles. "You'll find out what I want soon enough, dirty dog."

He returned the glasses to the bridge of Matthew's nose.

Crooked and broken.

"And then you'll wish you never asked."

Whistling, he swiveled away, the whistles eventually morphing into a familiar song.

The man hummed the verses of *Karma Police* by Radiohead before trudging back up and disappearing through the door.

I couldn't stop screaming.

I couldn't stop crying.

Matthew continued to grunt and growl through his attempts to escape the metal binds.

The song lingered in the air, a haunting soundtrack.

And the stars had the audacity to twinkle and gleam on the other side of the window, cruelly out of reach.

CHAPTER 8

GABE

Present Day

I swerve into my driveway at half-past eight and kill the engine of my Challenger.

Tabitha's car is parked in front of the writer's house, three properties down from mine, so I'm guessing the interview is still in session.

I pop my keys in my hand as I stare down the lamplit sidewalk and wonder if she's okay.

"She is stronger than you think," comes a familiar voice from a few feet away. "This won't break her."

My head snaps right. Oliver is seated on his front porch, his hands dangling between his knees while he gazes over at the quiet bird feeder that swings lightly when a breeze rolls through.

I stuff my hands into my pockets and saunter toward him. It's nice having my stepbrother and best friend living right next door; especially on nights like this when my mind is spinning with a mess of madness. "Yeah, part of me knows that," I reply with a shrug, stepping closer. He's haloed in muted yellow porch light, his chestnut-brown hair glinting with gold. "Part of me doesn't."

"That is the part of you that cares." He sends me a small smile, tapping at his chest with the palm of his hand. "The heart has a grave tendency of overriding logic."

I simmer in those words.

The heart is hope.

Logic is truth.

And then there's me, swimming right between the two, flailing in the tragic balance.

Stepping up beside him, I watch as Oliver scoots over and allows me space to join him on the cement step.

He looks up at the stretch of stars with a long sigh. "I can't pretend to know what it's like for her," he muses, his gold-brown eyes squinting skyward. "I have lost a lot, yes, but lost time is nothing compared to losing something as fundamental as love."

He *has* lost a lot.

Twenty-two years of his life were lost to awful circumstances after he was abducted as a little kid and held in captivity, fed lies, and hidden from the outside world.

My asshole father had a fuck-ton to do with that.

I nod slowly, teeth grinding together. "You probably think I'm wasting my time, pining over a woman still in love with a ghost." I don't mean to sound bitter, but the words taste like lemon peels on my tongue. "Can't really compete with that."

"I don't think that at all." His eyebrows crease as he glances at me. "Time spent loving another is never time wasted. In fact, I'm apt to believe it's the only time that truly matters in this life."

"That's easy to say when the person you love loves you in return. This isn't the same."

He frowns, then turns away. "Mmm."

I wait for him to continue, but he doesn't. "What does that mean?"

"What?"

"*Mmm.*"

One shoulder pops up slightly with a shrug. "I suppose *mmm* is what I meant."

Leaning forward, knees to elbows, I ruffle my hair with both hands. "That's not an answer."

"There was no question." I hear the hint of a smile in his voice as he adds, "If there had been, perhaps I would have told you that, no, it is not the same, but no love is ever the same. It's up to you to decide if your love is worth all of the harrowing moments you may suffer as a result of it."

Damn him and his Oliver wisdom.

He always makes me think, and I don't really want to think

tonight. I just want to sulk and be miserable because the woman I love is probably crying her heart out right now, trapped in a hopeless past, losing herself to demons and darkness, and I'm not there to quiet her tears.

Sighing, I decide to pivot. "What's Syd up to?"

"Reading," he says.

"One of her sex books, no doubt."

"Indeed. I dared to take a peek at an excerpt and there was talk of knives in precarious places." He blows out a breath. "I can't find the appeal in sharp objects in the bedroom. Perhaps I need to try it before I pass judgment."

I snort a laugh. "Let me know how that goes." Pondering the notion, I cringe and change my mind. "On second thought, please don't. Tell me absolutely nothing."

He chuckles under his breath. "I wouldn't. Unlike you, I'd never divulge such things."

That's true.

Oliver lived with me for months before moving in with Sydney and was privy to a flurry of different women in and out of my bed. I wasn't shy about it. My vivid storytelling often made him blush, especially because he was still a virgin at the time.

Now I'm the one who's celibate and lonely, while he's probably living it up, acting out Sydney's smut-filled romance novel fantasies.

I'm not jealous.

If I wanted to get laid, it wouldn't be hard.

I just…don't want to.

All I want is her.

I give Oliver a slap on the shoulder and pull to a stand. "On that interesting note, I'll leave you to your precarious knife play. Tell Syd I said hi."

"I shall. Goodnight, Gabe."

"'Night."

Sparing a quick glance at Tabitha's car, I send my stepbrother a wave and make my way across the yard to my own house.

It's quiet.

Too quiet.

Maybe I should get a dog or something.

Or a bird—birds are never quiet.

Oliver and Sydney have a pet raccoon, but I squash that idea immediately.

Kicking off my work boots, I busy myself by turning on some music then slapping American cheese onto slices of bologna and calling it dinner before I trudge to the bathroom to take a quick shower.

I'm freshly cleaned within ten minutes, swiping a towel through my still-damp hair and pulling on a pair of gray sweat-pants as I jam out to a song by one of my favorite bands.

I'm reaching for my T-shirt when the doorbell rings.

My heart stutters.

It could be Lorna, the crotchety neighbor lady, asking me to turn my "noise" down.

Or it could be Tabitha.

Forgoing the shirt, I traipse out of the bathroom and race down the short flight of stairs to the landing area of my raised ranch. When I pull open the door, she's standing there, her white blouse shimmering against the pearly moonlight, dark hair framing her wide-eyed face.

Those big eyes lock on mine before dipping lower, skimming over my bare chest.

She swallows, lingering for a beat, before glancing back up. "I saw your car in the driveway," she murmurs. Her eyes flick over my shoulder, as if expecting to discover that I have company. "Is this a bad time?"

Warmth floods me. While I was anticipating a text or a phone call tonight, I didn't think she'd actually stop by.

I shake my head, unable to hold back the smile. "Nah. I'm alone."

I'm alone because I haven't been able to look at anyone but you since you stepped through my front door eight months ago.

I don't say that part because it sounds delusional.

She nods. "I can't stay long…I need to get home to Hope and relieve Mandy, but I wanted to stop by since I saw your car. I hope that's okay."

"That's always okay." I catch the relief that touches her berry-balmed lips. "Come in."

Tabitha steps inside, toeing off one tan and one ivory sandal, and drops her purse by the door. She glances at my chest again, her long, inky eyelashes nearly touching her brows when she peers back up at me. A light blush stains her cheeks.

Clearing my throat, I palm the nape of my neck. "Let me go finish changing. Feel free to raid my fridge if you're hungry. I'll be back in a sec."

"All right. Thank you."

I hear her shuffle up the staircase while I half-jog into my bedroom to snag a clean shirt.

When I return fully clothed a minute later, Tabitha is seated on my couch with her face in her hands, sheets of waist-length midnight hair curtaining the sadness I know she's wearing.

"Hey," I say softly.

She pulls her chin up in slow motion, turning toward me with eyes rimmed red and cheeks bright pink, both glinting with tear stains. All she does is shake her head.

She shakes her head like words are too hard, or maybe there aren't any words that will convey the things she's feeling.

She shakes her head, and it's a small plea, a request for comfort.

It's all I need.

I close the gap between us, collapsing beside her on the couch, and let her fall against me, my arms enveloping her with the hug I know she craves.

But she does more than hug me back.

She climbs into my lap, cages me in with her knees, and buries her face in my T-shirt as my arms instinctively wrap around her middle, and my hands graze up and down her spine.

I know she feels the way my chest nearly caves in, and how my breath stops short, and the erratic thump against my ribs as my heart fumbles for its next topsy-turvy beat. And yet my arms hold tighter, my fingers continuing their up-and-down sweep along her back.

My arms don't question it. They only know how to hold her.

"I'm sorry," she whispers. Taut fingers cling to the fabric of my shirt as she nuzzles her face against me and trembles on the inhale. "This isn't fair to you."

I choke down a hard swallow. "What's not fair?"

"This. Me."

Frowning, I swing my head back and forth, not understanding. "What do you mean?"

Tabitha lifts up, her hands trailing up my chest and latching onto my shoulders, our pelvises flush together. A glimmer of regret lights up her eyes. "I'm not naïve, Gabe. I'm not oblivious to the way you feel about me. And I know this isn't fair." She squeezes me. Her hands on my shoulders, her thighs around my hips. "I'm being selfish. I'm taking comfort from you when I desperately need it, and I'm giving nothing back."

I freeze at her words. I wasn't expecting them.

But they don't ring true.

"Tabs, look at me." I frame her face between my hands, pulling our eyes together. She tries to look away, as if the eye contact only amplifies her guilt, but I keep her attention from wavering. Stroking my thumbs along the skin below her ears, I send her a soft smile. "The fact that I'm the one you think of when you need comfort means a hell of a lot. I'm not expecting anything in return. That's not how this works."

She flicks her eyes away, lips parted and wobbly. "You don't have to wait for me, you know. I'm not sure when I'll…" A tear slips. "I'm not sure if I'll ever—"

"Hey, listen." I force her focus back on me, my smile still intact. "If you think for a second that I don't have all the time in the world for you, then you've got me all wrong."

A sharp breath falls out of her, a warm plume of wonder skimming my lips.

She blinks.

And then she collapses against my chest with a heavy sigh, clinging to me harder, her hands rising to clasp around my neck in an intimate grip.

I keep the groan at bay as my lips drop to the crown of her head.

I force back the shot of desire that sweeps through me when the scent of jasmine shampoo and cherry body lotion wrap me up in a cloud of temptation.

I ignore the way I'm all too aware of the warm juncture between her thighs pressing into me.

The girl of my dreams is in my lap, holding on to me like a lover while telling me I'll only ever be a friend.

Get it the fuck together, Gabe.

I close my eyes and release a slow sigh.

And then my arms wrap around her again, doing what they

do best.

Tabitha is quiet for a long time. A minute turns into two, then three, and within the span of those minutes, her body becomes weightless and lax within my arms.

"Do you remember our first date?" she asks me. Her words are muffled by my chest, voice scratchy from grief.

She says it like we've had more than one.

She says it like I could ever forget it.

"Of course."

That December night sails through my mind, a swarm of ancient memories.

DJ strobes lighting up the dance floor with magenta and indigo.

Music pulsing through my bloodstream.

The way her raven-winged hair flapped around her face, trying to hide the beaming smile she wore as genuine thrill glittered in her eyes brighter than the strobes.

We danced.

We danced for hours, unrefined steps and clumsy arms swinging to the music.

Oliver and Sydney had been tangled up in each other beside us, lost to their own music, while I felt myself falling for the girl in a mustard sweater with the eyes of a wounded soldier, the spirit of a fallen angel, and a heart I was determined to win over.

I can't recall a single song that played that night, but I'll always remember the cadence of her laughter. The pitch of it, the buoyancy in it.

It wasn't an act or a ruse.

She was happy.

She'd left her demons at home that night, allowing herself a few hours of true peace, and she'd found that peace with me.

It kills me that we couldn't hold on to it.

"I think about that night a lot," Tabitha continues, her fingers curling at the nape of my neck. Her head is still bowed, pressed into the planks of my chest. "It was the first time I'd felt truly happy in over a year. I'd been faking it well, practicing my smile, rehearsing words that would keep people from questioning my mental state." She inhales and lets it out, each breath more unburdened than the last. "I didn't need to fake it with you. The moment I met you, I just felt...safe. I didn't need to hide."

Safe.

She felt safe until I crossed a line, thinking it was a line meant for me to cross.

I kissed her and fucked it all up.

The thing is, I'd kissed her before the night it all came undone. A few pecks on the lips here and there, quick and sweet. I never lingered, never pushed for more. Not until that night in February when my kiss grew wings and sent her flying in the other direction, straight into a pitch-black sky.

The darkness swallowed her up.

I've been trying to catch her ever since.

She twirls a finger around the hair at the base of my neck. "I still feel safe with you," she says. "So I'm sorry if that feeling has me running into your arms every time I need a friend. I'm not trying to…confuse you. Or lead you on." Raising her chin, she straightens again, her hands around my neck, fingers playing with my hair. "If it ever gets too hard, I'll understand. I'll leave you alone."

I don't answer right away because I'm too focused on the caress of her fingertips dancing along my nape. Her gaze floats to mine, locking, waiting, questioning, and it's almost like she suddenly realizes the position we're in. It's not exactly innocent, despite her intent.

Heat warms my skin the longer our eyes tangle.

I spent all day outside in the blistering ninety-five-degree heat, yet nothing compares to the hot flush that scalds my blood at the image of her straddling my lap, her hands on me, her attention dropping to my mouth for a split second before she blinks rapidly and inhales a quick breath then glances back up.

And nothing, *nothing*, compares to the warmth that steals my heart, knowing that I'm her safe haven. After all she's been through, I can't think of a better thing to be.

So I say the only thing I can muster that won't scare her away. The only words that will keep her safety bubble fully intact, free of holes and cracks.

"I'm happy being your friend."

Her eyes flare, like she expected me to say something else.

Yes, it's too hard.

Yes, it's eating me from the inside out like a slow-killing cancer.

Yes, this one-sided love makes me feel hopeless and stranded, and it'll be the death of me one day.

Tabitha pulls her bottom lip between her teeth, chewing on it, toying with her next words. "But…" she whispers, her tone sad, a little guilty. "You'd be happier being more."

I don't hesitate. "I'm happiest being exactly what you need."

My heart clenches.

I suck in a sharp breath because I realize it's the truth.

I meant that.

A genuine, surprised smile tugs at the corners of her mouth as total relief sets in. The guilt in her eyes dissipates, replaced with gratitude.

Maybe even a little love.

It's not the love I crave, but it's a gift nonetheless, so I accept it for what it is.

Returning the smile twofold and adding a touch of a levity, I reach over to the adjacent side table and snatch my earphones. I hold them up, leaning back into the couch as she fully straightens on top of me. "Music?" I suggest.

She nods. "Sure."

I power up a song from one of my playlists as she untangles herself from my lap and sits beside me on the couch. Our shoulders fuse and our thighs smash together, as if the couch isn't big enough to hold five people, let alone two.

I take one of the earbuds and pop it in my ear while handing her the other. She doesn't question it. She just takes it and sticks it in her own ear, harnessing that sweet smile.

Music comes alive—a song by the mash-up band Neverending White Lights. It's fun, lighthearted, free of pain and melancholy.

Tabitha closes her eyes and rests her head against my shoulder, letting the song drown out any trace of the darkness that sank its teeth into her today.

Oliver's words echo in my mind. They mingle with the music, ringing loud over the chords and melodies: *"It's up to you to decide if your love is worth all of the harrowing moments you may suffer as a result of it."*

Smiling, I wrap an arm around her and pull her closer, breathing her in, perfectly content.

Yeah, it's worth it.

She is so fucking worth it.

CHAPTER 9
TABITHA

Two Years Earlier

An orange globe crested outside the dust-sheathed window and I had never in my life been more jealous of the sun.

The way it rose without question.

The way it shined without burden.

The way it dawned a new day, tempting hopeful beginnings that would never come to pass.

I was grateful for it, too.

I was grateful for the way it set his eyes aglow.

He was watching me, swirling aimless shapes along the dirty concrete with the toe of his shoe. I hadn't slept since our captor abandoned us down there in that hellhole, my temple pounding, my head spinning, my heart wondering if it would be better off dead.

All I'd done was wait.

I'd waited for daybreak, half craving it, half hating it, needing to see that he was real.

He was with me.

Matthew's eyes stayed fixed on me and I could finally make out the blue of them. A blue two shades darker than his sweater. My throat was dry and swollen, making it hard to breathe, let alone speak. But I attempted words because it was the only thing I had control over at the moment.

"I'm scared."

Those two words cut through the air like a dull blade.

His blue eyes stared back at me, blinking slowly, and I'd never seen the color blue look so hopeless. I pulled my splayed legs up until my knees were level with my chest. My calves and thighs were ice cold, having been glued to the cement for hours.

We'd been alone and trapped down there for *hours*; four, maybe five, until the dark sky brightened with daylight.

Matthew finally stopped tracing patterns in the dust and pulled his own khaki-clad legs up to mimic my position. His head dropped back to the pole, arms tied behind his back. "What were your plans for the day?"

My heart skipped.

And somewhere within that skipped beat it considered giving up again.

Emotion burned behind my eyes and stung my throat. He was only trying to make conversation, but the question felt like that dull blade was twisting in my gut, puncturing something vital. I shook my head and looked away, tears blurring my vision.

"I was going to get an oil change this morning," he said. "After I took my dog for a walk, I was going to stop for coffee at that little café off Fullerton, the one that looks like an old row house, and then I was going to bring my car in for an oil change. I'd likely grade some assignments while I waited. Scroll Facebook. Refill my coffee with the crappy Keurig selections at the auto shop."

My head continued to swing back and forth, rejecting his words. Rejecting his ordinary day that sounded so appealing right now.

"I had classes to teach this afternoon," he continued. "I knew you'd be there, but I'd force myself not to think about you sitting in the front row, tapping your pen, your chin in your hand, your pretty brown eyes following me as I paced the classroom."

"Stop."

"I'd fail, though. I'd think about you anyway, and then I'd hate myself for it."

"Please, stop," I cried. A tear fell, and then another. I wondered how long we'd be deprived of water, and then even crying would become a stolen privilege. "I can't...I can't do this."

"I'm going to get you out of here," Matthew told me.

"You can't know that."

"I believe it."

I tilted my head to look at him and found conviction staring back at me. Hopelessness lingered, but there was conviction, too. He believed it, even though he had nothing tangible to hold on to.

I guess they called that faith.

But faith was useless in a place with silver chains and skittering rats and a sun too far away to warm my skin.

"Tabitha, listen to me." Matthew sat up a little, squaring his shoulders in a way that made him appear strong and sure. "Listen carefully, okay? I'm going to tell you how to get out of this—at least as a way to buy time until I figure out a concrete plan. You have to trust me."

My heart twisted between my ribs. "What about you?" I croaked.

"I'll be fine. I'm going to figure something out."

Tears tickled my cheekbones. My fingers itched to swipe them away, but I wasn't even allowed the simple task of doing so. I glanced down at my pale-purple dress spattered with blood stains, streaked in dirt, torn at the hem. My porcelain legs were also smudged with filth and hadn't even had a chance to bronze before winter rolled in again, eclipsing the warmth of spring.

I returned my attention to Matthew across from me, just out of reach. I was pretty sure our toes wouldn't touch, even if we'd tried. "What do you think he wants with us?" I asked softly. It was hardly above a whisper because part of me didn't want to know the answer.

A hazy sunbeam highlighted the way his throat bobbed as he swallowed. He looked away briefly, then cut his gaze back to me in a slow slide. "I think this is a game for him and he gets off on our fear."

I squeezed my eyes shut like I was blotting out his words. "But…what does he *want*?"

"You, Tabitha," he said hoarsely. "I think he wants you, which means you might have a semblance of power here. We've seen his face. Right now, I don't think he has any intention of letting us go, so we need to find our own way out."

My throat was tight, my insides pitched with dread.

"Everybody has a weakness—even those with evil, psychotic minds. They are still human," he continued. "We need to study him, observe him. Pinpoint his weakness and use it as a tool. The more we can learn about him, the better chance we have."

My head whipped back and forth, new tears brimming to life. "He's going to kill us."

"But he hasn't yet. His motives go beyond killing." Matthew paused, his words fading out so only the sound of my whimpers filled the space between us. "This was premeditated. He took your keys, knowing you'd be stranded. My guess is he intended to offer you a ride home and then abduct you, and I was a crime of opportunity."

I let his words settle in. I tried to taste their truth, but they were sour on my tongue. Something didn't add up.

Swallowing, I glanced around the dimly lit basement, eyeing our surroundings. Surroundings I'd been assessing from the moment my eyes had opened.

I blinked, my chest swelling with awareness as my eyes swung back to Matthew. "I disagree," I murmured.

He cocked his head with interest. "Explain."

Licking my lips, I panned my gaze around the cellar. "Two poles. Two sets of handcuffs."

"Convenient."

"Calculated," I countered. "He called me 'Kitten.' He called you a 'dirty dog.' Everything feels rehearsed, so he's probably done this before—I think it's always involved two people." My heart pounded. My skin prickled with icy chill, with sickly alert-ness. "This isn't about me…this is about *us*. Whatever he has planned, you were always meant to be a part of it."

Silence festered.

Matthew watched me through busted glasses that had slid halfway down the bridge of his nose. He didn't respond for a while, soaking up my theory and testing its weight. Running the tip of his tongue along his top teeth, he nodded slowly. "Maybe."

Maybe.

I supposed there were nothing but *maybes* for us.

Maybe we'd escape.

Maybe we'd be strewn with bullets and buried in the backyard.

Maybe we'd starve to death.

My stomach grumbled at the thought, reminding me that there were several ways to die. I drank in a shaky breath and leaned back against the pole while I spent the next several minutes dissecting every option and debating on which one would be worse.

"Will you listen now?"

I popped my head up. "Listen?"

One leg stretched, the other bent at the knee, he sent me the faintest smile. It was a sad smile, and I'd never understood the point of sad smiles.

"I'm going to tell you how to get out of this alive," he said.

My eyes watered again. "I'm listening."

Matthew's smile faded, though the sadness of it lingered. "You'll have to pretend, Tabitha. Pretend until it feels real, pretend until it feels like you're not pretending anymore. Manipulate him."

"M-manipulate him?" I stammered.

"Yes." The word was nothing but a choking sound, a single syllable that pained him to say. "Pretend to enjoy whatever he does to you. Pretend to like him, to sympathize with him, to understand him. Create a rapport." Another pained sound fell out as he darted his eyes away. "We don't know what his motives are yet. It's possible he's incapable of feeling empathy, but establishing a bond is your best chance of survival at this point."

Horror and disgust churned my stomach, overriding the hunger pangs.

All I wanted to do was retch.

"No...that's impossible," I shot back, my words clipped with the audacity. "That's *impossible*."

He smacked his chains against the metal pole, making me flinch. "Dying down here in this shithole is *impossible*," he said through clenched teeth, throwing his head back. "You can do this. There's a life waiting for you on the other side of this wall, and I'll be *damned* if I don't do everything I can to put you on that side of it." Chest heaving, tone grave, he lifted his head back up. "Please, you have to try."

No.

No, no, *no.*

Tremors sluiced me from head to toe, my body violently shaking at his words. At the notion of offering myself to that slimy pig willingly, at the mere thought of allowing him to think for a second that I *wanted* him. That I *cared* for him.

Fury burned through me.

"If I do this, you have to fight with me," I volleyed back. "If there's a way out of here, it will include *both* of us. Do you hear me? It's both of us or it's neither of us. I won't leave this basement without you. I refuse."

He stared at me for a long while, his throat moving with trapped emotion.

Then he nodded.

A quick, terse nod, letting me know my conditions had been heard.

That's when I broke.

Finding a burst of strength, I pulled myself up to trembling legs and rattled my chains, slamming them against the pole, over and over, one, two, ten times. I started screaming. I shrieked away my pain, my horror, my incredulity, until my vocal cords were stripped raw, my mouth desert dry.

The final cry fell out as a heartbreaking moan of disbelief.

A ragged wail.

I could hardly catch my breath as bile climbed my throat and I glanced down at Matthew seated stone-still below me, both legs sprawled out in front of him as he watched me come apart.

A tear slipped from the corner of his eye.

I watched its slow-motion descent down his cheek until it dangled from his jaw and fell loose.

His prior words spiraled back to me: *"We do have a weapon."*

My eyes snapped shut as I tried to breathe, tried to latch on to an ounce of courage amid this harrowing Hell.

Our minds.

Our minds were the weapon.

I dropped back down to my butt and toppled sideways, tears leaving little puddles beneath my cheek as I silently wept onto the dirty cement.

My mind was all I had.

And him.

I still had him.

I⊤ WAS a miracle I'd managed to drift away at all, my body too weak and withered to stay awake any longer. Sleep had stolen me from the nightmare for as long as it could, a valiant attempt to protect me from reality. But the sound of steel-toed boots eventually stomped through my dreamworld, and the stinging of my scalp had me snapping awake with a shriek of pain when a cruel fist yanked me up by the hair.

I blinked away the sleep fog and came face to face with our abductor.

He grinned at me.

A snarling, curling grin that pulled at his bulbous cheeks.

"Welcome back, Kitten," he crooned.

I clung to the dream I was having. It had been a simple dream —me, sitting atop a grassy hill, my legs dangling over the edge. Water had glittered from down below, the sun lighting up the ripples, the breeze creating slow-cresting waves. I was scared of heights, but I hadn't felt afraid. I felt utterly weightless and at peace as I'd stared down at the lake from fifty feet above.

I thought I was going to jump, but the moment I'd scooted forward and slid down the jagged ledge the monster had returned and wrenched me away from the dream.

His gray-black eyes narrowed with devilry.

Whimpers crawled up my throat. "No...no, no, please..." I kicked my legs, but my strikes were just weak little knocks to his shins. "Don't hurt me. *Please*, let us go."

He laughed in my face, tugging my hair back. A scummy-slick tongue jabbed at my collarbone, then slithered up the side of my neck as the man groaned with lust. "Mmm. You taste real pretty."

Matthew went wild with his chains from the corner across from me. "Get away from her," he shouted, catapulting forward so hard his glasses fell off his nose. "Fuck, please. Leave her alone. *Leave her alone.*"

The man laughed again, his foul breath making my stomach pitch. My body heaved, wanting to vomit, but my stomach was empty and nothing came out. Only dry, barren gags.

Still laughing, the monster shoved me back against the pole until I slid down and landed in a heap on the floor. Then he turned and stalked toward Matthew.

Matthew pulled to a standing position, his cuffs hissing against the metal pole like a fork dragging across a chalkboard. He lifted his knee and planted a flat foot to the stranger's belly when the man approached, causing his heavy frame to totter backward with a sharp huff.

He tried to do it again when the man regained his footing, but was caught by the ankle, flying upward, then back down, hitting the ground hard.

The man snatched him by the hair, lifting him halfway off the cement, and twisted Matthew's attention toward me. "Look at her, doggie," he ordered. "Look at her now, so sweet and pure." An evil laugh rumbled in his chest. "She won't look like that much longer. You're gonna watch me fuck her."

Matthew growled, grunting his horror, spit glistening on his chin as he bared his teeth.

"You're gonna watch, and you're gonna remember every sound she makes when I pound her into that pole," he continued with a smirk. "And if you're a very good dog, maybe you'll get a reward."

He shoved him back to the floor.

I scampered to my feet when the man beelined toward me.

No.

Oh, God, no.

This was it.

I cried out as his stumpy legs carried him over to my corner, his eyes gleaming with anticipation. My mind tried desperately to latch on to Matthew's orders, but I couldn't hold on to them.

Pretend.

Manipulate him.

Trust me.

I couldn't pretend.

"Tabitha…it's okay, it's okay," Matthew yelled to me, rattling his chains to steal my attention. "You'll be okay, I'm here. You're not alone. You're not alone. I'm right here…"

I tried to catch and hold his words, but all I heard was the jangle of a belt buckle. All I felt were rough hands pulling at my dress and dragging my underwear down my thighs. All I could muster was a horrible wail when he settled between my legs and gripped me by the hip with one hand, by the hair with the other, and destroyed me with one violent thrust.

All I knew was true fear.

Hopelessness.

Nothing.

Matthew's words of solace morphed into howls of despair and I zoned out.

I felt nothing as I closed my eyes and pictured myself dangling at the edge of that cliff, sun on my skin, wind in my hair, and Matthew sitting beside me as our hands locked and our bodies pushed forward over the ridge.

I free-fell, I fluttered, I plummeted.

I was *free.*

I fell until I breached the water's surface and floated weightlessly to the bottom of the lake.

I fell because I couldn't stay there.

Present Day

The click of a tape recorder pulls me back to the sunlit office.

Evan sits across from me, hands steepled in front of him as he taps at his chin with his fingers, eyes glazed over. Silence hovers between us, only fractured by the sound of preteen-girl giggles floating from down the hallway.

I swallow, glancing at my bleached-white knuckles fisted in my lap.

"Are you okay?"

His voice is gritty and raw, almost like he was choking down my pain right along with me.

I nod slowly.

I nod because lying feels easier than telling him that my resolve is dismantling, memory by memory, minute by minute.

Maybe this was a mistake.

I don't feel any prickling of healing, no telltale wave of therapeutic relief.

All I feel is smothered.

"I want you to know that we can stop at any time," Evan says. "If this ever becomes too much, too triggering, we'll wrap it up. You never have to feel obligated to continue."

Inhaling a quaking breath, I lift my eyes and find his truth shining back at me. That alone has the anxiety ebbing, my chest feeling lighter. "I'm…okay. But thank you," I tell him. Sincerity bleeds with uncertainty, but I'm not ready to give up just yet. The bigger part of me wants to see it through. "It is hard, of course, but I think I need to do this. I want to keep going."

He gives me a small nod. "All right."

"Doing these interviews in chunks is easiest. I know I'm taking up a lot of your time, but—"

"No, hey, I've got nothing but time," he assures me. "Seriously, don't worry about me. I agree that slow and steady is best, so just let me know your availability and we'll make it work."

I smile my thanks. "I appreciate it, Evan. I think I've reached a stopping point for the night, but maybe we can reconvene in a few days? My schedule is a little swamped this week."

"Absolutely. Just send me a text."

Drinking in a full breath, I reach for my purse and move to stand. Evan walks me out of the office and down the hall, where Summer finds me from her perch on the couch, her legs pulled up beside her as she munches on a chocolate peanut butter cup.

"Hey!" she chirps, oblivious to the nature of the interview. "How'd it go?"

"Um, it went well." I force an easy smile to stretch. "We got a lot accomplished."

Summer's eyes pan up and down my figure as I slip into my sandals. "I like your style, by the way. It's fun."

"My style?"

"Yeah. Last time you were here, your shoes didn't match. Today you're wearing a purple shirt with green pants. It doesn't really match either, but it works somehow."

"Oh." I glance down at my outfit choice, realizing she's right. Shrugging, I chuckle lightly. "I guess I like things that don't always fit together in a conventional way. Keeps life interesting."

"Totally." She grins. "It's like you're finding magic in the flaws. I like that."

I blink, absorbing her words as I squeeze the strap of my

purse and move toward the front door, my smile blooming. "Thank you." Glancing at Evan leaning back against the far wall, hands in his pockets, I offer them both a little wave. "See you again in a few days."

They send me off with a goodbye and I step outside into the setting sun.

A hazy, orange glow lights up the pathway to my car as I glance down the neighborhood street, noting Gabe's car is absent from his own driveway.

He's not home.

I suppose there will be no heedless comfort tonight, no taking of things that don't belong to me.

Tonight, it's just me and the slow-dipping sun.

The sun, setting without question, beaming without burden.

And me, wondering how it can still glow so brightly when he's no longer here to watch it shine.

CHAPTER 10
TABITHA

She must be teething.

The pediatrician said her molars should be coming in any day now.

Hope wails against the crook of my neck as I murmur soft hushes into her dark ringlets. "It's okay, Pumpkin. You're okay."

I, on the other hand, am not okay.

I haven't gotten more than two consecutive hours of sleep in days, as my nights have been filled with awful, dark memories that have kept me restless and awake until dawn. Within the small pockets of sleep I *am* granted, come nightmares.

Grisly ones. Frightening ones. Hopeless ones.

Sometimes I see him—I see Matthew. He's as handsome as ever, his glasses whole, his faith unimpaired, his smile still intact. He's asking me to trust him.

I do, I always do.

And fate punishes me for that trust.

I pace around my bedroom in a cotton-lace nightgown, bouncing my toddler along my hip as she splays across my chest, her tears dampening the fabric. The hem of the dress tickles just below my knees as my bare feet pad back and forth, right to left, my hand sweeping up and down Hope's spine. As I move toward the dresser, I glance over at the partially-open drawer filled with clutter and a familiar vintage watch I consider slipping over my wrist.

A good luck charm.

But I know better than to believe in luck. I know better than to pretend that a wristwatch will gift me with a few hours of restful sleep.

Turning away, I touch the back of my hand to Hope's forehead. She feels warm. Fevers are often common with teething, right?

That sounds right.

I've done this before—dealt with early-stage teething—and yet those infant months feel like a fog-filled blur.

Traipsing into the kitchen, I give her a sampling of fever reducer and collapse onto my floral-swathed sofa. It doesn't match the rest of the home décor with its bright-tangerine marigold print, but I found it at a rummage sale and couldn't say no to the bold piece.

Hope's shrieky cries fade into ragged little breaths against my neck and I take a moment to drink in my own calming breaths.

My mind shifts to Gabe.

It often does that in the quiet moments.

When my world is dark and tumultuous, I think of Matthew and his pleas and mourning, his usual neatly-styled hair in disarray, his eyes wild.

And when the sun peeks over the clouds, a balmy warmth on my skin, I think of Gabe and the way his arms feel wrapped around me.

Comfort.

My cell phone sits beside me, charging on an end table. I reach for it, noting the time is nearly one a.m., and send Gabe a text message, knowing he'll be asleep. He sleeps with his earbuds in, so I won't disturb him.

ME:

> Does the teething stage ever end? I hope sleep has found you better than it has found me.

Sighing, I drop my head against the back of the cushion, still idly bouncing Hope in my lap, soothing her squeaky cries that keep threatening to reappear.

The phone buzzes in my hand.

Startled, I glance down to find a response.

GABE:

Sleep, you say? An elusive privilege only given to some. ☕

My smile is instant.

ME:

You're awake! Hi :)

GABE:

Hi ;)

ME:

My arms are full of a feverish toddler who agrees with that sentiment.

I'm trying to tell her I have to be at work in five hours and my tips are dependent upon whether or not I resemble a zombie or a bright-eyed pancake server.

And her puff snacks are dependent upon my tips.

I don't think we're making any headway because she keeps crying.

A tipless, zombie future feels imminent.

I'm trying to locate the zombie emojis when he responds.

GABE:

Lucky for you, you'd make a damn cute zombie, so I can't imagine your tips will suffer.

ME:

You'd let me eat your brains?

GABE:

In a heartbeat.

My smile widens to a teeth-flashing grin as I chew on my lip. Not wanting to keep him awake any longer, I send him a slew of heart-rimmed smiley faces and return my phone to the end table.

Hope starts crying again.

The smile fades.

"Oh, Pumpkin, it's okay," I soothe, anxiety brewing in my chest. I'm tired. I'm next-level exhausted. "Shh. Mama's here."

"Owie," she cries, tapping at her jaw with two chubby fingers.

Definitely teething.

Poor baby.

I stand and begin pacing the room again, humming a lullaby into her hair, the one about mockingbirds and diamond rings. I offer her a warm cup of milk, which she declines, and it only makes her sob harder. My own tears leak out as we dance around the room, my lullabies bleeding with despair, and I attempt an assortment of new distractions. Her favorite teething toy. A piece of a cereal bar to nom on. The little stuffed pig given to her by Cora on her first birthday because the sound of snorting pigs would make her crumble into a fit of baby giggles.

Nothing seems to work.

Thirty minutes later, we're collapsed on the sofa again and I'll be lucky to get three hours of sleep at this point, if any.

That's when I hear a knock at the front door.

Immediately, my blood runs cold.

I clutch Hope to my thudding chest as my head whips left, eyes flaring with fear.

The door is locked, at least. Triple locked. I'm a stickler for locked doors, sealed windows, and curtains that stay closed, even when the sun is happy and bright.

The knocking starts up again and I flinch, squeezing Hope tighter. Blowing out a breath, I set my daughter down on the couch, asking her to stay hushed, and slowly make my way to the front of the house. I creep open the baby-blue curtain and peek outside, hoping to catch a glimpse of the visitor.

My heart skips.

Gabe.

It's Gabe.

Relief washes over me as I swing the door open and reveal my friend looking not nearly as tired as I feel. His hands are filled with two cups, his jade eyes sparkling even brighter against the porchlight and a playful smile lifting his mouth.

"Gabe," I whisper. "What…what are you doing here?"

He shrugs like it's the most nonchalant thing in the world.

"Can't sleep, but there's still hope for you. Here." Extending a hand, he offers me one of the cups. "It's sleepy tea."

I take it, stepping aside to allow him entry. The drink is warm inside my palm. "Sleepy tea?"

"Yeah, the kind you like. With the flowery shit in it."

"Chamomile?"

"Yup." He moves inside and toes off his sneakers. "I figured there's no point in both of us being awake. I don't work tomorrow so I can take a nap whenever."

I'm staring at him in wide-eyed wonder, lost for words.

He takes my silence the wrong way and backpedals. "I mean...if you want my help. Which you probably don't, because you're a badass mom who has it covered, and I'm just being presumptuous." He chuckles with self-deprecation and scratches at his mop of wavy hair. "Shit. Am I an idiot? You can be honest."

"No...no, sorry. I just...I wasn't expecting you."

"I'm an idiot."

"No!" Letting the smile loose, I reach for his arm, giving his bicep a tender squeeze. "Not at all. This is incredible. The sweetest."

"Mm."

"I'm serious." My hand trails down his arm and locks around his wrist, tugging him farther inside. "Thank you. I haven't slept in...God, I don't even know. Are you real? Am I hallucinating?"

A crooked smile twitches on his mouth as he steps closer to me, his gaze dropping south for a quick beat before panning back up. The grin fades as a flickering of heat steals his expression.

I realize I'm wearing nothing but a thin white gown, almost transparent against the yellowy lamplight. A knot furls deep inside my belly, glowing and tingly.

The tingle feels real, so *he* must be real.

Which means the fact that I'm hardly dressed, my nipples on full display, is also very real.

"Gab!" comes a voice, and then a little hand tugging at my nightdress. "Gab play?"

Hope has climbed her way off the couch and toddled toward us, her cheeks bright pink and wet with tears. I scoop her up with one arm, noting how Gabe swivels away from the dipping of my gown and how I manage to flash him completely. My own cheeks pinken to match Hope's.

Clearing my throat, I rearrange my clothes as Gabe pretends to become enraptured by the uneven planks of my knotty pine flooring.

"These floors are really great."

He says it with all the enthusiasm in the world.

"Gab," Hope babbles again, reaching for him and pulling his attention away from the riveting floorboards.

Spinning back around, he sets down his own cup, likely filled with coffee, and shows no hesitation in plucking the red-cheeked, tear-stained toddler from my arms. Gabe is one of the few people I fully trust with my daughter. Even when Matthew's parents are in town for a visit, I find myself faltering before handing her over, hovering as they hold her, making up excuses not to leave.

His mother and father live in Canada, so their visits with their granddaughter are infrequent. They are kind people, and as welcoming as they can be toward the woman who was abducted with their son, the student who fell in love with her professor, the traumatized girl who managed to make it out alive while their only child was found buried beneath a gravel pit on that monster's property. They've done more than they've needed to in helping me provide for Hope—most notably, purchasing this home for us and keeping a roof over our heads. I don't feel right taking their money. Hope is my responsibility. So, when they send me checks periodically, I deposit the funds into an education account for my daughter.

Overall, they are kind but wary.

Welcoming but cautious.

And I can't blame them for that. I can't blame them in the same way I can't blame myself for the falters and the hovering and the excuses I give when they fly in for a visit and steal Hope from the safety of my arms.

My trust resides in a fragile, thin thread, ready to snap at any given moment.

And Gabe…

Somehow, he managed to weave that thread into thick, sturdy rope in the few short months I've known him.

So I don't even flinch when she goes to him.

I just watch, transfixed and charmed, as he totes her around the room, bouncing her on his hip, sweeping her through the air as her cries morph into belly laughter.

"Teething shmeething," he quips, rocking her side to side, humming a song under his breath. "Sydney said the only thing I'd ever be nurturing toward is my car, but take a look at this."

Oh, I'm looking.

I'm looking and yearning and wanting.

Mostly, I'm brokenhearted that all I can ever do is look.

Hope slithers from his grasp and teeters across the room on clunky feet. "Book," she says, rounding the corner toward her nursery. "I get book."

I cross my arms over my chest in an attempt to cover myself before glancing up at Gabe. He stuffs his hands in his pockets, his smile soft.

"Thank you for coming," I tell him, unable to prevent the slow lift of my hand and the way it reaches for him, reaches until my fingers are sweeping along his corded forearm and idly tracing his veins like they are something artful. My eyes lift to find his fixed on me. I drop my hand, exhaling sharply. "And for appreciating my floors, of course." I clear my throat. "They don't get the recognition they deserve."

He blinks, a grin pulling. "They're great floors. Shame how people just walk all over them."

I bark a laugh. "On that note…" Smile still beaming, I can't help but reach for him again. He's here, and he's warm, and he's real, and my hand believes it was made for touching him, even though my mind knows it shouldn't. "If you're serious about staying, I guess I can attempt a few hours of sleep. I really appreciate it."

My fingers glide from his arm in slow motion, giving him plenty of time to reach back.

He catches my wrist before I spin away.

All humor leaves his eyes as he swallows, his grip as searching as his gaze. "Tell me you're okay," he murmurs. "Please."

My throat tightens.

I'm an expert at faking it, but I can't seem to get the lie out.

I just stare at him, silent.

His jaw clenches. "Tabs."

"I will be," I opt for, not wanting him to worry. I don't know it to be true, but I believe it because I *have* to believe it. "I'm getting there."

The muscles in his bicep flex and twitch as his hold on me strengthens. My eyes lock onto the scar peeking out beneath his shirt sleeve, a stamp of true bravery, a mark of love and devotion.

It's beautiful, but it's also evidence.

Evidence of his mortality.

Proof that he's human, flesh and bone, just like all of us.

He's not untouchable.

He can still leave me.

I suck in a breath and wiggle my wrist free of his hand. My arms drop to my sides, but his attention doesn't drop to the outline of my breasts through the gown. It stays rooted to my face. It stays glued to the lie in my eyes shimmering back at him.

I don't know if I'll be okay.

I don't know if I'll ever be okay.

"Thank you again," I say meekly, turning around and making my way to my bedroom.

I give Hope a hug and a kiss before retreating into the darkness.

I sip my tea and set it beside me on the nightstand then slide beneath the covers and wait for nightmares to find me.

I fall asleep within seconds, my belly full of sleepy tea, and my heart filled with warmth as sweet dreams whisk me away…

IT WAS TOO good to be true.

Evil seeps into my subconscious and spoils the sweetness.

I'm flailing, scratching, fighting.

The man found me.

He regrets letting me go and now he's here, taking what he thinks is his, while I bite and claw and scream, desperate not to be dragged back into that basement.

"My Kitten escaped," the man sneers, hauling me over his shoulder and taking me from the comfort of my warm bed. "Naughty little pet."

"No!" I shriek, raking my nails down his back until I draw blood.

He laughs. "Feisty thing, you are. You know how much I like it when you fight back."

Hope chases after us, somehow escaping from her crib and running toward me as I extend my arms and reach for her. "My baby…I need my baby, please!"

"Mama, come back!" she cries.

The monster pays her no mind and ignores our pleas. He stomps through my living room and pulls open the front door until a chilly winter draft shocks my skin. Snow tumbles down. It's a blizzard, a freezing, lonely Hell.

He takes me to his car and opens the trunk, tossing me inside like I'm trash. Like I'm nothing. Like he owns me.

"I missed you, Kitten," he says, his gurgling laughter following the ice of his words. "Can't wait to take back what's mine."

The trunk slams shut, locking me inside.

No, no…no!

"Please, no, Hope…I need my child. Please, please, let me go…let me go!" I scream, terrified, kicking at the trunk, hardly able to breathe. It's dark, frightening.

Familiar.

"Let me go!"

I keep kicking and pounding and shouting, knowing there's no way out.

Knowing it's useless.

And then I feel arms around me, trying to tame my flailing limbs.

Soft hushes in my hair trying to quiet my screams.

Warmth trying to melt away the frost in my bones.

"Tabs, hey, you're okay…Jesus, wake up…shh, you're okay…"

My eyes ping open.

Shadows cloud my vision, darkness yearning to prevail. A trace of moonglow brightens the face looming over me as my body still fights back, confused, caught between a nightmare and the real world. His face comes into focus, and it's not the monster.

It's not my captor.

It's Gabe.

A sob of relief spills out of me as I yank my arms from his grip and fling them around his neck, pulling his weight onto me until his weight is the only weight I feel. I hold him tight, coiling my legs around his waist, feeling him blanket me, feeling his heart pound desperately with mine. I can't think about the position we're in because I don't want to think at all.

I just want to feel.

"Shit," he pants into the crook of my neck while I continue to cry and shake. "Christ, I heard you screaming. I thought you were—"

"Just hold me," I beg, squeezing him tighter, latching onto him like an anchor. My anchor to reality, to safety, to anywhere but there.

He obeys. He buries his face deeper into my shoulder, fingers burrowing in my hair and making a loose fist while his other hand finds one of mine. Our palms lace together, and my legs tighten around his middle. I cling, I hold, I weep.

I come back.

As my breathing finally steadies, Gabe shifts his weight to the side, taking me with him.

"D-don't let me go," I breathe against his chest, inhaling his scent, my one leg still parked over his hip as my hands clutch his T-shirt.

"I've got you," he murmurs. "You're safe."

I suck in a shallow breath. "I'm t-trying to fly, but…"

"I'll be your wings," he says, smoothing back my hair, his chin pressed to the top of my head. "You don't have to save yourself this time. You're not alone anymore."

My tears leak out in buckets. My body tremors as the adrenaline ebbs, leaving me a quivering mess of pain and confusion.

My hands snake beneath his shirt.

He goes still, a sharp breath fluttering against my hair.

I don't know what I'm doing, but I need to get closer—to feel him, to truly *feel* him. Warm skin, blood pumping, pulse racing and alive. My fingers travel up the planks of his abs, his chest, as one hand trails to his shoulder and my fingertips graze along the puckered flesh of his scar.

I trace it.

He shivers.

"I'm sorry," I whisper. "I just—"

"You can touch me."

His voice is low and gravelly, and I know he's affected by

this. He's trying to be strong for me, selfless, but I know what I'm doing to him.

Guilt gnaws at me but I keep touching him.

I drag my shaky hands back down his torso until I'm fisting the hem of his shirt and tugging it up, a bold request for more contact.

There is no hesitation as he yanks the shirt over his head and tosses it to the floor. His chiseled physique, bronzed from long days of working under the sun, stares back at me within the muted glow of moonlight. I keep my focus trained on his chest, his scar, his body, unable to meet his eyes.

He takes my hand and presses it to his chest.

His heart.

My tears still fall, quietly, more subdued, as my feather-light touch grows full-feathered wings.

I explore his body.

It's the only male body I've touched in years, having been too broken and scarred to invite intimacy back into my life.

Too afraid.

His breathing is unsteady. His skin vibrates. His muscles twitch as I roam and touch, as I trace his lines and divots, memorizing the edging of his scar. It takes up most of his upper right arm, tapering up his neck and fading at his jawline.

My fingers follow.

I realize my palm is now cupping his jaw, my thumb gently caressing the delicate skin while my other hand rests atop his chest. Our faces are centimeters apart; so close, his breaths feel like warm kisses on my lips.

Swallowing, I brave a glance up.

It's a mistake to look at him when he's half naked in my bed, our bodies dangerously entangled. My nipples pebble beneath my gown. My thighs clench, his legs trapped between them.

I watch his eyes flutter closed and his jaw tighten, and I hate myself for doing this to him.

The moment is sensual, raw, intimate.

And it's teetering the line of mass destruction.

"Tell me what you're feeling," he grits out, eyes still closed, as if it's too painful to look at me while we're like this.

It's as if his control is as delicate as my thread of trust and it's my turn to weave it into rope.

I feel his heartbeats kick up speed beneath my still-grazing palm. "Protected," I tell him. "Grateful that you're here."

He nods once. "Good."

Gabe slowly drops his forehead to mine, nearly every part of us touching. My heart fumbles in my chest. I feel whole, weightless, free of nightmares.

I feel like I could fly.

When I shift against him, instinct pulling me even closer, my breath catches when a part of me brushes against a part of him it shouldn't.

There's a hardness between his legs he can't hide, straining against his blue jeans.

His eyes are still closed, but he must notice the sound I make, something like a whimper or a fleeting gasp. He holds me tighter and repeats in a fraught tone, "You're safe."

I want to cry again.

Not from haunting memories, not from sadness.

I want to cry because he feels the need to remind me that I'm safe when it's impossible to feel anything *but* safe when I'm in his arms.

I whisper back, "I know."

Gabe tucks my face to the front of his chest and strokes my hair while inching his hips away from me. He doesn't want to scare me. He doesn't want me scurrying free of his hold, triggered and panicked, like I did the night he kissed me.

The truth is, I wanted that kiss.

Craved it, needed it, savored it.

Yet a buried, wicked part of me rejected it, too. His kiss sent me spiraling in the wrong direction as it tore away my mask so I couldn't hide any longer…couldn't pretend.

I reach for his hand, braid our fingers together, and squeeze.

I'm not running away this time.

The room is dark as the sun still sleeps, resting peacefully and lulling me back to my dreamworld now that the nightmares have been chased away. Before I drift off, I murmur, "Is Hope okay?"

He nods, pressing a kiss to my hair. "She fell asleep in my arms an hour ago. She's in her crib."

I smile against his chest.

Like mother, like daughter.

Comfort sweeps through me in waves of warmth, and when

my dreams find me once again, there are no monsters creeping in the shadows.

There is no darkness, no terror, no screams.

This time, there is only his hand in mine, a starlit sky, and two green eyes instead of blue.

CHAPTER 11

TABITHA

Two Years Earlier

Another day had passed.

I stared at Matthew seated across from me, his legs sprawled out in front of him, his feet tipped to each side as if his ankles, too, had lost their strength. His usual meticulously groomed hair was disheveled, pointing up, pointing side to side, making it look like gravity had become confused. His glasses were a mess of crystal shards and distorted frames lying beside his legs, and the blueness of his eyes looked desaturated and gray, even in the daylight.

We'd hardly spoken.

There was nothing to say.

He'd hummed a few songs, and I'd whimpered my own mourning hymns, but words were jumbled and hard to catch. Conversations felt like a strenuous climb up a never-ending mountaintop, where the peak was so tall it bled into clouds.

In other words…*pointless.*

I sighed heavily, training my breath not to morph into sobs.

After hours of silence passed between us, I tried to find words because there was nothing left to do but speak. It felt like I'd been pacing the base of the mountain for days and days, and now there was nowhere else to go but up. "You…you have a dog, right?" I asked.

My voice was a whip, slashing through the quiet.

He blinked, eyes squinting in my direction. "Yes."

"What kind?"

"A husky. Her name is Echo."

"Echo," I parroted, envisioning Matthew with his styled hair and unwrinkled clothes traipsing down the city streets with a leash in one hand, a hot coffee in the other. "That's a pretty name."

"She's all alone in my apartment right now. Likely out of food and water. Soiling herself, whimpering by the door." His eyes closed, posture stiffening. "No one is there to check on her."

I felt burning pressure behind my eyes but the tears didn't well. I was too dehydrated to cry. "She'll be okay. I'm sure someone has noticed our absence by now…I bet the police are at your apartment right this minute, looking for you, taking her for a walk."

"Mmm," he muttered, unconvinced.

He was still squinting at me and I wondered if he could see me without his glasses. Maybe I was nothing but a blur.

Maybe it was better that way.

To see was to know, and I was certain he'd rather be blind than see a reflection of his circumstances staring back at him with a torn, bloodied dress, matted hair, and hollow eyes.

Dropping his head to the pole, Matthew made a croaking sound like he was in pain. "Are you hurt?" he wondered through clenched teeth.

I just blinked, not knowing how to reply. There was a stinging ache between my legs and purple bruises along my inner thighs, but he didn't need to hear that. "No."

"You don't have to lie. There's no point."

"I'm fine." My voice cracked terribly. "I'll be fine."

"Fuck…" he gritted out. "I've never felt more helpless."

"We're going to get out of here," I said with all the conviction I could muster—which, decidedly, wasn't much. "We have to. There's no other alternative."

The other alternative hovered between us like the Grim Reaper, but Matthew allowed me to pretend.

"I almost fucking died watching him do that to you," he said.

Bereavement laced his words.

Tortured, awful bereavement, as if part of him *had* died.

"I wanted to look away," he continued. "I wanted to block it out, but I couldn't. If *you* couldn't, then I couldn't either. It didn't seem fair to let you go through it alone."

A strangled cry escaped my lips. "Matthew, I—"

The basement door burst open.

I instantly cowered, curling around my pole in an attempt to hide. My naked feet skidded along the cement, but my legs were too weak to pull me upright. I had no strength, no fight, no hope.

"Potty break for my pets," the man announced, his boots stomping down each step, one by one. "Kitten goes first." He yanked a pistol out from his waistband, pointing it at me. "Pull any tricks and I'll put a bullet between lover boy's eyes before you can take your next breath."

I nodded quickly. "I won't."

A touch of relief swam through me.

My bladder was painfully full.

"You'll get one minute to eat something. Can't have you withering away before I'm done with you, amiright?" He snickered. "There's still fun to be had."

Matthew pulled himself to shaky legs. "Don't hurt her."

"Kitten'll be safe so long as she behaves and keeps her claws away." Sniffing, he sauntered toward me and pulled a key from his pocket with his free hand.

My wrists tingled with anticipation. My muscles sang with joy, aching for release.

I didn't know what to say, so I muttered a pathetic, "Thank you."

Laughter was his response. A roar of belly laughter, like my gratitude was the funniest joke he'd ever heard. "They always thank me," he chuckled, a warbly noise that sounded like phlegmy amusement. "But they sure as fuck don't thank me when they're bleeding out all over my floors and the life is draining from their eyes."

My body started to tremor, my heart sinking with terror.

Oh God.

He was going to kill us.

It was no longer a *maybe*; it was a staunch fact.

It was only a matter of when.

Matthew growled from his corner, yanking at his chains. "Let her go. Keep me, do whatever you want to me," he begged. "Just let her go."

He laughed again, nearly choking on his glee. "They always say that, too. That's why I take the pretty ones. My dogs like to throw themselves on the sword for the pretty ones." He moved in closer and slapped a pudgy hand between my legs, squeezing until I cried out. "Good pussy makes stupid men even stupider."

"Please," I pleaded through a tearless sob. "Please…"

He let me go, his evil eyes gleaming. Moving behind my pole, the man grabbed my linked wrists and freed me as he hummed a jaunty tune, the chains clanking against the cement.

For a moment, pure relief overpowered my fear as my arms fell to my sides. Both of my wrists were bleeding and bruised while I massaged them, savoring the feel of skin on skin.

Savoring the feel of touching something, anything.

"Let's go, bitch," the man snarled, tugging me to my feet by the hair, severing my small pocket of solace. "You've got three minutes to piss and eat a sandwich. Time starts now."

My hair was tangled in his grimy fingers as he dragged me through the basement, away from Matthew. I gasped as I struggled to stay standing, my feet tripping over themselves while I twisted toward the man still chained and trapped. "M-Matthew…"

"It's okay," he called back, voice cracking. "You're going to be okay. Remember what I said. Trust me."

Manipulate him.

Pretend to enjoy whatever he does to you.

Create a bond.

I couldn't.

God, I couldn't.

Three minutes later, my bladder was lighter and my belly was fuller. My thirst was quenched for the time being, but none of that seemed to matter because the monster was between my legs again. He'd replaced my tattered dress with a musty, oversized T-shirt, and his hands were exploring my body underneath the itchy cotton as his grunts and groans echoed off the basement walls.

I found Matthew's eyes over the man's shoulder.

He was watching me.

Stunned and helpless.

Tears streaked down his dirt-smeared face as he shook his head with hopelessness. Apology shimmered in blue-gray eyes.

And then he mouthed, *"Trust me."*

I slammed my eyelids shut and floated away.

Everything was earth and sky.

Flesh and bone.

Stars and waves.

I was drifting and weightless and nothing, because nothing was so much better than what this was.

The man wrecked me.

Sullied me.

Ruined me.

He stole another piece of my soul with every awful violation.

To him, the only thing in the world that held more value when it was broken...*was me.*

After the man finished, he hauled his pants up his hips and secured the buckle into place, and I leaned back against the pole, defeated and used.

But there was a prickle of survival churning in my blood.

A desperate need to break out.

To live.

It wasn't just me down there.

Matthew thought I held the power, that I was the one who could get us out.

And if I succeeded...he was coming with me.

The man grinned as he took a single step back and hiked up his zipper.

I looked him dead in the eyes.

And I smiled.

Present Day

"EARL HUBBARD." Evan leans forward on his elbows and folds his hands together, the tape recorder still drinking in my dark secrets. "That was his name. Earl Timothy Hubbard."

"Yes." I nod. "He never told us his name at the time, so I just referred to him as 'the man.'"

He jots down some notes. "He told Cora Lawson and Dean Asher his name."

Tucking my hair behind my ear, I nod again. "I think he'd become more confident by then. More certain they wouldn't escape."

"Do you think he always had the intention of letting you go? Maybe he thought you were different?" he wonders. "More… special, somehow?"

"No, I think he planned to kill me. Just like the others."

"But you built a rapport with him," Evan says, confirming while also questioning. "You created a bond."

"I did. It was the only way."

A slight frown creases his browline. "Hmm."

"What is it?"

"Nothing," he says, setting down his pen. "That must have been difficult."

"It was."

There's a fine line between difficult and impossible, and I teetered on it tenfold. But it was never *entirely* impossible—not compared to the alternative.

And I know, with absolute certainty, that the lean toward difficult is the only reason I'm still alive right now.

Evan looks contemplative as he picks his pen back up and clicks the end with his thumb, almost like each click represents a beat in which he wants to ask me something but can't seem to get the words out. He sucks in a deep breath, a question gathering in his throat.

Then he drops the pen again.

I swipe my clammy palms along my thighs. "Is that all for today?" When I stopped by this evening, I'd been inclined to press forward, to dive deep into the horrors of the two weeks that followed, but I'm tired. I'm running on less than three hours of sleep and I don't think I can handle any more tonight. I need to mentally prepare for the nightmares that will come when I slip into bed and close my eyes.

They are greedy and draining.

Evan pushes back in his chair, the legs screeching against hardwood. "We're good," he says. "You look exhausted. Did you want some coffee for the road?" He closes his notebook and shuts down the laptop, sparing me a quick glance.

"No, thank you. Can I come by tomorrow?"

"I'll be here. Get some rest."

Rest.

What a concept.

What a luxury I'll never take for granted again.

After collecting my belongings, I step out onto the small front porch and discover Summer already seated on the stoop watching the cloud cover eclipse our remaining daylight.

She doesn't look at me as she says, "I think it's going to rain soon."

My eyes pan across the graying horizon as my skin prickles with the slight drop in temperature. The breeze picks up, causing my hair to dance across my vision. Cicadas sing from nearby trees and I shiver at the sound of them. Their thrumming, pulsing drone reminds me of the single-worst moment of my life.

Summer turns to me with a smile. "I love thunderstorms."

"Do you?" Hesitating, I move forward and take a seat beside her on the cement step. "I don't, really. Thunder makes me nervous. Storms are unpredictable, and I don't like unpredictable."

"I can understand that," she says with a nod, tipping her chin skyward. "I guess I like the reminder that not even the sky is ever truly at peace. It's breakable, just like we are."

I blink at her, studying her profile, her slender jaw and curious blue eyes. "How old are you again?"

"Nine. Almost ten."

"You're very wise for your age."

She shrugs. "My friends say I'm weird, but I take it as a compliment. I think our weirdness is what makes us unique, don't you think?" Summer picks at her fingernails as she turns to me, nibbling her lip. "Like that necklace you're wearing. It's kind of weird, but it's cool, too. Are those rings?"

I glance down at my necklace and finger the two rings I laced through the brassy chain. One is made of tungsten, the other of rose gold. "Yes. They mean something to me."

"What do they mean?"

Matthew's face flashes to mind as he tugs the ring off his

trembling finger and shoves it into one of my cuffed hands, curling my fingers around the metallic token.

"For good luck. A keepsake. Just in case—"

I suck in a breath. "One of them was given to me by the man I loved. The other I found when I was just a child. It was buried in the dirt beside our cherry tree."

Summer's eyes glisten with intrigue. "I love that." She perks up a little, straightening on the stoop and twirling one of her own rings. Plucking it off her thumb, she hands it to me. "Here. You can add this to your collection. I found it at the park and thought it was neat."

I extend my hand and she drops it in my outstretched palm. It's chipped and tarnished, ringed with silver stars. My heart pounds as I squeeze it in a tight fist. "Are you sure? I'd hate to take something of value from you."

She dismisses me with a flick of her hand. "It doesn't mean anything to me. But maybe it'll mean something to you. You should add it to your chain."

I open my fist and stare at the circle of stars. My chest feels strangled.

"You don't like it?"

"No, no…I love it. Thank you. This is so thoughtful."

She smiles, then swivels forward to stare at the gray clouds moving in. "You should probably get going before the storm hits. I think it's going to be a bad one."

Nodding, I rise to my feet and stuff the little ring into my front pocket. "I'll see you tomorrow. Thank you again."

She grins, bobbing her head. "See ya."

Sending her a wave, I move across the walkway toward my car, glancing down the street to Gabe's house. His Challenger sits idly in the driveway.

My stomach pitches with memory.

Heat warms my cheeks.

I imagine his strong arms around me, his heartbeats lulling me to sleep as I drifted away against his bare chest the night before, then awoke in the exact same position.

Selfish.

I was so selfish, clinging to him, holding him, *touching* him in ways I shouldn't. Giving him hope when I am only made of hopelessness. I'm just a lost soul, wandering and wilting.

THE STARS ARE ON OUR SIDE 109

I have nothing to offer him.

And still, I take.

My feet carry me down the sidewalk, toward his house, the pull of him trumping my common sense. My selfishness leading the way.

But I stop short when my cell phone pings from my purse.

I can't help the relieved smile that stretches, thinking it's him, thinking he's the one pulling me because I'm on his mind, but when I open the text message, it's not him. It's not Gabe.

It's Martha Gleason.

Matthew's mother.

MRS. GLEASON:

> Hello, Tabitha. Pat and I are in town for the remainder of the summer and we would like to spend time with our granddaughter. I apologize for the short notice, but my e-mails have gone unread. We purchased a summer home in Galena and are hoping to take Hope for a few weeks. Call me as soon as you get this.

I teeter on the sidewalk.

I sway and wobble as the stormfront rolls in, stealing my balance, my breath hitching with dread.

A few weeks.

They want to take my baby, my anchor, my whole life, for a few *weeks.*

Galena is nearly three hours from here.

My hand glides up my chest, latching onto my rings and squeezing. I've never been away from my daughter that long; no more than for a few hours at a time.

Not even a full day.

Not ever.

The idea of her not being around is debilitating.

My thumb hovers over the call-back button, my body quivering as I try to process the request. A few raindrops slip from the clouds and dapple my phone screen. The wind picks up.

I lift my chin, my eyes landing on Gabe's house and drinking in the lamplight glowing from his front window. It beckons me forward.

Comfort. Solace. Reprieve.

Safety.

But I turn in place, instead, and jog back toward my car, flinging myself inside just as the thunder cracks, the lightning strikes, and the rain falls down in buckets.

I sob into my steering wheel and break apart, right along with the sky.

CHAPTER 12

GABE

My cell phone buzzes in my hand as I'm clocking out of work two days later and I answer it on instinct.

"You're receiving this call on a pre-recorded line from inmate Travis John Wellington at the Marwick County Corrections Facility. To accept this call—"

I decline it and shove the phone into my pocket.

Fuck that.

Fuck him.

My skin prickles with ice and loathing, trumping any curiosity as to why my piece-of-shit father keeps calling me from prison while he awaits trial for crimes I can't even begin to wrap my head around. He doesn't deserve a second of my time.

He deserves a needle in his arm.

A barren, deserted funeral swarming with bees because bees are the only thing in the world that can shake him up.

He deserves a shallow grave, where the feasting maggots will choke and gag, his flesh too vile for even the lowliest creature.

I cringe at the mental image.

The sun hangs low in the sky, still a burning ball of death despite the recent rain. I'm supposed to meet Sydney at our favorite taco joint in twenty minutes, but work ran late, as per usual, and I'm sweating my ass off in my canvas pants and long-sleeved shirt.

A shower first feels like the compassionate thing to do.

I make a beeline toward my black Challenger, ruffling my

sweat-damp hair as I pull the hard hat off my head. I'll be honest…my car is my baby. I don't have a child or a pet, and I don't even have a girlfriend, much to my own crippling disappointment, but I do have a car to dote upon.

Considering my house is paid off—the title transferred over to me years ago by my father the felon—the obscenely high car payments on a newer-model Dodge Challenger with a V8 engine are actually manageable. It's not a Hellcat, because that's bucket-list shit, but she's still a dream.

As the sun beats down on me, I almost don't notice the man lurking beside my prized possession. Raising a hand to my forehead, I block the hellfire from my eyes and squint.

It's that creepy dude in the newsboy cap, the one who was staring at me at the jobsite days ago.

Weird but okay.

I ignore him since I have no idea who he is, so it seems unlikely that he's here for me, and move to the driver's side of my car.

"Mr. Wellington."

Shit.

I stutter to a stop, tapping the hard hat against my thigh as my mind reels with who this guy could be. He approaches me with a slight limp in his gait, his cap shadowing his eyes. "Do I know you?" I face the man fully, watching as he inches closer. There's a grisly scar roping down the left side of his face, cheekbone to jaw, while tufts of salt-and-pepper hair fly loose beneath the hat.

He looks like he just stepped off the set of Peaky Blinders.

"Not yet," he says with an off-putting smile.

I have no idea what that means. "Did you need something?"

He stuffs his hands into tweed-like trousers and lifts his chin, revealing two pale-blue eyes that look transparent. "I'm here to collect a debt."

I blink.

Awesome.

That's not at all ominous.

"I think you have the wrong guy," I tell him dismissively, my jaw ticking. "But I'm sure I can put you in touch with a debt collection agency. I know a guy who owes a lot of people a lot of money, and they keep harassing me. Happy to hand over the dozens of numbers I've blocked."

He glances at his fingernails, totally composed. "That won't be necessary."

"Sorry I can't help you, then." I reach for the car door handle.

"I've been informed that you, specifically, *can* help me."

Sighing, I pause mid-reach. "Someone lied to you."

"Unlikely."

The guy isn't overtly threatening, but there's something about him that has my duck-and-run instincts firing. Given the scar, the limp, and the icy, fear-instilling persona, I'm guessing he's been through some shit. Worse, he's probably the cause of it. "Listen," I try, deciding it's in my best interest not to provoke him, "I think you've mistaken me for someone else."

A grin curls on his mouth, causing the scar to stretch and skitter like a menacing snake. "I assure you, Mr. Wellington, I don't make mistakes."

"Gabe," I correct, eyes narrowing. "Wellington is my asshole father."

Silence is his reply.

Nerve-rattling silence that chills my blood, despite the sun dead set on melting off my skin.

A joyless smile still paints his mouth as those eerie eyes bore holes into me, almost like he's trying to tell me what I owe him without using words.

Unfortunately for him, I don't speak laser-beam eyes.

I yank open the car door.

I'm expecting him to stop me, my adrenaline spiking, defenses flaring, but he makes no move to prevent me from slipping into the front seat and collapsing onto the black leather interior. I glance at him before closing the door.

The smirk doesn't wane as he says, "I'll be in touch, Wellington. By the way, I suggest answering the next phone call from your asshole father." He sniffs. "I have a feeling things will become a lot clearer."

The guy spins around and moves away, hands in his pockets, whistling under his breath.

Of course he whistles.

"I'll give you two weeks," he calls out before half-limping

toward the edge of the parking lot. "My boss doesn't like delays."

Two weeks.

Debt owed.

Talk to my father.

Yeah, right.

That's never gonna happen. This prick is just going to have to acclimate to a never-ending delay.

Shaking off the bad mojo crawling all over my skin, I let the guttural purr of the engine replace my anxiety while making a mental note to change my last name.

It's something I've been wanting to do anyway, but hearing it roll off that creep's tongue, all filth and venom, definitely bumps it up the priority list.

I'm going to take my mom's last name—Kent.

Mom lives in Delaware now. After a messy divorce, my father managed to gain full custody of me due to having money and connections. He only did it to be vindictive because that's the kind of person he is. I saw my mother one day a week for years until I reached adulthood, then she moved to the east coast to take care of my grandparents.

There was always a distance between us, but we've become closer lately.

In fact, I'm due for a visit soon.

After sending her a quick text to see if she'll be around next month, since I'll have some time off of work between projects, I finally cruise out of the parking lot.

Because of the hold up, I don't have time to grab that shower, so Sydney will just have to suffer the consequence of my labor-intensive day in the heat.

Parking my car toward the back of the lot, I jog inside and find Syd already perched at one of the booths, scooping tortilla chips into homemade salsa.

"Yo. Sorry I'm late."

She perks up when she spots me. "Always preferable. More chips and salsa for me."

"Opportunist," I tease, sliding into the space across from her and collapsing with a bone-weary sigh.

She leans over the table to sniff me. "Ooh, you smell good. New cologne?"

My eyebrows lift as I swipe the basket of chips and dig my hand in. "Yeah, it's an intoxicating mix of silicone sealant, sewage, and sweat stains."

"Well, it works." Licking a dab of salsa off her finger, she adds, "Nice alliteration, by the way."

"Thanks."

"How's Tabitha?"

The subject shift has the tortilla chip stopping just before it reaches my mouth. I sit on the question for a beat, then take a bite before chewing thoughtfully. "Is that why you wanted to grab food? To bust my balls?"

"Maybe."

I huff. "I'm worried about her."

Sky-blue eyes soften with sympathy through her black-rimmed glasses. "Understandable," she says. "How are you?"

"Fine." I steal another chip and avert my attention to the salsa dish. My answer comes too quickly. It's too rehearsed.

Sydney knows me better than anyone.

We've been friends since childhood, becoming closer and closer as the years pressed on in Oliver's absence. At first, the loss of him was the main thing we shared in common, until time shed light on all of our other striking similarities.

We both love Mexican food, raunchy sitcoms, the same music, and we share a similar sense of humor.

We're kind of a hot mess.

And most notably, we've both built up walls. We've guarded our respective hearts with jokes and ill-timed sarcasm, loveless connections, and a variety of vices that have never really served us beyond a temporary peace.

Until Oliver returned, anyway.

Until Tabitha.

We always say we're basically the same person, which is why romance has never been in the cards for us. Honestly, Syd feels like a sister to me.

She's my family.

We order the same thing we always order, and when the plates arrive, Sydney swirls designs into her enchilada sauce with the tines of her fork. Sighing, she glances up at me. "Remember when we were sitting at this exact table eating enchi-ladas last year and you warned me to keep my distance from

Oliver because he was vulnerable and breakable?" She sets the fork down and folds her arms on the table. "You were afraid I would hurt him."

I wince, still feeling mildly guilty for that.

I knew Sydney would never *intentionally* hurt him, but I also knew that my stepbrother was completely head over heels for her. He was handing his heart to her on a silver platter while Syd had spent a lifetime shunning handed-out-hearts and true intimacy. It sounded like a recipe for disaster.

Now…I get it.

Sometimes you meet your match and those walls come tumbling down, brick by brick. You no longer want to run from potential heartbreak anymore, because heartbreak feels like a welcome risk when it means you have a fighting chance at love.

My love seems to be more fighting and less chance—but, *fuck* if it doesn't feel worth it.

Replying through a bite of food, I finally mumble, "Yeah, I remember."

She stares at me knowingly.

I sigh through a swallow and wipe my hands on a napkin. "Look, I know Tabs has been through a lot and, on paper, I'm probably not the best guy for her. She has a kid and I still can't figure out how to put a diaper on the right way. She was kidnapped and assaulted, while my father sits in a jail cell on similar fucked-up charges. I totally know that I'm not—"

"Gabe, that's not what I'm implying at all."

I blink, my brows pinching with confusion. "I thought this was one of those moments where I'm a giant hypocrite."

"Oh, you are." She smirks at me. "But I'm not worried about you hurting her. I'm worried about her hurting *you*."

The words settle in my gut like the loose bricks from my crumbling walls.

I push my plate away and lean back in the booth, tilting my head to the side. "I know what I'm up against. She wouldn't hurt me."

"I know she won't mean to."

Grumbling, I look down at my feet, fairly certain I used those exact words on Syd at some point.

A vision from two nights ago flickers in my mind, a vision of

Tabitha's arms clinging, her legs squeezing, her hands exploring. She was so fragile. So desperate for comfort, for physical contact.

Of course, my dick decided to read the moment all wrong. I couldn't help my body's reaction to her warm palms grazing up and down my chest and torso, or how she was pressed so fully into me, we were nearly becoming one.

God, the way she trembled and swayed in my arms. The crackling, all-consuming tension I felt between us. The feelings, the love, the heat.

She set me on fire, leaving me nothing but a pile of ashes come sunrise.

And I guess that's the trouble with fire.

It only knows how to burn.

Sydney puckers her lips, flipping her flaxen-blonde hair over her shoulder as she levels me with her signature squinty eyes. "Tell me."

I shake away the memories of Tabitha's limbs wrapped up in mine, her thin gown the only physical barrier between us, before this conversation isn't the only thing getting hard. "Tell you what?"

"Where you went just now." Somehow, she squints harder, almost like the narrowing of her eyes is enough to pull the answers out of me. Then she gasps. "Something happened."

"No."

"You're getting all flushed. You never do that."

I shoot her a glare. "It's called a sunburn, Syd. It's two-hundred fucking degrees outside."

Sydney cocks her head and makes a pouty face, not buying it. Digging into her meal, she pops a forkful of rice into her mouth and talks through the bite. "Well, don't say I didn't warn you, dude. I think Tabitha is amazing and sweet and the epitome of strength, but I don't think she's ever going to be what you want her to be. She's been through too much." A smile tips her lips, softening her words. "You can't wait around forever."

Heart, meet dagger.

I don't say anything as I smash my refried beans with a fork, pretending that her words aren't a flame to my weakening thread of hope.

Truth be told, I realize she's not wrong.

Tabitha is a raven around my heart.

Soft feathers and sharp claws.

She soothes me while shredding me to pieces at the same time.

And yet I'll take every claw mark, every painful laceration, just for the chance to fly with her one day.

If waiting is all I need to do, it's a damn small price to pay.

CHAPTER 13

TABITHA

I cancel my interview with Evan the next evening for an emergency girls night with Cora and Mandy.

My baby girl is leaving me.

When the sun comes up, Hope will be taken from the safety of my arms and toted three hours away with two people who haven't even heard the sweet sound of her laughter yet.

It doesn't feel right.

It feels like I'm losing a limb.

Hope is entertained in a giant plastic playpen that takes up half of my living room when my friends breeze through the front door with a bottle of wine and take-out food from a local Chinese restaurant.

I don't drink wine and haven't touched alcohol since my twenty-first birthday. I had two strawberry margaritas that were more slush and syrup than liquor, but I still recall the way they clouded my mind, making me feel incapable. A friend of mine had to drive me home.

I've never liked the idea of having my common sense compromised and that feeling only grew stronger after my…*ordeal*.

I need to be in control.

I can't let my power slip.

Mandy tosses the bag of takeout onto my marigold couch and sweeps her hair to one side, eyes instantly panning to Hope bouncing up and down in her playpen. "The little munchkin missed me," she says breezily, racing toward the toddler with arms stretched wide. "Maybe Reid and I should have a baby. Do you think we should have a baby?"

Cora plops down on the couch and sticks the bottle of wine between her thighs. "My answer will always be yes." She drops her head to the back of the couch, only her eyes trailing to me with a soft smile. "You've given my sister baby fever. I never thought I'd see the day."

"Hey, I'm maternal," Mandy insists, scooping up Hope and parking her on her hip. "A natural-born nurturer."

Cora coughs through her next words. "Plant Fiasco of 2007."

"What? I hate it when you do the coughing thing."

"The plants, Sis."

Mandy glares. "How dare you bring that up."

Cora's smile stretches as she watches me move toward her and take a seat beside her on the sofa. "Mandy managed to coerce our mother into turning her bedroom into a greenhouse. All the plants were dead within a week."

"I was too busy to water them, okay? I had an active social life." She shrugs. "We were learning about plants in school and it sounded really appealing," Mandy says. "I wanted to be a lobotomist."

"Oh, my God." Cora laughs, cupping a hand over her mouth as her shoulders shake. "I think you mean botanist."

"You're such an English teacher."

I lean back into the couch, my anxiety easing as I take in the sisters' bantering. It warms my heart that they've made it to this point after a messy fallout involving Cora's boyfriend, Dean.

Dean, who was once *Mandy's* boyfriend.

Her fiancé.

After Cora and Dean were kidnapped by Earl Hubbard months after my escape, they fell in love with each other. I wasn't a part of Cora's life just yet, so I never witnessed the grisly breakdown firsthand, but I was there to comfort Cora as she tried to put the pieces of her dismantled life back together. It was a long, uphill journey. But Mandy found love again, and I think that was the key to everyone's healing.

Love.

It's the one thing in this world that can be both a killer and a healer.

While Mandy fusses over Hope, Cora turns to me, setting the wine beside her feet. Her knowing emerald eyes see right through my smile. "I think this will be good for you," she tells me gently, extending a hand to cup my knee. "A break. Some quiet moments."

My eyes dip, the smile fading.

She has no idea that it's within the quiet moments that I die a slow death.

I've had my fair share of quiet moments. When Matthew left me, all I had was the awful silence, only severed by curious rats skittering along the walls, tree branches smacking against the roof when the wind mocked me, and the sound of my own grief as my heart cracked in two.

Still, I nod, pretending she's right.

Pretending this will be good for me.

"And let's face it," Mandy adds, returning Hope to her playpen and traipsing toward us, "you won't *actually* be all alone. You have us. You have me and my big mouth to keep you entertained." She shoots me a Mandy smile. "And Gabe, of course. I bet that man won't let you out of his sight."

My skin warms at the thought of Gabe. I haven't seen him in a few days; not since the night he held me until dawn, keeping me safe and free of nightmares.

We've texted, talked on the phone, but I've tried to keep my distance because I know my clinging and needing doesn't serve him in any way.

I care about him...*a lot.*

Maybe a buried part of me even loves him.

But my love is the killing kind, and he doesn't deserve to go like that.

Mandy collapses onto the couch to my right after fetching the sparkling wine and unscrewing the cap. "How's it going with Gabe, anyway? Have you guys gotten your freak on yet?"

"Mandy," Cora scolds, leaning around me to scowl at her sister.

"What? Gabe is hot. Tabitha is hot. I'm not an English major like you, Cor, but I know my math." She wiggles her eyebrows at me.

I slink back into the cushions, my cheeks growing hot. "We're just friends." It's mostly the truth. Sure, maybe we'd be more if my past didn't follow me around like a dark phantom, but it does, and I refuse to let it haunt him, too.

Cora offers sympathy instead of sass. "You know I get it. Ignore my sister. She loves being a matchmaker—" She freezes, her words turning to dust as we both choke on the grit.

I clear my throat and look away.

"Shit, that came out wrong," she says.

"No worries, it's fine." My pounding heart and trembling knees tell me it's not fine, but again, I pretend. I'm good at that. "Anyway…Gabe is amazing, but I'm not looking for a relationship any time soon. Probably never."

"What about sex?" Mandy wonders, seemingly oblivious. "Maybe it'll help. He'd probably worship you. Treat you like a queen."

"I-I can't…I mean, I don't think I—"

I swear Cora growls beside me, leaning forward and glaring daggers at her sister. "*Mandy,*" she repeats through clenched teeth. "Seriously."

Mandy cowers a little. "Jeez, I'm just trying to help. Calm down."

"That's not helpful. Tabitha was raped by a lunatic for months. Do you really think sex is going to be her go-to healing solution?"

Tension swirls between us. A thick, palpable pressure in the air.

Flustered, Mandy sets her jaw and lifts her chin. "Seemed to do the trick for you."

My eyes pop.

Oh no.

Cora's jaw unhinges, a glassy look of stunned pain claiming her eyes.

Dean is never really a topic of discussion between them— especially in regard to their complicated past. I'm aware of the details. I know that Cora and Dean started sleeping together after he finally broke things off with Mandy, and apparently, it's still a sore subject.

I suppose no amount of time and healing can ever truly erase something like that.

Cora scratches at her forehead, blinking away the shock, then jumps from the couch. "I'll go get some wine glasses."

I watch her storm away, her golden-blonde tresses floating behind her as she disappears into my kitchen.

Mandy drops her face into her palms beside me, her elbows perched atop her thighs. "Shit. I'm such a bitch," she mutters miserably. "I didn't mean to say that."

I'm not sure how to respond. I bite my lip and watch as Hope flips through one of her board books, babbling at the animal pictures.

"I'm over him, Tabitha. I swear it. I love Reid."

"I know," I agree. "But you're not over the fact that the man you *used* to love is with your sister."

She lifts up from her hands, her cheeks stained pink. "I mean…I am. Mostly. I forgive her, and I've learned to understand how it all happened. *Why* it happened. I know she never meant to hurt me. And I know she fought it," she explains. "I'm just programmed to lash out when I'm feeling attacked. I've always been like that. My therapist told me it stems from deep-rooted insecurities or something." She sighs, shaking her head. "I don't know. I'm just a mess. A never-ending work in progress."

"We're all a mess," I tell her, empathy bleeding into my tone. "We're all a work in progress."

Tugging her hair back with her fingers, she links them behind her neck and blows out a breath. "I guess."

Cora reenters the living room with her head down, her hands filled with tumblers because I don't own any wine glasses. "So, when are the Gleasons coming by?" One of her sleeves falls to her elbow, revealing a heartbeat tattoo inked across a patch of tiny scars. When she sets the glasses on the coffee table, she massages the underside of her wrist with her thumb then fiddles with a heart-shaped locket around her neck. "They're taking her for the rest of the summer?"

My eyes trail back the tattoo when Cora tucks her hair behind her ear. I considered getting a tattoo for a while. A butterfly. I love butterflies and have always reveled in the way they fly and flutter so effortlessly. But they don't hold any true meaning for me, no underlying sentiment.

I'm not sure what I'd get now.

It's not like I have the funds to pay for a tattoo, anyway, so I suppose it's a moot point.

I blink away from Cora's wrist and swipe my palms along my

thighs, my attention shifting to Hope. One of her little curls is sticking up, prouder than the others, and it sends a tickle to my heart. "They'll be here at nine a.m.," I respond. "They're taking her through the end of August, and then they fly back to B.C. over Labor Day weekend. They said I can come visit any time I'd like."

Mandy is leaning into the couch with her feet pulled up beside her, scrolling through her phone, avoiding the sting of her barb that's left us feeling like we're sitting in a thorn bush.

Cora folds her lips between her teeth and nods, pouring wine into two tall glasses after I refuse a glass of my own. "Don't be afraid to call or text me anytime you need a friend. I'm happy to make the drive over."

"Thank you. I'm sure I will."

The evening presses on, a lighter mood eventually seeping in, thanks to the now-empty bottle of wine discarded on my coffee table. Mandy's comment dissolves amid inside jokes, workplace gossip, and television-show catch up.

Hope starts to whine shortly past seven and I rise to pluck her from the playpen, dancing her around in my arms to ease her fussing. The two sisters also stand, traipsing into the kitchen for munchies. Hushed chatter meets my ears as I move to the couch and plop back down.

I hold my daughter close, breathing in her flowery shampoo that smells like lavender. My eyes mist at the scent. "It's always been you and me," I murmur against her temple. "It's always been Hope and me. What am I going to do without you, Pumpkin? You're my foundation."

Without a foundation, there's no stability.

You lose your balance.

You fall.

And I'm so damn tired of falling.

Hope bounces in my lap, tugging at the chain around my neck. "Gab," she says.

My heart thumps. Of all the words she could utter, she chose that one syllable, the one name that sends a warm shiver down my spine. It's almost like an answer.

I pretend it's an answer as I smile through my tears and kiss her curls.

When she collapses against my chest, her tiny fists clutching my blouse, I glance into the kitchen and watch as Mandy grips Cora by the shoulders and whispers words too quiet for me to hear. Cora nods, her cheeks flushed. Mandy stretches a watery smile, nodding right back. Then Mandy pulls her sister into a hug while Cora wraps her arms around Mandy's waist.

They hold each other for a few beats, while Hope plays with the rings along my chain, her chubby cheek pressed up against my heart.

I close my eyes and savor the moment.

THE NEXT EVENING, I'm sitting on Gabe's front stoop with my knees tucked to my chin, my arms locked around them at the wrists. I'm not sure how long I wait. It's long enough that the sun dips lower and kisses the treetops, dusk settling in and stealing all color from the sky.

I tap my feet in opposite time, glancing up whenever an engine rolls past.

He's working late again. He texted me that he's putting in extra hours to finish up this project so he can take some time off to visit his mother in Delaware next week.

I know I'll be lost without him.

I'll be wandering through the awful quiet moments alone, without Hope, without Gabe, with only my ghosts and night-mares to keep me company.

I shudder at the thought.

As the sky darkens to a deep-cerulean blue, a throaty engine roar has my head popping up, my eyes landing on Gabe's prized muscle car cruising down the street. It swerves into the driveway, a Bad Omens song blaring through the open window. I watch as he spots me curled up on his stoop, as he hesitates for a breath before killing the engine and hopping out, blinking at the sight of me.

"Tabs."

I stand. The summer breeze sweeps my hair up until the strands are tangling wildly in front of my face, the skirt of my sundress dancing around my knees. He looks awestruck for a moment. Like he's staring at a ghost, or a mirage, or the love of his life. His car keys are fisted in one hand, his neon work vest glowing in the porch light. There are dirt smudges on his cheeks and soot staining baggy canvas pants, telling me of his laborious day. A mess of dirty-blond hair falls across his forehead, and he pushes it back, never taking his eyes off me.

The awe never leaving them.

I part my lips and let out a wobbly breath. "They took her."

My whispered words are enough to break the spell. His brow-line furrows with concern as he takes two steps forward, inching closer. He doesn't reach for me just yet, doesn't come close enough for me to reach for him. Maybe he's remembering the way I reached and reached, clung and took, only a few days prior, leaving him empty and depleted.

I don't blame him for the distance. He needs to protect himself before I drain him dry.

Gabe thinks on my words, flicking his tongue across his lips. "What do you mean?"

"They took her," I croak, the words falling out of me like heavy weights. "Hope. They took her this morning, and they're keeping her for nearly four weeks."

Another step, then another.

Closer, closer, and closer still.

Before I can take my next breath, he's right in front of me, reaching.

I reach back.

Gabe's hands frame my cheeks, lingering gently before he smooths back my hair, taking my whole head along with the gesture. We're eye to eye, his face hovering directly above mine. "Who took her?"

"Her grandparents," I murmur. "They wanted to spend time with her."

"Your mom and dad?"

I shake my head.

Awareness lights up his eyes. He knows I'm referring to Matthew's parents, but I don't say that name. I can't utter those two syllables to him after those two syllables once broke him in two.

His throat bobs. "You're okay with that?"

"No," I say, but then I exhale and try again. "Yes. They

deserve to see her. They deserve to get to know her. I can't be selfish forever."

"Selfish?" The word hits the air with disdain, almost like it personally offended him somehow. He tightens his hold on me. "You're not selfish. Don't ever say that. Don't even think it."

He's wrong.

I'm standing in front of his house right now with reaching hands and a closed-off heart, which is a glaring contradiction to his claim.

Gabe's handsome face looms over me, pinched with worry. Worry for me. I feel like I break further apart with each new day, and it only pulls him closer.

I wonder if he likes me broken.

"I'm sorry I came here," I whisper, the words ragged. "I don't mean to worry you. I shouldn't keep doing this."

We're so close, I feel his breath beating against my lips. I feel his body heat vibrating my skin. My hands are curled around his upper arms, reveling in the hard, firm muscle, my fingers digging and clinging.

Safety. Protection. Warmth.

His eyes dip to my mouth.

I don't think he means it, and it's only for a fleeting second, but my body reacts. Just like it did a few nights ago when I felt his need brush up against me, heating me from the inside out.

There's a riot in my chest.

Heartbeats, spasms, tangled breaths.

For a startling moment, I want him to kiss me. I want his tongue to stroke away my pain beneath the blackening sky and brassy porchlight, and for his arms to wrap me up and hold me tight, while he fixes all of my broken pieces with only a kiss. I want him to make me whole again.

But the uproar is quelled by a single touch, his palm curling around my neck, his thumb grazing just below my ear. The gesture always soothes me. Soothes my demons, my fears, my selfish desires.

My heartbeats steady, the spasms ebb, and the breaths cut loose, one by one.

He always tells me not to look down, but I couldn't if I wanted to.

How could I look down when his eyes are two inches above mine?

"Don't ever apologize for coming to see me," he finally says, an easy smile pulling at his mouth. "You can always land here."

Gabe steps back, his hands falling away from me, the loss of him weakening my wings. I swallow and nod, folding my arms across my chest and glancing out at the skyline. "Thank you."

We take a seat on the front stoop, side by side. Shoulder to shoulder. It's a quiet moment, and I realize it's not the awful kind of quiet that I'm used to. I'm relaxed and calm. Oddly burdenless.

A few minutes pass when Gabe turns toward me, bumping my shoulder with his in a playful way. "Music?"

I smile, meeting his eyes. "Sure."

Sifting through both pockets of his pants, he pulls out his cell phone and a pair of headphones he always keeps on him. He pops an earbud in my left ear, then sticks the other in his right. We sit together on his porch step while my temple drops to his shoulder and a song by Black Lab spills out of the little speaker, stealing away any lingering stress.

It's that easy.

It's that easy for my fears to float away, for my anxiety to dissipate, and for the horrors of my past to become nothing but a blur.

Two wires.

A song.

And his warm body pressed to mine.

CHAPTER 14

TABITHA

I have been dreading this day. This moment, these words. Having to see the look in Evan's eyes when I detail Earl Hubbard's true motives, when I explain why my captor was given the nickname of "The Matchmaker" by riveted reporters. I'm sure Evan has done his research; he's seen the endless news reports that still manage to clog my social media feeds and make headlines.

But I'm just as certain that nothing compares to hearing it all laid out, firsthand, from the mouth of one of the surviving victims.

I fiddle with the three rings on my necklace chain, lingering on the one made of silver stars.

Evan sets a glass of water in front of me then idles beside me for a beat while he rubs the nape of his neck, thinking on his next words. There's a different kind of tension in the air today. Almost like he knows the twisted tale is about to take an even more twisted turn.

I glance up at him, dropping my palms to trembling knees. "I assume you know what happens next."

Evan presses forward on his desk, head bowed. "We can take breaks. Whatever you need." His eyes lift to mine. "There's no pressure."

"I know."

"Are you ready to get started?"

"Yes." My heart pounds between my ribs, the opposite of

ready. It will never be ready to relive, to recall, to retell. It only wants to forget.

But I can't forget. The only way out is through.

"All right." Sighing through a nod, Evan straightens from the desk and moves around to his chair, faltering briefly before taking a seat.

Maybe he's not ready, either.

My knees knock together, restless and twitchy. I watch him prepare. He opens his laptop, flips through the pages of his spiral-bound notebook, picks up a pen, and casts his attention to me.

And then he presses the button on the tape recorder.

I close my eyes and freefall back in time with one little sound.

Click.

Two Years Earlier

"What scares you?"

His face was cloaked in shadow as nighttime stole the final trace of sunlight. Only a fragmented moon allowed me to gaze upon the man across from me, highlighting his sagging frame slumped against the pole.

I glanced out the window.

An inky, midnight sky stared back at me, shrouded in stars—a canvas for dreams and wishes. They twinkled brightly, beckoning for an enchanted prayer, but my eyes were only focused on the crescent moon glowing among them.

A half-moon.

A half-moon to mimic my shrunken half-heart.

Five more days had come and gone. Five days of abuse and hopelessness, of briny well water that I'd gulped down with my palm from the bathroom sink, and of stale turkey sandwiches with Miracle Whip. On one of the days, there'd been a slice of processed cheese stuck between the bread and turkey, and I'd nearly collapsed with tears of joy.

But that ounce of joy was ripped away when the man grabbed

me by the hair moments later and dragged me down to the bottomless pits of Hell.

My head dropped back to the pole, tilting sideways.

We were deteriorating down there.

I saw it in his eyes, in the chalky color of his skin. He was gaunter, quieter. I felt like I was losing him with every passing minute, and the moment I lost him, I lost me, too.

He was my anchor.

My only wish.

I blinked back to Matthew, his question finally registering. The words were like sludge and my brain was a backed-up drain trying desperately to suck them in.

What scares me?

I wasn't sure how to answer that.

A lot of things scared me: heights, cockroaches, missed opportunities, a failing grade in school, the thought of never finding real love.

But the only thing that *truly* scared me was watching the man across from me die while I was helpless to save him.

I swallowed, choosing to give him a less grave answer. "Flying," I told him. "I've always been terrified of flying. I feel like feet are made for solid ground."

Matthew shifted slightly, his cuffs clinking against the pole. "I love to fly. I love to travel."

"I like road trips," I said. "My friends and I drove from Arizona to Disney World one year, and the drive was even more memorable than the theme parks."

I couldn't see his expression, precisely, but he made a little sighing sound, so I imagined his lips parted and his dark brows taut and furrowed.

"My father has a private jet. I'd like to take you on it one day."

My breath caught. I wasn't sure what was more terrifying— the thought of flying on that private jet, or the notion that I never would.

"He was a pilot for thirty years and he's a certified skydiving instructor," Matthew continued, his tone gravelly and subdued. "He'll make sure you're safe. I'll even hold your hand the whole time." I thought I heard a smile in his voice. "Promise."

A tear leaked from the corner of my eye and I was grateful for it. It meant I was hydrated, still alive, still capable of escaping the basement. There was a chance I'd step on that plane one day. "I'd like that," I said softly.

I would.

I would love the chance to stand inside that jet, even if I ended up running right back out of it.

"I think, sometimes, the things that frighten us become more bearable when you don't have to face them alone," he said.

Nodding, I yearned to swipe the tear tracks from my cheeks. "I'm really glad I'm not alone right now. I'm sorry you're here, but…" My voice trailed off when I realized how terribly selfish that sounded.

I'm so happy you're shackled to a pole in a madman's basement, awaiting a death sentence, just so I don't have to suffer all by myself.

It wasn't at all what I meant, but I couldn't help but feel grateful for him anyway.

"I understand," he assured me. "You don't need to explain."

I swallowed. "What are you afraid of?"

My question was met with a long stretch of silence. I tried to count the seconds between, but I lost track, my mind too blurry to focus. I wondered if he'd fallen asleep as I stared at the dip of his chin, the extra slack that stole his shoulders.

But then he answered as he extended his legs and shifted in place. "I always wanted to be a father one day. The thought of never meeting my child is my greatest fear."

Pain.

Pain was what I felt when his gentle, broken words reached my ears. My heart felt like it shriveled up like a dying rose, the wilted petals fluttering to the pit of my stomach and turning into rocks.

"Matthew—"

"You're doing good, Miss Brighton."

I tripped over my next words when his eclipsed mine. They stalled on my tongue as I stared at him across the darkened room, just barely making out the way his eyes skimmed over my face through the shadows.

He said it again, even more tortured sounding than before. "You're doing…so good."

A whimpering sound fell out of me. A frayed little moan. "I'm trying."

"I'm proud of you," he told me. It sounded like he'd poured every ounce of remaining energy into making those words sing. "So proud."

I was trying, but not hard enough.

Never hard enough.

"I've been taking notes of my surroundings upstairs," Matthew muttered, his tone reflective. "During the bathroom breaks."

"Me, too. I haven't seen anything of relevance."

He made a humming sound. "I've noticed something. A photograph, hanging in his hallway. He doesn't seem like a senti-mental man by any means, so it caught my attention."

I slid my lip between my teeth. "There was a picture of a woman. She was pregnant. It looked like an older photo."

"His mother, perhaps."

"That's what I was thinking."

"There was something else." He hesitated for a moment before adding, "She resembled you."

My insides pitched.

Yes.

I'd noticed that, too.

Long, dark ribbons of hair and wide eyes. Alabaster skin, willowy frame.

It wasn't a dead ringer, but there had been…a likeness.

Still, I couldn't imagine how a picture would help get us out of there.

Clearing my throat, I added, "I've considered smashing the bathroom mirror and using the glass as a weapon, but I'm too afraid I won't be quick enough. He waits on the other side of the door and taps the gun against the frame like a warning. A reminder that he's there."

Matthew nodded slowly. "I know. It's too risky, especially because you're weak and malnourished. You'd need to be quick," he explained. "The fact that he's still feeding us and keeping us alive means there's more of a chance we can escape through other means. I'm trying to read him. Trying to pick up on anything that might—"

I wished we had more time to discuss and think it through, but the basement door flew open, crashing against the stone wall.

I flinched.

I squeezed my eyes shut, blotting out the horrors that awaited me.

Was tonight the night I died?

Who would he kill first?

I hoped it was me…God, I hoped it was me.

"Wakey, wakey," the man barked, storming down the steps. "Boy, do I have somethin' fun in store for my pets tonight."

Fear blanketed me; a smothering cloak.

Matthew and I both glanced at each other, his features brightened by the artificial light seeping in from atop the staircase. I saw the same fear shining back at me in his blue-gray eyes.

I'd spent the last few days trying my best to build a connection with the monster. It had been unbearable. Sickening. If I died tonight, it would be my greatest regret—using my final days on Earth pretending to *feel* something for such a disgusting excuse for a human being.

It didn't seem like it was working. The man had been indifferent toward my attempts, but it still felt like it was our only hope. My only power.

I didn't know what else to do.

Casting the fear aside as much as I could, I rose to unsteady legs, my cuffs sliding up the pole with me. "H-hello," I greeted timidly. "What…did you have in store for us?"

The man stopped a few feet short of me, his dark eyes twinkling. "Did my Kitten miss me?"

I wanted to vomit, but I forced a nod. "A little."

I'd tried to take it slow, making my feelings more believable. It wouldn't have made sense to flip a switch overnight and suddenly care for him. I had offered a smile first, and then a kind word. I'd even allowed a horrible moan to slip out as he violated me.

While he gave no reaction, we were still alive. I was trying to take that as evidence.

He sniffed. "My favorite pet missed me, eh?"

I nodded again. "I don't know why, but I just…did."

Every word shredded my throat like white-hot needles.

Taking another step toward me, then another, the man extended a hand, and I trained my body not to cower or wince.

"You remind me of her," he said.

I blinked.

I managed a quick glance at Matthew who had risen to his feet and was studying the interaction closely. Then I looked back to the man as his calloused fingers grazed my jawline. "Her?" I wondered.

"This pretty jaw." His eyes narrowed thoughtfully, like he was imagining a different face. "These eyes. This hair, too…" He twirled a piece of my long, dirty hair around a stubby finger.

Gently. Carefully.

And then he snapped back, his face contorting with rage as he gave my hair a violent tug. "Are you playing me?"

I tried not to cry out as my scalp burned. "N-no…of course not."

"I don't like games. Don't like tricks."

"I would never."

He snarled, a smile lifting, yellow teeth bared. "The only end to this game is your lithe little body rotting away in my barn while I scrape your brains off this floor." Yanking on my hair a final time, he released me. "Remember that."

Bile shot up my windpipe and I choked it back down.

My whole body shook in the aftermath of his threats, knowing they were not baseless threats. He still planned to kill me. The plan would take time and I wasn't sure how much more of it I had.

Our captor pivoted away from me and sauntered toward Matthew.

I wanted to cry out, stop him, beg for him to leave Matthew alone, but he wouldn't believe that I had feelings for *him* if I showed feelings for Matthew, too.

I needed to pretend.

I needed to be the ideal student Matthew thought I was.

Folding my lips between my teeth, I bit down.

Matthew stood stock-still, only his eyes following the man. "The photograph on your wall," he said, fusing his words with a touch of sympathy. His head cocked slightly. "She was beautiful. Is that your mother?"

"Shut your trap. That's none of your damn business."

"You must have been very fond of her. I couldn't help but notice a resemblance to Tabitha." He paused with his arms linked behind him, his shirt rumpled and untucked, his khaki trousers smeared with grayish stains from the cement. "Don't you agree?"

The man ignored him, immediately changing the subject. "I think it's time to give my doggie a bone," he chortled, reaching for the pistol behind his back. He slid it out of his waistband, and it glinted in the moonlight. "I think you'll like this treat."

Matthew's eyes shifted over to me, then back to the man.

Shock stole both of our expressions when our captor moved behind Matthew's pole, plucked a key from his pocket with his free hand, and unchained Matthew's wrists.

I gasped, stunned.

We'd already had our bathroom break today. We'd already eaten our sandwich and guzzled water from the sink.

What was happening?

"Be a good mutt. Any funny business and I blow you away. I won't think twice." The man nodded his head at me, gun aimed at Matthew's forehead. "Go."

"What?" Matthew was breathing heavily, his attention shared between me and the armed madman. He was assessing the scene, trying to understand. "Go where? You have a pistol pointed at my head."

The man chuckled. "Go pet the nice Kitten. She's begging for you." He spared me a grin. "She's even purring."

Matthew shook his head. "I don't—"

"Go!" he shouted, taking two steps back, the gun still aimed at Matthew.

Matthew hesitated for another beat, then moved toward me. Slowly, cautiously, his brow pinched with confusion.

Was he going to let us go?

No…he wouldn't.

This was it. He was going to kill us.

My eyes stayed locked on Matthew as he continued forward and glanced over his shoulder, once, twice, his features coming more into focus the closer he got.

He stopped once we were toe to toe.

Face to face.

My legs tremored. My fingers tingled, aching to touch him. My heart longed and begged and wanted.

Matthew waited, not knowing what to do. Not knowing what he was *allowed* to do.

We held our breath.

And then, the man gave his next order: "Now…fuck her."

The air left me.

I watched as Matthew's eyes flared, his complexion going ashen in the dim lighting. His temples pulsed, the purple-tinged bruise left behind from the man's gun thrumming along with the beats of his heart.

We'd misheard.

There was no way our abductor had just told him to…*do that.*

Matthew didn't move, didn't blink. Didn't question. He just stared at me, the most haunted expression etched into every line, every shadow, of his face.

I sucked in a sharp breath, breaking eye contact to glance over at the man. "What do you mean?"

My question was met with amusement. "Didn't think there was room for interpretation." He unlatched his belt buckle, looking eager. As if this was the climax of a compelling show and he couldn't wait to see how it all unfolded. "My dirty dog is going to fuck you, Kitten. And I'm going to watch."

"I…I don't…" My eyes panned back to Matthew, who stood still and lifeless in front of me. I tugged at my cuffs, my chains, my legs ready to give out.

"Do you need another demonstration?" the man blared.

Matthew finally blinked, finally moved. His hands twitched at his sides, chin dipping to his chest. "Tabitha…" he whispered.

The man marched forward, belt hanging loose, and pressed the barrel of the gun between Matthew's shoulder blades. "Do it." He forced him forward with a snarl until Matthew stumbled, almost falling into me. "Do it now, or I'll gut you with my hunting knife. She'll be next."

I cried out, jangling my chains. "Matthew…j-just do it…"

Oh, my God.

Oh, my God.

Matthew lifted his head, hopelessly skimming my face. I must have looked like a wreck. A mask of disbelief, my hair matted to my scalp, my pale skin colored in green and brown bruises.

"I'm sorry," he murmured. His throat bobbed with a hard swallow as he shook his head back and forth. "I'm so sorry."

The man took the apology as concession and inched the gun away. He stepped to the side, into the shadows, where he lurked in darkness as he watched. Waited.

Enjoyed.

Matthew took a slow step toward me until I felt what little warmth he had left radiating into me. He was the sun on my skin. Starlight in my bones. I needed more, so I begged him to come closer. "Please."

His arms trembled as they lifted from his sides and tentatively reached for me, landing first on my bony shoulders, then dragged down my biceps and squeezed. He dropped his head again, features contorting with pain. "I'll be gentle," he told me. "I won't hurt you."

"I know." Tears glided down my dirty cheekbones. "I know."

Our eyes locked as his hands gripped. Gently, as he'd promised. Tenderly. And then they traveled lower, to my elbows, falling from my arms and grazing my hips. His fingers slipped beneath the hem of my oversized shirt. I had no underwear, no barrier. The feel of his fingertips brushing my bare skin sent a shiver down my spine.

"Look at the stars."

His words froze me and I blinked slowly, not understanding.

I didn't look. I only looked at him.

Matthew's fingers curled around my waist as he pressed his forehead to mine. "Look at the stars, Tabitha. Let them be your anchor. Let them give you comfort."

My lips quivered, our mouths only separated by his breath and mine. I didn't want to look at them. I didn't need comfort when his hands were on me, when his beautiful, worn face was only a millimeter from my own.

And then something magical happened. Something I never thought I'd witness again.

He smiled. Matthew trailed a finger down the side of my face, inching back to stare at me. There was hope in the upturn of his lips. There was solace in the slow glide of his finger. "I can see you."

I blinked up at him, both mesmerized and bewildered. "See me?"

"Yeah." He swallowed. "I can hardly see you without my glasses. You've just been this…beautiful blur."

My lip wobbled hopelessly at the thought. Matthew had been stripped of everything down there. His freedom, his dignity, and even his sight.

But he had his touch, at least, and it was as much of a gift to me as it was to him. My wrists chafed against my cuffs, aching to touch him back. I drank in a shaky breath. "Will you kiss me?"

My question sounded darkly romantic. Kisses were borne from fairytales, not from something so grim and nightmarish. But I asked him anyway, and he didn't hesitate.

He didn't hold back.

His mouth crashed to mine, less of a kiss and more of a devouring. I cried out with a moan. My mouth parted on instinct and his tongue plunged inside, stroking and taking. I tugged at my restraints, my eyes squeezed shut, desperate to pull him closer, to clutch him. To scratch and claw and take everything I could grasp.

One of his hands disappeared from underneath my T-shirt and I heard the telltale sound of a tinkling buckle. A zipper. Rustling of fabric as it slid down to cement. His hand returned to cup my face, his thumb brushing along my cheekbone, smearing the trail of tears. Our mouths kept tasting, our tongues kept tangling. Hot, needy, searching.

I was whimpering. Forcing my body closer and closer, as close as it could get to his.

Matthew lifted my leg with his other hand, curling it around his hip. He pulled back from my mouth, whispering raggedly, "Look at the stars."

I opened my eyes, lashes fluttering and still damp with my tears. His lips were swollen and kissed raw. A trace of vibrant blue overshadowed the dimming flecks in his eyes, almost like our kiss had breathed new life back into him. New colors.

The moment my gaze panned to the window, he pushed inside me.

I gasped. My fingers curled into fists behind the pole, my leg coiling around his lower back. My eyes stayed locked on the narrow window, watching as the stars twinkled and shined from the other side of it.

The man grunted and groaned beside us, but I blocked him out. I was too full of moonlight and star glow to let the darkness in.

I made wishes. I said prayers. I begged for every star to fall from the sky and pluck us both from the nightmare.

Save us. Please, save us.

Matthew's face fell to the crook of my shoulder, where he

peppered kisses along my neck, his tongue flicking out to taste my skin. I must have tasted dirty, but he didn't seem to care. He moved slow, careful, kind, one hand gripping my waist, the other cupping my jaw.

It didn't last long.

It was only minutes before his body shuddered, a tortured sound muffled by my clumps of tangled hair as he buried his face into my neck. It was over far too soon. The warmth, the pocket of comfort. The bubble of make-believe, where it was just us, his hands on my skin, his heart pressed to mine. It was just a gasping breath as I breached the water, only to be yanked right back down.

He was torn away from me the second his pants were secured around his waist.

"No," he bit out, fighting, reaching. But he couldn't reach me; he couldn't touch me any longer. "No. Fuck you, no, no—*fuck you*!" He was growling, shouting, flailing, as the man curled a fist around Matthew's shirt collar and jabbed the pistol into his abdomen.

"Shut the fuck up," our captor barked. "Know your place, dog."

Still, he fought.

He knew his place was with me.

I watched with horror as Matthew lunged at the man. There was a gun digging into his stomach, yet he lunged, uncaring that he was one finger-flick away from having his insides blown apart. Matthew had always tried to be calm and collected, relying on his mind instead of violence and force.

But now, I watched him snap.

And there was nothing I could do about it.

"Matthew, don't!" I shrieked.

The man only had a split second to react, and he didn't pull the trigger. He lifted the pistol and slammed it against Matthew's head until he slumped to the ground, just a pile of boneless limbs.

"No! Please…p-please, no…" My knees bent and shook, but there was still nothing I could do.

There was nothing I could do.

"Stupid asshole," the man grumbled, more annoyed than angry. He dragged Matthew's unconscious body to the pole and pulled both of his wrists around it. "Lucky for you, I'm not done with y'all yet."

He secured the cuffs with a single sound that had me falling to my butt, utterly defeated.

Click.

And then he stormed away, latching his belt buckle and stuffing the gun inside his waistband.

I sat there, collapsed, sobbing, hating the quiet. "Matthew…" I repeated his name over and over, just so the awful silence wasn't my only companion. "Matthew."

He remained unconscious until dawn and I'd never felt more alone.

I wanted to break free, to climb out the window and take Matthew with me.

I wanted to run back home with what was left of my half-heart, guided by the light of the broken moon.

But the window was too far away.

My chains were too sound.

And the stars had never felt more out of reach.

Present Day

HE FINDS me in my car, curled into the fetal position in the backseat. I sailed out of Evan's driveway twenty minutes ago and only made it a few feet down the road before I pulled over and broke.

It's possible he heard my cries. My terrible weeping. The window is cracked because it's a beautiful midsummer night, a night spun with warm breezes and songful crickets. I cracked it to let some air in, to allow the night's beauty in; I thought it would help. I'm suffocating on my own grief, so I wished for reprieve. A full, lung-easing breath.

And I got my wish.

I should probably be mortified by my current state. I'm a blubbering mess, my thick sections of hair glued to tear stains and snot bubbles. My eyes are so swollen I can hardly see through my puffy lids. It's for the best, I'm sure. I don't want to see the look of horror on his face while he's yanking open the back door and hurling himself inside, leaving it hanging open to let in more breezes, more summer sweetness that doesn't hold a torch to the man gathering me in his arms.

But I push him away. I wiggle out of his grip because my burdens are too heavy for him to try to carry. "Don't," I croak through my sniffles. "Please go."

Don't go.

Stay with me forever in this self-serving limbo of mine.

"Not a chance." Gabe fights back, and it's not much of a fight because my own fight lacks any valiant conviction. His arms envelop me, hauling me backward until I'm sprawled in his lap, my back to his chest. All it takes is a squeeze, a kiss to the top of my head, and three words whispered near my ear, and I melt. "I've got you."

I still can't see much through the ropes of damp hair draped over my eyes and the film of tears blotting my vision. But I feel him. I feel his heartbeats heating my back, both of his arms clasped around my middle, caging me in.

I feel guilty for all this taking.

"Please, Gabe…just go, will you?" I say with little conviction, weak words spilling from a weak heart. In fact, I press closer to him, the lie in my plea clear as day. "I don't want you to see me like this. I'm a wreck, and I don't want your pity. Just go and be done with me."

"Stop," he whispers, his lips grazing the top of my ear. "That's bullshit."

"It's not." I try to pull away, but he holds me tighter. "Gabe, please let me go."

"I know that's not what you want."

Twisting around in his arms, I face him with grief-soaked eyes. His hair looks darker than it is in the night's shadows and I can't even see the green of his irises. But he's warm and alive and my arms aren't tied behind my back, so I reach out, my hand landing on his chest. "Fine. Kiss me, then."

This is what has his hold loosening, his body stiffening. He swallows. "Don't do that."

His answer angers me. I simmer in it, enjoying the heat it brings to my blood. It's something. It's a feeling. I crawl into his lap, a desperate scramble, until I'm straddling him in the back-seat of my junky car, my hands latching onto his shoulders to lift me up. "Kiss me."

"I can't."

I lean forward and he pulls back.

He shakes his head, his gaze tortured.

The anger blooms. A growl of frustration rattles my chest as I leap out of his lap. "Then just go. Leave me alone." I scurry to the other side of the seat, not out of the car, but as far left as I can go, until I'm smashed up against the opposite door, my legs curling to my chin.

Gabe inches toward me. "Tabs," he says, the word free of any frustration. There's torment in it, though, and that sounds worse. "You can't ask me to kiss you when I know you plan on regret-ting it. I won't survive it."

"You'd be surprised at what you're capable of surviving," I say back.

I'm mad.

I'm so mad.

But I'm not mad at him—he's just here, in the aftermath of my harrowing interview while I'm missing my baby girl desperately, so I'm hurling my bottled-up grief at him. It has nowhere else to go.

I press both palms to my face.

My shoulders shake.

And I sob.

Miserable, choking sounds. I'm in his arms again before I can catch a full breath and I let him hold me this time, my guilt fusing with anguish. "I-I'm…s-sorry," I stammer, my voice hitch-ing, my body wracked with tremors. "That was…c-cruel. I don't want to be cruel to you."

When I lift my chin, Gabe smooths my hair back and I finally look at him. Truly look at him. And there's no pity in his eyes, no resentment, even.

I don't understand why he won't be done with me.

Why he's torturing himself.

He's still in his work clothes, having likely just gotten home and spotted my car stalled a few houses down from his. Heard my pathetic whimpers tainting the night. He could have gone inside the comfort of his home to relax after a long, hard day.

Instead, he's here. With me. Accepting my misplaced anger and holding me tight.

"I don't understand it," I mutter, my words strewn with gravel. "Why do you still want me? What are you waiting for?" The space between his eyes creases and I wonder if he's questioning himself. Doubting his patience, his loyalty. "I've given you nothing. No promises, no sex. You could be with anyone, enjoying your youth."

It's dark, but it's not too dark to see the look on his face.

An expression steeped in strained devotion.

"I don't give a shit about that," he tells me. "I don't want anyone else. I think I've made that pretty clear."

I turn away from him, shaking my head. "It doesn't make sense."

"There isn't any sense in how I feel. Feelings just *are*."

Rejecting his declaration, his feelings, I keep inching away, keep swinging my head back and forth. "You shouldn't—"

"I'm going to Delaware next week," he interrupts. "Come with me."

The words dissolve on my tongue.

I freeze.

At first, I want to laugh at his offer.

I'm in no state to travel, to sightsee, to meet his *mother*.

I can hardly keep myself properly fed.

I can't even sleep, my mind too muddled with evil things, my heart too empty, missing my child.

He senses the knee-jerk rejection and drops his head to my shoulder, pressing a light kiss to my collarbone. "You need a break. You need to get away for a few days, to clear your head and recover," he tells me. "Take advantage of the free time. Use your vacation hours at work."

I blink.

Somehow, I'm considering it.

Images of open roads and endless playlists sweep through my mind, overtaking the fear. Thoughts of spending uninterrupted time with this man who refuses to give up on me warms me from toes to top. I tilt my head toward him. "Would we be able to…drive?"

He nods. "Sure. I'll cancel my flight and we'll make it a road trip."

"Are you sure it's not too long?"

"Thirteen hours. It's doable."

Anticipation lights up my chest. A tingle of excitement. I can't even remember the last time I did something spontaneous, something so reckless. Over the last two years, I've only ever been a mother, a provider, and a victim.

When was the last time I was simply…*me*?

Tabitha Elise Brighton—the girl who loves road trips, wild-cherry pie, mockingbirds, and boys with crooked smiles and arms that feel like home.

My reply slips out, and it's effortless. "Okay."

His head pops up from my shoulder, surprise lacing his tone. "Yeah?"

"Yes. I want to go with you."

A pause. Perhaps he's giving me a moment to change my mind, to overthink my decision. When I say nothing and my acquiescence hovers between us, he pulls me into his lap again. This time, I don't fight to get away. "Okay."

Gabe wraps both arms around me and pulls me closer, his forehead falling against the crown of my head as we stare out at the blackened sky through the cracked window.

The breeze seeps inside, drying my tear stains.

The twittering of crickets is sweet music to my ears.

His arms squeeze, holding all of my broken pieces together.

And suddenly, the stars don't seem so far away anymore.

CHAPTER 15

GABE

I've never seen her look so light.

Tabitha leans back in the passenger seat of my Challenger, her eyes closed, fingers dancing out the window while her hair floats around her like abstract art.

The smile hasn't left my face for eleven hours. Seeing my girl so untroubled, so relaxed, is like warmth on my skin after a long, sunless winter.

I prop my sunglasses on top of my head, sparing her a quick glance as I turn the music down. A Jimmy Eat World playlist has been filtering through the speaker for the last hour. I let her pick the music. In all the months I've known her, I realize I didn't even know what kind of music she liked. We always listened to mine.

It's like she'd forgotten.

She bounces in her seat a little, shoulders bobbing to the song. She catches my eyes on her and looks my way, a soft smile peeking through her tangled hair. "I love this song."

"Yeah?"

"Mmm-hmm. It's called *Night Drive* and I played it over and over on a road trip one summer with some college friends, the summer before—" Glancing out the window, she rethinks her words. "A few years ago."

I turn the song up, listening to the lyrics.

Sounds like a perfect road trip song about cherry kisses,

engine fumes, and moonlight. I picture her a few years ago, before that evil bastard stole her shine.

I want to know more about her.

"Where did you go on the road trip?"

"Phoenix," she murmurs, gaze still trained on the open window, voice pitching to overpower the wind. "I grew up there. My friends came with me and we went camping at Estrella Mountain."

"What are your parents like?" I've been curious about them. She hardly talks about her mom and dad, and all I've been told is that they separated when she was young. "You're not close?"

Glancing down at her clasped hands, she shakes her head. "My father hasn't been in the picture for years, and my mother… well, she never really had time for me. There was little affection growing up. No long hugs, no bedtime stories, no '*I love yous.*' I was forced to be independent from an early age, so becoming a young, single mother wasn't as daunting as it could have been."

"I'm sorry you've grown apart." I shoot her a sympathetic smile. "My mom is a sweetheart, but she's very logic-centric and tells you like it is. You'll understand when you meet her. Oliver's mom raised me for most of my life before she passed away, and she was overly empathetic and maternal. I had pretty badass women in my life growing up."

"Must be why you're such a softie," she teases. Her finger pokes out to jab me in the bicep.

"Hey, I resent that."

"You shouldn't." Tabitha's gaze softens, her finger falling from my arm. "It's my favorite thing about you. Your heart."

My lips purse as I weigh the compliment.

I guess I've always been softhearted, which isn't a terrible thing to be.

The downside is, soft hearts are susceptible to leaks. Just the smallest puncture can have it bleeding out. They're prone to breaches, too, which makes it so easy for a knife to slide through. For the bad stuff to sneak inside. Pain, betrayal, regret.

The dull ache of one-sided love.

Tabitha sighs, shifting in her seat and picking at a sewn-on patch on her denim shorts. It's a multicolored butterfly, kind of quirky and avant-garde, and it looks like she added it herself. "My mother was all about order. Precision, cleanliness. Everything needing to be meticulous and in its place," she muses. "I think as I got older, I rebelled against those things. I liked adding bright, funky prints to a neutral palate. I wanted the eccentric outfits sprinkled into a color-coordinated closet, and the old, falling-apart books placed among all the pretty new ones on a bookshelf." She finds my eyes for a beat, smiling. "I prefer flaws over perfection."

Well.

I've got plenty of those.

Maybe there's hope for us yet.

"Tell me more about your mom," she continues, one leg crossing over the other. "She's strict?"

"Nah, I wouldn't say she's strict," I answer. "She's just...practical. She tackles life with rational thought versus idyllic hope and fantasy. Drove me nuts sometimes, but it also made me a little envious. I've never been like that."

"Nothing wrong with having a hopeful outlook."

"There's plenty wrong with it. Feels like a curse most of the time." My fingers curl around the wheel as I switch lanes. "She's always wanted the best for me, though."

"Does she want you to settle down? Start a family?"

"Definitely. Mom told me the next time I came to visit, I better be engaged." I laugh lightly, scrubbing a hand down my face. "She hates being so far away, especially after that shit with my father and the fire, but my grandmother is in hospice care so she can't really leave. She plans to move back to Illinois soon." I press my lips together. "I guess she just wants to make sure I'm not alone. That I have someone, you know?"

Tabitha stares at me, her back flush to the seat but her head twisted in my direction. There's a thoughtful expression glittering in her copper-brown eyes, the little green flecks dancing with whimsy. She fingers the chain around her neck that holds three rings. "We could be engaged."

I nearly hit the brakes and my heart fumbles around in my chest as I glance at her, then glance back out the windshield. Then back at her.

Maybe I should pull over.

"I mean...we could pretend," she says.

"You want to pretend to be engaged?"

She squeezes all three rings in her fist before looking down at her lap. "That's a bad idea, huh?" Shaking her head, she flusters in place, biting at her lip. "Sorry. We shouldn't lie."

"We should absolutely lie. It's a great idea."

She laughs. "Gabe…"

"I'm serious. It's brilliant." I can't hold back my slap-happy grin as my wrist dangles over the steering wheel. "I proposed to you last month and it was romantic as fuck. You said yes, of course, because I'm irresistible like that. You couldn't say no to that amazing ring I picked out, the dirty one with the stars that looks like I dug it up alongside someone's grave. Money is tight, you know? But it's fine because our love is everlasting."

My grin only broadens when I catch her giggling into her palm, shaking her head at me.

"Picture this—" I wave my hand through the air as if I'm unveiling a grand scene "—a grassy little hill overlooking the water. Fireworks. Me on one knee. Everyone is there, cheering us on."

"That was how Oliver proposed to Sydney."

"It worked. She said yes."

"I think we can be more creative." Tabitha inches up in her seat, fully facing me. There's a light in her eyes I haven't seen since the night we danced among DJ strobes and techno music, oblivious to anything but each other. "You took me flying."

"I did?" I glance at her and nod. "I did."

"You did, and it was amazing. I've been scared of heights my whole life, so you rented a helicopter to take us flying because you said we could face anything as long as we're together. You held my hand. You sang to me."

"That I did not do."

"Fine, you hired my favorite local band to sing to me once we landed. Because music is our thing. You had them play our song."

"What's our song?"

She worries her lip between her teeth, pondering. "It can be anything."

"Details matter, Tabs. Mom is freakishly observant."

"Okay, um…I love U2." She glances out the windshield briefly, her eyes glazing over as if stolen by a memory. "Before my father left, he would play the Joshua Tree album on repeat every summer during backyard barbecues. The smell of lavender would fuse with burgers on the grill, and mockingbirds would sing along from our little cherry tree. My favorite was always *With or Without You*, so we can use that one if you like it."

"Kind of tragic, but it slaps." It's hard to keep my eyes on the road when hers are damn near twinkling. "Perfect. So I was able to afford a helicopter and a band, but I couldn't scrounge up a single cent to get you a ring better than the graveyard ring."

"Maybe I love this ring." Her smile blooms twofold in my periphery. "It's sentimental."

I scratch at the stubble on my chin, going over the details in my mind.

I think it'll work; Mom will buy it.

The problem is, I might buy it, too.

"All right, Tabs. You'll have to pretend to really like me." A grin curls, half of my mouth turning up. "You might even have to hold my hand."

She smiles right back, slipping the star ring through her index finger and twirling it as she drags her eyes away and murmurs, "I like holding your hand."

Yep.

There's an obscenely high chance that my too-soft heart won't make it out of Delaware alive.

Worth it.

We cut through a small town in Maryland, hardly two hours from Mom's house in Seaford, and pull into a gas station to fill the tank. The air is sticky and I yearn for the refreshing salt breeze on my face that only a seaside town can bring. Mom and I went to Atlantic City the last time I came to visit and it was a highlight of that trip.

Maybe Tabitha and I can take a drive there before we head home.

Images of watching her pop colorful saltwater taffy into her mouth on the boardwalk, her raven hair catching on an ocean-drenched draft, fills me with an untouchable sort of magic.

Tabitha hops out of the car to stretch her legs as I fill up the tank and watch her lean back against the black exterior, her long, shiny hair nearly bleeding into the paint color. She's wearing a baby-blue tank top with thin straps and those little denim shorts that fringe along the edges, tickling her milky-white thighs.

An intoxicating image that I should definitely ignore.

I force my eyes up to hers when she points across the street amusedly.

She's looking at an adult store titled *Sexy Stuff*—only, one of the letter *F*s is burned out on the flashing marquee sign. "It's missing a letter." She giggles. "Sexy Stuf."

I follow her gaze, the pun coming easy. "Clearly, they don't give an eff."

It takes a second for the joke to register.

And then her laughter startles me.

It's a whispery burst of breath at first, becoming full-on belly laughter as she bends over, arms draped across her stomach, hair curtaining the joy on her face. The sound of it strangles my chest. It has my own smile fading, but not because I'm not happy—it's because I'm sucker-punched with the notion that her laughter is so rare, so unanticipated, that I don't even know what to do with it.

I want to hug her.

Kiss her.

Both…neither.

Maybe I just want to stare at her and ingrain that sound in my bones until it's a physical, forever part of me.

When she catches her breath, she pops up, straightens, and sweeps her hair out of her face. It's such an ordinary gesture, but not for her. It's so breezy and free of pain.

I take a step toward her and extend my hand, reaching for her necklace made of rings. "May I?"

She pauses, then gives me a small nod.

My feet move forward until we're inches apart and her jasmine-scented shampoo and fruity skin overpower the smell of gas-station hotdogs and engine fuel. I fiddle with the three rings, weighing each of them in my hand. One looks like a man's ring— her father's, maybe? The other is tarnished rose gold, and the third is made of silvery stars. I tug the chain up over her head and unclasp it, letting the star ring fall into the center of my palm.

She watches, nerves skittering across her face.

After I return the chain around her neck, I hold up the little ring in front of her face. "Tabitha."

She ducks her chin and shuffles from one sandaled foot to the other. "Gabe."

I fall to one knee.

"Gabe!" she exclaims, looking mortified, reaching for my shoulders to yank me back up. "Oh, my God. Please get up."

"I'm proposing."

"You don't need to actually propose." She glances around the parking lot, her eyes bugged out, cheeks stained crimson. "Stand up. Please."

"I'm method acting. It needs to feel real."

"*Gabe.*"

She's beyond flustered, so I begrudgingly stand and fall beside her against my car. I don't miss the tiny smile that tips her lips, though. She can't hide it.

Grinning, I stuff one hand into the pocket of my dark-gray jeans and finger the ring with the other. It's dirty and blemished. Riddled with flaws.

It's perfect.

And I realize how much those two things go hand-in-hand sometimes.

"Can I at least put it on your finger?" I wonder, hip-bumping her playfully. "Let me have my moment here. I've always wanted to propose at a gas station. Specifically, a Kum & Go, but I can be flexible."

She chuckles, her hair hiding the expression she's wearing. "Sure. If you want to."

I really fucking want to.

I try to not act too excited as I steal one of her clasped hands, her fingers trembling as I stretch them apart and focus on the ring finger. She doesn't look at me. I think she's afraid of what she'll see. "Tabitha," I murmur, stroking her knuckle between my thumb and finger. "Tabs. I would love nothing more than for you to be my pretend fiancée for the next few days so we can trick my mother into believing I've somehow scored the most beautiful woman alive. Will you fake-marry me?"

Finally, her chin lifts. A lift and a tilt, and her eyes latch onto mine, and I know, I *know* she sees the flicker of yearning buried beneath the ruse.

I try to shut it down.

I try to bury it deeper.

But I wear my heart on my sleeve, let it bleed into my words, and it's definitely in my eyes.

She swallows. "Yes."

I slip the ring onto her finger as my heart dances pathetically between my ribs.

And that's where I fake-propose to the girl of my dreams.

In the parking lot of a sketchy gas station in Maryland, across the street from the Sexy Stuf kink store, with a billboard of Bambi the buxom blonde and her come-hither eyes as our only witness.

When I think back on this day, I'll probably forget that part.

I'll only remember the whimsical smile on Tabitha's face, the way she laces her fingers with mine, and the laughter in the air, feeding me with a false sense of hope.

I let it fill me up. I let it suffocate me.

There's no better way to go.

We take a selfie to capture the moment, then I sneak a quick kiss on her cheek, catching the way her eyes flare and her skin flushes a perfect shade of pink.

I shoot her a wink and whip open the driver's side door. I've never been more eager to lie to my mother.

I've never been more eager to lie to myself.

"Let's go, Wifey."

CHAPTER 16

TABITHA

I've lost my mind.

I realize that, yes. I know it's true. But I suppose there are worse things to lose when one's mind is as messy and destructive as mine.

Sunset pours in through the open window, causing my ring to glint as I twist my hand from side to side in my lap. I do it inconspicuously, pretending to inspect a small scratch along my knuckle. I don't want Gabe to know how nice it feels to wear it. To stare at it, to pretend.

To pretend I'm not falling apart, a walking disaster, a beacon of tragedy.

Instead, I'll turn my tragedy into a travesty. There are only a few letters separating the two, after all. Just a flurry of pen strokes that will transform my pain into a harmless, silly charade.

How I wish it were that easy.

I wasn't really thinking when I blurted out the idiotic idea of fooling Gabe's mother into thinking we were betrothed. And that's the thrilling appeal of Gabe Wellington—the draw of him. That's what keeps me running into his arms, keeps me tethered to him, has me agreeing to an eight-hundred mile road trip across the country. He makes me feel like I can be anything.

Do anything.

With him by my side, I could fly.

It's a reckless feeling, and I am anything but reckless these days.

I used to be, though, and maybe that's the true appeal. Gabe brings me one step closer to the woman I used to be with every hug, every burdenless laugh, every playful look in my direction.

Like right now. I see him glance at me, and it's just a glance, but it makes me want to sing at the top of my lungs, jump out of an airplane, travel to new, exciting places, and kiss him until I can't catch my breath, can't even think straight.

I can only feel.

There's a fine line between dangerous and liberating, and I dangle precariously between the two whenever he's an arm's reach away.

As the latest playlist hums along with the purr of the engine and the howl of the wind, I feel my phone vibrate between us on the center console. We're a few miles outside of Seaford when I get a video call from Martha Gleason.

My pulse jumps with anticipation; I've been craving a glimpse of my baby girl since the sun came up this morning. Martha said they were taking her to a church picnic today and would send me pictures throughout the day. A video call is even better.

I quickly hit accept. Hope stares back at me, the camera posed at an awkward angle, giving me a prime view up her nostrils. "Pumpkin!" I exclaim, sluiced with a shot of relief at seeing her face. There's a violet-colored sunhat on her head, the string tied with a bow beneath her chin. A banana is fisted in one sticky hand, while the other hand waves madly at me through the screen.

"Mama! Miss you, Mama." She presses the smashed banana up to the camera, leaving smudge marks behind. "Yum-yum."

"A banana! How tasty. I bet you're having lots of fun." My grin is stretched so wide, my cheeks ache. "Are you being good?"

"Good girl," she babbles. "Ice cream."

I told the Gleasons that strawberry ice cream is her favorite and the ultimate source of bribery.

Hope presses a juicy kiss to the screen, then pulls back and says, "Gab."

I can already see Gabe's smile cresting in my peripheral vision, so I spin the camera in his direction, twisting to get both of us in the frame. He pulls his focus off the road as we cruise to a stop at a red light, waving to Hope.

Her dark-blue eyes sparkle with recognition. "Gab!" she squeals. "Read book."

"Eh, I can't read right now, Peanut. I'm driving," he tells her, his grin wide.

"Car?"

"Yep. A fast car. Maybe I'll teach you how to drive it when we get home." He throws me a wink. "How about I read you a book tonight before bed?"

"Yay!"

Our shoulders bump together as I lean in closer and tilt the screen toward me. "I'm so glad you're having fun. Can you put Gramma on the phone?"

Martha comes into view, plucking the grimed-up cell phone from Hope's fist. Her chestnut hair is spattered with snowy-white threads and tied into a tight bun at the base of her neck. She smiles into the screen. "She's been lovely, Tabitha. Just a joy. Thank you for allowing us to spend this time with her," she says wistfully, tone genuine. "It means the world to Pat and I."

I smile back, my heart twisting with equal parts warmth and melancholy as I resituate in my seat. "Of course. I appreciate the updates and video chats."

"You're on your way to Delaware, yes? The free time must be refreshing."

"I am…and yes, it is. I miss her, but I think I needed this."

"You're with your boyfriend?"

My stomach pitches, my fingers plucking at the fringe along my shorts.

"*Fiancé*," Gabe coughs beside me.

I spare him a quick glance as he steps on the gas. Blushing, I opt for, "Um, just a friend. A good friend."

"Well, that sounds wonderful." Martha reaches for a tennis ball on the picnic blanket beside her and tosses it to her right. "I'll give you a ring later tonight before Hope goes to bed."

A flash of white and silver fur darts behind her through the grass, chasing the ball.

Echo.

Matthew's beloved husky.

My palms clam up and I drink in a deep breath to keep the anxiety from climbing. "That would be great. Thank you so much."

Hope waves goodbye and blows me a kiss before we discon- nect the call and I slump back into the seat, watching the cars zoom by in streaks of red, white, and black.

His hand finds my knee.

My head pops up to look at him, but his eyes are on the road, his left hand on the wheel. If it weren't for his other hand gently cupping my kneecap, his thumb carefully dusting along my skin, I would assume his mind was elsewhere. He says nothing, does nothing else, but I feel that he is fully with me, just by the way he holds my knee. And that's where his hand remains, my fingers resting on top of his, until we turn off the main drag and into a waterfront subdivision fifteen minutes later.

We pull into a circular driveway off of a street called Rivers End. My eyes light up when a charming colonial comes into view on a sprawling property that overlooks a wooded lot and creek. "Oh, wow," I murmur, taken aback by the beauty of it as I straighten in the seat. White siding, charcoal shutters, and a cozy front porch lined with shrubbery and multicolored flower bulbs stare back at me. There's a tree perched to the left side of the house, boasting some kind of yellowy-orange fruit on its branches. The tree looks so happy, so welcoming.

The image is breathtaking.

Gabe kills the engine and leans back, exhaling deeply, head canting in my direction as his jade eyes soften against the hazy sunset. "You like?"

"I *love*. This is a beautiful home," I tell him, mesmerized. I'm not sure what I was expecting, but it wasn't this. My gaze trails back to the tree that reminds me of summers spent lying beneath my childhood cherry tree. "What kind of fruit tree is that?"

"Persimmon," he says. "Mom makes persimmon pie with the fruits when fall rolls in. It's fire. Tastes kind of like a honeyed pumpkin pie. Weird, but good." Pulling the key from the igni- tion, Gabe pops open the driver's side door. "Ready to share the good news with my mother?" He winks at me before pulling himself from the car.

Butterflies burst to life with dizzied wings inside my belly.

God. What have I done?

My heart kicks up speed as I twirl the star-rimmed band around my ring finger. I nod and follow suit, inching my way out of the car on jelly-like legs. My muscles ache, sore from hours of sitting, but nothing aches more than my chest when Gabe's glowing smile meets me as he moves around the car. He looks so happy. So eager to introduce me as his new fiancée.

Maybe it was cruel to suggest such a thing.

I hate being cruel.

I hate being selfish.

My cheeks are burning, despite the light breeze coming off the water.

"Gabriel, you made it." A petite woman with a golden-blond bob and cranberry-red pantsuit appears across from us, waving from the front stoop, her shoulder propping open the screen door.

Gabriel.

I've never heard him called by his full name before.

The name makes me think of the biblical Gabriel, a messenger, the bearer of good news and hopeful visions. An angel.

Angels have wings.

Perhaps that's the reason he makes me feel like I can fly.

I shake away the silly thoughts and fix my hair, feeling unprepared to meet Gabe's mother after a long car ride of sweating and gorging on sugary gas-station snacks. Nerves race through me as I lift my hand with a small wave.

Before my arm falls back to my side, Gabe takes that hand in his and laces our fingers together. My cheeks heat, the nerves growing wings. I glance up at him, petrified, but I don't let go of his hand and only squeeze tighter.

"You okay?" he murmurs, his lips dipping to my ear. "We don't have to do this. We don't have to pretend."

Oh, but I want to pretend.

In fact, it's all I want to do. I only have three days to live inside this magical bubble of make-believe and daydreams.

"I'm okay." Looking up at him, I catch the colors of sunset swirling in his eyes, dancing with green. It's like a painting I could get lost in. A whole new world. "It's harmless, right?"

Those eyes tell me it's anything but harmless. Not to him.

Not to me.

"Of course." He nods anyway, deciding to dive inside the dreamful bubble with me. "It's all in good fun. We'll laugh about it one day."

Gabe's mother calls to us again, the screen door slapping shut behind her as she steps forward onto the walkway of stone pavers. "Is this your friend?" she inquires, similar green eyes pinned on me, shimmering with curiosity. "Tabitha, right? My son has told me so much about you."

My chest tightens. "Yes, it's wonderful to finally meet you."

She glances at our clasped palms. A crooked smile emerges, again, so similar. So familiar. "More than friends, I'm guessing?" Her eyes drift to Gabe, knowingly.

He unlocks our fingers to drape his arm around my shoulders, tugging me close. "Uh, yeah. Yep. Yes." He clears his throat. "We're engaged, actually."

Halting her steps, she blinks, the statement registering. Then her eyes pop.

"You know, to be married."

"That's implied, yes." She laughs, caught off guard.

"We wanted to surprise you," he continues. "It happened so fast. A whirlwind of...crazy love..." His arm squeezes tighter and I wonder if he's regretting this. He sounds nervous. "So... well, surprise."

My smile is useless. Strained and terrified.

His mother drinks us both in, attention trailing from his face to mine. And then her grin broadens, charmed and beaming, as she closes the gap between us and pulls me into a warm hug.

Guilt.

Guilt slithers down my spine the moment her arms wrap around me.

"Oh, I'm so happy for you both," she whispers, squeezing gently. "I've been waiting for this moment. I knew Gabe would find a wonderful girl."

A wonderful girl.

I realize then, Gabe must not have told her *all* about me.

"Come inside, both of you. I can't wait to hear more." She pulls away, still smiling from ear to ear. "I'm Janie, by the way. Janie Kent."

Gabe's palm slides from my shoulder to the small of my back, resting there, sweeping along the slender arch. His eyes are on his mother, his mouth moving with a flurry of words, his opposite arm reaching out to hug her, but his hand remains on my back.

He's with me.

We stroll toward the front of the house while Gabe and his mother make small talk about the long drive. When I step through the threshold, I immediately feel warmth. There's a homeyness that was always missing while I was growing up in Arizona. Something cozy.

"You have such a beautiful home," I tell her, glancing around at the ceiling beams and shiplap walls. "Do you live alone?"

She nods, guiding us through the foyer and down a narrow hallway. "I do. I love the quiet, and it's so relaxing out here in nature."

It's interesting how I've lived alone for most of my life and have always felt so lonely. I've hated the quiet, but Janie makes it seem like a peaceful oasis. I think that when your mind is full of serenity and sweet blessings, you find solace in the quiet moments.

It's harder for people like me.

"Let me get you two something to drink. Tea? Wine?"

"I'd love some tea," I say with a smile. Gabe sends me a conspiratorial glance before nodding me toward the couch. We plop down, side by side, and he cups his hand around my knee. My insides flutter and sing at the contact, causing me to stiffen.

He pulls his hand away. "Sorry."

Janie returns from the kitchen and I grab Gabe's hand, returning it to my knee. Then I graze my fingertips up and down his forearm, watching his skin come alive with goosebumps. He stares straight ahead, jaw clenched tight, gaze trained on his mother as she sets two tall glasses of iced tea in front of us.

We both speak at the same time.

"Tabitha is just—"

"Gabe is so—"

My eyes bulge. "We're so in love."

"Madly," he adds.

Wow.

We suck at this.

Janie glances between us, her eyes lowering to Gabe's white-knuckled grip on my knee. A smile hints. "Tell me how you two first met."

I'm pretty sure my expression goes blank, my face draining of color. We didn't discuss this part. Do we tell her the truth? Do we make up a whimsical, fairytale-esque story?

Gabe takes the lead, coughing into his fist before proceeding. "She came by my house when Oliver was still living with me. For a date."

Janie's grin is bright. "How romantic."

"A date with Oliver."

Color returns to my face in patches of bright red. I slink further into the couch as I place my hand over Gabe's. "Um, yeah…" I laugh lightly, awkwardly. "Oliver and I connected at the library, and we had a few things in common, so we decided to go to dinner."

"Oh?" Janie frowns as she sips her tea. "That didn't go well, I'm assuming?"

"It went great for me," Gabe says.

My hand trails to his thigh, and I dig my nails into his shorts. I think I hear him groan, so I loosen my hold because I'm probably drawing blood. "Oliver and I definitely worked better as friends. We had a nice time, but I—"

"She couldn't stop thinking about me."

Well…

That's mostly true.

He'd looked at me like he was staring at some prized piece of art hanging in a gallery. Awe-struck. There was a heated curiosity in his eyes, as if he'd been trying to uncover exactly what the artist had envisioned when they'd dipped their paintbrush into the colors and made careful strokes.

He was smitten.

And throughout the entirety of the dinner, I'd felt like I was on a date with the wrong man.

I wonder if I should tell her that, but I can't manage to get the words out. All I mutter is, "Um, yes. He made quite the impression."

"Mm," Janie replies, bobbing her head. "My son has never lacked any charm. So, it was a whirlwind romance after that?"

"Well, not quite—"

"Totally," Gabe answers at the same time. We look at each other, both blinking rapidly. He backpedals. "No. Not at all."

My eye twitches involuntarily. "I-I just mean, we took it slow…at first." I have no idea what I'm doing. Maybe I should feign muteness. I'll magically become a mime. It could happen. People turn into mimes all the time. "My past is complicated and

Gabe knew that, so he was a total gentleman. He was patient with me. Kind and loving. He made it easy to fall for him."

Gabe's grip slackens on my knee. He dusts his thumb along my skin, slow and tender. I'm too scared to glance at him, too afraid of what I'll see, but I catch the soft smile that touches his lips from the corner of my eye.

"And now you're engaged?" Janie presses.

I hold up my star ring as evidence and wiggle my fingers. "He proposed…in an airplane." My mind desperately tries to recall our rehearsed story, but the details are hazy. I'm butchering this. "And he sang to me."

"Helicopter," he coughs.

"Helicopter."

Janie's eyebrows raise. "He sang the proposal?"

"Well, he sang *after* the proposal. It was *With or Without You* by U2. That's our song."

"Great song," Gabe says, tilting toward me further as our shoulders kiss.

"I've never heard you sing, Gabriel."

"And you never will."

I reach for my tea and start gulping it down.

A few seconds tick by as Janie continues to study us carefully. Her perusal has me rubbing my palm up and down Gabe's thigh with bruising force, while leaning into him more and more as I try to salvage what I can of this charade. When my hand feels like it's on the receiving end of rug burn, I promptly stop accosting his leg. I'm only making it more obvious that I'm over-compensating for something.

Gabe wraps an arm around me and kisses my cheek. "Well, that's our story. One for the books, really. How have you been, Mom? Still selling houses like a boss?"

Thankfully, the subject shifts to Janie and her real estate business. The tense mood dissipates as we fall into easier conversation and untangle ourselves from the web of lies, thread by thread.

I notice, though, as laughter trickles its way in and the smiles bloom and grow, that Gabe and I never inch away from one another on the couch. His hand remains on my knee, his thumb dusting and grazing every now and then, like the contact is normal and effortless. His arm stays tucked around my shoulders, and my own hand doesn't move from his thigh, my fingertips dancing over the hem of his shorts to tickle his skin.

Janie watches us, drinking us in.

Assessing our dynamic.

And I think, as evening settles in, that she's wondering the same thing I'm wondering:

Is this real?

CHAPTER 17

TABITHA

Dusk transitions into nightfall, and we're perched at the kitchen island, shoveling homemade pie into our mouths.

We just got off the phone with Hope after saying our good-nights. Gabe read her a story, as promised, after Janie brought out a box of his childhood belongings to show me. One of my favorite stories growing up was tucked inside the mementos: *The Very Hungry Caterpillar.*

She was captivated. It was only a ten-minute chat, but my little girl was clinging to his every word. Gabe is so good with her, and watching them interact together made my heart squeeze.

"It's not quite persimmon season yet, so I hope you like the rhubarb," Janie tells us while separating leftovers into Tupperware containers and sealing the lids. "I added a touch of coconut. It's my secret ingredient."

"It's incredible," I say through a mouthful. "My mother never baked when I was growing up. She hardly cooked, either. Most nights I made myself ramen noodles or we had fast food." The memories seep in like a cloud of melancholy so I shake my head, dislodging them. "This is a nice treat. I try to cook for Hope as much as possible, but baking has never been my strong suit."

She smiles. "We'll change that. The next time I come to visit, I'll teach you everything I know."

"I'd love that." I really would. Baking cookies and pies and sweet treats was something I missed out on as a little girl with an inattentive mother.

"Oh, I also made up the guest room. Originally, I'd put an air mattress in the office, thinking you'd be sleeping separately. But the bed in the guest room is a queen, so it's plenty big enough for the both of you." Janie says it casually, expecting us to sleep together in the same bed. Because we're engaged. "I'll grab some extra pillows."

My cheeks grow warm. I duck my head and pull my hair from behind my ears to cover the evidence.

"Awesome," Gabe says, clearing his throat. "Thanks, Mom."

When Janie breezes out of the kitchen and down the hallway, I start smashing the tines of my fork into the pie. Our knees bump together underneath the kitchen island and I realize mine are bobbing restlessly. Nervously. It's not like we haven't slept together in the same bed before. It's not like I didn't fall asleep in the crook of his shoulder with his bare chest pressed up against me after my hands boldly explored his body, desperate for physical touch. But I suppose that moment was borne from trauma and desperation, and this feels…different.

Intentional.

"I can sleep on the floor."

My head jerks toward Gabe. His attention is on his plate of food as he gathers remaining pieces of flaky crust onto his fork. "No…no, that's not necessary. I would never make you sleep on the floor at your mother's house. This was my idea."

"An idea I don't think you really thought through," he says. His tone isn't disappointed, just practical. "It's fine, Tabs. The last thing I want to do is make you feel uncomfortable."

"Gabe, the *last* thing you make me feel is uncomfortable. I promise." I watch his eyes lift to mine and I offer a smile. "It's okay. We've slept together before."

Those eyes flare, just marginally, glittering like dew-tipped grass.

I stumble over the implication. "I-I mean…when I had that nightmare…and you held me as I fell back to sleep. And—"

"I know what you meant," he cuts me off with a smirk.

He does know what I meant. But I also know what he was thinking the moment those words slipped out, and they were not the same.

We finish our rhubarb pie and I stand to collect the plates, rinsing them before popping them in the dishwasher. Then I move on to the rest of the dirty dishes in the sink.

"Don't you worry about that. You're my guest—no cleaning allowed." Janie appears from around the corner, shooing me away with a flick of her wrist.

"Oh, sorry." Chuckling under my breath, I swipe my palms along my shorts. "Habit, I guess."

"A fine habit. You could teach Gabriel a thing or two, I'm sure." She spares Gabe an amused glance. "My son will treat you like a queen, that I can promise. The drawback may be wading through his piles of clothes to get to your throne."

"Jeez, I'm not a slob," Gabe grumbles. "I've lived on my own for years now."

I smile.

He's not wrong. While his house has some clutter, it's never a disaster. Never dirty. And the occasional mess is actually something I appreciate—it looks lived in.

Perfectly flawed.

"I suppose I've taught you well, then," Janie relents, her smile blooming. She turns to me. "Why don't you two call it an early night? I'm sure you're exhausted. There are plenty of fresh linens and extra pillows in the guest room." Adjusting her glasses, her dark-green eyes sparkle back at me. "A nice breeze spills in from the east, so I left the window cracked. Please let me know if you need anything else."

My palms clam up.

I glance at Gabe as he rises from the kitchen stool.

"Thanks for dinner, Mom," he says, sounding eager. "See you in the morning."

He nods toward the staircase, so I follow, saying goodnight to his mother before trailing him up the older wooden steps. They creak beneath my bare feet and it's a welcome sound. I prefer steps that creak and groan, versus blocks of cement that echo under heavy boots.

The guest room is subtly lit by the moon and a ledge adorned with flickering electric candles. There's a wax warmer in the corner on an antique table, leaving traces of lavender in the air.

My eyes water at the scent.

Gabe closes the door behind us and the sound of it clicking

shut causes my heart to teeter. I pivot around until we're face to face, his eyes finding mine and dancing with shadows and firelight.

I realize I don't have anything appropriate to wear. Without knowing we'd be sharing a bed, I only packed my nightgowns made of thin satin and lace.

I swallow.

"The offer stands," he murmurs, only a foot away from me. "I can take the floor. It's not a big deal."

Biting my lip, I shake my head. "No. I don't want you to."

"Okay." His throat bobs as he nods. "Did you need to change?"

There's a small bathroom attached to the bedroom with a pedestal sink and vintage mirror. "I do. I'll just be a minute." I slip away into the shadows, plucking a gown from my suitcase and stepping into the bathroom to change my clothes.

As I flatten out my gown, my eyes lift to my reflection. I drink in my bony shoulders and collarbone, my willowy frame, my chest that looks nearly skeletal against the dim lights above the oval mirror. I haven't been eating well. I haven't eaten well since my escape, which is strange after being deprived of hearty meals for two months. Food should be a delicacy, a true privilege, but the thought of it makes my stomach churn. I eat to get by—a necessary routine instead of an indulgence.

Insecurity races through me as I inspect my curves; rather, my *lack* of curves. I used to be filled out and healthy, my breasts full, my belly trim but well-fed. My gowns and dresses would never hang off of me like this, making me look gaunt and shapeless.

I have no idea what Gabe sees in me. Why he claims to *want* me. He's attractive, virile, toned, and fit. I've seen the way women look at him when we're out in public.

He's a catch.

And I am nothing but the deficient scraps of a girl long gone.

Tucking my loose hair behind my ears, I turn away from the mirror and head back into the bedroom. Gabe is dressed in a white T-shirt and gray sweatpants, perched at the edge of the bed, swiping through his phone. He looks up at me when I enter, his eyes briefly trailing me before pulling back up. A smile claims his gaze, tips his lips, as if the sight of me has brought him joy.

I don't understand.

And I hate this feeling—this feeling of lacking, of unworthiness. I never used to see myself in such a dismal light.

I clear my throat and move forward, quickly hiding myself beneath the covers and burrowing deep. My eyes are closed but I feel the mattress shift and creak beneath his weight as he slips in beside me. My heart pounds. I'm not sure what to do, what to say. I want him to hold me as I fall asleep, but I can't ask him that. He already gives me too much.

Suddenly, anxiety ripples through me.

I shoot up with a flicker of worry. "Are the doors locked?"

"Yes. I made sure."

"The windows?" I glance at the window Janie said was cracked but it's shut and latched now. Gabe must have closed it.

"Yep. All of them."

I'm already throwing off the covers and sliding from the mattress. "I should double check. Just in case—"

He pulls me back down, his arm curling around my middle and tugging gently as he presses a kiss to my hair. "You're safe. You'll always be safe when I'm with you."

I allow his words to quell the anxiety as he unravels his arm from around me and leaves a gap between us. It's as if he realized we were too close, too intimate, and he's afraid I'll try to leap from the bed again.

I wouldn't.

I prefer his arm around me over the gap.

"Tabs?"

His voice is low but loud against the quiet. I feel his body heat behind me as I face the opposite way. "Yes?"

"Tell me what you're thinking."

I breathe in deeply, my eyes fluttering open and landing on the wax warmer across the room. Lavender wafts around me and I instantly feel sad. "It smells like lavender in here. The scent of lavender makes me want to cry."

I've never confessed that to him before. He doesn't say anything for a few moments but I hear the confusion in his silence.

I twist around, facing him. He's partially under the covers, one hand propping his head up on the pillow as he stares at me, waiting for more context.

"When I was just a little girl, my father liked to set firecrackers to our wild cherry tree where the mockingbirds would sing. He said they were too loud, too pesty. He enjoyed sitting on the patio with his beer and a book and the birds would disrupt his solitude," I explain. "So, he'd try to scare them off with firecrackers. I never understood it—I loved those birds. I loved the songs they sang."

Gabe watches me, the artificial candles illuminating his thoughtful expression.

"Lavender bloomed along the back of the house, right beside the tree. One day, after my father laughed at the birds as they scattered from the branches, he went back inside while I knelt beside the tree where a tiny bird had fallen." Tears spring to my eyes, my heart clenching. "One of the birds had died. I think it was so frightened by the firecrackers, its heart stopped."

"Shit." His brows crease. "I'm sorry."

I swipe away a loose tear, embarrassed that I'm getting emotional over a fifteen-year-old memory. Over a little bird, who no one remembers but me. "Anyway," I say through an exhale. "Every time I smell lavender, I think of the bird. It was potent that day, sailing through the backyard and overpowering the cherry blossoms in the air. I watched the bird's wing twitch a final time before it went completely still. Lifeless. I was only eight years old at the time, so I didn't really understand death. It affected me, though. I kept thinking about the bird's last day. What it did, what it saw." I glance away and finger the rose-gold ring on my necklace chain. "Later that day, I went to bury the bird beside the tree and I found this ring hidden in the dirt. I kept it as a reminder that life is fragile. Fleeting."

Gabe seems to have inched closer to me on the bed, close enough that my naked toes creep underneath his legs for warmth. He stares at me like he's completely invested. Like he only sees me, only hears me. "Are you afraid of death?"

Instinct has me wanting to say yes. I think everyone is scared of dying.

Except…that's not really true for me.

I shake my head. "It's not death itself I'm scared of—I've already faced it, head-on, day after day, expecting it to come. Accepting it," I tell him. Finding his eyes, I hold for a beat before continuing. "It's the last day that scares me."

His brows furrow, contemplative. "The last day?"

I nod. "What if I run out of my favorite coffee and have to settle for gas-station coffee? What if I lose my temper and snap at my child? What if I didn't have time to shower one last time, or eat my favorite candy bar, or what if I accidentally cut someone off in traffic and that's my final moment on Earth? My swan song." I inhale a deep breath, a chill snaking down my back. "The last day is your last chance to get it right. To leave your mark and do everything you want to do. The idea of those final moments not being brilliant or memorable is terrifying to me."

My thoughts grow dark and I think back to Matthew's last day.

I wonder if he felt validated, fulfilled. It was an awful, terrible last day, following a nightmarish two weeks, but that final moment…

Perhaps it could have been worse.

He left his mark, and I think he knew that. I think that brought him comfort.

Gabe drops his hand from underneath his head and scoots closer to me, our faces only inches apart. Our eyes hold. He reaches for my hand, the hand that's trembling beneath my cheek, and pulls it out from under me to clasp it inside his. "I hope the next time you smell lavender, it doesn't make you sad." He presses a kiss to my knuckles. "I hope you'll think of this moment instead of the bird. This day. This room." Another kiss, and then a whisper. "Me."

My lips wobble and my eyes glaze over, but not from sadness.

It's the complete opposite of sadness.

He reaches for me until his strong arm is tugging me closer, until I'm curled into him with my nose burrowed against his swiftly beating chest. Our hands are still clasped, his thumb brushing over the star-rimmed band on my ring finger.

I breathe in the lavender and let it chase away the melancholic memories, replacing that moment with this one.

This day. This room.

Him.

"Goodnight, Tabs."

I smile, pressing closer to him. "Goodnight, Gabe."

I know it's reckless, letting him hold me like this. Allowing our bodies to mesh and twine as we share a bed and drift to sleep like lovers.

I'm being so damn *reckless*.

And I think, maybe…

It's within the reckless moments that we truly live.

I close my eyes with a contented sigh, the soft smile lingering on my lips.

If this were to be my last day…I know I would die happy.

CHAPTER 18

GABE

I've always been an early riser when visiting my mother.

I think it's the birds.

Mom's house is surrounded by giant basswood trees, so the birds sound closer, more songful, pulling me awake just as dawn begins to crest. Tabitha lies curled up beside me with one knee tucked to her chest, the other twisted up in the blankets. She's a vision in white; white blankets, an ivory gown, pale skin. She looks like a snow queen draped in sheaths of inky-dark hair.

I decide to let her sleep, knowing she needs it.

When I enter the kitchen after freshening up in the hall bathroom, Mom is already perched at the large island with a cup of coffee as she flips through a home and garden magazine.

She looks up over the rim of her glasses. "Good morning," she greets with a smile. "Coffee is still hot. I made plenty."

"Thanks." I make my way over to the coffee pot and fill a ceramic mug decorated with smiling foxes. "How are you always awake so early?"

She closes the magazine as I face her on the other side of the island. "Same as you, I'd imagine. It's hard to oversleep in a place like this."

Sipping my coffee, I glance out the floor-to-ceiling windows, drinking in the undulating tree branches as they come alive with the glow of first blush. "Valid."

"Is Tabitha still upstairs?"

"Yeah." I nod, returning my attention to my mother. "She

needs the rest. That girl hardly gets a full night's sleep with Hope and the long hours at her job."

"Mmm," she muses. "She's strong. She's been through a lot."

It's no secret what she's been through. I made sure it wasn't a topic up for discussion this weekend, but Mom is aware of Tabitha's backstory, thanks to never-ending news coverage about The Matchmaker killer and his three surviving victims.

Tabitha hardly ever goes on social media, but her Facebook profile has over a million followers. She's basically a household name.

"She has a child."

I lift my chin, my eyes narrowing at my mother. "Shit, Mom, thanks for that stunning revelation. How did I miss that?"

"I'm just saying, that's a big responsibility. I hope you're ready for it."

There she goes, trying to be rational.

Thinking I'm incapable.

"You think I can't handle that? You think I'm destined to be a bachelor for the rest of my life, chasing tail, partying, without a care in the world?" My glare turns icy. "Well, you're wrong. I can step up to the plate. I can fucking *leap* up to the plate. She's worth it."

Mom glances down at her coffee cup, spinning the ceramic between her hands. "That's another man's child, conceived during a terrible, traumatic situation. Is Tabitha's abductor the biological father?"

"No. She had a DNA test done. Hope belongs to the other man who was down there with her. The professor. That sick bastard, Hubbard, made them…" I wave my hand around. "You know."

"God. How awful."

"Yeah." I nod through a hard swallow. "But I can handle it. I *want* to. That little girl is incredible."

"I just worry. You didn't have the best role model growing up, so I—"

"Trust me, I'm well-versed in subpar parenting thanks to the piece-of-shit you decided to procreate with. I know exactly what *not* to do." My heart jumps, my pulse tripping with a shot of anger. "I can't believe you'd even compare me to him."

Her head snaps up. "I'm not *comparing* you to him. I would

never." She swallows, her shoulders squaring. "I just hope she doesn't, either."

"She doesn't. She knows I'm nothing like that monster." The anger continues to climb. I can't believe we're even having this conversation. "I'm a good fucking person."

"Yes, you are," she agrees. "That's why I worry. I worry you're chasing a happy ending that doesn't end happily for you. I worry you're too busy hoping, instead of seeing the situation at face value."

The back of my neck prickles. "What do you mean?"

A look of pity shimmers in her eyes as she leans forward on her elbows and plucks the glasses from her nose. "You're not engaged, are you?"

How?

How the fuck does she know that?

My fingers curl around the mug handle, my other hand pressing forward on the countertop. "What makes you think that?" I try, as if I can still hide what she's already pieced together.

Mom sighs. It's the same sigh she makes whenever she's about to say something she knows I don't want to hear. "You look at her with love," she says gently. "And she looks at you like she doesn't know what to do with that love."

There are a million ways to die and my mother settles on the most painful.

She must sense the way my heart shrivels up inside my chest and my light snuffs out. A mother's instinct, I suppose.

"Sweetheart, I didn't mean…" She grabs my cold, stiff hand. "I didn't mean it like that. I think she cares…she wants to love you. I think she's trying."

Trying.

I pull away, retreating into my coffin while that remaining sliver of hope spits on my grave. "Thanks, Mom. You always know how to make me feel all warm and gooey inside."

"Gabriel, I'm just trying to be the voice of reason. I don't want to see you get hurt."

"I don't want reason. Can't you pretend, for once in my life? Can't you fucking *pretend* that everything is going to work out perfectly?" I set down my coffee as my fingers ball into fists at my sides. "That's what mothers do, right? They sprinkle fanciful things into their kid's ear; fairytales about Santa Claus and leprechauns and unicorns. Shit like that. Why can't you do that?"

"I've always been honest." She frowns, hurt. "I've always been true."

"I was four years old when you told me Santa wasn't real."

"Gabriel—"

I slam my hands down on the countertop. "Why can't you just fucking *lie* to me?"

Both of our heads jerk sideways when a figure appears at the entry to the kitchen. Tabitha stands there, her eyes wide, newly changed into a summery, coral-colored dress.

She wrings her hands together, blinking as her attention drifts between us. "Good morning."

Mom gifts me a look of apology before painting a smile on for Tabitha. "Good morning. How did you sleep?"

"Very well, thank you." She clears her throat and fiddles with the star ring. "I was just coming down for some coffee."

"I can pour you a cup," Mom says, standing. "Then I'll get breakfast ready. Do you like omelets?"

Tabitha nods with appreciation.

Fuck.

I press forward on both palms, tucking my chin to my chest.

I'm not sure how much she heard.

Regardless, I realize the act is up. It was pointless and stupid anyway. I think I only agreed to it to fool *myself*, knowing my mother was too perceptive to believe that I was mature and responsible enough to take care of someone like Tabitha—a single mom, a survivor of unspeakable horrors.

A woman too in love with a dead man to see a future with me.

Pushing up from the counter, I storm out of the kitchen and sweep past Tabitha. She snatches my wrist before I can get far.

"Gabe…"

I stall my feet, glancing off to the side before meeting her eyes. "I'm going to hop in the shower. I was thinking we could go to the boardwalk today. Atlantic City," I tell her, trying not to show how fucking defeated I feel. "It's about a three hour drive from here. You up for another road trip?"

She bobs her head. "That sounds fun."

Fun.

It'll be so much fun plodding through another day in hopeless purgatory with my mother's wicked truths ringing in my ears.

"Great." My smile is forced, and I know she can tell. Apparently, I'm incredibly easy to read. "We can head out in about an hour."

The smile evaporates the moment I'm stomping up the stairs, two at a time.

After I lock myself in the bathroom, I hop in the shower and crank the water on high heat, then simmer beneath the jets while I try to conjure up an image of the prior night. Tabitha, spilling her heart out to me, sharing her fears, and letting me hold her until birdsong pulled me from the reverie I hoped would last forever.

The image doesn't stick.

The dream dissolves, just like dreams do.

All I can see is the look of trying in her eyes.

OLIVER:

> Hello, Gabe. It's Oliver. There's a dapper-looking gentleman at your front door inquiring about your whereabouts.

MY BLOOD CHILLS as I glance down at the phone in my hand. I bump into three separate people, my focus on the text message, the sounds of carnival rides and a trumpeting mariachi band fading out when realization sets in.

Fantastic.

The Peaky Blinders prick knows where I live.

"Oh, my God, Gabe, this view is incredible!"

Tabitha's voice pitches with a range I've never heard before; one octave above pure joy.

It's a defibrillator paddle to my heart, and it's enough to distract me long enough to forget about Oliver's text. Charmed by her enthusiasm, I hand over the half-eaten plate of funnel cake we've been sharing while itching to swipe away the dollop of powdered sugar above her upper lip. "Your hat is ridiculous." I throw her a grin. Her hat is fucking awesome.

She grips the oversized brim decorated in neon-yellow flowers. The hat practically swallows her whole, but I saw the way her eyes lit up when she spotted it at a seaside boutique, making it the easiest forty dollars I've ever shelled out.

"I know, right? I love it." She laughs again, another electric shock to my chest. "Thank you. I promise I'll pay you back."

Yeah, right.

She's already paying me back plus interest right now, just in the way her smile glows brighter than the Ferris wheel lights. She looks so goddamn free. I want to bottle her joy in a glass jar and store it away for a rainy day. It's easy to turn off my miserable thoughts when the woman I love is backlit by glittering sunshine reflecting off the ocean, her laughter bleeding into saxophone melodies played by street musicians.

My cell phone pulls me from the moment with another metallic ping.

OLIVER:

> He's impressively persistent and is now snooping around your property. Perhaps I should speak with him?

Frustrated, I scrub a hand over my face. I can't deal with this shit right now. I have no idea why this guy thinks I owe his "boss" money, or why he thinks I'd even have extra money lying around on a blue-collar salary. I'm not my father. I'm not a shady businessman who's made his living laundering money through a slew of high-end restaurants and God knows what else. Drugs, hits, a fuck-ton of illegal activity, I'm sure.

The dude said to talk to my dad; said that good 'ol Pops will know what to do.

Well…

1. Fuck no.
2. Double-fuck no.
3. I'd rather scoop my eyeballs out with a melon baller and dive face-first into an acid bath than have a conversation with that man.

That leaves me with my only other option: option *D*.
Denial.

I'll avoid the situation and pretend it's not happening.

ME:

Tell him I died.

Then tell him to fuck off.

D for Dead—that works, too.

I watch the little speech bubbles burst to life, wiggling with an impending reply.

OLIVER:

If it's all right with you, I may word it differently.
But I'll attempt to get the point across.

I drop my arm to my side and tap the phone against my thigh, anxiety eating at me. This shit is stressful. Apparently, losing my stepbrother for twenty-two years, then having to save him from a house fire along with my best friend, while nearly losing my arm, all because of dear-old Dad, isn't enough pain and suffering to satisfy the universe.

A few minutes pass, and I glance up at Tabitha. She's picking at the funnel cake and licking her fingers, her eyes roaming the boardwalk littered with tourists, performers, and musicians. "Should we request a song?" she asks me. Her gaze lingers on the saxophone player covering *Careless Whisper* as she sways to the music, her sundress kissing her knees. When she discovers my eyes on her, the smile she wears turns almost flirty. "Maybe we can request...*our* song?"

Shit.

I can't even remember what song it was we'd decided on. It feels like every song is ours.

The notion that she wants someone to play it for us in the middle of the iconic boardwalk does something stupid to my heart.

Grinning like a fool, I watch as Tabitha spins the ring around her finger. The one she hasn't removed despite the fact that I'm dead certain she heard my mother shredding my heart to smithereens in the kitchen this morning. "Only if you'll dance with me," I reply with a shrug. It's a casual pop of my shoulders, exuding the exact opposite of how I feel. "I've been dying to recreate those amazing dance moves from our first date."

She huffs a laugh. "I was stepping on your toes the whole time."

"Gouging them, honestly. Those heels could have doubled as a weapon." We share a smile as I stuff my hands into my cargo shorts along with my phone and tilt my head, wondering what she'll say or do next.

"No heels this time." Tabitha lifts an ankle, showing off her petal-pink toenails peeking through a strappy sandal. "The damage will be minimal."

I'm pretty sure we're still talking about shoes, so I nod and saunter forward. "All right, Tabs. Put the song in and I'll sweep you off your non-hazardous feet."

There's a giddiness on her face, mimicking the last time we danced together.

And I feel it all spiraling back. That debilitating flicker of hope.

Tabitha discards the funnel cake remains in a trash can and makes her way over to the saxophone player, holding her hat with one hand as she leans over to tell him the song. He smiles, nods. His pale, golden eyes brighten, looking striking against dark skin and a black hat.

The first few notes ring out, and I remember the song now.

U2.

Thorns twisting, hands tied, bodies bruised.

So romantic.

She swivels around after popping a wad of money into the man's tip jar, inching toward me as I move forward. One step, two steps. There's an invisible string between us, one end tied around her heart, the other tied to mine. We pull together until she's pressed against my chest and we're both teetering left to right, swaying in a lazy circle in the middle of the boardwalk.

It's not a grandiose movie moment. The crowd doesn't part, doesn't *ooh* and *ahh* as they watch with lovestruck eyes. It'll never make the big screen, or even a book, and it won't be dissected in college courses or literature classes one day.

But it's us.

Implicitly, perfectly flawed.

I spin her around, letting her fall against my torso, and I nearly collapse under the weight of it. Not from the weight of *her*, but from the weight of what she does to me. The weight of painful, one-sided love. It will forever be the heaviest thing I carry.

Her hand is small and trembling as I hold it in mine, my other arm draped around her back, my palm splayed across her spine. I saw Sydney's parents dancing like this in their driveway one night when I was just a curious kid. I was in Oliver's old room, peeping outside after hearing classic music pour in through the cracked window. My father never danced with my stepmom like that. In fact, they hardly touched each other at all. Dad was too busy, too cold. And Charlene was an independent woman, practically raising us by herself, leaving little time for a romantic, late-night rendezvous in the driveway.

It felt like I was watching a fairytale as Sydney's mother pressed her cheek to her husband's chest while his lips caressed the top of her head, his eyes closed with contentment. They danced and swayed beneath stars and string lights, uncaring of the cars that slowed down to take in the scene.

I think about that moment as Tabitha nuzzles her cheek against my own chest, inhaling a shaky breath, and as I press my lips to the top of her head, breathing in her jasmine shampoo.

That moment had felt a lot like love. And so does this one.

Her hands curl around my upper arms as the saxophone fades out and transitions into a new song. Pulling back, she gazes up at me with cheeks stained pink, likely from sunburn. Or maybe from the same thing that has my own skin sweltering.

"Thank you for the dance," she whispers, her fingernails biting into my skin.

I'm wearing gray cut-off sleeves, so her eyes are drawn to the gnarly scar decorating my bicep and she quickly loosens her grip. I'm not ashamed of my scar. I wear it with pride, showing it off, because I know it was borne from something good and selfless.

She dusts her thumb over the puckered edges before glancing up at me again. I can hardly see her face underneath the wide-brimmed hat.

"I brought sunscreen," she says. "For your scar." She pulls me away from the crowd by the wrist until we're huddled in a less-crowded area beside a seafood stand. Her hand snakes into her satchel to retrieve the tube of sunscreen.

I watch her untwist the cap. "I'm good. You don't need to worry about my scar."

"I can't help but worry. You're always in the sun." She squeezes a handful of cream onto her palm and starts lathering it along my arm, traveling up my neck and jawline.

I go still, swallowing hard at the feel of her fingers sliding over my skin, the cream cool but her touch warm. I keep my eyes trained just above her head, staring blankly at a colorfully dressed man on stilts, simply to avoid our gazes from tangling.

"I care about you."

Her words float over to me, magnetic enough to drag my attention down to her face. Tabitha tilts her head back so I can see beneath the brim of her hat, so I can witness the truth of her words shimmering in copper-spun eyes.

She does care.

It's natural for someone to care about their almost-everything.

I reach for her hand just as it ascends back up, about to cup my jaw. I reach for it to prevent the contact, to keep it from grazing the side of my face and making me believe and hope, but I forget to let it go.

Our hands hold mid-air and my thumb starts tracing the divots of her palm, landing on the star ring she still wears.

She stares up at me, pupils dilated.

I think about kissing her. The idea of spinning her around and pressing her up against the side of this building, our mouths fusing together as an intoxicating salt breeze swirls in the air, nearly consumes me. But all I can think about is the last time I kissed her beneath the stars on a chilly February night.

She was willing, at first. Responsive. My tongue slipped between her lips as her hands clasped both sides of my neck to pull me closer, to keep us connected, to keep the flame from dying. She opened her mouth wider, sliding her tongue against mine. Moans, whimpers, surrender. My fingers were buried in her hair, fisting and tugging, desperate to keep her with me. Heat bloomed hotter than any midday sun. The flame kindled and burned.

Ignited.

And then it snuffed out with a single word.

A name.

Another man's name.

Matthew.

The look of abject horror that wrenched her eyelids open and had her scrambling away from me will forever be seared into my memory. I can't forget it.

How could I?

The woman I love uttered a different man's name while my tongue was in her mouth.

Part of me died that day.

And that same dead, rotting part is what has me letting go of her hand and inching back. Away. Far enough away so that the temptation of another kiss evaporates in the ocean breeze.

"Excuse me…"

I shake away the misery that has seeped back into my psyche and turn my attention to a redhead tentatively inching her way closer. Tabitha catches her breath, severed from whatever spark of magic flared between us, and also turns to eye the young woman.

The girl approaches, looking nervous. "A-are you Tabitha Brighton?"

Tabitha blinks. Even the beaming sun can't mask the shadows that cloud her eyes when she's recognized—knowing she'd only be recognized for one thing. "I am, yes." Her arms wrap around her middle like a protective shield.

"I'm so sorry to intrude. I hate to be a bother. I just…" The twenty-something-year-old woman ducks her head bashfully before glancing back up, tucking her reddish hair behind her ears. "I just had to tell you what an inspiration you are. I've followed your story for years. It's incredible what you've overcome."

Tabitha's eyes glass over.

All of my instincts have me reaching for her hand again, just to let her know I'm here. She's not alone. I'll always be her friend.

She gives my fingers a squeeze. "Thank you. I appreciate that."

The woman smiles, and I've seen that smile before. It's a product of trauma, of survival, of many gruesome secrets.

"I can't begin to imagine what you went through. I wanted to tell you that I also found myself in a dangerous situation. With an ex. I know it's not the same, but…you really helped me through it. You allowed me to believe that I'm stronger than I ever thought possible." Tears glimmer in her eyes. "You don't post much on social media, but you have a huge following. I think it would be amazing if you used your platform to encourage other women to find their strength."

Tabitha squeezes me harder. Her nerves feel like a tangible thing.

"Oh…wow, thank you for sharing that with me. I'll, um…I'll consider it. I don't have much time for social media, but it would be rewarding if I could help others." The tension wanes slightly, her grip loosening. "It's a great idea."

"Really?" The woman blushes as her eyes twinkle. "Gosh, that would be so wonderful. You're a blessing, truly. A gift. Thank you for allowing me to stop over and say hi."

The woman doesn't wait for a reply and only offers a timid wave before retreating backward, then spinning away into the crowd.

Tabitha watches her go, lost in thought.

My pocket vibrates.

I fish out my phone and skim over Oliver's message.

OLIVER:

I told him you were in Uganda on a mission trip and may never return. I panicked a bit, and I don't believe he bought it.

Uganda.
Works for me.

ME:

Did he leave?

OLIVER:

Yes. He sauntered down the sidewalk and disappeared into the fog. It was quite ominous.

ME:

Good enough.

Thanks.

OLIVER:

Would you mind filling me in on what all of this is about?

I rub at my forehead, warding off an inevitable tension headache.

ME:

Your guess is as good as mine. Probably some supplier or subcontractor hassling me about the new-build subdivision we're working on.

OLIVER:

All right, then. Be safe, Gabe.

ME:

You know it.

When I glance up, Tabitha is simultaneously fiddling with her own phone while peering over at a roller coaster that stands tall before us. She eyes it warily but with a twinkle of curiosity.

I revert back into the land of denial and decide to enjoy the rest of my day.

Clicking off my phone screen, I shove it into my pocket and arch an eyebrow at Tabitha when she glances at me. "You want to go on that roller coaster."

"No." She swallows. "It looks terrifying. The track sounds rickety."

"Part of the appeal," I say breezily. "Let's do it."

"I don't think I can."

"You can do anything with me by your side." I bump her shoulder with mine, in time with the wink I send her. "Even fly."

She hesitates, then pivots toward the ride again, watching as the train stuffed with shrieking people and raised arms inches over the lift hill.

When it falls back down, she visibly shudders.

And then I don't even think.

I rush toward her, bend, then haul her onto my back as her huge hat flies backward, the tied string catching underneath her chin, keeping it from billowing away. She squeals right into my ear, her hands linking around my neck. The dress she's wearing bunches up around her thighs, but she doesn't seem to mind my forearms latching under them, digging into her bare skin. There's no flinching, no pulling away. It's just effortless.

Too effortless.

The line is mercifully shorter than usual, so we make it onto the ride in less than twenty minutes after Tabitha deposits her hat and satchel into a storage bin. We hop into the two-person bench seat and squish together, side by side, as the safety bar falls down and presses into our laps.

The train begins to move.

"Oh God. Oh God, what am I doing?" She's close to hyperventilating.

I'm not entirely sure what she's doing, but I can tell she wants to do this, despite her fear. Despite her protests. I lean over to whisper in her ear, "Don't look down."

Her hand slashes through the air to squeeze my thigh.

She closes her eyes.

And then she pops them back open.

A fleeting expression dances across her face, one I can't decipher. Whatever it is has her digging in her front pocket with a shaky hand until she's clutching her cell phone.

With one arm tucked around her shoulders and one curled around the safety bar, I watch as she opens up her Facebook app and scrolls until she finds what she's looking for.

She presses the "Live" button.

I stare at her ashen profile in astoundment.

It's evident she's never used the feature before because the screen is pointed down at our kneecaps smashed together as she flusters through the prompts and buttons. "I don't know what I'm doing," she mutters with panic as we ascend toward the top.

Her viewers climb, just as we do.

I jump in to help her, lifting the phone until it's aimed at the track and then I press the front-facing camera button. Her windblown hair and wild eyes pop into frame.

"Oh, my God…um, hi," she squeaks out, clasping a hand over mine so we're both holding up the phone. "Hi, everyone. I felt compelled to do this. I've never really used this platform before, but I was recently informed that I have a lot of people who follow me. Who are inspired by me." The number of viewers shoots up by the hundreds every few seconds. Soon, there are over four-thousand people watching as comments flash across the screen and we inch halfway to the tip of the peak.

Hi!

Where are you??

Is that a roller coaster?

Tell us your story!

You single?

How is your daughter doing?

She's flustered. Nervous, petrified.

And so fucking brave, I want to kiss her in front of all of these people.

"A-anyway, this is a weird time to do this, but I'm on a roller coaster right now. I've never been on one before. I'm scared of heights." She stumbles over her next words, locking up. Then she turns the camera toward me and murmurs, "I'm going to throw up."

I tilt it back to her, grinning. "You got this. Keep going."

Who's the hottie?!

Is that your boyfriend?

What would you say to the Matchmaker Killer if he were here right now?

She gulps, ignoring the questions. "We're about to go over the top, so I thought it would be fitting for anyone watching who needs a dose of bravery. A lift. I'm going to face my fears with all of you watching, live on camera, and if I manage to make it off this roller coaster in one piece, I know it'll be worth it. That feeling of overcoming is always worth the uphill climb." Tabitha glances my way, blinking rapidly. "I think."

Gears creak. The track wobbles underneath the wheels. Fellow riders howl from behind us.

I can see pillowy clouds bleeding into the wooden railway as we crest. Below us, sunlight pours down on ocean water like glittery white lace.

Tabitha swaps the phone into her left hand, her right hand finding my leg again, nails burrowing into the skin below my shorts. We reach the top. A heartbeat of tense silence hovers within the train car as everyone holds their breath, ready to unleash their screams.

And then we plummet.

She manages to keep her hold on the phone as she latches onto the safety bar with her other hand and releases a high-pitched screech into the sea-spun wind. I watch through the phone screen as her hair flies every which way, her eyes tipped skyward, refusing to look down.

I swear there's a smile in that scream as she stares at the clouds.

As we fall.

As she flies.

When the ride finishes after consecutive loop-di-loops, mini-hills, and sideways zooms, we jerk to a stop, the other riders clapping and hollering in celebration.

I stare at her, mesmerized. Proud as hell.

For a moment, I think she's going to burst into tears. All color has drained from her face and her hair is a tangled mess over her eyes. Her chest heaves with gasping breaths. A hand flies up to cup her mouth, and I wonder if she's going to actually throw up.

Instead, she surprises me.

She lets out a shriek of unparalleled laughter. Her shoulders shake, her entire body quivering head to toe with adrenaline and pure relief.

Accomplishment.

More comments flash across the screen, one after the other.

`You did it!`

`Woohoo, this makes me want to go bungee jumping or something. What a rush!`

`This was so inspiring. Thank you.`

`Now kiss the cutie by your side—I'll wait :)`

Tabitha lowers the phone to her lap, the camera facing up, both of us in the frame. She links a hand around the back of my neck and tugs me toward her with a beaming grin, her lips coming in for a kiss on my cheek.

I turn.

I turn at that precise moment, and our mouths lock together for a soul-sucking beat. It's nothing but closed lips and startled breaths, but it sends a shockwave straight through me.

She freezes, briefly, her instinct to pull away, her eyes shooting open.

But she lingers.

Just for two precious, frozen-in-time seconds.

Tabitha retreats back in slow motion, eyelids fluttering, her hand sliding from my neck and off my shoulder. A hard swallow works her throat as she glances down at the phone that captured those few seconds in which my heart tore through my chest to tangle with hers.

Her hands are violently trembling when she lifts the phone

back up and inhales a choppy breath. Then she smiles into the screen and ends the live video.

We shuffle off the ride, my stomach in my throat, my heart still on that train.

She reaches for my hand the moment we're on solid ground. "Gabe?"

I glance at her, memorizing her euphoric smile. "Tabs."

"Thanks for flying with me today."

Fuck.

She makes it so damn easy to believe she's mine.

And now?

Thousands of people all over the world believe it, too.

We stroll away from the ride, hand-in-hand, as my phone dings from my back pocket. I use my free hand to pull it out, thinking it's Oliver, prepared to tell him that I'm too busy to chat. I'm too busy trying not to fall even more in love with the woman on my arm whose smile is glowing brighter within the beam of the sun.

Instead, an unknown number stares back at me.

UNKNOWN NUMBER:

Time is ticking.

CHAPTER 19

TABITHA

P ale skin is a curse on days like this when my own reflection resembles the bright-red fruit that oozed from Janie's post-supper rhubarb pie. I slather aloe vera over my shoulders and collarbone, then dab the cool gel along the tip of my nose and cheekbones, soothing the parts of me most affected by our carefree day under the Atlantic City sun.

Studying my image, I twirl from side to side in the vintage mirror off the guest bedroom. My stomach is still flat and caved in, bordering on sickly, despite all the treats I gorged on today. It's probably the most I've eaten since before—

Since before.

It's also the most fun I've had.

My hair is thick and freshly blow-dried after a lukewarm shower, so I twist it into a loose side braid to contain it. The door is cracked and I hear rustling behind me. When I peek through the narrow opening, I watch as Gabe sifts through his suitcase looking for a change of clothes, his hair damp and mussed from his own shower.

His toned, bare skin glistens beneath the overhead light, his muscles flexing as he combs through his pile of T-shirts. My cheeks burn hotter, giving my sunburn a run for its money.

He's perfect.

In every possible way.

Instinct has me twirling the star band around my finger. I haven't removed it yet, despite being privy to the conversation between Gabe and his mother this morning in the kitchen as I hid behind the wall and listened to the despair lacing Gabe's tone. She knows we're not engaged. She saw it in my eyes and I hate that it was *me* who gave us away. My darkness and demons couldn't allow me a single weekend to pretend. To believe I'm worthy of engagement, of a new relationship, of love.

Of *his* love.

I'm not sure what Janie saw, exactly, but I don't think it was entirely accurate.

She didn't see the whole picture.

I press against the door too heavily, and the creak of it permeates the silent room. Gabe pops up, a fresh T-shirt in hand, and spots me ogling him from the bathroom.

Embarrassment fizzes in my chest as I push the door open and fiddle with my braid, glancing down at my naked toes, then back up at him.

"Sorry." He palms the back of his neck, averting his eyes from my inappropriate attire. It's another ivory, nearly-transparent nightgown. "I was just grabbing some clothes. I can sleep in the other room tonight. The air mattress is still inflated and ready to go."

My heart jumps with anxiety. "That's not necessary. We can share the bed again."

His eyes lift. "Mom already knows we're dirty little liars." A subdued smile crests, something etched with sadness and defeat, even though his tone is playful. "There's no point."

"There is a point," I hear myself say, unknowing of the point but believing in it, nonetheless. "Please, stay."

Gabe's fingers curl around the T-shirt hanging at his side as his eyes skim my face. He's searching for the point.

Truth slithers through me, so I offer him part of it. "I don't like sleeping alone."

The real truth is too dangerous to say; the part in which it's his arms, specifically, I want to be cradled in until dawn.

Swallowing, Gabe nods once. Slowly. He doesn't seem to catch on to the hidden, suppressed point, and takes my answer at face value. The T-shirt is pulled over his head in record time, messing his already rumpled hair into further disarray.

"All right," he says. There's a subtle bite to his reply and it chews at my heart. "Want to watch a movie? I'm still a bit wired."

"Sure."

I watch him throw back the coral-and-cream quilt and slide into bed, reaching for the remote on the bedside table. There's a Saxe-blue mug billowing with steam from my own nightstand and the image stabs at my heart. Feeling guilty, I shuffle forward and reach for the ceramic handle, bringing the beverage to my nose and inhaling the familiar scent.

Chamomile.

Sleepy tea.

He made me sleepy tea, and the notion sends a trickling of pitter-patters to my heart.

I'm careful to leave a gap between us on the mattress when I join him, sipping on the piping-hot tea as a television show bursts to life.

I hardly notice it.

I'm not sure what show it is, and I wouldn't be invested anyway. I'm just as wired as he is. Wound up and topsy-turvy. My heart is doing cartwheels between my ribs, too aware of his proximity, too tempted to leap over to his side of the bed and ruin his.

My heart would, too; I know it would.

It would ruin him.

Flush travels across my skin, and I'm not sure if it's the sunburn's doing, or if it's my own reckless thoughts heating me up, so I try to focus on the show. Two characters start kissing and tearing at each other's clothing after a heated argument, their moans and desires doing nothing to temper the fire in my blood or the dappling of red splotches on my chest, staining my cheeks and ears. My breathing quickens, matching my heart rate. I stare at the erotic images flickering across the screen as a dull ache pulses between my thighs. Something foreign and deeply buried. The characters topple to the bedroom floor, bare skin slapping together, hands fisting hair, tongues dueling.

It's been so long since I've experienced that.

I squeeze my legs together and brave a glance at Gabe. His hands are linked behind his head as he leans back against the headboard, attention on the screen. I inhale a sharp breath and blurt out, "I haven't been intimate with anyone in years." I'm not sure why I confess such a thing. Right here, right now, as moans from the television show thicken the tension in the room.

Mortified, I pull my eyes away and slam my lids shut, setting the mug back down beside me. "I don't know why I said that."

I wait for him to say something, but he doesn't. A few seconds tick by before the room goes silent, the television noise snuffing out. All I hear are my chaotic heartbeats laughing at me.

Mocking me.

Burrowing deeper into the blankets, I tug them to my chin and open my eyes. I stare up at the ceiling, my stomach in knots.

Finally, he replies. "I know."

It takes all of my willpower to twist my head in his direction. He's looking at me, his emerald eyes glinting with both heat and sympathy. My curiosity gets the better of me, and I blurt out more foolishness. "Have you…been with anyone?" I croak. "Recently?"

Since me.

Since that kiss.

Since I broke your heart.

He shakes his head. "No."

My heart stutters. I've been witness to many conversations between Gabe and Sydney, and it's no secret that Gabe has never been shy when it comes to women. He'd been living the typical attractive-bachelor lifestyle before I came into the picture. While I knew he wasn't actively dating, I was certain he was at least partaking in one-night stands and fleeting trysts.

Gabe shifts positions, turning toward me and propping his head up with his hand. His expression is curious, engaged. "Why are you asking?"

I don't know.

Maybe I do know, but I don't know how to tell him that any answer other than "no" would have felt like poison injected into my veins. And that's borderline irrational.

My shoulders lift with a tiny shrug. "I assumed you were enjoying yourself."

"I am enjoying myself. I'm here with you."

"I just meant…" I nibble the inside of my cheek, wondering why this sudden curiosity has developed wings. Has bloomed like a winter rose. "I thought you were still having sex."

Considering that the word alone has me blushing from toes to top makes me wonder if I'm even ready for it.

Part of me figured I'd never have sex again. I was too damaged, too afraid of someone's hands exploring me. Bare skin touching. Lips discovering my scars and bone-deep bruises.

But it's been on my mind lately.

My body is responsive whenever Gabe is near. Heart flutters, belly clenches, flushed skin. Just the scent of his nautical cologne and oceanic body wash prompts a physical reaction from me.

I catch the way his throat rolls as he studies me, likely confused by the sudden turn; by the seductive subject matter hovering between us like a third force.

"I haven't had sex in a long time," he murmurs. "Not since you walked through my front door."

My words tangle with the breath stuck in my throat. "But you want to?"

"Not particularly."

Feeling brave, I rephrase the question. "But you want to…with me?"

His jaw ticks, eyes flare. He bites at his lower lip as his focus slips to my mouth. "Yes."

The pulsing between my legs amplifies.

I gather my strengthening courage and slide closer to him on the mattress until our legs brush together beneath the covers. I see it unfold within his hooded eyes. The conflict, the want, the confusion. It all bleeds together, a striking shade of green.

"Tabs…"

"Maybe we could," I say, reaching for him and gliding my fingers underneath the hem of his T-shirt. His body stiffens, his abdominal muscles twitching beneath my touch. He hisses between his teeth, eyes fluttering closed. "Maybe I want to."

Those eyes reopen as a crease forms between his brows. "I can't do it on a maybe."

"It's all I have."

"It's not enough."

My fingers trail higher, landing on his chest beneath the cotton fabric. My nails graze his skin as I pop my hips closer, seeking more warmth. He smells like oakmoss and driftwood. "Do you want to kiss me again?"

I swear my racing heartbeats may result in detonation.

We'll both ignite.

A pained sound falls from his lips as his hand whips out and cups the back of my head, pulling me closer. "I want to kiss you again. Of course I want to kiss you. It'll be like fucking Heaven," he says in a ragged, tortured tone. "Or…*fuck*, I don't know. Maybe it'll be Hell."

I stare at him, waiting. Wondering. My heart is in my throat, in my ears. I can hear my blood pumping furiously like a roaring river. A ticking time bomb.

Gabe drops his forehead to mine. "I want to kiss you. I want to know which one it'll be," he whispers. "But I don't want to have to die to find out."

Shrapnel pierces my skin. There's rubble in my throat.

And still…

I kiss him.

I'm a selfish, terrible person because I don't think; I just take. I take what I want, what I need. And right now, I need him. I need him to show me that I'm not irrevocably broken or damaged. There's still a spark of life in me. A woman who is capable of experiencing pleasure and intimacy.

Gabe groans against my mouth, his grip on the back of my head tightening. Fingers digging and twisting in my hair. There's no lingering this time, not like our kiss on the roller coaster.

His tongue is in my mouth when I take my next breath.

Oh God.

I'm alive again. My body is singing, my core achy, humming with an ancient feeling. He's dusting me off and breathing new life into my bones.

In an instant, my hands are yanking his shirt up over his head. As soon as it's tossed across the room, I'm on him again, my arms linking around his neck, my pelvis thrusting against his erection, my leg hauling itself over his hip. My tongue plunges into his open mouth desperately. In and out. Sliding, probing, discovering every inch of him.

His hand curls around the front of my neck, cupping with a possessive hold as he tips my head back and makes love to my mouth.

I'm shaking everywhere. Utterly vibrating with fear and need.

I hardly remember what to do, where to touch.

My hands trail lower, one slipping into the waistband of his sweatpants to grip his cock. It's a steel rod. Huge, hard, pulsing for me.

I squeeze him.

He nearly buckles with a moan, his face dropping to my shoulder as his hands snake up my nightgown.

I can feel how wet I am. My underwear is uncomfortable, sticking to me.

I'm not broken.

My body is reacting just as it should.

"*Fuck*, Tabs…" he grinds out, his hands palming my backside as he bucks his hips against the fist wrapped around his erection. "You're killing me."

I'm killing him.

And he's bringing me back to life.

Somewhere between the two, the perfect balance must exist.

I stroke him, feeling him hot and heavy in my hand. I arch my neck until my spine is bowed and he has full access to my throat, his open-mouthed kisses a mix of venom and comfort seeping into my skin. Everything is a blur, a dream, an awakening.

I want this.

I need this.

My mind is mindless, hardly coherent, as I yank his sweatpants down his thighs.

Reaction over reason.

I reach underneath my gown to tug my panties aside, then buck forward until his hard length is flush against my slippery center.

So close.

So close to absolution.

Gabe freezes on a stifled moan when the tip nearly slips inside of me.

Tension ripples through him. War. A battle between his own reaction and reason. "Wait, wait," he finally rasps, dropping his hands from my bottom and inching backward.

Away from me. Away from what I need.

No, no, no.

"Gabe, please." I swear I sound like I'm on the verge of hysterics. "Please don't stop. I need to do this. I need this."

He pulls back far enough that I can make out the utter torture he wears through my cloud of lust. I try to bring him back to me, my hands grabbing at his shoulders.

Shaking his head, he squeezes his eyes shut, then pulls away fully, collapsing back onto the bed and scrubbing both hands over his face, chin to forehead. One hand reaches down to tug his pants back up over his hips before he drapes an arm over his eyes, his chest heaving up and down.

It's over.

Just like that, it's over.

I don't know what to do. I'm frozen beside him, my gown bunched up around my waist, my underwear twisted and damp with shunned desire. My heart thunders in my chest as my lips start to wobble. "Gabe…I-I thought you wanted this. I thought you wanted me."

He pinches the bridge of his nose, as if trying to calm himself down. "Not like this."

"Not like *what*?" I'm so confused. Rejected.

A deep breath leaves him. A long, tapered exhale that sounds a lot like resignation. "You want *this*. I want *you*," he says. "It's not the same."

I frown. "I don't understand."

"It's like you weren't there. You were racing toward a finish line, but it wasn't with me." He tilts his head on the pillow to look at me, his eyes gleaming with torment. "If we do this, I need you *with* me. I can't just be a vessel, or a stepping stone to the other side of what you're trying to work through." Rubbing his forehead, he finishes softly, "I don't want to be your practice run, Tabs."

His words dig into me like a pickaxe. A sharp spade. "I didn't mean it like that."

"I don't think you know what you meant, or what you want. Which is why I can't do this. I can't." He pulls up from the bed, rising to his feet.

Panic inches its way through me.

Hurt, longing, guilt.

I suppose he's right, in a way.

I was laser-focused on the end result, hardly willing to appreciate the beauty of getting there.

With him.

I'm not sure what to say as I watch him lean over to pick up his discarded shirt, his sweatpants still tented with slow-dying lust. All I muster is a single question. "Which was it?"

Gabe turns to me, pulling the T-shirt over his head. "What?"

"Heaven or Hell?"

Silence hangs between us, an insidious hum of nothing. His throat bobs, his eyebrows creasing with pain as he stares at me clutching the bedsheet to my chest. Then he murmurs, "Both."

I watch him walk out of the bedroom, closing the door behind him.

Tears stream down my cheeks as I stare at the empty space beside me on the bed. Then I roll over, feeling just as empty, and glance at the little blue mug on my nightstand that has since cooled. I whisper to no one at all, "Thank you for the tea."

"I TOLD you I'd always be with you."

There's a clearing through the trees. It's nighttime and the world is a chasm of darkness, save for the starry spotlight brightening his smile. "Matthew!" I race toward him in my dirty T-shirt, my bare feet cutting on stones, my ankles tangling in hedges. "I've been looking everywhere for you. We got separated." I'm out of breath when I reach him, winded and doubled over. "I thought I lost you."

A new pair of dark-rimmed glasses rests on the bridge of his nose and his eyes sparkle navy blue through the glass. "I didn't go far," he tells me. "I'll never be too far."

"We made it, Matthew. I knew we would." Once I catch my breath, I leap into his outstretched arms. "There was no way I was leaving that basement without you by my side."

I glance skyward over his shoulder, thanking the stars.

Matthew holds me against his chest, fingers braiding through my mess of hair. I need a shower. A warm meal. A blanket and a soft pillow to rest my head.

But first I need this moment; this moment with him. Feeling his arms around me, feeling my arms around him. It feels like a tiny miracle.

"I had no doubt you'd make it out," he whispers, his chin propped atop my head. He strokes my hair, massages my scalp. "You're smart. Clever. I knew it the moment you stepped foot in my classroom." He

lets out a long sigh. "A girl like you could outsmart the Devil himself."

My mind races with thoughts of the future. It'll be a hard road ahead, no doubt, but nothing could ever be harder than what we just went through.

He inches back, drinking me in with a soft smile. "I'm still looking forward to reading your thesis, Miss Brighton. The one about dreams."

I blink up at him, confused. I'm not sure why he's thinking about my thesis at a time like this. We only just escaped the pits of Hell after weeks of torture and neglect.

"I think they're far more complex than we could ever imagine, don't you think?" He cups my jaw, grazing his index finger down the length of my chin. "Are they the manifestations of our deepest fears? Our truest desires? Or are they a glimpse into another world?"

"I-I don't know." I frown. "The only world I care about is this one… this one, with you," I tell him. Something doesn't feel right. He's too far away, but he's hardly moved. "I'm sick of dreaming."

"I hope you never get sick of dreaming. It's the only way for me to see you." His hand reaches down to clasp mine. "To touch you."

My heart beats erratically. My ribs feel like they're cracking inside my chest. "That's not true…I'm right here. I'll always be right here."

"I know."

His smile is sad. So sad.

This can't be right. He should be happy, celebrating, overjoyed.

Anything but sad.

"Matthew…"

My words trail off when I notice a blood-red stain blooming on his sweater.

Memories flash behind my eyes. Grisly images flood my mind.

His face, contorting with pain. Blood trickling from the corner of his mouth. His eyes, his beautiful blue eyes, dimming to a forever shade of gray.

No, no, no.

Please, no!

He glances down at the crimson stain with a look of painful acceptance, while sickly realization has my stomach twisting into knots. My heart breaks all over again.

He's not here.

He's not by my side. The stars failed me.

I'm not sure why I ask him this, why this is the one question that *passes through my lips. But it's all I want to know. "Was it...good?" I murmur, my voice horribly frayed and torn.*

I don't need to explain.

He already knows.

"Yes," he whispers. "I was with you." Tears glitter in his eyes as he steps away from me and starts to fade into the black of night. "That made it...a good last day."

I crumble, just like I did then. The day I watched him leave me. He always knew he'd never see the other side of those walls. He knew, but I didn't.

I stupidly believed.

I lunge forward, wrapping my arms around nothing, around the barren space where he once stood. "Matthew! Please, don't leave me... please, I'm not ready..."

But then all I hear is a shrieking alarm sound, like dying cicadas. It assaults my eardrums and I want to scream. Cry. Crumble.

Eventually, the noise fades out, morphing into the soft echo of his voice as dawn lights up the treetops, calling me home.

"Goodnight, sweet girl."

I STARTLE AWAKE.

For a moment, I'm crippled with confusion. Daybreak bleeds in through lace drapes, shining light on the floral, mauve wallpaper I'm staring at.

I'm facing the wall.

I'm just standing in the corner of the room, half in a daze and half here, clueless as to why I'm not burrowed beneath the bed covers.

The dream slithers through my mind, raw and real.

My stomach pitches.

Matthew.

I suck in a gasping breath, wrenching forward until my fingers are curled around the edge of a dresser to keep me upright.

Oh God...it felt so lifelike. So vivid. I can still hear the shrieking alarm bell mingling with the timbre of his voice, and feel the way his fingers felt sifting through my hair. I feel the tree branches digging into my bare feet while the moon watches from its throne among the stars.

Hands grip my shoulders before I buckle to the floor.

I flinch.

Still disoriented, I whip around and shove at the chest that has come up behind me.

Gabe stumbles back, his eyes tired. More than tired.

Wounded.

All I seem to do is make people bleed.

My breaths come in quick spurts of adrenaline and madness, my limbs shaky. "S-sorry," I murmur, watching as his arms fall at his sides. "I had a dream. I was sleepwalking, I think." Blinking through the fog, I bite down on my lip to keep it from trembling. "I didn't mean…"

No, I never mean it, but I still do it.

And I think he's beginning to realize that.

I'm a lost cause. He's waiting in vain, being patient for nothing.

Gabe swallows, the glimmer of hope fading from his eyes.

Tired, wounded.

Done.

He steps backward. "I heard you yelling."

"I'm sorry. I didn't mean to wake you."

"You didn't." He glances off to the side, rubbing the back of his head. "I'm going to visit my grandmother today. Maybe you should take it easy, get some rest. It's a long drive home tomorrow."

Home.

I don't even know where home is.

My baby is in Galena, Gabe is checking out, and my heart is aimlessly wandering between a *now* I crave and a *then* I can't escape.

I'm lost.

I feel homeless.

All I send him is a nod, curling my fingers into fists so I don't pathetically reach for him. I can't bear to see that hope flicker back to life, knowing it only serves one purpose: inevitable ruin. "Maybe I'll go for a walk. Read a book." I shrug, noncommittally. "The weather is supposed to be beautiful today. I'll give the Gleasons a call and talk with Hope while I sit out on the deck."

"All right." He wants to say more. I see the words tickling his throat, teasing his lips. "Tabs, about last night—"

"You were right."

His shoulders slump, his browline creasing with a frown.

"I was being selfish. Using you for my own benefit." That's not entirely true. There's no one else in the world I would do that with, no one else who makes me feel so safe and worthy. He makes my soul seem salvageable. And yet, telling him that will only string him along, keep him stunted, keep him tethered to the idea of me. A future I could never promise. "I'm sorry."

An emotion claims his eyes, one I can only describe as devastation.

But he blinks it away as quickly as it came and takes another step backward. "Right."

"I truly am sorry that—"

"You don't need to explain what I already know," he cuts in, shoving both hands into his pockets. He continues to back away as the space between us grows. "I think when we get back we should keep our distance for a while. I need to…clear my head."

I won't cry.

I refuse to cry.

This is for the best.

"I understand."

Forcing a thin-lipped smile, Gabe gives me a single nod then pivots around, stalking out of the bedroom.

I collapse back against the dresser, my knuckles bleached-white as my hands grip the edge. I know it's for the best, I do, but I still cry. My tears don't care about reason or logic. They only know how to fall when I fall.

People love to say that time heals all wounds.

They're wrong.

Time is nothing but a fingernail picking at the scabs, reopening those wounds the moment they start to itch, so they never truly heal. They just bleed out every now and then. Get infected. Cause deeper scars with every scratch and poke.

Time doesn't heal anything.

It's a pretty lie to help us cope.

Time just makes it worse.

CHAPTER 20

TABITHA

Janie helps toss my luggage into the trunk of the car while Gabe is inside collecting his own bags. I glance over at the beautiful colonial as a bird family flies overhead through the cloud cover. I'll miss this place. Being here felt like a beginning and an ending all at the same time. To what, I'm not sure. Only the elusive, wicked time will tell.

"I saw your video."

Pulling my attention off the persimmon tree where two songbirds landed and camouflaged themselves within the leaves, I find Janie watching me with a soft smile. I chuckle, ducking my head. "That was a spur-of-the-moment break in sanity. I'm not sure why I did it."

"I do." Her hands fall from her hips as she takes a step toward me. "It's a first step."

My chin lifts. I process her words as they tighten my chest. "It's been two years," I murmur. "Seems like a long time for a first step."

Her lavender blouse billows in the breeze as her hair takes flight. It's the exact same color as Gabe's hair—golden-dark, like shadows on barley fields. His curls and waves must come from his father's side, as Janie's hair is perfectly straight.

She glances up at the sky, almost like the answers lie within the bird-vee swooping above us or the marshmallow-white clouds lighting up the blue. "Children start walking at their own pace, too," she muses, eyes still aimed high. "It doesn't matter if it's at eight months or eighteen months, even though people like to tell you that something is wrong. They'll say your child is falling behind if the process doesn't line up with their own ideal timeline." She tilts her head to the side, a silver earring glinting in a sunbeam. "Then, suddenly, those babies are all grown up, running and chasing and thriving, and you realize you hardly remember them ever crawling. All you see is how far they've come."

My heart kicks up speed, my throat burning with clogged sentiment.

Finally, her eyes find mine. They soften to the same comforting green I always see in Gabe's. She wraps her hand around my elbow, giving it a gentle squeeze. "The *when* doesn't matter, Tabitha. The amount of time it takes to pull yourself up on shaky legs is irrelevant," she whispers. "One day, you just start walking. And you don't look back."

I suck in a breath as I twist the star ring around my finger. Her analogy hits close to home. Hope was a late walker—she only just started walking at fifteen months old, hardly five weeks ago, much to the whispering and gossip of fellow daycare mothers. But even in that short amount of time, it's hard now to picture her doing anything but charging into my arms on toddling legs.

As Janie's hand falls from my elbow, Gabe appears over her shoulder, dragging his suitcase across the stone walkway. She leans down to mutter one last thing into my ear. "I know you heard me in the kitchen the other day, and I want you to know...I was wrong about what I said I saw when you look at him," she says, her voice hardly above a whisper. "The truth was in that video."

I lose another breath, her words sinking deep.

I haven't watched the video.

It's saved on my profile for playback, the views at a startling one-point-four million, but I haven't had the guts to press Play. I'm not sure what Janie saw, but I don't think it really matters now. Gabe is done with me and I don't blame him. It's for his own benefit.

He hauls his suitcase into the air and throws it in the trunk beside mine. He's wearing another cut-off shirt, a shade of vintage-silver. I can't help the pang of anxiety that shoots through me when the sun beams down on his exposed scar. It's still too fresh, too new. He should keep it more covered.

I watch as Gabe slings one arm around his mother, tugging her to his chest for a hug. "Always a pleasure, Mom. Thanks for letting us visit. But mostly, for feeding us."

Janie's eyes close over his shoulder as she hugs him back. "I'll come see you soon. Thanksgiving is on the books."

"All I heard was persimmon pie."

I giggle, the sound of my laughter tearing through their moment. Gabe pulls away from his mother and twists toward me, the smile on his face dimming ever so slightly.

My heart falls.

I don't want to be the cause of his smile turning to ash.

He studies me for a moment in my pinstripe jumpsuit and ratty-brown sandals, my hair tucked back in a ponytail. I wonder what he sees. All I know is what I see right now, which are visions from thirty-six hours ago when my fingers were wrapped around him and his tongue was in my mouth.

Shivers scatter across my skin at the memory. "Ready?" I squeak out, still fidgeting with my ring.

Gabe blinks, shaking himself from whatever memory *he* was in. Likely, the one where I lied and said I was only using him for my own pleasure, after all he's done for me.

"Yep." His eyes dip to my ring for a beat before his jaw tenses and he swerves around me, heading to the driver's side of the car. "See ya, Mom."

"Bye, Gabriel. Text me when you get home."

I wave goodbye to Janie as I make my way to the passenger's side and hop in, sparing the persimmon tree one final glance.

Gabe pulls out of the circular driveway, honking the horn as we depart.

And then it's quiet.

Too quiet.

I don't know what to say in the wake of our last conversation. I don't know what to do, what to think. Slouching back in the seat, I spin the star band around my finger and close my eyes, my heart pounding with uncertainty.

Gabe breaks the silence with a single word. "Music?"

My eyes open.

A smile lifts on his mouth. A real, authentic grin.

It's all I need to smile right back. "Sure."

CHAPTER 21

TABITHA

Three days later, a text message lights up my phone as I wander up to Evan's front door to continue my interview.

GABE:

I'm throwing a party tonight. Come over.

I glance to my right, but Gabe's Challenger is missing from the driveway. He went back to work yesterday. Pausing on the walkway, my thumbs hover over the keyboard as I debate my response. Gabe throws a lot of parties, but I haven't attended a single one of them—I've always had Hope, making my free time scarce and sacred. I don't drink, either, so the idea of hiring a babysitter for an evening that involved alcohol, smoking, and people hooking up in random spare rooms never felt like a responsible decision.

Tonight, I don't have Hope.

Tonight…

I think I want to go.

ME:

What time?

GABE:

7 or 8.

> Stop by whenever you want.

I slide my teeth across my lower lip.

ME:

> I thought you wanted distance...?

It's not like we haven't corresponded over the past three days, though it hasn't been anything like it used to be. A few text messages. A phone call to check in.

The thirteen-hour drive home was torture, and not because we didn't talk or get along, or fall into a familiar, friendly routine despite what happened between us—it was because I was certain it would be the last thirteen hours in which Gabe would be within arm's reach of me.

That doesn't seem to be the case.

GABE:

> Tried that.

> Hated it.

> Come over.

A buzzy feeling travels south. A tickle.
Warmth.

ME:

> Okay. I'll stop over for a bit.

> Thank you for inviting me.

GABE:

> :)

We haven't discussed that night.

The night when I shoved my hand down his sweatpants and tried to have sex with him like I was starved and deprived after months of dodging his advances.

We didn't discuss the following morning, either.

The morning when I told him I was using him.

It was a wicked thing to say. Shameful. And if there's any reason I should stop by Gabe's party tonight, it's to apologize profusely, having been too much of a coward to do so during our road trip in fear of spoiling the mood.

I tuck my phone back into my purse and continue the trek up Evan's walkway.

He meets me at the door as soon as the doorbell chimes. "Tabitha." Flashing me a white-toothed grin, he ushers me inside, holding the door open. "And so we meet again."

"Sorry for my absence the past few days." I slip out of my sandals and plop my satchel near the door. "I hope I didn't mess up your creative flow or anything."

"You did not. My daughter, in fact, did."

"Oh?" I chuckle, following him down the hallway to the makeshift office. Evan pulls the rolling chair out and signals for me to take a seat while he moves to the other side of the desk.

"Summer hosted an end-of-summer sleepover party that turned into a camping extravaganza in my twelve-by-twelve living room. There were tents. There were marshmallows stuck to sofa cushions. There were leaves and tree branches everywhere to make the set-up more *authentic*." He scrubs a hand down his face as he sits down across from me. "I even found texts on my phone to Sydney—sent from my daughter pretending to be me—asking if we could borrow their pet raccoon for dubious reasons."

"Oh, my God." Laughter spills out of me. "What were the reasons?"

"A test run, supposedly. We were torn between domesticating a raccoon and a wallaby. Pivotal research."

I can't stop giggling. "What did Sydney say?"

"She said: *Hi, Summer. Your dad wants his phone back.*"

"Then what did you do?"

"Moved that vasectomy up my priority list."

I laugh again.

The easy chit-chat has my nerves dwindling, and it's something I've come to appreciate with Evan. He's always trying to make this better for me. More bearable. He never has me feeling judged or ashamed, unlike most people.

Unlike my old friends from school and at least eighty-percent of the internet.

Unlike my own mother.

But the time for easy soon fizzles out, replaced with the

harrowing hour ahead, in which I'll delve back into my haunting past.

We're getting closer to the moment my heart dropped out of me and bled into the cement cracks, never to fully return. I searched for parts of it the day that monster let me go, tried shoving the battered pieces back inside my chest so I could live a semblance of a life outside of those basement walls. But those pieces were dirty, stepped-on, and compromised. A broken heart doesn't work the same as a heart unscathed. There are always complications.

Poorly stitched holes. Faulty beats.

And I suppose that's why Gabe never stood a chance.

If I gave any more of my heart away, there would be nothing left of it.

I straighten in the chair and cross my legs, centering myself with a full breath as I conjure up the right words. The worst words.

My words.

My story.

Evan encourages me with the click of the tape recorder, his smile dimming. "Ready?"

I'll never be ready.

"Ready."

Two Years Earlier

HE STIRRED awake the moment sunlight poured into our cell.

A groan filtered over to me.

Pained, disoriented. Tortured and weak.

"Tabitha."

It was the first thing he said when his eyes fluttered open, his focus hardly aimed in my direction. He must have only seen me in his mind. Maybe I'd been in his dreams.

"I'm here."

He was sprawled out on the concrete, dried blood crusted underneath his head from where the butt of the pistol had clob-

THE STARS ARE ON OUR SIDE   213

bered him. He hadn't moved all night. Not for five long hours, causing my chest to remain strangled with an impending panic attack as I'd stared at him through the shadows. I hadn't slept at all, my worry dominating any promise of rest. I hadn't even been sure he was still alive.

It had been too dark to monitor the slow rise and fall of his chest.

I couldn't hear him breathing.

It was so quiet.

Matthew still didn't move from his position on the floor, despite the way his arms were twisted behind him around the pole in a painful, ungodly position. He just laid there.

Didn't speak, didn't flinch.

My tears began to fall, despair hovering all around us. Suffocating us. I hated that he woke up to this because nothing had changed. If anything, it all felt more hopeless. "I-I thought…you were dead…" I croaked, unable to keep the sorrow out of my voice. "I wouldn't have survived it."

He didn't say anything for a long time, and he still hadn't moved.

Panic crept into my chest again. "Matthew, please…stay with me."

"I'm here," he finally echoed. "I'm still here."

I wished he wasn't.

I was so, so glad he was.

I watched through the cloak of darkness as he began to pull himself up into a sitting position. It took a while; three or four minutes. It hurt to watch him struggle against his chains and head wound, deprived of nutrients and strength.

He'd always carried himself with fortitude. A silent force. The students who weren't lusting after him had been intimidated by him. To see him reduced to this was just another dull dagger twisting in my gut.

His breaths were labored and strained when he was eventually seated across from me, legs splayed out in front of him. "Did I hurt you?"

"No," I answered quickly. "Not even a little. Not at all."

"Did *he* hurt you?"

"No, he…he just left. He left me here wondering if you were

even still alive." Inhaling a tear-laced breath, I rethought my answer. "So, yes, I suppose he did hurt me."

Matthew stared at me from his pole. My eyes had adjusted to the shortage of light, so I was able to make out the way he watched me, silent and studious. I recalled the way he used to look at me in the classroom sometimes when fellow students had been immersed in their work—curious, his gaze steeped with a trace of wonderment. The connection wouldn't last long, and the moment I'd catch him, he'd pull away and distract himself with paperwork.

I'd seen it, though.

I still saw it.

"He'll be done with me soon," Matthew muttered, almost choking on the words. "I can feel it."

My stomach dropped to the cement. "No…you're wrong. He's still feeding you, still giving you water. He's not finished with you yet."

"He will be. It's coming."

"*No.*"

Chains grated against metal as Matthew shifted in place, shaking his head at me. "You have to promise me something, Tabitha. You have to promise me you'll keep fighting, keep trying, even if I don't—"

Audacity stole my voice. "Stop it. I won't."

"I can't die down here thinking you've given up."

"Stop!" I cried. "Stop, please. Don't talk like that."

"*Dammit.*" He smacked his cuffs against the pole, his desperation bouncing off the walls, echoing through both of us. Hopelessness was seeping into his psyche. "I have nothing. Absolutely *nothing* of value I'm leaving behind. No legacy, no last hurrah to check off the bucket list. Fucking nothing, except for you."

Tears leaked out, streaming down my cheeks. "You swore you'd keep fighting, no matter what. You *promised* me, Matthew. Don't you dare give up now."

He heaved out a long breath, his chin dropping to his chest. A few quiet moments ticked by while he regrouped, forcing away the bleak thoughts. Pushing through the dark cloud. "He said you reminded him of someone. That's a good sign. It means there used to be a shred of humanity in him at one point—a connection to someone, likely his mother. We can use that."

I swallowed. "There's no humanity. His eyes are long-past dead."

"There's something."

"There's nothing there. He has no affection for me, so all of this is pointless. All I'm doing is spending my final days on earth trying to empathize with a monster." I choked out a joyless laugh. "How's that for a last hurrah?"

His head dropped back to the pole, eyes closing. He knew I was right. He knew it was futile and far-fetched, and a terrible way for me to go. But, it was all he had to latch onto—the hope that I would still try to make it out of there alive, even if he didn't make it out with me.

So, I did what I'd been doing all along. I pretended, faked it. I promised him I would keep going, keep trying, because that was the only thing I could offer him. And maybe it would be enough to keep his head above water. "Okay," I whispered, my throat burning. "I promise I'll keep fighting. I won't stop. Even if…" My words dissipated, turning to dust on my tongue. It was too hard to push them through.

But he understood what I'd meant to say. Seconds turned into minutes before he whispered back, "Thank you."

I fell asleep.

My brain allowed me to rest knowing Matthew was still alive. I wasn't alone down there. Time passed me by as I was graciously whisked away to some other place. Frolicking through purple fields of lavender and wildflowers, chasing mockingbirds and butterflies. Eating cherry pie while music danced in the air. Matthew faded in and out of my dreams, only a mirage. I could never reach him, never touch him. But he was there, close by, watching over me.

I wasn't alone.

Sunset rolled in hours later, and that was when the man came barreling into the basement, severing my dreamlike state.

I startled awake, reality crashing down on me.

Fear sluiced over me.

"Howdy, pets." He chuckled, his belly jiggling as he advanced on me. "Sleep well, Kitten?"

I swallowed, pulling myself up to unstable legs. "Yes, thank you."

He spared Matthew a quick glance, a sneer curling on his lips. "I see my dirty dog is more alert. That'll train you to behave."

"I'm not a dog," Matthew refuted. "I'm a person. We're *people*. We're people, just like you. You don't need to do this."

The man made a few barking noises, then moved toward me, panting through a grin.

I stood still, waiting for the inevitable. Preparing for another assault in which I'd act like it wasn't the most horrifying, disgusting experience of my life. I'd promised Matthew I would.

The man sauntered up to me and began untucking his shirt that barely reached his waistband. Lechery twinkled in his eyes. A trace of *fun*. Reaching for his belt, his tongue still hung out of his mouth like a thirsty dog.

And then…he paused, his eyes glassing over.

Briefly, subtly.

It was as if he'd zoned out, floated away. It was the same look I imagined came over me every time the man forced himself between my legs.

I waited, still and silent, trying to be good.

The man squinted at me, head tilting curiously as he studied my face.

When he leaned in closer, I flinched.

"Don't be scared, Fiona."

Confusion swept through me. Matthew quietly watched from his corner, taking in the scene. Assessing the moment, storing it away.

The man had his belt unhooked, his zipper halfway down, when the unfamiliar name flew past his lips. His fist was tangled in my hair, fingers catching on the knotted strands. Dark, beady eyes drifted across my face, clouded with something I couldn't pinpoint.

I pretended to want it.

I begged him for it, even though the words bled with bile on my tongue.

The fact that there was a slight change in our abductor's demeanor gave me more courage, more will to act the vile part.

But something strange happened.

Instead of taking me, his hand fell from my hair in a gentle slide and then cupped my cheek.

I forced my body to press closer to him through a swell of

nausea, batting my eyelashes in his direction, attempting flirtation.

Nothing.

A growl rumbled in his throat as he took a step backward, his pudgy features twisting into something frightening.

"What…what is it?" I tried, keeping the quiver out of my voice. "You don't want to?"

The growling sound escalated, echoing off the stone walls, sounding demonic. His eyes narrowed at me like he was trying to read me somehow. See me.

See someone who wasn't *me*.

I wasn't sure what to do, so I did nothing. I just waited, too afraid I'd agitate him.

He dropped his hand.

There was a new rage simmering inside of the man as he paced back, farther away from my side of the basement. He was inching toward the opposite side, toward Matthew, who immediately tensed up, the veins in his arms popping as he tugged at his manacles.

It was useless, of course.

He couldn't escape.

And to my horror, the man swiveled around and charged at Matthew, unprovoked.

Snarling and untamed.

"No!" I shrieked, lurching forward, my arms nearly ripping from my shoulder sockets. I couldn't pretend right now. I couldn't pretend to not care that Matthew was about to be on the receiving end of a violent attack when he was already wounded and weak.

"You motherfucker," the man seethed.

He curled angry fingers around Matthew's collar, then held him in place as his opposite arm whipped back, hand balled to stone.

I watched with sickening disbelief as our captor started pummeling Matthew with his fist, while I remained trapped and tied to a metal rod, helpless to stop it. Even my screams were drowned out by the sound of knuckles cracking against Matthew's skull.

"You fucking…" *Thwap.* "…piece…" *Thwap, thwap.* "…of disgusting shit…"

Blood spattered to cement. It oozed from torn flesh and broken teeth. It stained his blue sweater like crimson rain on an ocean tide.

He was going to kill him.

Oh God, he was going to kill him.

My mind raced with ways to stop it. I tried to think, tried to piece things together.

Who was Fiona?

The name had triggered him. And looking at *me* had triggered the name.

Thwap, thwap, thwap.

He'd told me I looked like her—*her*, seemingly being a woman named Fiona. It must have been the woman in the picture; a woman he was fond of. And the moment he associated that name with me, he had stopped touching me. He'd frozen up, turned almost gentle, and had been unable to sexually assault me.

A family member?

A sister or an aunt.

Most likely his mother.

I went with it because I had no other cards to play. If I was wrong, Matthew would be dead and nothing else would matter anyway.

"Be a good boy!" I cried out, pitching my voice as shrill as it would go as I slammed my chains against steel, trying to garner his attention. "Stop this. Please, be a good boy!"

My heartbeats accelerated, my stomach hollow and queasy.

I was stunned silent when the man's fist stalled midair and Matthew crumpled like a bloodied ragdoll to the concrete. His face was a mess of mutilated flesh and red gore. He was hardly recognizable and I wanted to sob and scream and beg to go back in time and drive out of that parking lot the moment we'd slipped inside his car after class.

The man was breathing heavily, strings of saliva swinging from his chin as he turned to look at me. I was lost for words, having not thought this through.

I had just needed him to stop.

Matthew.

Oh god, Matthew, please be okay.

"What'd you just say to me?"

Vomit climbed my throat. I felt ill.

Dizzy and uncertain, I scrambled for something to say. He seemed more coherent and I had succeeded in breaking the moment and halting the attack, so my instincts told me to play dumb. "I-I don't remember. I blacked out for a moment. Got confused."

"You fuckin' lying to me?"

"No, no, I can't remember what I said," I insisted, panicked. "You were scaring me. I was out of my head."

Hysterics were inching up my throat. Sobs demanded to be unleashed. Burning pressure swelled behind my eyes.

Matthew moaned at the man's feet.

Beaten bloody. Half dead.

A cry slipped out and I couldn't even use my hand to hold it in.

Still enraged, the man pivoted back toward Matthew, issued a final kick to his ribs with the steel toe of his boot, then turned around and stormed out of the basement looking frazzled and tugging at his hair by the roots. The door slammed shut.

And I lost it.

I was flailing, screaming, crying, calling his name, over and over.

"Don't you leave me," I begged, voice wobbling with grief. "Don't you *dare* leave me."

Matthew's knees curled up until he was shivering in the fetal position, one cheek stuck to the cold cement. I didn't think he could see me from where he laid, so I slithered down my pole and contorted my body to mimic his position on the floor. He blinked slowly as I came into view. My tears turned to ice when they dripped onto the pavement and pooled beneath my cheekbone and I forced a small, mournful smile, watching his gaze skim my face.

The sun set lower, a peachy glow bathing the room in false light. Hollow warmth. I had no more tears to cry and no arms to hold him. No hands to fix him.

All I had were words.

"I've completed my assignment, Professor Gleason," I said into the void, numbness seeping into my bones.

Matthew swallowed, inhaling a wrought breath. His breathing was weak and shallow, clinging to life. He was in so much pain, unable to speak, so all he managed was another sluggish blink.

"The assignment you gave us during class that last day," I continued. "Maslow's Hierarchy of Needs. The five levels."

Awareness lit up his gaze. His jaw tightened, a muscle in his bloodied cheek jumping as he recalled the assignment he'd doled out on the night we were taken.

"I've rearranged the order of needs like you requested. Number one is love."

My focus stayed locked on his face as we stared at each other across the room, curled up and sideways. I thought I saw tears in his swollen eyes, the sunset reflecting off the hopeless gleam shimmering back at me.

He didn't say anything; just waited, collapsed, heartbroken, and irreparably battered.

"Love, physical touch…intimacy," I told him. "I know, without a doubt, that I'd give up food, water, safety, and shelter. Just for a moment." The words broke on a small cry. Devastation drenched me from head to toe. "I'd give up all my basic needs for one single moment free from these chains. I'd sacrifice them in exchange for wrapping my arms around you and holding you tight."

My words died out on a bone-weary sigh and I closed my eyes, finishing the rest in a whisper.

"I'd give up everything," I croaked, "just to touch you one more time."

Present Day

MATTHEW'S BRUTALIZED face is on my mind as I wind through the plethora of cars lining Gabe's driveway and push through his front door. Loud music hammers my eardrums. Crowds of people have my head spinning, my feet itching to backtrack and carry me home.

Panic creeps its way inside me, tightening my chest.

This is a mistake.

I'm too broken for this, too worn down.

But then I realize—going home is even worse. Home is quiet and Hope-less—the perfect recipe for self-destruction.

"Tabitha!"

I glance up the short staircase and find Sydney waving at me from the kitchen in an oversized Nirvana T-shirt tied at her hip with a scrunchie, a flash of skin peeking out above her denim shorts. Her blue eyes smile at me through a pair of cat-eye glasses as she lifts a cocktail high above her head.

I wave back, meekly.

Setting down my purse, I traipse up the steps to join her in the kitchen, where people are flocking for beverages, crammed shoulder to shoulder. I squeeze my way between two sweaty backs, and Sydney pulls me all the way through by snagging my wrist and launching me forward with a laugh.

"Thought I was going to lose you there for a minute," she jokes. "You finally make it to a party, and you're smooshed to death by the Delaney twins."

"A fine way to go," one of the twins provides, holding up his beer.

Smoothing my hair down, I chuckle as I glance around, taking in the crowd. My eyes dip to a plate of appetizers displayed on the counter. "Did you make the snack tray?"

It's more like a charcuterie board with an assortment of cheeses, spreads, fruit, crackers, and meats all displayed like fine art. I pop a cheese square into my mouth and practically moan, hardly able to remember the last time I ate something.

Sydney glances at the tray and snorts a laugh. "My sister made that. Credit by familial affiliation?"

My stomach clenches. "Oh…Clem is here?"

"Yep." She pops the *P* and reaches for a grape. "Out back with Gabe."

I step to the side and peer over someone's shoulder, out toward the sliding glass door to the patio. I spot them instantly. Clementine is hard to miss with her light-blonde hair strewn with chunky streaks of bright blue and her tall, fit frame with tanned skin. Gabe is facing her, arms draped across his chest while a beer dangles from his hand.

He laughs.

He laughs at something she says and I die a little inside.

"Hey, don't worry." Sydney's fingers curl around my wrist, tugging me back. "That's old news. Trust me, it's over."

Pathetically, I hold back tears.

As if Gabe is mine.

As if Clem is a threat, or some kind of competition. I'm aware of their history—I know they were sleeping together last year before he met me, and I know that he liked her.

I'm being ridiculous.

Unfair.

"I'm not worried," I lie through my teeth. "Gabe is single."

Another snort slips past her lips. "Yeah, okay."

"I mean…he is, right?"

I guess I'm fishing now. I'm jealous and fishing, and I hate myself for being so irrationally petty.

I'm also waiting for her reply like I wait for the Amazon delivery driver to pull up to my house after a sleepless night of random purchases.

Shoveling a slice of summer sausage into her mouth, Sydney shoots me a "use your brain" look before scrolling through her Spotify app to pull up a new playlist. "Gabe is very much involved with someone. My ride-or-die is riding the Tabitha Brighton train until he dies." Loyalty toward her best friend shimmers in her eyes, though she softens it with a smile. "I suppose it's his funeral. I just hope you'll make it quick." She winks at me, teasing.

There are no sharp barbs hidden in her words, but they still slice into me, painfully.

My throat clogs with a lump of black coal.

"Brie de Meaux-Style Brie and clothbound cheddar. A pleasant surprise." Oliver's voice interrupts my small death as he reaches over to rummage through the snack tray. "Tabitha," he acknowledges, tone pleasant. "It's great to see you at one of Gabe's gatherings. How was your trip to Delaware?"

I hardly hear him. "Um…great…"

Nineties music spills out of Sydney's phone, prompting her to leap at Oliver and pull him into a flurry of silly dance movies. A cheese wedge sticks out between his teeth, and he grins around it, spinning her in aimless circles as they uncaringly bump into fellow party guests.

I back away.

Turn to run.

And then…

I change my mind.

I glance around the living area, watching strangers laugh, sip their beer, flirt, and dance. Let loose. Be free of stress and burdens.

I want that.

I want that, too.

Pivoting, I traipse back into the kitchen with nerves fizzing in my chest, my heart pounding with adrenaline. There's a half-full bottle of Malibu rum sitting beside the platter of snacks, and I go against everything I believe in, reaching for it and pouring a generous serving into a red Solo cup.

I take a few swigs, ignoring the burn as I glance out the back door again.

Clem is glowing and alive, backlit by the setting sun, grinning wide at Gabe.

She is summer.

And I'm that cold front that comes in, stealing away the warmth with the chill of early winter.

But not tonight.

Tonight…I want to be anyone but me.

I want to be the sun.

CHAPTER 22

GABE

I glance at my cell phone for the hundredth time, checking to see if Tabitha texted me back.

Clem is rambling about some frog exhibit at a reptile rescue as I nurse my beer and pretend to seem engaged. I offer a few smiles. Laugh a couple of times at appropriately spaced intervals. She's oblivious to my lack of interest in the fact that poison dart frogs aren't poisonous in captivity, so I'm playing the part of the immersed friend well.

Go me.

"Yo. Mason." Darius comes up behind me, slapping me on the back as he takes a swig of his beer. "Hot drunk girl at nine o'clock. Never seen her before. Lexi dumped me last weekend, so I'm going to act like you invited her just for me."

Sure, we'll go with that.

Guess I'm playing the part of the charitable friend well, too.

"Have at it, but my bedroom is off-limits."

"You're the man."

He gives me another slap and saunters away. I don't bother to look up. It's probably one of Sydney's friends from the bar she works at.

Clem collapses onto one of my lawn chairs on the patio, sounding exasperated. The conversation must have changed from frogs into something more dire in the span of the last thirty seconds and I missed it.

She blows out a breath, her lips vibrating. "Kip probably won't stop by. He's pissed at me."

"Kip?"

Multitasking, I send Tabitha another text.

ME:

You still coming? :)

"Yes. Kip. Haven't you been paying attention?"

"Not really."

"Ugh." She levels me with an unamused glare. "C'mon, Gabe. I need advice from a guy and the only other guy I know is my ex-husband, who thought screwing his secretary took precedence over his marital vows. And Oliver, but he doesn't count."

I pocket my phone and narrow my eyes at her over my beer. "Who's Kip again?"

"The guy I'm seeing. My post-divorce rebound."

"I thought I was your post-divorce rebound."

Her face scrunches up with distaste. "You were my post-divorce mistake."

"Mm." I shrug. "That's fair. Tell me about this Kip character. Is he good with Poppy?"

Poppy is her daughter and her entire world. He must be good with her or Kip wouldn't be anywhere near her radar right now.

"Yes, he's great with her. He's a cop, too, so he makes me feel safe." She sighs, glancing off over my shoulder. "But I think I'm scaring him away with all of my baggage. I've been feeling really unbalanced lately." Her attention turns to her cuticles as she studies them, lost in thought.

"Balance is overrated. Instability makes life interesting."

She sighs again, not looking up. "You'd make a terrible psychiatrist. So many lawsuits."

I nod in agreement. "This is why I fix soil instability for a living—not people."

Luckily, my phone buzzes in my pocket before I can offer up any more inferior wisdom. Fishing it out, I glance at the new text and my heart skips.

TABITHA:

That depends on you ;)

I frown. Then I reread my previous text and my skipping heart nearly flatlines.

That sounded thoroughly suggestive.

And very unlike Tabitha.

Some kind of fluttery intuition has my chin lifting, my eyes casing my living room through the glass door and ultimately landing on the woman staring back at me with a red cup in her hand.

Fuck me.

Tabitha is the hot drunk girl at nine o'clock. Darius is drooling all over my nine o'clock.

I book it off the patio.

The sliding door creaks open as I bust through and beeline toward Tabitha, worry tightening my chest. She's swaying back and forth to *Don't Speak* by No Doubt, sipping on a beverage that smells increasingly like coconut and bad decisions the closer I get.

Darius's hand is pressed to her lower back, and I see red. Shoving it away, I glower at him. "She's off-limits."

"Thought you only said your bedroom was off—"

"She's my girl."

Realization claims his expression as he holds his hands up and backs away, connecting the dots. I've told him about Tabitha—he knows exactly who she is. "Heard, brother. My bad."

Tabitha doesn't spare him a parting glance, her attention solely on me, smile flirty. She lowers the cup from her mouth. "I'm here."

"You're drinking."

"I am."

"You don't drink."

A glimmer of uncertainty flickers in her eyes, but she blinks it away and takes another sip. "My parental duties are on hold. Tomorrow is my last vacation day before I go back to work. I wanted to let loose a little."

Frowning, I reach for her wrist and lower the cup, swallowing down a knot of concern. "I didn't invite you here for this, Tabs. I just wanted to see you. Apologize."

She sucks in a breath, her lips parting. "I'm the one who needs to apologize." Glancing down my hallway, she fidgets on both feet with consideration before sliding her focus back to me. "Maybe…I can make it up to you? A redo?"

I blink, the context registering slowly.

A redo of the night she tried to fuck me.

She wants to have sex.

As if this scenario is any better than the last one.

"Hey." I slide the nearly empty cup out of her hand, trying not to zone out on her full bottom lip when she pouts. "This isn't the time for a redo. Maybe we should talk."

"I'd rather not." She snatches her cup back and swallows down another sip. "Talking is depressing and I'm tired of being depressed. It's a heavy weight. Tonight, all I want to do is fly."

"I've got Red Bull." I reach for the cup again in vain, but she keeps it out of reach. "Gives you wings."

Lame.

The joke falls flat.

She takes a step away from me, lifts a hand in the air, and starts shimmying back and forth like her body was made for music. Her hips are swinging with chords and notes, her smile full of lyrics. She closes her eyes and gets lost in the vibrations. "I'm a grown woman, Gabe. Let me have this one night." Her cup sloshes with rum as she holds it high above her head and flips her hair back.

A hand scrubs down my face, unease weaving with acceptance. She's right, of course. She's twenty-three years old and deserves to shed her turmoil for a night of fun. I'd be a giant hypocrite to stop her, considering I'm on my third beer.

The problem is, I'm a hypocrite in love.

And the lovesick part of me knows this night can only end in more turmoil.

Oliver is buzzed.

An hour has rolled by, the sky darkening to dusk, and my stepbrother is slouched beside me on the couch, trying to be philosophical.

"What if the only reason we cannot pass through mirrors is because our own reflection is stopping us?"

I sigh.

Part of me wishes I was still drinking, but I tossed my last beer the moment I realized I was going to be on Tabitha-duty tonight. We couldn't both be intoxicated.

I need to keep an eye on her, make sure she's okay.

"It's perplexing to me."

"Life is perplexing," I agree mindlessly. "So are mirrors."

"Perhaps it's a metaphor for every hindrance we endure in life. We, ourselves, are the only thing standing in the way of achieving true greatness." Oliver's eyes narrow, deep in thought.

"Perhaps."

Sweeping a hand through my humid-damp hair, I lean forward and watch as Tabitha and Sydney stand a few feet apart in the kitchen and toss Cheetos into each other's mouths. They haven't succeeded yet, so my floor looks like a lava pit of flaming-hot Cheeto failures.

Darius strolls over in my periphery and collapses beside me. "You look positively sober, Mason," he notes, knocking his knee against mine like I'm being scolded. "Very unlike you."

"I guess I'm not feeling it tonight." My eyes are still locked on Tabitha as she doubles over with laughter when a Cheeto bounces off her forehead and gets tangled in her hair on the way down. "More important things on my mind."

"Ah," he says, nodding slowly, his own eyes finding the source of my distraction. "Can't blame you there. That girl is a ten." He glances at me. "You hit that, yet?"

My skin feels itchy. Darius and I used to talk about women and hook-ups all the time, but lowering Tabitha to the same meaningless category feels wrong somehow.

I shake my head, jaw tensing. "It's different with her. I want more than that."

"I hear you, man. Some women make you want to leave all the bullshit behind and never look back, you know?" He sighs, getting more comfortable as he dangles a beer between his thighs. "Thought Lexi was the one. I felt it. I should've given her a ring."

Tabitha drags Sydney out to the center of the living room when a new song comes on. It's one of Syd's moody nineties songs. They start dancing in front of us, arms raised high, swaying in slow motion as their bodies move suggestively with rhythm.

The star ring glints off my ceiling light.

She's still wearing that fucking ring and I have no idea why.

"So, give her a ring," I mutter, sparing Darius a quick glance as he watches the girls dance. "Why not?"

He purses his lips. "Too late for that."

"Nah." My eyes slide back to Tabitha. "Time is relative. Action is what matters. People don't remember how long it takes for you to do the thing; they just remember if you do it, or if you don't."

Oliver perks up beside me, half listening. "Pragmatic of you, Gabe." He discards his empty cup and stands from the couch. "After considering your sound advice, I'll be taking Syd home now to partake in an assortment of…things."

I watch as he strolls over to Sydney and whispers something in her ear that makes her eyes pop. A mischievous smile floods her face.

Less than five seconds later, they're racing out my front door, shouting a hurried goodbye before the door slams shut. She didn't even grab her phone.

Darius chuckles. "On that note, I've got a girl to try to win back. You good?"

"I'm good."

He pulls out his cell phone and disappears onto my patio.

I hardly notice.

I'm still watching Tabitha's hips sashay back and forth, seemingly unaware that her dance partner has just ditched her. She flicks her fingers through her hair, holding the dark ribbons out of her face, then turns toward me. Her gaze glows with heated interest, a stark contrast to the shadows I normally see swirling in those light-brown eyes.

I freeze up when she heads my way, tipsy but full of purpose. Emboldened. She holds out her hand and reaches for me.

My heart stumbles over logical thought as I rise to my feet and reach right back. Our hands clasp together. She tugs me forward, back to the center of the living room, while the song continues to play. *Falling for You* by Jem.

Painfully appropriate.

"Hi." She spins around to face me, simultaneously tugging at my arms and wrapping them around her midsection until I'm holding her. Moving as one. "Dance with me."

Fire drenches my veins. Reason flies out the window as she wriggles against me, our bodies flush. All I can think about is how her hand felt wrapped around my dick, stroking me. How it felt when she slid me against her heat and tried to push me inside of her.

I have no idea how I scrounged up even an ounce of willpower to stop it from happening.

Tabitha twists around, holding my arms in place as she grinds against me, her back to my chest. My lips drop to the top of her head, eyes closing as I breathe in her flowery scent, my hips moving with hers and my hands splaying across her stomach. She interlocks our fingers and lifts both arms, taking mine with her. I inhale sharply, leaning into her even more, my face lowering to the side of her neck. My fingers trail down the length of her forearms in a slow-motion seduction as my mouth finds her ear. I nip the lobe with my teeth, out of instinct, out of madness, and she lets out a breathy gasp and arches into me. I groan when she presses her ass into my erection.

I let my hands trail lower down her arms, to her elbows, until they're sweeping across her slim waist and curling around her hips. That same madness has me tugging her to me. Grinding her against my hard cock.

Fuck.

I need to stop.

"Tabs…" It's a ragged whisper, a tortured plea. She ignores me and keeps grinding, keeps moving those hips as the song dies out. We're practically dry humping each other in my living room in front of all my friends, but she doesn't seem to care. Somehow, I don't either. "You're driving me crazy," I murmur, my forehead falling to her shoulder as my grip on her tightens.

This is the third time we've danced together. The first time was playful and fun, the second time was full of sweetness, and this time…

This time feels like annihilation with a side of blue balls.

Finally, she pulls away and spins back around to face me. Her cheeks are flushed pink, her hair mussed, eyes half-lidded. My hands are still all over her, my fingertips sneaking up the back of her ombre V-neck tank top.

She says nothing.

Instead, she takes me by the hand and pulls me from the living room.

Blindly, I follow, knowing it's a mistake, knowing how this storyline plays out.

Tabitha guides me down the hallway to my bedroom like a fallen temptress, her sheaves of black hair swinging back and forth with confidence. The second we're in my darkened room, she shuts the door behind us, locks it, and flies at me.

I'm frozen with weakness.

Helpless against my need for her.

Swallowed whole by love and hope.

Her hands cup my face, pulling it down to hers until our mouths crash together.

I moan.

She moans.

The sound of her desire sends electrical currents through me.

Her mouth opens wider, her tongue clumsy as it fills my mouth with needy strokes. Warm, slick heat invades me, tasting like pineapples and coconuts. My own hands grip her face, fingers braiding through her hair while our tongues tangle and twist, faces angling side to side, trying to get deeper. Moans escalate. Hands search and tug through the shadows.

Pressing closer, she grinds herself against my thigh, seeking friction between her legs. Her moans turn into whimpers, almost like she could come like this.

I wonder how long it's been since she's had an orgasm.

I wonder if she ever touches herself.

Thinks of me.

Fuck, stop, no, goddammit.

I have to stop this.

I need to.

Before I can speak, Tabitha drops to her knees in front of me, her face level with my groin.

I watch, rooted to the floor, as her shaky fingers slide up my denim-clad thighs and start unhooking my belt buckle. Her hand brushes over my throbbing erection and I nearly collapse.

Jesus Christ.

I debate letting her—shamefully, I consider it.

Almost every fiber of my being longs to slide my cock between her lips and finally feel what I've been craving for nine torturous months.

Almost.

She tugs my zipper down.

And somehow, I find that micro-pocket of willpower again and grab ahold of it, pulling her to her feet by the shoulders.

Bee-stung lips stare back at me, glistening with hot kisses.

Her eyelids flutter as her balance wobbles from the liquor, her long, black lashes tickling her brows. Blinking slowly, drowsy with lust, those brows dip into a confused frown. "Why are you stopping?"

She teeters from foot to foot and I know this is the right thing to do. I blow out a breath, forcing back the debilitating need, and look her in the eyes. "Tabs. We can't."

Her gaze is still a cloud of bewilderment as my words register. Then her eyes narrow, the confusion morphing into frustration. "You're rejecting me again."

"I'm not rejecting you—I'm rejecting the shitty timing. You're intoxicated."

"Barely. I know where I am, who I'm with."

My teeth gnash together. "And who are you with?"

She frowns. "What?"

"Who are you with?" I slam my palm against my chest, desperate to know how she sees me. "Who am I to you? Who do you see?"

Does she see a friend? A sad puppy dog trailing her heels, waiting for meager scraps?

Does she see a poor imitation of the man she once loved?

A back-up plan?

Tabitha wrenches herself from my grip, stepping away from me. "I see a man who claims to want me, yet consistently turns me down. It doesn't make any sense."

"You know that's not true."

"Prove it." She takes another step backward and yanks her tank top over her head in one fluid motion. Before I can blink, she unhooks her bra from behind and lets it fall to the floor at her feet. She stands before me, brightened by the light of the moon, close to bare.

I can't help my gaze from lowering to her perfect breasts.

Rosy-pink nipples, tightly beaded. Flat belly, tiny waist.

And a scar I've never seen before.

Two letters carved into pale skin along the upper, center part of her abdomen.

F.H.

I lose my breath, my gaze skating back up.

My brows pull together with pain. Pain for her.

Her chest is heaving, fists balling at her sides. "You're repulsed by me. Admit it," she says. "I'm too skinny, too pale. Too picked over." Her cheeks are stained crimson, more from anger than from lust. The alcohol breathes fire on her tongue, fueling her words. "It's like opening up your bank account and seeing insufficient funds."

What the fuck?

She can't think that. She can't possibly believe those heinous lies about herself.

"No." I shake my head, dumbfounded. "Christ…*no*. You're the sexiest thing I've ever seen. You're perfect. I want you more than I've ever wanted anything else, but not nearly as much as I want for it to be the right timing, the right circumstances. That timing isn't when you're drunk and breaking down in front of me."

"I'm breaking down because I've offered myself to you *twice*!" she shoots back. "And you've said no. Both times. You've turned me away."

Guilt nips at my ankles like a goddamn pest. "It's not because I don't want you, Tabitha."

"I want this," she begs, tears filling her eyes. "I *need* this."

This.

Again, she says *this*.

Not me.

This isn't about me; this is about exploring her sexuality, about rediscovering herself, and maybe I could get behind that if things were different. Hell, what guy wouldn't? Maybe in a different reality I'd be willing to be that guy—the guy she's chosen to reawaken the buried, sexual side of her.

But I can't be him. Not with her. Not with this woman whom my heart is fully, cripplingly invested in.

They say that self-preservation is the first law of nature, and I'm clinging to it with everything I have left.

I steeple my hands at my chin and let out a deep breath. "I'm trying, Tabs. I'm trying to be a good person, do the right thing," I tell her, pleading with her to understand. "But it feels like I can't win here. If I say yes, I'll hate myself. If I say no, you'll think I'm rejecting you."

"You are rejecting me. It's a blowjob, Gabe. What man wouldn't want that?"

My eyebrows arch to my hairline. "Really? You think I don't want it? Come on." I throw my hands up at my sides. "I don't want it *like this*. You've been drinking. You have a history of sexual assault and a fuck-ton of trauma—I'm not taking advantage of you."

"Maybe I want you to."

My jaw ticks. "If you wake up tomorrow, sober, and decide you still want to do this with me, then yeah, I'm more than willing to oblige. Of course I am. But not now. Not like this."

"Fine," she bites out, bending over to retrieve her top. When she pops back up, she bares her teeth and adds, "I'll find someone who will."

My heart shatters.

Implodes.

Her eyes flare, horror claiming her face.

"Whoa." It's just a breathy whisper, a single syllable of pain. "Are you serious?"

She squeezes the fabric of her tank top, knuckles turning white as she holds it up to her chest. Her head swings back and forth as she gapes at me, unblinking. Stunned silent.

We stare at each other through the dimly lit room as the ashes of my heart thicken my blood with black tar.

"Fine," I grind out. "Go."

She cups a hand over her mouth, still shaking her head. "I-I'm sorry."

I turn away and stare out the window. "Please, just go."

"Gabe, I'm so—"

With my back to her, I point a finger at the door. "Go,

goddammit. Pulverize my fucking heart." My voice lowers to a wrought whisper. "Just get it over with."

She crumbles behind me.

I hear the snap, the break.

The sound of her heartache spins me in place until I'm looking at her, seeing her. Seeing how much she regrets saying that.

Painful tears twist up her features before she runs into my arms and collapses against me, her tank top fluttering back to the floor. "I'm sorry. I didn't mean it, Gabe. I'm so sorry," she cries, dampening my shirt. "Forgive me. I didn't mean it." Her arms coil around me, locking behind my back like she can't bear to let me slip from her clutches.

My own arms dangle at my sides, steeped in defeat.

I'm at a loss, a crossroads.

"Hold me," she murmurs helplessly. "Please hold me." Not willing to wait, she tugs my arms up and forces them around her.

Dammit.

I can't help but hold her.

I can't help but gather her in my defeated fucking arms and squeeze her to me, closer than ever, and bury my face into her shoulder. "I'm trying to do everything right, Tabs. I'm really trying."

"You're doing everything right," she says, choking on her sobs. "I'm the one broken. I'm the one hurting you. Please, please don't hate me."

"I don't hate you. I could never hate you." I stroke her hair and press a kiss to the curve of her neck. "It's okay."

"It's not okay. I can't believe I said something so horrible to you." She sniffles. "I would never do that. I swear, there's no one else I want. No one else who makes me feel the way you make me feel."

Slowly, warily, my heart pieces itself back together inside my chest.

I think of her scar. I think of all of her scars.

I *am* trying, but she's trying, too. She's trying so hard to heal, to keep fighting, to overcome the worst possible thing a human being could go through.

I was right about one thing: this isn't about me.

None of this is about me.

I don't let myself think and fall to my knees at her feet, my hands gliding down her waist and tugging her to me.

She gasps, reaching for my shoulders. Her whole body trembles with tears, regret, uncertainty, unfulfilled desire.

Closing my eyes, I curl my fingers around her hips and press my lips to the jagged scar above her stomach. "Tell me what he did," I murmur. "Tell me what he did to you, baby."

I feel her shiver.

Her stomach heaves with labored breaths against my face as I press more kisses to the cruelly carved letters, nuzzling them with my nose. "Tell me."

"He...he carved initials into me with a pocket knife. He branded me, making me his."

Jesus.

I can't even begin to fathom what she went through, how she suffered.

"Fuck," I exhale, my breath feathering against her skin. "You're not his. You don't belong to anybody."

She's still trembling in my arms, her nails digging into my shoulders. "I hardly felt it. It's like I wasn't even there."

"You're safe now." Pressing my cheek to her concave belly, I feel her fingers move to my hair and sift through the strands. "I promise."

She sighs. "Hold me, Gabe."

That's all it takes.

I straighten from the floor and bend down, lifting her up by the thighs, and carry her over to my bed. We collapse onto the mattress, wholly entwined.

She's still shirtless, still shivering. Her bare chest is flush against me, legs wrapped around my hips. I pepper kisses to her collarbone, her neck, her jaw. I tamp down the flickering of desire funneling through me and focus on keeping her warm. Protected and safe.

Loved.

"Do you forgive me?" she whispers gently, her lips grazing my collar.

I nod, squeezing her. "There's nothing to forgive."

My reply has her relaxing in my arms, becoming weightless. Warm. At peace.

Party noise seeps in from the other side of my house, but I

drown it out, only listening to her perfectly timed breaths. Only feeling her heartbeats vibrating with mine.

And with the stars as our nightlight, she finally gives me an answer.

"I see *you*, Gabe," she murmurs on a sleep-laced breath. "I only see you."

CHAPTER 23

TABITHA

I still have a pounding headache when I sit down with Evan the next morning, graciously accepting the hot coffee he provides me. My eyelids feel like paper-weights every time I blink.

I had a quick video call with Hope on Evan's front stoop, and even my toddler wondered, "Mama sick?"

"Something like that," I told her.

Heartsick, homesick, lovesick.

Mostly, rum-sick.

"Rough night?" A shadow of a smirk finds me across the desk as Evan clicks something on the laptop and the printer purrs to life. It appears to be a news article, with a black-and-white photo attached. "You look like you just discovered what vodka does."

My lips purse. "Pineapple Malibu, actually." I chuckle lightly, embarrassment tingeing my cheeks. Then I cock my head with curiosity. "I'm impressed you were able to differentiate a hangover from my perpetual state of exhaustion."

"I'm a writer. We know all." He leans back and pulls the pages from the printer. "Just kidding. We actually know jack-shit and are heavily reliant on private, untraceable search engines and making things up while hoping nobody notices." Evan's attention skims over the article, brows furrowing, as he adds, "However, your car never left my driveway last night and you're wearing the same outfit you wore yesterday, so I suspected you made it to Gabe's party."

I slouch back in the rolling chair and tilt it side to side with my feet, wallowing in my terrible choices. Truthfully, I hadn't even realized I'd forgotten my car at Evan's until I left Gabe's house this morning. I'd raced out of that interview so fast, I'm surprised I even remembered left from right.

And then I raced out Gabe's front door this morning when my post-drunken tirade exploded in my mind, ricocheting through me like a bad dream. In the harsh light of day with a sober mind, humiliation warmed my skin. I quickly scuttered off the bed in search of my tank top while Gabe slept soundly beside me, still fully clothed.

He held me all night.

He held me in his arms, despite my cruelty, despite my unkind words and false assumptions.

The alcohol had clouded my rational thought, and all I could see was him not wanting me. I had it all wrong, though. I was so wrapped up in my physical insecurities, I was missing the big picture. The thing that really mattered.

Gabe wants more than just my body.

He wants my heart.

And I punished him for wanting the most precious thing I own. I penalized his patience, cut him down for his unwavering commitment.

Then I abandoned him this morning like a coward, leaving him with nothing but a note:

> *I do see you, Gabe. I see you so very clearly.*
>
> *But I see me, too, and I don't like what I'm seeing right now.*
>
> *Forgive me. For everything.*
>
> *— Tabs*

I then dragged myself to Evan's for our scheduled nine a.m. meeting, determined to get as much interview time in before I head back to work tomorrow. Gabe sent me a text a few minutes later, likely stirred awake by my hasty departure.

GABE:

Your note sounded an awful lot like goodbye.

Please tell me I'm wrong.

I haven't responded yet.

I have a lunch date with Cora this afternoon and I plan to pick her brain on the subject of post-abduction romance, hopeful of gaining some new insight into where to go from here.

I'm a mess.

Twirling my thumbs, I offer Evan a look of apology. "Sorry about the car," I mutter. "I hope I didn't block you in."

"Nope. That would imply I have a social life, which is debatable these days." He lifts his eyes to me, then sets the loose pages on the desk, spinning them around to face me. "Do you recognize this woman?"

I glance down.

Ice inhabits my veins, the coffee freezing on my tongue.

I look away from the photograph and nod. "Yes. It's a picture of Earl Hubbard's mother."

She's pregnant in the photo, seemingly far along. According to a rigorous police investigation, the image was taken shortly before she was beaten to death, prompting a premature delivery.

The baby didn't make it.

The easy humor in the air chills, too, as Evan taps his index finger on the article, his smile dimming. "I've been digging into the case. Wondering about the whys. What turns men into monsters, what fuels them, what makes them tick. What motivates them to commit these heinous crimes." Leaning back in his chair, he folds his arms across his chest and studies me. "I couldn't find anything connecting the couples—his selection seemed to be random, based solely around the relationship dynamic between the man and the woman. Specifically, he abducted two people with zero romantic involvement. It was part of the thrill, establishing a connection between the victims and then watching them suffer when he ended their lives." He pauses. "One thing stood out, though."

My muscles tense up as my knees bob up and down. "What's that?"

"Every female victim before and after you had blonde hair."

I blink, processing his words.

I didn't know that, but then again, I didn't *want* to know anything about the other victims. The ones who didn't make it. The ones who succumbed to that basement.

It's been hard enough grieving the man I lost. Getting to know the others felt like too much for me to carry when I was already bearing an unfathomable amount of weight.

Swallowing, I glance down at my tightly-fisted hands resting in my lap, the nails leaving little half-moon prints on my palms. "That's interesting."

"It's telling," he says. "I think Earl Hubbard had a type, but it's not because he had a fixation on blondes, per se. It's because he had a trigger with brunettes. Women with dark hair and light skin." His head dips thoughtfully, focus returning to the photo. "Women who reminded him of his mother?"

He poses it as a question, the inflection lifting at the end.

I suddenly feel trapped, caged.

Chained.

This new direction makes me uneasy.

"He hardly knew his mother," I state. "She died when he was only six years old."

Evan runs the tip of his tongue along his upper lip, studying me, working through his thoughts. "Valid. I guess I'm trying to find logic in the way a psychopath's mind works...which is about as productive as my daughter on summer break." He sends me a smile and inches forward, elbows on the desk. "Anyway, are you okay to continue today? I know you had a tough night."

Straightening, I let out a breath and try to get more comfortable. "I'm okay. Unless you have other things you need to do. I don't mean to commandeer your Saturday."

"Nothing major—just a diabolical revenge scheme I'm concocting against my mortal enemy, but it can wait." He winks at me. "For a book, of course."

"Of course." I clear my throat and offer a laugh. "I'll make sure to read that one when you're finished."

He presses Record on the tape recorder.

"Whenever you're ready," he says. "Take your time."

I zone out into the past, picturing gray walls, buckets of rain pouring down outside the window, and the smell of mildew mingling with coppery old blood.

Matthew's face forms in my mind's eye. His battered, swollen face.

My heart pounds, hands shake.

Releasing another slow breath, I slip away.

And I pray I return.

Two Years Earlier

THE MAN DIDN'T TOUCH me for three days.

And on that third day, when drizzle beat against the lone window, I wondered if he'd had his fill of me. Perhaps he realized we'd suffered enough and he was working on a way to set us free. The idyllic, hopeful part of me pretended he had developed a conscience in the span of seventy-two hours; after all, he was still feeding us. Giving us bathroom breaks and palmfuls of water.

It was as if we were dying flowers in the dead of winter, and he was giving us just enough to hold on to the promise of spring.

Matthew stared at me from across the cellar as the sound of raindrops echoed throughout the hollow space. He'd managed to pull himself into a sitting position as he leaned back against the pole. It killed me that he could hardly keep his head up. His face was terribly wrecked, bruised and broken, painted in deep gashes and slow-healing wounds.

But he was still hanging on.

Still waiting for spring, while the snow tumbled down and tried to bury him in frost.

"You always wear that ring and that watch," I said aloud. My words thundered between us as I recalled the tungsten band around his right ring finger and the antique-looking watch around his wrist. I'd been curious about them, wondering if they had sentiment. "Do they mean something to you?"

We hadn't done much conversing due to Matthew's condition.

He hadn't been able to speak at all during those first twenty-four hours post-attack. I'd offered one-sided conversations, hummed a few songs that reverberated like a dirge, but mostly, I'd watched him. I'd watched him slip in and out of consciousness as he clung to life, knowing he didn't have much life left to cling to.

Rain poured down on the other side of the window. The drizzle turned angry, rattling the glass pane across from me.

"They were...my grandfather's," Matthew said, voice strained. "He passed away. Last year."

Immediately, I felt terrible for bringing attention to a painful topic.

As if he needed any more misery.

"I'm so sorry."

"It's...all right." Inhaling a ragged breath, he raised his head as much as he could. "My grandfather...he was my role model. He taught me a lot. How to drive. How to...fly an airplane. How to love, with no conditions." He swallowed, gathering more words. Gathering more breath. "He met my grandmother at war. Vietnam. She was...a nurse. She tended to him once, a flesh wound, and he fell in love. Told me...she had eyes like a perfect spring sky. The ideal sky for flying.

"She had no interest in him, at first. But...he was persistent. A bit of a comedian. He won her over with laughter and jokes. It took months, but...he didn't let up."

"That's so romantic." I drifted away, imagining his grandparents in their youth, envisioning a simpler time. Now I knew where Matthew got his beautiful blue eyes. "They were married?"

"Eventually, yes," he murmured. "First, she got injured. Enemy rocket fire."

"Oh," I gasped. "How awful. We don't have to talk about it."

"I...don't mind." Matthew winced as he tried to straighten, lift up. "She survived, despite losing an arm. I think...I think it made him love her more. He said to me once...he had less to hold, but no less to cherish. He took care of her. Worshiped her." A smile crested, a marvel of a thing. "My grandfather always told me...his greatest effort in life was not the war he fought. It was the battle...to win my grandmother's heart."

My own whittled-down heart burst back to life, my blood pumping with vitality.

I sniffled, emotion clogging my throat. Tightening my chest.

"On his deathbed, he gave me his wedding ring to symbolize love…and his watch as a token of luck. The watch was…special to him. It brought him good fortune at war, he said."

Smiling at the sentiment, I murmured, "A ring for love, and a watch for luck."

"Yes." He offered a tiny smile back. "There was a Chinese philosopher I studied deeply…when I was in college," Matthew continued, hardly able to catch his breath between words. "Confucius. One of his quotes has always…stayed with me." His gaze found mine across the dreary space and held tight. "I had the passage engraved…into that ring."

My eyes watered, glazing over like the rain-laden window. "What is the quote?"

"It says—"

The basement door plowed open.

No!

No, no, not now.

Not ever, but please not now.

The man whistled as he stomped toward us, tearing, ripping, shredding our perfect moment like a twister funneling through a peaceful town. Downed trees, broken buildings, my heart in dust-tossed tatters. He appeared almost…*rejuvenated.*

"Morning, Kitten," he purred with menace.

He hadn't called me 'Kitten' in days, but it seemed the nickname had returned.

I didn't have the strength to pretend today. I didn't have the will, and I certainly didn't have the heart. Tatters could only do so much.

I stared at him, eyes glazed and blank.

"I need to watch today." A grin curled as he swerved over to Matthew and hauled him upright by the front of his sweater. "C'mon, dog."

Free from his chains, Matthew could hardly maintain his balance. The man dragged him across the room and thrust him toward me, while Matthew's legs tripped and stumbled, both of his hands catching on the pole above my head to keep us from colliding.

The man backed away quickly, pistol pointed in our direction. He didn't come near me, didn't touch me. Hardly looked at me.

"You know the drill, mutt."

I looked at Matthew.

Crusted, dried blood riddled his handsome face. One eye was swollen shut, the other half-lidded, and his bottom lip was split wide open. He was masked in bruises and partially opened wounds. All I wanted to do was heal him, take care of him, but I wasn't even allowed to touch him.

I pumped my fingers into fists, digging my long, brittle nails into the heel of my palms. A sense of panic overtook me as my mind punished my body for being unable to do the one thing it wanted more than anything.

Matthew lowered both trembling hands to cup my face, his touch the antidote to my brewing panic attack. It was a small comfort when there was otherwise none. "You're...so beautiful." He inhaled wheezy breaths that resembled high-pitched gasps, like a lung had been punctured. "You're the only thing keeping me going. I live for these fleeting moments. When I can see you... touch you."

"Yes...yes, me too. Don't stop touching me," I begged him. "Show me you're here, that you're still alive."

The one eye I could see glistened, as if what I'd said was painful.

"Matthew." His name fell out in hopeless syllables. "Kiss me."

His fingers were calloused and dirty as they cradled my jaw in a tender grasp. Moving in to kiss me, his other hand dropped from my face and reached behind me, finding my chained wrists. He laced our fingers together, allowing me the sensation of touch. Giving me a tiny piece of what I craved.

I cried out through the kiss, the moan parting my lips and inviting his tongue inside. He was still warm, still wet. It was proof of life in the sweetest form. I squeezed our palms together as much as I could, my hand twisted awkwardly yet tingling with relief.

It was the third time he'd been forced to make love to me.

I called it making love because that was what it felt like. That was what it would have been if there were no cement walls, no guns pointed at our heads, and no curious rats watching us from the shadows while a madman got off on our imminent death.

My thoughts were a slow-moving carousel as Matthew lifted my T-shirt and fumbled with his zipper. He entered me slowly.

Everything was slow, an unhurried, dreamlike haze. Partly to savor our few moments of reprieve, and partly because Matthew had the look of dying in his eyes.

He didn't let go of my hand as his opposite hand trailed to my hip, holding me steady. His grip was less firm, less needy. It felt an awful lot like giving up, and the notion had me sobbing through our kiss.

Pulling back, he whispered against my lips, "Don't cry... sweet girl." Swallowing, his throat bobbed with his own anguish. "Look...out the window. Picture the stars."

I hated the stars.

They'd rejected my wishes, mocking them with their carefree shine.

I preferred the rain; it fell and wept like I did.

Mostly, I preferred the man in front of me, my only tangible sliver of hope.

So I looked at him, instead.

I saw only him, instead.

Matthew moved inside me, our hands squeezing tight. He leaned forward to brush my tears away with his bruised lips, stealing a little of my lifeforce for himself. I'd give him it all if I could. I'd give him every tear, every breath, every shredded piece of my heart.

His face fell to my shoulder as he released, filling me with warmth. Giving me *his* lifeforce, which seemed backward and wholly unfair.

I was still crying, unable to keep my tears from falling as he lifted his head ever so slowly.

A smile reached his half-open eye, and it twinkled back at me, brighter than any star. Then he moved to unclasp the wristwatch, to pull it over his hand, to place it around my wrist. I quickly shook my head. "No...no, don't." I swallowed. "It's your good luck charm. Please, keep it."

He paused for a moment, and instead of unlatching the watch, he twisted the tungsten ring off his finger and shoved it into my bound hand. He closed my fingers around the precious piece of jewelry and said, "For you...for good luck. A keepsake. Just in case—"

"Hey, time's up," our captor barked. "Step away from the pretty kitty."

I clutched the ring, holding onto it for dear life, wishing I could hold him, too.

Matthew bent to whisper something in my ear just as our captor approached to drag him away. He resisted, clung to me, and then he murmured softly, so only I could hear him:

"To rank the effort…above the prize…may be called love."

Moments later, he was chained to his pole once again as the man disappeared up the stairs and left us alone with the rain and ghosts.

Matthew lay slumped over, drifting out of consciousness, his breathing weak and unsteady.

All effort and no prize.

I squeezed the little ring in my fist and quietly sobbed.

Present Day

MY LUNCH DATE with Cora is a welcome reprieve.

We sit across from each other in a two-person booth, munching on croissants and sipping a midday coffee as sunshine filters in through the tall window beside us.

I fiddle with the tungsten ring still attached to the chain around my neck. Twirling it aimlessly, I watch as the sunlight catches on the silver and glints like starlight.

Cora laughs under her breath as she types something on her phone, her smile broad.

I close my hand around the ring, stamping out the false gleam. "Is that Dean?" I wonder, knowing what that smile implies, knowing who it's meant for.

Blushing, she sets her phone down with a love-laced sigh. "Yes." Her grin widens. "He's in town this weekend. He drives back to Bloomington tomorrow night." The next sigh she releases is less blissful, more melancholy. "I can't wait for a job transfer to open up. He thinks it'll be soon."

I instantly feel guilty for pulling her away from quality time with her boyfriend who she only sees on weekends. "We could have rescheduled, you know. I hope I'm not intruding on your plans."

Shaking her head, Cora flicks her hand at me with an air of dismissal. "No way. You're important, too. Besides, Dean and Reid have been meaning to get together for bro-time, whatever that consists of. Pretty sure they're counting down the days until football season."

"Sounds riveting."

"Mm. As riveting as me counting down the days to the Puppy Bowl, I suppose. I bought my dogs jerseys this year. I'm insane."

Giggling, I cup my palms around my hazelnut cappuccino and blow into the mouth hole to counter the steam.

Cora reaches for her phone again. Smiles. Bites her lip a little.

And then I pivot, deciding to taint this easygoing conversation with my fears and bottled-up trauma. "Um, can I talk to you about something?" I gulp. "Something kind of…personal?"

"Of course." She takes a sip of her iced coffee and glances my way, returning her phone to the tabletop. "Shoot."

My face heats. I'm not sure how to talk about this. It's almost like I'm a teenaged girl again, asking my school friends about sex as we huddle in our sleeping bags and gossip about boys.

I'm twenty-three years old and I feel like a virgin.

Tucking my hair behind my ear, I force myself to continue. "I've been thinking about sex again lately." My throat burns, catching on the words. "With Gabe."

She doesn't look surprised. She doesn't look mortified, either—I'm the only one with bright-red cheeks and the beginning of a rash mottling my chest and collarbone.

"Oh, yeah?" All she does is send me a soft look as she fiddles with her straw. "You really care about him."

"I do." Nodding, I duck my chin. "I've been handling it all wrong, though. I keep rushing to the finish line like I'm trying to prove something to myself, and I don't want it to be like that. I want to enjoy every moment, savor the experience." Embarrassment climbs when those blurry, rum-fueled memories seep into my psyche. "I got drunk last night and threw myself at him. Said mean things when he told me he wasn't comfortable with it since I'd been drinking." I sigh, ashamed. "I felt rejected, so I accused him of not being attracted to me, which he's never once indicated. He's only ever shown me the exact opposite."

Cora's eyes glisten with sympathy as she sets down her coffee. When she leans forward, her long, golden-honey hair spills over her shoulders. "That's completely natural. It's not uncommon to carry around misplaced insecurities. It can take years, decades, to move past those feelings."

I twist the star ring around my finger, considering her words. "He's being so patient with me, Cora. So loving. I'm afraid I'm pushing him away because I can't see past my trauma. I can't see what *he* sees when he looks at me."

Her head tilts to the side, thoughtfully. "What do you see?"

"Someone unworthy of a good man like him. Someone undeserving." I swallow. "Someone ugly."

She reaches across the table to clasp my hand, a frown twisting her pretty face. "Those are lies. Your self-worth was warped by a fucked-up, soulless monster. You *are* worthy of love. You're worthy of sex and healthy relationships. I promise, that's not what Gabe sees. That's not what anybody sees." Tears reflect in her eyes as she squeezes my hand. "You've always been worthy, deserving, and beautiful. The fact that you survived that basement is just a testament to those things. A reminder. It only makes you *more* beautiful."

My breath quivers as I hold eye contact. "Do you ever feel that way about yourself? After all this time?"

I think I just want to feel validated, like I'm not alone in feeling this way. Cora says it's normal, but is it? After two years? I realize she's had access to better mental health resources and parents who live locally and are fully supportive, but part of me needs to know that she felt like me, once. Even for a little while. Even for a moment.

"*Of course.*" She answers firmly, without question. "I still fight those dark thoughts. I absolutely do. What happened to us…it *changed* us, Tabitha. We can do everything right, take all the recommended steps, utilize every option out there to help us heal —and still, we don't forget. We don't ever go back to the person we used to be."

A tear slips from the corner of my eye; I can't help it.

"I'm going to share something with you that's a little personal." Cora pulls away and sweeps her hair to one side, then tinkers with the flowy sleeve of her blush tunic. "When things were bad with Dean—really bad—I asked him to do something. Something I didn't understand at the time. Something that made him run the other way because he didn't understand it, either."

I blink at her, hanging on to every word, squeezing my coffee cup until liquid dribbles out the top.

"I asked him to tie me up. During sex."

"Oh." My lips part, not expecting that confession. "Did he?"

"No. He saw it as a red flag...he thought I was still living in that basement, unable to move on." Flush turns her cheeks pink, staining her tanned skin. "At the time, he was right. I was drowning. Sinking. And in that moment, it wouldn't have been a healthy route to take—we were too toxic, too codependent. We needed time away from each other, room to heal as individuals before we could ever dive into a thriving relationship.

"Anyway, as you know, we found our way back to each other when I was in a much better place. I'd brought that moment up to my therapist, and she assured me that my request was completely normal. Sometimes, acting out those triggering scenarios are therapeutic for rape victims. It's a way of taking back control and replaying those experiences consensually, on our own terms." Cora worries her lip between her teeth and glances down at the table. "Dean understands, now. He gets it. And it's only brought us closer together."

Curiosity filters through me. I wonder if they do that now—act out those *scenarios*. Part of me wants to dig deeper, ask more questions, but I don't want to pry. It feels too intimate.

Inhaling a deep breath, Cora offers me a small smile. "I think the key to moving forward is learning to love yourself first. That's what I needed to do. That was my breakthrough. The moment you truly believe you are beautiful, sexy, and deserving of sex and love, is the moment you'll start believing that other people see that, too."

My grip on the coffee cup loosens as I consider her advice. "Where do I even start?"

"You start small. Baby steps."

Pondering that, I glance out the window, my eyes landing on two robins teetering on a tree branch. Birds start small. They hatch, and they grow, and they flap their wings until those wings are strong enough to fly. It's instinct. It happens when their wings are ready.

They never doubt that they will fly one day.

They just know.

When I glance back at Cora, she's watching me, new thoughts dancing across her face.

"What is it?" I wonder.

A sparkle claims her eyes as she reaches for her purse, slurping down the rest of her coffee. "I have an idea."

CHAPTER 24

TABITHA

I stare at the brand-new lingerie laid out across my bedspread.

It's siren red, made of satin and lace.

I can't imagine it'll cover much of me, but I suppose that's the point.

My stomach pitches, nerves climbing.

It feels like I'm about to go deep-sea diving into uncharted waters with half an oxygen tank, which is ridiculous because it's only lingerie.

But it feels like another step, and those first few steps are always the hardest.

Bending over, I graze my fingertips along the silky fabric, testing the feel of it against my skin. I've never owned real lingerie before. The truth is, I've only ever been intimate with two people—the first being my crush on prom night during my senior year of high school, which was awkward and uncomfortable and only lasted thirty seconds, give or take.

The second, of course, was Matthew.

He never got to see me in lingerie.

Gathering my courage, I unbutton my tie-knot blouse and let it flutter to the floor. My jeans follow; then my undergarments. Soon, I'm working my way into the lacy, push-up corset, sliding the spaghetti straps over my shoulders. I step into the satin G-string panties that hardly cover anything and make a slow spin toward my full-length mirror hanging on the back of the bedroom door.

My eyes fly open at the sight.

I pull my dark hair over both shoulders, fluffing it for volume, and twist side to side, admiring the image staring back at me. My breasts aren't as full as they once were, but they're not nothing. My cleavage is ample, especially with the added lift of the corset. My skin is pale, but it's not sickly like I often believe it to be. Against the rich-cherry color of the material, my complexion resembles white rose petals blended with red. Something beautiful.

A shot of giddiness surges through me.

With a wildly beating heart, I move back toward my bed and climb atop the sheets, reaching for my cell phone. I open up the camera and flip the lens around until I'm in the frame.

My hand is shaking.

My cheeks are so red, they almost match the lingerie.

The lighting isn't great with my closed blinds and faint lamplight, but it's a baby step. The next step will be bright, natural sunshine highlighting every inch of me.

Choking down a breath, I lift the phone and angle it so the majority of my body is visible. I snap a few pictures, look them over. Delete all of them.

Try again.

Snap, snap, snap.

Delete, delete, delete.

I close my eyes and center myself, taking more deep breaths. I tell myself I'm pretty, I'm loveable. I'm an irresistible sexpot.

If I pretend long enough, maybe I'll grow to believe it.

Baby steps.

I take a few more photos, all in different poses, and refrain from deleting them this time. Studying each photograph, I try not to pick apart my flaws. My scar is covered by the corset, but the rest of my skin isn't unblemished—I have smaller scars scattered across my flesh, a few moles, a birthmark on my hipbone, and a faded sunburn from the boardwalk that shadows my collarbone in uneven patches.

I look past those things and focus on the good parts.

A strong heart beats beneath these ribs. My lungs breathe clean air, granting me life. My body isn't supermodel-worthy, but it has two legs that carry me places, two arms that allow me to hold precious things, and two eyes that let me look upon the world that was still waiting for me on the other side of those basement walls.

I smile.

I'm still swiping through the photographs, learning to love every one of them, when my phone dings with a text message.

Gabe.

Guilt punctures me when I realize I never texted him back this morning. I've left him worried and wondering all day and allowed him to believe my note was a poor excuse for a goodbye.

As if I could ever say goodbye to him.

GABE:

> Judging by your radio silence, I'm forced to believe that your note was indeed a goodbye. And, well, I'm here to say…I think you can do better. I'm disappointed. Where's the angst, the breakdown, the tears, the heart-wrenching climax? Our friendship deserves more than a measly note. The fallout needs to be epic. Overdramatic telenovela kinda shit. If we go down, we go down in a fiery blaze of glory and barely make it out alive.

> Don't you agree?

> Am I wrong?

Somehow, some way, he manages to bring a smile to my face.

He could have been angry, could have hurled cruel words at me, could have written me off forever, and it would have been justified.

Instead, he makes me smile.

I nibble my lip and slide my feet up the mattress, resting my chin between my knees. My thumbs swipe over the keypad with a response.

ME:

> You're absolutely right. What was I thinking? How's this…

I type "blaze of glory" into the GIF bar and proceed to send him an endless string of explosion animations.

He starts typing back.

GABE:

> Much better :) also, I miss you already. Can we undo all that?

ME:

> I'd love to.

He sends back a GIF of the "reverse" card in Uno.

Giggling, I pull up my search engine and save a funny telenovela meme to my phone that says "gasps in Spanish," then I send it off to Gabe. I'm still grinning like a fool as I lean back against the headboard and set my phone beside me.

A few minutes pass by when his reply comes through.

I glance at the screen.

GABE:

> Um

> Holy shit

When his texts register, my brows bend with confusion.

I blink.

I have no idea why a meme would garner that reaction.

Frowning, I pick my phone back up and open our message correspondence all the way.

It takes less than three seconds for me to discover that I accidentally clicked on *two* photos from my gallery—one being the silly meme.

The other?

Yep.

The other is me in a come-hither position with my boobs spilling out over a corset of red lace, paired with an itty-bitty piece of fabric between my legs that leaves little to the imagination.

I freeze.

I choke.

I teeter on the realm of the afterlife, fairly certain my mortal soul has been summoned by God himself.

My hands shake as I attempt damage control.

ME:

Oh my God.

I didn't mean to send that to you.

I'm so, so sorry.

Oh my God.

The speech bubbles move in time with my sporadic heart rate. All he says is:

GABE:

Fuck.

I send him a string of sobbing emojis because I'm shutting down and can't produce words that even remotely resemble one of the seven-thousand known languages in the world.

GABE:

A better man might tell you it's fine and that no harm was done.

I wait for more, my heart thumping irregularly and possibly cracking a rib. His response dots dance and dip, and then more messages come through, back to back.

GABE:

But I'm not that man

It's not fine

Harm was done

My limbs are shaking, skin flushed hotter than ever.
I brace myself for the final text.

GABE:

Pretty sure you just destroyed me, Tabs.

I chuck my phone across the bedspread, hoping the action will erase the last thirty seconds of my life. It doesn't. The phone just tumbles over the linen sheets and slides off the edge, toppling to the hardwood floor. The sound ricochets through me like a hammer to my dignity.

I stare into space for a few moments, debating my next move.

Then I scramble to retrieve the fallen phone.

ME:

I'm mortified.

Please erase that from your mind.

It never happened.

Delete the picture.

A beat, and then…

GABE:

Is that what you want?

Of course that's what I—

I pause.

I swallow, hold my breath.

Is it?

Madness churns. Curiosity blooms.

My baby steps pick up their pace until I'm running full-speed ahead, destination unknown.

I click the call icon and bring the cell phone to my ear, hardly feeling sane.

Gabe picks up on the first ring. "Jesus," he mutters into the receiver. "Do I even want to know who you meant to send that to?"

I place a hand over my heaving chest, squeezing my eyes shut. "I-I took some pictures for me. Only for me. Cora took me lingerie shopping. I wanted to feel…sexy," I explain, voice wobbly. "I sent it to you by mistake, but…" My words trail off.

Silence hangs.

"But?" he hedges.

I gulp, nearly choking. "But…do you like what you saw?"

More silence, more labored breathing. He's debating where to go from here, and I'm waiting for direction. I feel scared, nervous, out of my element.

Strangely intrigued.

Finally, he husks, "If you were here right now, you'd see exactly how much I liked it."

Heat unfurls down below and I clench my thighs together. "I'm glad," I whisper back. "Are you...aroused?"

He groans. "Painfully."

"Tell me where you are. What you're feeling," I say, strengthening my voice, trying to be brave.

A few seconds tick by before he looks for confirmation. "Are we doing this?"

This.

This, meaning phone sex.

I've never had phone sex. I hardly remember what *real* sex feels like.

Still, I press forward, owning it.

I want to do this.

"Yes."

"Christ, Tabs." Rustling filters through from the other end of the line. "I'm in my living room, on the couch. I'm feeling insanely pent-up, thinking about what I'd do to you if you were here with me."

My skin is burning, turning fire-engine red. I part my knees, my fingertips drifting to my silky panties and lightly grazing. "What would you do?"

"You'd be sitting on my face before you could take your next breath."

Oh, God.

Tingles race south as I rub the pads of my fingers over the fabric, arching my back against the headboard. "No one's ever done that to me before. I wonder what it would feel like."

"You've never been eaten out?" he questions, tone gritty with lust. "Fuck...I'd make you feel so good. You'd beg me for more."

"Do you like doing that?"

"I fucking love it."

I close my eyes and picture him doing that to me. His face between my legs, his tongue dipping inside me, tasting, eager. It makes me hot imagining him enjoying it.

"Give me a safe-word," he says.

I suck in a breath, my eyes fluttering back open. "What?"

"A safe-word. Something you're going to say if anything goes too far or makes you uncomfortable. I'll shut it down the second you say it. I promise."

My mind races.

I try to locate a word that will break the moment if my fears get the better of me. A word that will slice through the tension and drag us from the deep end until we're wading in the shallow water again.

Somehow, two words come to mind. "Tabula Rasa."

It means "clean slate."

It's a redo. A fresh start.

Gabe doesn't question it. "Okay. Tabula Rasa," he echoes. "Say it, and we stop. No questions asked."

"Okay."

"Where's your hand?"

My throat is tight. It feels like something is squeezing it, but it's not the familiar noose of shame. It's not even anxiety, or the makings of a panic attack.

It's...adrenaline.

Excitement.

Power.

Inhaling a breath, I prop myself up higher on two pillows and slip my fingertips inside the waistband of my red panties. I use my other hand to hold the phone to my ear. "In my underwear."

His breathing sounds unsteady.

"Where is yours?" I murmur.

He doesn't hesitate. "Wrapped around my cock. I'm ridiculously hard thinking about you touching yourself. It won't take long for me to come."

Moisture pools between my legs, slicking my fingers as they slip inside to explore. His words fuel me. The breakage in his voice has my skin hot, my hairline damp with sweat.

I'm turned on.

I can't remember the last time I felt this...*free*.

Sexually, emotionally, mentally.

"Do you want to...have a video call?" My heart thunders between my ribs as lightning flashes inside my chest.

Gabe makes a sound. Something like a tortured groan. "You're killing me, baby."

Baby.

I nearly fainted when he called me that last night.

The lightning quiets to moonglow as warmth trickles through me. "Do you?"

"Yes. You have no idea how much I want that."

My fingers are shaking as I fumble for the video-call button.

"But," he interrupts, "not yet. We should take this slow. One step at a time."

I pause, my thumb hovering over the button. He's probably right. My nerves are fragile, my boldness dangling by a thin thread. "Okay."

"Are you still wearing that red lingerie?"

"I am."

"Your fingernails are painted red, too. So fucking sexy." His voice is hoarse, strained with desire. "I'm imagining those red-tipped fingers wrapped around my dick right now."

"Ooh," I moan softly. I'm imagining that, too. The vision has my fingers dipping deeper inside, exploring parts of me long forgotten. "I-I remember how big you felt in my hand. The night I touched you."

"Yeah?"

"Yes. I wanted you inside me," I say breathily. "I still want that. So badly."

"Fuck…you have no idea how much I want that. Tell me how you'd let me take you," he probes. "You'd want to be on top, wouldn't you? You'd want to be in control and ride my cock until you make yourself come."

I rub my clit with the heel of my palm, my neck craning back as I close my eyes and fantasize. "I…I don't know. I think I'd want you to take charge," I admit. "I think I'd want it…a little rough. I don't want you to hold back with me, like I'm delicate or something."

The notion surprises me.

But I think that's what I'd want—I don't want to be treated with kid gloves. I wouldn't want him to treat me any differently than anyone else.

Gabe moans, his breathing ragged. "I'm close," he says. "Tell me how wet you are."

"My…my fingers are soaked. My panties, too."

"Mmm. Jesus," he grinds out. "Do you touch yourself often?"

"No. I haven't done this in a long time." I keep rubbing myself, biting down on my lip. "But I've been thinking about it lately…thinking about you. You make me feel alive again," I confess. "Desirable. Real."

"You're the sexiest girl I've ever seen. The sweetest, the bravest. I…" His words trail off, fading into another moan. "God, Tabs. I'd kill to be between those pretty legs right now."

I release a long sigh, a breath of longing, of needing, of missing.

I picture him between my thighs, thrusting and filling me. His strong arms caging me in, corded and veined, his hips bucking into me, green eyes blazing above me as he makes me feel things I never thought I'd feel again. Skin to skin, heart to heart. Safe, protected, adored.

The world falls away when he's near.

My demons scatter, taking to the shadows when I'm in his arms.

"Please…come over," I blurt out, desperate to make my vision a reality. "Make love to me."

"Shit," he groans. "If you mean it, I'm there. I can't say no to you again. If you want me to fuck you, I'll come over, I'll take you rough like you want me to. I'll make you come until you see stars."

A touch of panic stabs my chest.

I don't want to see stars.

I force away the dark thoughts and mutter like a coward, "Next time. I-I'm too close."

"All right," he rasps, his breathing heavy. "Next time."

Collapsing further into my pillows, I dip two fingers inside me, blocking out the past. I find my way back to Gabe, only Gabe.

I wasn't lying. I'm close.

I whimper, mewl, feel myself peaking.

"You're going to come, aren't you? I hear it in your voice. Your breathing. The sounds you're making are driving me straight over the edge." He moans. "Fuck."

His own breathing picks up. I imagine him stroking himself faster, harder, chasing the feeling that teases me, too. "Yes."

"You first. Let me hear you," he tells me. "Don't hold back."

I spread my legs wider, my knees parting as I pick up my pace. I rub my swollen clit as tingles spark and climb, the knot of heat in my lower belly moments away from unraveling. "Oh, God...Gabe..."

"That's it. Say my name."

"Gabe..." I chant his name, over and over. "Gabe, yes..."

"Let it go, baby." More groans, more heated breaths. "Let it go."

I let myself tumble over the edge.

I'm freefalling, parachuting, nosediving.

Flying.

My hips lift off the bed as my body is doused in shimmery heat. Pure magic. I moan loudly through the intense climax, almost dropping the phone, as Gabe's groan of pleasure rings in my ears and causes my chest to thrum.

The tingles ebb and I buckle back down onto the bed in a heap of sated bliss. I drape the back of my arm over my eyes and try to catch my breath.

"I wish you could see what you just did to me," Gabe says, tone gritty with his own post-release. "How much I want you. That was...everything."

Everything.

I don't know what to say. I'm not sure where we go from here. A line was crossed, that much I know. And I don't regret it...I know that, too.

I also know we're changed now.

Things will be different between us.

Silence hovers and holds as I tuck the phone between my ear and shoulder, as we both come down from the high, processing this new dynamic. I should say something. I should assure him that I'm fine, that I harbor no regrets.

But then Gabe speaks up first, and it's the simplest, easiest thing he could say. "Music?"

I close my eyes and smile. "Sure."

A few moments pass, then the sound of music filters through the speaker. It's an immediate relief, an instant calming. I realize he could listen to his music, and I could listen to my music, and we don't need the phone between us, but there's something cathartic about listening to it together. It's not two wires, but we're still connected, still tethered.

He's with me.

Pulling the blankets up to my chin, I burrow into the soft sheets. "Gabe?" I murmur.

I hear the affection in his voice. "Tabs."

"Thanks for flying with me today."

He doesn't say anything for a while, and only *Blurry* by Puddle of Mudd hums between us, filling the space with chords and lyrics.

Finally, he whispers, "Any time."

Smiling, I drift away to music, to Gabe's quiet breaths, the phone still resting against my shoulder.

He has no idea that I said my true safe-word; I've said it thousands of times.

One syllable of solace.

Four letters of sweet relief.

A safe place to land when my wings get tired.

Gabe.

His name is my safe-word.

He's my solid ground.

CHAPTER 25

GABE

Oliver and Syd invite me over for breakfast the next morning before I head into work, and I can't downplay the overly enthusiastic grin I'm wearing when I breeze into their kitchen. "Yo." I lift my hand with a wave. "Egg me."

"Don't you ever knock—" Sydney does a double-take from the table when she spots me in all of my grinning glory. "Oh, my God."

"What?"

"You got laid."

"No." I shrug off her claim, but my smile takes a sharp left turn onto Unhinged Avenue.

"Liar. I know that look. You and Tabitha finally had sex." I'm met with a celebratory fist-pump. "Hell, yes."

"Jesus." I pull out a dining chair and plop down, collapsing against the seatback. "You're acting like my sex life is some kind of breaking-news story."

"So, you admit you have a sex life." She leans forward on her arms, her grin matching mine. "You have to tell me everything."

"Not a chance."

"Seriously? You're my ride-or-die."

"Fine. I choose die."

"He's right, Syd," Oliver adds from his position near the stove, whisking an omelet mixture while donning a raccoon-printed apron. "A true gentleman never discloses details pertaining to his intimate encounters."

"Yeah, Syd." I wink. "A true gentleman."

She scoffs. "Oh, please. If you're a gentleman, then I have the etiquette of a dignified Victorian lady."

"Honestly, you'd kind of rock a bonnet."

"I do have the bone structure for it."

Oliver chops up bits of green pepper and tosses a handful into the eggs. "I take it you and Tabitha are progressing nicely, then?" he asks me, without *over*-asking. "It was a pleasant surprise seeing her at your jamboree."

Slurping down a flute of orange juice that most definitely contains ninety-seven percent champagne, Sydney snickers as she glances up at her fiancé. "Nobody says that, honey. It's called a party." Her nose crinkles. "Pretty sure Jamboree was a kids' show from the nineties with creepy puppets. Thanks for breaking through those repressed memories."

I scroll through my phone, unable to tamp down the budding smile. "Yeah, things are going well. I'm feeling hopeful."

"How's Tabitha's interview going with the hot writer?" Sydney inquires.

This earns her an over-the-shoulder glower from Oliver.

"Undetermined," I reply. "I'm still not sure if it's really benefiting her. She usually comes out of the sessions triggered and emotional." My heart pangs, thinking of her sobbing in the back of her car the night I discovered her pulled over to the side of the road a few houses down from mine. "At the same time, she seems to be opening up, having some breakthroughs. She's starting to *see* me, where, for a while, I felt like she only saw him."

"The deceased professor?" Oliver wonders.

I swallow. "Yeah."

"A painful situation, indeed." He pours the egg mixture into a frying pan and reaches for a spatula. "How is that other situation unfolding, by the way? The one with the peculiar man I discovered on your property?"

Sydney pops her head up, tugging at her messy topknot. "What? Who?"

I swipe my hand down my face. "He's nobody. Haven't seen him since I've been back."

His forbidding text message flashes through my mind.

Time is ticking.

"What man? Who are you talking about?"

"He left me feeling uneasy," Oliver notes. "I certainly hope he found what he's looking for and leaves you alone."

"Dude. Answer me." Sydney leans over and smacks me, her eyes flaring with alarm. "What guy? Are you in trouble?"

My knees start bobbing restlessly because I know it's something I'm going to have to deal with eventually. I'm confident he hasn't found what he's looking for, because what he's looking for is money, and I'm giving him none of mine. "It's nothing," I lie. "Just a contractor. Weird guy."

"Is he dangerous?"

"Why would he be dangerous?"

"I don't know." Her knuckles go white as she squeezes the stem of her champagne flute. "Is Travis involved?"

My eyes drift left, breaking eye contact. I'm reluctant to confess that I have at least a dozen ignored phone calls from my felonious father in relation to the matter. "Of course not. He's in jail."

"Gabe—"

"Syd." I glance at her pointedly. "It's just work-related bullshit. It's nothing."

Silence permeates the small kitchen, only fractured by the sound of bacon popping in the pan.

Oliver clears his throat. "The mood has become fairly uncomfortable now. My apologies. Perhaps bacon will help." He proceeds to carry multiple plates over to the kitchen table, two in his hands, and one balanced on his forearm; a juggling act that has my eye twitching.

And I jolt backward when their pet raccoon, Athena, comes barreling in from the other room, chased by their orange tabby cat. Both animals vault themselves onto the tabletop just as Oliver deposits the plates.

Food goes flying.

Dishes clatter to the floor.

"Athena!" Oliver scolds. "Bad raccoon. You're incorrigible."

"Ack!" Sydney leaps to her feet when the pitcher of the dubious orange-juice concoction topples into her lap. "Shit, shit, shit."

I stare blankly into the chaos, rubbing at my forehead. "Great. IHOP, it is."

We all watch as Athena snatches up a piece of bacon and darts back out of the kitchen, pleased with her prize, while the knocked-over syrup oozes into the divots of the kitchen table.

"This new oaken table, ruined," Oliver grimaces.

I frown. "Oaken? What the fuck is oaken?"

"The material of the table."

"So, wood. You mean wood."

"I'll clean up and we can make our way to the pancake house," he relents, shaking his head with a sigh. "I'll meet you in the car."

I shuffle outside first, after helping with the cleanup, and wait for the other two while they attempt to get their animals contained. Taking a seat on the front porch step, I mindlessly browse through my phone.

I'm mid-scroll when a text message pops up.

UNKNOWN NUMBER:

> I hope you've used your free time wisely. I'll come by to collect your debt at six p.m. sharp. Meet me in the parking lot of your jobsite.

My throat closes up, mouth going dry. I glance up at the late-morning sun and squint, my mind reeling with ways to avoid this mess until the end of time.

Maybe Uganda isn't such a terrible idea.

Swallowing the lump of dread in my throat, I scroll through my missed-call log and hover my thumb over the repetitive number associated with the prison.

I consider scheduling a visit, itching to get to the bottom of this shitshow.

Ultimately, I pass, letting my thoughts land on something sweeter.

Tabs.

It's my girl's first day back at work after using her vacation time to take a road trip with me, meet my mother, and pretend to be my fiancée. The vacation is over, the ruse long-since ended, but she still wears that little ring made of rusted silver stars.

Before I put my phone away, I send her a quick text.

ME:

> Can't stop thinking about last night :) ...you?

It is, in fact, a terribly inconvenient time to be thinking about last night as Sydney comes barreling out the front door complaining about period cramps, while their tabby cat zooms past us all, rejoicing in her escape and causing Oliver to chase her through the lawn still holding a spatula.

But it's also impossible not to.

We had phone sex.

And she was into it, she was *there* with me. She touched herself, made herself come to the sound of my voice. Begged me to make love to her, to take her roughly because she doesn't want to be seen as fragile or delicate.

I can't help but wonder if that's what comes next.

Sex. Romance. A relationship.

A chance that I'll go from her almost-everything to her *everything*.

And maybe, one day, she'll wear a real engagement ring on her finger.

She'll be mine.

A new message dings, and I quickly swipe open her reply.

TABITHA:

> Me too.

> No regrets. 🩶

I hold back the groan but not the grin.

ME:

> You busy tonight?

TABITHA:

> I have an interview with Evan after work, but I'll be free after. Maybe I can come over?

ME:

> It's a date ;)

A date.

A fucking date with the woman I'm crazy in love with, the woman I'd risk everything for.

With a lovestruck smile, I slip my phone into my front pocket and join Oliver and Sydney in the car, completely forgetting about my other date.

My six p.m. date with the Devil.

I HIGH TAIL it out of my jobsite at five-thirty, grateful to have clocked out early and avoided whatever shady parking-lot confrontation awaited me.

Unfortunately, my gratitude dissipates the moment I swerve into my driveway and kill the engine.

He's here.

That creepy asshole is standing on my front porch, leaning against the stone pillar with a cigarette pressed between his fingers.

Motherfuck.

He stares at me with ice-blue eyes as smoke that matches the color of his hair billows from the glowing embers.

My heart does jumping jacks as I scrub both hands up and down my face, trying to figure out a game plan. I probably should've contacted my father. I should've gotten to the bottom of this, figured out what this prick wants with me.

Either way, I don't have any money.

He's barking up the wrong fucking tree.

Gathering my courage, I step out of my Challenger and face him in the center of the driveway, folding my arms across my chest. "Leave."

He smiles, releasing a plume of smoke into the cloud-covered sky. "So demanding," he mutters. The man tosses his cigarette stub to the cement and crushes it under the toe of his boot. "And entirely unwise. We had an appointment."

"I never RSVP'd. Get the fuck off my property before I call the cops."

Another chuckle, and he steps down from the porch and saunters toward me with a limp in his gait. "You failed to speak with your father, didn't you?"

I glare at him, unmoving. "If you're referring to the useless waste of human life currently stinking up a jail cell, then no. Didn't pique my interest."

"That was a mistake."

My hackles rise as he steps closer. I can't imagine him doing anything overtly threatening in broad daylight, smack in the middle of quiet suburbia, so I hold my ground. "Take your creepy-ass riddles and leave. I don't owe you anything."

He cocks his head, stalling a few feet in front of me. The scar veining the left side of his face twists with menace. "Boss says otherwise. Your father owes quite a bit, actually, and unfortunately for you, he's not here to pay up."

"Because he's a pedophile and an attempted murderer." My eyes narrow, my pulse tripping. "How much does he owe?"

Glancing at his cuticles, almost boredly, he mutters, "One point two."

"One-point-two percent of what?"

Rich laughter echoes throughout the peaceful street, sending a chill down my spine. The man looks up at me and parks his hip against the hood of my car. "One point two million," he states. "That would be in American dollars, in case your feeble brain is having trouble computing numbers."

I blink.

My veins freeze.

I cup a hand around my jaw and close my eyes, hating my father more than I ever thought possible.

"Ah, yes," the man muses. "I'm sure you're experiencing a bit of sticker shock right now—which, might I add, could have been avoided if you had only taken my suggestion two weeks ago. Dear old dad has accumulated quite the outstanding debt thanks to private loans he secured for his doomed-to-fail restaurant. I'd wager he's been eager to offer you his fatherly advice and help you sort out this mess he's made. Too bad you were unreceptive."

The world is spinning.

Everything is spinning.

This has to be a fucking joke.

"I don't have that kind of money," I murmur, shaking my head, chest tight. "Not even close."

"You've had plenty of time to fix that."

My eyes fly open, glaring daggers, shooting fire. "I'm a

goddamn construction worker, you fucking parasite. I have zero relationship with my father. I'm not involved in his shady bull-shit, and I have absolutely no way of coming up with a million dollars. That's insane." I slice an angry hand through the air. "It's impossible."

"One point two," he clarifies.

"I'm calling the cops." My fingers are trembling as I fish through my pockets for my phone, my eyes drifting a few houses down to where Tabitha's car sits idle in the writer's driveway. I need to get this son of a bitch out of here before she walks out that front door.

I can't bring her into this.

Heart racing, throat burning, I unlock my phone and open up my keypad.

"I strongly advise you don't do that," the man says. "It would not be in your best interest to involve the police."

I pause, glancing up. "And why's that?"

"Because I know everything about you, *Gabe*. I have the ability to ruin your life and take away all the things you love most."

He's bluffing.

I press the nine. Then the one.

Then—

"She's very, very pretty," he says, ever so subtly, leaning back against my car. "It would be a shame if anything were to happen to her."

His words stab into me like buckshot, almost stopping my heart.

A sharp breath leaves me.

A white-knuckled fist to the gut.

"Especially," he adds, our eyes locking, "after everything she's been through."

No way.

No fucking way.

I don't even have time to process what he's implying when he lets out a whistle.

Digging through his tweed trousers for the pack of cigarettes, he plucks one from the box, lights it up, and cups a sun-spotted hand around the cherry. "I told you, Wellington...my boss doesn't like delays." He blows a puff of smoke right into my face, his see-through eyes glinting with malice, scar stretching as he leers at me. "I'm afraid these are the consequences."

A hand grabs me by the shoulder.

Spins me around.

I stumble, not expecting it.

Shock laces my blood when I'm faced with a wall of muscle towering over me, dressed in all black, a long-sleeved compression shirt stuck to him like a second skin. "What the fu—"

My words are cut short by a slug to my jaw. I reel backward, swiping the back of my hand along my jawline.

The muscleman reaches for me, stoic and expressionless, his meaty hand curling around my vest. He's a big dude, bigger than me, looking like a roided-up gym rat who wants to try and sell everyone he meets his one-of-a-kind keto meal plan program.

His fist flies back, then slams into my jaw for a second time.

Blood spills from my split lip.

Stars flicker behind my eyes.

I regain my balance and charge at him, spurred by adrenaline, and attempt to tackle him to my driveway. He doesn't even budge.

All he does is laugh.

When I pull my arm back to strike, he stops it midair, throws me to the ground like I weigh nothing at all, and starts kicking me in the ribs before tugging me upright.

Another punch to my face.

Then another, and another, until my eyes bruise, my jaw throbs, and blood spurts from my nose and mouth. I'm in good shape, but this guy is a brick-fucking-wall. I don't stand a chance as I'm tossed to the ground again.

More kicks to my abdomen.

To my hips.

To my stomach.

The man hardly breaks a sweat as he looms over me, chuckling under his breath when I'm teetering the line of consciousness, collapsed in a heap in my own driveway.

The fucker spits on me before storming away, readjusting his black beanie and muttering, "Sure you don't want me to kill him, Stoney?"

I lie there, dazed.

Bloodied.

Bruised and broken.

A cigarette butt is tossed onto my chest, then snuffed out with a firm stomp of a boot. I heave, my eyelids fluttering, pain exploding between my ribs.

"Not yet." The man called Stoney looms over me, his sneer and scar backlit by the slow-dipping sun, as he slides his cell phone into his back pocket. "It's your lucky day, Gabe. The boss is feeling generous," he says, grinding the toe of his boot into my chest before lifting it off me. "Talk to your father. You have one more week."

His face inches out of my line of sight, until all I see is a flock of birds flying overhead, fading into the pillowy-white clouds.

I think of her.

She's all I see as I inhale a wheezing breath.

And I black out.

CHAPTER 26

TABITHA

My grin is borderline deranged as I reread his last text message over and over.

GABE:

It's a date ;)

I bite my lip, slipping my cell phone back into my apron as Smithers hollers at me to hurry it up from his station by the stove.

Work has been an abrupt change of pace compared to the last few days of open roads, little responsibility, and a head-first slide into this budding new romance with Gabe.

Romance.

I never thought I'd experience that again.

Technically, I'm not sure I ever really have before. My connection with Matthew was something else entirely. Brutal, life-or-death madness borne from trauma and suffering.

It was love, though.

I felt it in my blood, my veins, my bones.

And this…this is something else.

Something sweeter, something more wholesome.

Something with the power to heal me, instead of break me in half.

Sighing, I fill my tray with plates of hot food and breeze through the kitchen doors, eager for my shift to be over. It's been wonderful seeing all the familiar faces sitting in the burgundy booths again, but my mind is preoccupied with thoughts of tonight.

Our date.

Knowing I would likely see Gabe after my interview with Evan, I made sure to pack a small overnight bag. Presumptuous, perhaps, but after our phone call, my thoughts have been flooded with visions of what's to come. I took an extra long shower this morning. Shaved, groomed the necessary areas. Kept my hair down and lightly curled. I even put on a little makeup, wanting to feel pretty.

Hints of my jasmine shampoo and cherry-infused body mist waft around me as I move from table to table. Smiling at a customer I've never seen before, I set down his plate of pancakes and a mug of hot coffee, and tell him to enjoy his meal.

He looks up at me, a cigarette pressed between his fingers.

The smile he stretches looks almost fearsome.

A chill slithers through me as I glance down at the feathering of smoke emitting from the glowing butt of his cigarette. Clearing my throat, I tell him, "You can't smoke in here, sir."

"Mmm," he murmurs, a gravelly rumble. "Is that so?" He takes a long drag, then snuffs it out on his stack of hotcakes. "My apologies."

Odd.

The smoke-free act in Illinois has been in effect for years now.

Maybe he's not from around here.

I force a smile.

A long, gnarly scar lines the side of his face when he turns fully toward me and reaches for his coffee. "You look like you're doing well, Tabitha."

I blink, then look down at my crooked nametag attached to my blouse. I sense the recognition in his eyes and realize he's probably seen me on the news. My skin heats, anxiety flaring. "Um, thank you. I am doing well."

"Stay safe out there," he adds, sipping his coffee, his eyes a haunting shade of clear blue. "There are a lot of nasties lurking in the shadows these days. You can never be too careful."

The warning sounds intentional, yet strangely out of place.

Instincts firing, I take a step back from the table and grip my empty tray with both hands. "Let me know if you need anything else," I tell him, keeping my voice level and my nerves in check.

As I spin away from him, he replies coolly, "I certainly will."

I feel rattled and out of sorts as I race back into the kitchen to collect my next order.

My breaths tangle. My heart skips.

In an attempt to avoid a scolding from my boss, I paint on a smile and fill my tray with more eggs, more pancakes, more bowls of jams and butter, and fill my mind with Gabe.

Don't look down.

Keep flying.

Inhaling a calming breath, I get back to work.

When I glance over to the booth where the man once sat, I see that it's now empty.

All that's left is his half-sipped coffee, a plate of untouched pancakes with a cigarette sticking out the top, and a twenty-dollar bill.

Two Years Earlier

THE MAN HADN'T BEEN DONE with me, after all.

It had only been wishful thinking. My own hopeful imagination.

To make matters worse, he was even more rough with me now, as if he were taking his anger out on me and making up for all that lost time.

I pretended to be okay with it, forcing back my tears and heartbreak. Bottling up my grief. Holding in the sickness that churned my stomach.

I'd been vomiting more regularly, even with hardly any food in my belly. The circumstances were making me physically, painfully ill.

And yet, through it all, I hadn't let go of the little ring tucked inside my hand.

It was all I had to hold on to.

After he finished with me and stalked back up the staircase, I collapsed to my bottom and leaned over, retching onto the cement. It was nothing but bile. Multiple puddles lay strewn beside me, so I scooted around the pole to get away from the evidence.

"You're…sick," Matthew murmured from across the room, casted in shadows and defeat.

My chest heaved as I tried to catch my breath. "I feel terrible."

"Do you have…a fever?"

"No. It's just my stomach and anxiety. That monster has been brutal with me lately." My voice cracked. "I'm not sure how much more I can take."

Thankfully, Matthew had been spared from any more bizarre attacks.

His face was still bruised and lungs still wheezy, but his cuts and gashes seemed to be healing as much as the conditions would allow. I didn't see any telltale infection.

"You look like you're…fading before my eyes," he whispered softly.

His words had the nausea swirling in my gut again, but I tempered the queasiness and tried to make light of it all. "I thought you couldn't see me without your glasses."

He tried to chuckle, but the effort made him wince. "That could be the reason."

A small smile stretched. My lips cracked with the gesture, chapped and brittle, but mostly because I couldn't remember the last time they'd turned up like that.

Silence hovered between us as the mood darkened once again.

Matthew watched me from his pole, his eyebrows dipping, a prelude to sadder words I was certain I didn't want to hear. "I'm worried…about you."

"I'm fine. I…" I wasn't fine. I had never been less fine. My throat stung with leftover bile as I added, "He didn't feed us today."

My stomach rolled. After our bathroom break earlier, the man had dragged us back down the stairs without our usual sandwich.

Matthew didn't respond, closing his eyes and leaning the back of his head against the pole. He knew there was nothing he could say that would ease my anxiety, because it only meant one thing—

The man would be done with us soon.

But we'd already survived two weeks down there. That had to mean *something*. He had kept us alive for that long, which meant he could still have a plan for us.

We could escape.

We could.

"Matthew, we need to start thinking. We need to figure a way out of here, fast."

He blinked his eyes back open but didn't lift his head, almost like the effort was too great. "You've triggered something in him. You remind him of…somebody. His mother; I feel confident about that. Keep going…keep wearing him down."

I shook my head. "We need a *new* plan. A different plan. This one isn't working," I exclaimed. "You've seen how he's been with me—he doesn't care about me at all. I'm nothing but a plaything to him."

I watched the slow rise and fall of his chest as he studied me through the darkened room.

A few seconds ticked by before he murmured, "I've seen it."

"So then you know that this—"

"I've seen it from a different perspective," he interjected. Matthew shifted against the pole, hissing with pain. When he caught his breath, he finished, "This bond I've encouraged you to create…it's not working, not in the traditional sense. He's a psychopath. It's impossible to make him fall in love with you, so you need to…pivot. Offer him a mother's love, instead. Be nurturing."

I gawked at him, stunned. "That's absurd. He's been absolutely vile with me. Evil and cruel."

"He's overcompensating," he stated. "He's reminding himself that you're just a toy, nothing of value. He hates that you remind him of Fiona, and he's taking that aggression out on you. But, the fact that he's associating you with her…that's hope, Tabitha. That's where I see hope for you."

"What?" I shook my head. "No. You're looking for reason when there is only madness. Look at what he did to you," I insisted. "There was no reason for it. It was senseless."

"There *was* a reason. It was because of you." Swallowing, he let out a raspy breath. "And then he stopped. Because of you. Because of whom he sees when he looks at you."

No.

There had to be another way. We were running out of time.

"Matthew…I think we need to utilize the time we have free of our chains. I know it's risky, but maybe we can think of a plan. Some way of getting the best of him, to distract him long enough to grab his gun. He's not superhuman, he's not undefeatable. We can do this."

Matthew let out a slow breath. "I'm at my lowest, Tabitha… my weakest. The chance of overpowering him is slim to none at this point. He's armed, he's unpredictable, and he's twice my size."

"We have nothing left to lose."

"*I* do," he gritted out. "I have something left to lose."

My eyes watered.

Me.

He was referring to me.

"Please…if we don't try, we'll both die down here. I'm sure of it."

His throat worked as he stared at me. "I'm not sure of that yet. I still see another way out, and until that route has been eliminated, I can't risk your life," he told me, his tone pleading. "The odds of me failing are high, and if I do…you'll never see the other side of these walls."

I threw my head against the pole and slammed my eyes shut.

The plan wasn't going to work.

There was no logic in the way that monster thought and acted. His mind was black, his soul blacker. His heart was made of nothing but ashes and—

Present Day

I'M PULLED from the interview prematurely by the sound of police sirens blaring right outside the house.

I freeze, my words drying up.

I realize there are many houses on this street, many houses other than his, and still, my heart beats wildly like a bass drum.

No…a snare drum.

The rattling, shrieky kind.

"Everything okay?" Evan wonders, pausing the recording. His brows furrow with concern as he stares at me across the desk. "You look pale."

"The…the sirens. They sound close."

He blinks twice, as if just noticing them. "Shit, yeah, you're right." Pushing away from the desk, he rises to his feet. "I'll check it out."

I follow.

I do more than follow, led by the tight knot of dread-filled intuition in my belly, and race ahead of Evan, wrenching open the screen door and poking my head out and to the left.

My stomach drops out of me.

Multiple squad cars and an ambulance are lined up in front of Gabe's house.

Medics are in his driveway, bent over beside his Challenger.

A crowd of people watch from the sidewalk.

There's a gurney.

A gurney.

My gasping scream hits the air as I shove my way through the doorway, forgoing my sandals. I run full-speed down the sidewalk with bare feet, my heels cutting on stones and rock, tears biting at my eyes. "Gabe!"

I hear Evan calling after me, but I keep going. Keep running. Keep barreling forward until I'm close enough to discover Gabe sprawled out in the middle of his driveway, spattered in blood.

Another scream shreds my lungs.

I'm in that basement again.

Matthew, Matthew, Matthew.

Gabe.

Both of their bloodied, battered faces stare back at me.

I can't breathe.

I can't breathe.

"Miss."

A hand curls around my upper arm, tugging me back when I lunge forward. "No…let me go!" I'm fighting, kicking, resisting. "He's my fiancé!" I shout, holding up the hand with the star ring. I don't care if it's a lie. I need to be near him, I need to get to him, make sure he's okay.

Please be okay.

The hand releases me.

I stumble toward him, my lungs caving in, my heart buried alive. He's still wearing his work vest, the setting sun reflecting off of it and lighting him up. I fall to my knees as EMTs continue to take his vitals. "Gabe…*Gabe*…"

His bruised eyelids flutter open at the sound of my voice, and I swear he smiles. "Hey…Wifey," he rasps.

"Oh, my God," I whimper, reaching for his hand. He's talking, he's breathing, he's alive. "What happened?"

"Just some…muggers."

He's also wheezing.

He's wheezing like Matthew wheezed in the days before he took his final breath right in front of me.

It's happening again.

I'm losing another man I lo—

My heart clenches.

I squeeze his hand as two EMTs carefully move him onto the gurney.

Gabe winces, hissing through his teeth. "Watch the…ribs." His eyes find me, swollen, black and blue. "Rain check…on the date," he murmurs, still holding onto that tiny smile.

I'm near hysterics.

I feel it climbing up my chest, so I breathe in and out, over and over, trying so hard to keep it at bay. The last thing he needs to do is worry about me, too.

"We need to go, Miss. You're welcome to meet us at Condell," a medic tells me.

Our fingers drift apart in slow motion as rubble from his driveway digs into my kneecaps and terror digs into my heart. "Gabe," I cry out.

I can't hear whatever he says as he's taken away and hauled into the back of the ambulance.

Evan stands off near the sidewalk, talking to a police officer, giving a statement, telling him he didn't hear anything suspicious.

My ears pick up bits and pieces while my eyes stay locked on the ambulance as it pulls off down the street.

Two men.

Multiple witnesses.

Robbery, mugging, ambush.

I grip the front of my blouse, calming my rattled chest, keeping my dark thoughts from overtaking me. As my eyes dip down to the driveway, something catches my eye.

I frown.

A half-smoked cigarette lies snuffed out beside my feet.

CHAPTER 27

TABITHA

I fly through the front door of his raised ranch shortly after Oliver and Sydney drop him off from the hospital the next day. "Gabe!" My feet trip over each step, my legs unable to catch up to my eager heart. I wanted to be the one to take him home. I wanted to be the one by his side when he was released.

But my boss threatened to fire me when I attempted to call in this morning. It's only been a day since using my vacation time and there was nobody available to cover my shift.

Liquid dribbles out the top of a cup of tea when I reach the top of his staircase, my attention flicking left, then right.

I hear water running. The sound of shower jets fuse with loud alternative-rock music spilling from the hall bathroom, and I exhale a deep breath, itching to hug him, needing to see him.

It's been a twenty-four-hour whirlwind.

Gabe was lucky. He only suffered some bruising to his face, a split lip, a concussion, and two cracked ribs. They kept him overnight to monitor the concussion, but ultimately, decided he was well enough to return home today.

Lucky.

I'm not sure that's the right word for what he went through, but given my first-hand experience with violent attacks, I know it could have been so much worse.

Oliver and Sydney had been at the mall when I called them from the ER, informing them of Gabe's mugging. They dropped everything and met me in his recovery room as police officers, nurses, and doctors filed in and out, checking his vitals and asking Gabe to recount what had happened to him.

He was vague, explaining that it had all happened so fast, and he couldn't identify the men who had attacked him.

It was strange.

He still had his wallet on him, filled with over one-hundred dollars in cash.

According to Gabe, the two men were solely interested in something called a Quad Cortex—a pricey, modern-day amp used for music and recording—that he recently purchased and had left in his car. I wasn't aware of it and hadn't seen it before, but he claims it was all they took.

Trying to calm my worried jitters, I take a seat on his couch and set the beverage beside me. I drop my head in my hands and tug my hair back with my fingers, waiting for the shower to turn off.

I ended up canceling my interview with Evan this evening, given the circumstances.

It'll be one of my final interviews.

Part of me wishes I could delay it indefinitely.

A few minutes later, my head pops up when the water shuts off and the music stops. Rising to my feet, I wring my hands together as I wait for the bathroom door to burst open.

Gabe steps out wearing only a pair of gym shorts as he dries his hair with a bath towel.

My breath hitches.

He spins toward me, startled at first; almost jumping back, as if he were expecting to see somebody else. Someone worse.

I understand that feeling all too well—the looking over your shoulder, the notion of being watched, stalked, followed. My arms drop to my sides, my eyes wide and glazed with fresh tears.

His body relaxes when recognition settles in, and a smile forms. "Tabs."

I run to him.

Adrenaline and sweet relief carry me down the short hallway, past the kitchen, until I'm leaping into his arms. He stumbles on his feet with a wince, and I jolt backward, cursing myself for being careless with his injuries. "I-I'm so sorry…I didn't mean—"

He grabs me.

Kisses me.

I moan, sagging helplessly against him, my hands flying out and landing in his hair. His bottom lip is swollen and split, but he doesn't seem to care, his own hands tangling in my loose tresses as he devours my mouth. Our tongues are hungry, needy, aching to taste and feel.

He's alive, he's alive, he's alive.

But he's not okay. He needs time to heal.

I pull back with a sharp gasp, cradling his bruised face between my palms. "Gabe, you're hurt. God, look what they did to you…" My gaze skims over his black eye, his cuts and scrapes. His torso is also riddled with purple splotches. I dance my fingertips down his collarbone, his chest, his abs. They stop at his waistband, and my eyes drop to the large tent in his shorts. Swallowing, I glance back up. His eyes are hooded, heated. "I was so scared. I thought I was going to lose you…"

"I'm fine," he grinds out. His voice is strained, either from lust or from the pain he's trying to hide from me. "Just a few scratches."

"Gabe…"

"Don't worry." He pulls me back to him, wrapping both arms around me and tugging me close. One hand cups the back of my head, the other splays across my spine. He breathes deeply into my hair. "I won't let anything happen to you."

Me?

He's worried about me, after he was just left for dead in his own driveway?

I inch away. "I'm not worried about me. I'm worried about *you.*"

A curious look dances across his expression, causing his eyes to darken. I can't read it, but my instincts tell me he's holding something back. "Were you honest with the police?" I wonder gently.

His hold on me loosens, his eyes dipping to the side. "I was mugged."

That wasn't a direct answer.

My body tenses up. "Gabe," I whisper. "Are you hiding something?"

"Of course not." He shakes his head, throat tight, then moves past me toward the living room. There's no limp to his step, but he moves slowly, clearly still in pain. "You brought me coffee?"

I watch the bare planks of his back ripple, muscles tautening as he strides over to the couch. "It's tea." Following behind him, still concerned, I add, "I thought it might help you relax."

He collapses onto the couch, unable to hold back the hiss. When I move into his line of sight, a crooked smile claims his face, injuries cast aside. "You got me sleepy tea."

"Yes." I nod, emotion catching in my throat. "Gabe, please—"

"Come here."

I pause in front of him, debating if I should press for more answers. More truths. But my attention snags on the look in his eyes staring back at me, something earnest, something filled with yearning, and I drop the questioning for now and pace toward the empty space beside him on the couch.

When I'm within arm's reach, he leans forward and captures me around the waist, coaxing me into his lap. I exhale sharply, not expecting it, my knees landing on either side of him, caging him in. I'm brought back to the last time we were in this position on his couch—the night after my first interview when I told him he didn't need to wait for me.

I was afraid he'd be waiting forever.

But he's still here, still with me, wanting me, and a wicked, buried part of me doesn't know why.

My hands graze up his chest and latch onto his shoulders as I tilt forward, pressing our foreheads together. "Gabe…"

He drags both hands up my thighs, curling them around my waist. Giving me a squeeze, he murmurs on a wrought breath, "You're all I thought about. All I saw."

I close my eyes and swallow. "What?"

His erection presses into me.

Right between my thighs, where I crave him most.

"I was lying on my driveway, hardly conscious, and all I could think about was you." His hips arch up, grinding into me. "I'm so fucking crazy about you." A groan rumbles through him, through us both. "I'd do anything for you."

I sigh, a blend of a moan and a sob. "Why?"

"Why?" he parrots, the word edged with disbelief, a frown creasing.

"With all the girls in the world, why me?" I need to know; I need answers. He could have anybody, yet it's *me* he wants. Me and my band of ghosts. Shaking my head, not understanding, I purge my insecurities as I pull away. "I'm broken, Gabe. I'm damaged. I'm—"

He grabs my face between his hands, forcing me to look at him. "You've got it all mixed up, Tabs," he tells me, our eyes locking together as his thumbs stroke the sensitive skin below my ears. "With you in the world, how can there be anyone else?"

Tears fill my eyes.

Air sticks like cellophane in my throat.

I blink at him, lost for words.

And when I finally breathe out, when I sigh again, it only sounds like untethered relief. It's a release; a different kind of purging.

It's a softening of my hard-bitten edges, a melting of my iron walls. It's a little light, newly emblazed, like a firefly that's been trapped inside my cupped palm, finally flying free.

He's shown me a thousand times, a thousand different ways, that he loves me.

But it's *these* words that break through.

It's *this* look in his eyes that breaches me soul-deep.

I kiss him hard.

My mouth finds his like I'm taking my first breath after only breathing in water for hours, days, years. It's more than hunger, more than thirst, more than basic need.

We're a tangle of groans and roaming hands. A flurry of wet kisses and desperate tongues. His mouth opens wide as he angles my face, taking everything I give him.

And it is, it's everything. I give him everything.

I pull on his hair, graze my nails down his neck, slide my fingers down his body and feel him shudder beneath my touch. Electricity surges. His hands disappear up my yellow sundress, warm skin on mine. My neck arches, offering him more, my long hair spilling down my back.

"You're so beautiful," he murmurs, sliding his tongue across my jawline. "So fucking gorgeous."

I don't fight his words this time because, right now, I do feel beautiful.

I feel untethered and deliciously alive.

Gabe's teeth nick down the side of my throat, leaving love bites, before he lifts my dress all the way up and pulls it over my head. My bare breasts meet his eyes, and he dips forward, sucking one into his mouth.

Yes.

God, yes, this is what I want.

This urgency, this need.

I moan, my eyes closing, head still tipped backward. I grind myself into his lap, already feeling like I could come from the friction alone. "Gabe…God, please, I need you inside me."

"Fuck, Tabs…" he murmurs around my breast, moving to suck on the other. "I want you in my bed. Not here."

Taking him by the hand, I scutter off his lap and help him to his feet. He tugs me to his chest, kissing me as he walks me backward down the hallway, but I pull away, panting, "You're hurting. We don't have to…"

His mouth drags across my cheek as we continue to stumble down the hall. "The only thing higher than the amount of ibuprofen in my system is my absolute determination to make you come tonight."

A moan slips out, my legs turning to jelly beneath me. Pivoting us both to the right, Gabe guides me into his bedroom, illuminated only by the moon and stars. He spins us around and collapses onto the edge of the mattress, pulling me between his spread knees and taking my breast in his mouth.

Another moan slices through the silence as I steady myself, my hands linking at his nape. My head falls back again, lust flooding my veins and revving my pulse. "A-are you sure?" I try once more, still worried I'll hurt him. "You're injured…"

He swirls my nipple with his tongue. Then he grips me by the back of my head and yanks me lower, nipping the shell of my ear as he husks, "My cock works just fine."

Wet heat pools between my thighs, shivers dancing down the back of my neck. My underwear is soaked through, and almost as if he's fully aware of that, he tugs the fabric down my legs and cups me there, two of his fingers slipping inside.

I watch the carnal look that claims his face, twists his expression, has his eyes slamming shut. "Jesus, you're wet," he says, pumping his fingers in and out, then sliding them forward and rubbing my clit. "Did I do this to you?"

I practically fall against him, weightless, boneless. "Yes."

"Do you remember your safe-word?"

I nod, swallowing. "Tabula Rasa."

"Say it and we stop. Say it and it's over." He kisses my fore-head, a touch of tenderness amid the frenzy. "You never have to worry about me taking more than you're willing to give."

"I won't say it." I bend to find his lips and kiss him once, twice. "I'll never say that to you." Three kisses, four kisses. "I trust you."

His hand slides up to lightly grip the column of my throat, a possessive hold that has my spine straightening, my legs clenching around him as I move into his lap and straddle him.

Gabe falls back onto the mattress and inches his way up toward the headboard. I crawl over him, pausing at his hips, at the rock-hard erection straining his shorts. My hands tremble as I curl my fingers into his waistband and work the shorts down his thighs. When his cock springs free, I take him in my hand and stroke him, relishing the sounds he makes and the way he tries to watch me fist his thick cock but can hardly keep his head up, too overcome with pleasure.

I lean forward and wrap my lips around the tip. Precum wets my tongue in salty musk, pulling a moan from my throat as I take him further into my mouth and suck.

His hips buck up with a sharp hiss. "Christ."

A hand tangles in my hair, holding me to him. A second hand joins, and he guides my mouth up and down his cock while I swirl my tongue and hollow my cheeks.

"Fuck...*fuck*," he groans. "Come over here and sit on my face."

The words drip with something primal. I slowly trail my tongue up his length as I lift my head and release him. My core pulses at his order, at the thought of his mouth on me there.

Nerves trickle their way in, too, causing me to hesitate.

He lifts his head, our eyes meeting through the dimly lit room as he curls his hands around my waist. "Kiss me first," he says, sensing my falter, my trace of jitters.

I tilt forward and drape my body across his, my breasts to his chest, holding my lower half up by the knees so I don't apply any pressure to his ribs. I feel his hands trail up my spine, feather-light. Reassuring. My lips fall to his, just as light, just as tender, and our tongues meet in a sweet dance. Ribbons of my dark hair curtain us like a veil as the kiss gains wings, causing my courage to take flight. The throbbing between my legs has me breaking the kiss, has me desperate for release, and I quickly crawl up his body, refusing to succumb to insecurities.

I position myself over him, my limbs vibrating as I hold on to the headboard.

My heart is pounding with anticipation.

I'm soaked with need.

Gabe groans, gripping my thighs and hauling me down onto his mouth.

I cry out.

Loudly, uncaged.

Oh, my God.

And then I glance down, my jaw dropped in pleasure, and watch as he eats me out.

I realize it was a mistake to look down because it hits me, instantly, with no warning.

Seconds.

An orgasm rips through me within seconds of his tongue plunging inside me, my clit grinding against his face. I clutch the headboard with one hand, the other reaching down to fist his hair, my knuckles turning white as I shake and shudder on top of him, shamelessly riding out the waves and moaning his name.

He doesn't stop when the tingles peter out, his tongue lapping up my release, his fingers digging into my thighs to keep me steady. His moans sound hungry as his mouth continues to feast on me. When his teeth lightly nip my sensitive clit, I almost collapse. "Gabe…"

His lips and chin are glistening when he pulls back, breathing ragged. "Fuck, that was hot. You came so fucking fast."

I wiggle my way south, my wet juncture sliding down his chest. "I want to taste you again. I want to do that to you."

I'm moving down his body when he reaches for my shoulders. "Tabs…fuck, wait," he says, sounding desperate. "The second you do that, I'm coming in your mouth."

The notion arouses me.

Knowing that I have that much control, that much power over him.

The thought that I can do to him what he just did to me has my thighs clenching with need.

"Maybe I want you to."

His moan sounds tortured as he tugs on my hair, coaxing me back up. "I need to be inside you."

I falter, knowing I need that, too. "Okay," I breathe out.

Gabe twists toward his nightstand, wincing as he moves. "Condom," he hisses.

I take over, climbing over to the drawer to fetch it instead. Part of me wants to feel him bare inside of me, free of barriers. Uncut intimacy.

But I'm not on birth control. It wouldn't be responsible.

Riffling through the drawer, I pull out a foil packet and hold it up, watching it glint in the moonlight streaming in through the window. I realize I don't even know how to put it on him, having never done it before. Inexperience squeezes my chest.

He must not notice because he takes it from my hand and tears it open with his teeth, pulling out the rubber and sliding it over his cock.

I gulp.

Gabe kicks his shorts all the way off and wraps an arm around my middle, tugging me back to him. "You'll have to be on top this time."

Climbing back over him, I lean forward for a kiss. I'm nervous. I'm scared to be in control, but I realize he's in no condition to take charge right now.

"I'll make it up to you," he says softly, nibbling my bottom lip. "Next time I'll ride you hard, fuck you like you want me to."

I dissolve into a puddle above him, plunging my tongue into his mouth as I let the fear fade away. His golden hair is a mess of soft waves, still shower-damp between my fingers as I tug on it and grind myself up and down his erection. Arousal ripples through me. His hips jerk, a groan rumbling in his throat while our tongues twist and twine in a wet dance. I lift up, positioning myself over him, inching back and forth and glancing down to watch his thick head glide along my slickness.

The image is erotic, stirring my desire. I let out a whimper as I lower myself, and he slips inside of me by an inch.

"Tabs," he rasps, my name falling out like a guttural plea.

My whimper morphs into a moan, feeling him stretch me. I look up and revel in the pure lust glowing in his eyes as he watches.

Holding on to his shoulders, I slide lower, lower, taking him all the way inside, throwing my head back with a frayed gasp as his fingers dig into my hipbones and he trembles beneath me.

I don't move for a moment, can hardly breathe.

Then I lean forward, skin to skin, wriggling my hips as I adjust to his girth. Our foreheads knock together, our breaths unsteady and beating against each other's lips. One of his hands moves to tangle in my hair, to cup the back of my head to keep our faces aligned.

I move a little. Watch his jaw tick, his teeth clench, eyes still locked.

His gaze is heated, engaged, skimming my face like he can't believe he's inside me.

My lips part, mewling sounds tickling my throat.

I move again, this time with more intent, raising my hips and inching back down.

Gabe's eyes close briefly, his head tipping back with a groan. "Fuck," he whispers.

The pleasure hums low in my belly, and I feel him there, filling me deep. He's everywhere, he's everything. Both of his hands sift through my hair, nails scraping my scalp as he gives me control, lets me set the pace. I move faster, lifting higher each time, falling harder.

My moans are squeaky and shaky as I grind against him, lifting and falling, drowning in the sensations, in the innate connection I feel.

"So gorgeous…watching your body moving above me, in control," he says, fisting my hair with both hands, his head elevating as our foreheads meld together. "Riding me. Taking my cock."

"Ohh, Gabe…" I moan, the waves of heat unfurling as I grind into him harder. My cheeks burn, my heart drums in my chest.

I feel powerful, feminine, free.

Our noses brush together, our eyes holding tight.

"Am I hurting you?" he asks.

"No," I murmur. "You're healing me."

He tugs my face down to his, our tongues colliding. The kiss has my hips pumping faster, my pelvis grinding, my internal muscles squeezing and taking. His moans vibrate right through me, telling me he's close. I straighten on top of him. Gabe lifts his knees as his hands fall back down to my waist, guiding my body as it moves up and down.

"Fuck, baby. That's it," he pants, practically growling as he holds on to me. "You're so fucking perfect. So sexy taking my dick."

My breasts bounce. My back bows.

His words spur me, making me feel like a goddess. Beautiful and worshiped. I dig my nails into his kneecap to keep me balanced as my other hand palms my breast.

"You're gonna make me come," he grits out, lips parted, eyes half-lidded.

Another orgasm begins to crest as I watch him come undone, knowing it's because of me, because of what I'm doing to him. I drape myself over him again until we're chest to chest and my hips are pumping furiously, chasing a second release.

When I peak, it's sky-born thunder rolling through me. Lightning heat and shimmering rainfall. Spasms seize me from toes to top, my thighs clenching through the pinnacle, my hand stealing one of his as I lace our fingers together and kiss him while I come apart.

I'm with you. I'm with you, Gabe.

He holds me tight, moaning into my mouth as his body shudders with his own release. I feel his cock jerk inside of me, his muscles tensing, his hand squeezing mine.

My movements slow, my skin sheened in sweat. We're both winded, lips still pressed together as we come down from the high. I can't help but smile against his mouth. "Hi."

His eyelids flutter open as his own grin stretches. "Hi."

I roll off of him to keep from collapsing on his injured ribs. "Are you okay?"

"Mmm." Gabe twists toward me, pulling me to him until we're lying on our sides facing each other. "Never been better."

"I didn't hurt you?"

"I'm sure tomorrow will say otherwise, but right now, I could fucking fly."

Snuggling into him, I press a kiss to the center of his neck, exhaling a tapered sigh. My eyes close with contentment when he strokes my hair, tucking it behind my ear.

"Be right back," he whispers.

I burrow into the bedcovers that smell like driftwood and salt breezes, my eyes peeling open to watch him slide off the bed, carefully, slowly, and pull himself up.

There's no hiding the flinch or the hiss through his teeth, telling me he's in pain. My heart aches, watching him trudge to the adjoining bathroom and pause in the doorway to grip the frame, catching his breath.

"Gabe—"

"I'm good," he says quickly, voice strained. "Promise."

He disappears behind the door and returns moments later, still naked, free of the condom. My skin heats as he climbs back into bed half-hard and uncaring that he's bare before me. I'm hidden beneath the bed covers, vulnerability sneaking inside now that we're wading in the aftermath.

Gabe scoots closer to me, gathering me in his arms, as one hand drifts under the blankets and trails to my backside. He gives it a squeeze. "No regrets?" he wonders, lips grazing my forehead.

"No regrets."

My knees curl up, my hands tucked beneath my cheek as exhaustion settles in and a sense of peace washes over me.

I don't need music to lull me to sleep.

I don't need anything other than this.

His arms around me. His beating heart. His warm breath feathering along my hairline.

I've never felt more cherished.

More loved.

More safe.

I'm finally flying.

CHAPTER 28

GABE

After a rigorous security screening including metal detectors, pat-downs, and a body scan, as well as providing ample identification, a background check, and my future first-born child, I'm finally guided to a visitation room by a guy who looks like Lou Ferrigno.

The maximum-security prison is cold, joyless, and smells like feet.

I don't want to be here, not by a fucking landslide, but I didn't have a choice.

I'm out of options at this point.

The open-table room I'm brought into is even more sterile and depressing. It resembles my old Catholic elementary school cafeteria with its white paneled ceilings, squeaky, checkered flooring, and brassy, artificial light. The few windows in the room are barred, and the wide-open space is only furnished with a bunch of tables and metal chairs that even a cadaver would find less than adequate.

The odor in the room is a marrying of chemicals and disinfectant fused with an overcompensating amount of lemon, pit stains, and, well—still feet, but feet with the makings of a fungal infection.

I try not to gag when Ferrigno leads me toward the prisoner I'll have to keep myself from mauling.

We wind through a plethora of tables, some housing cuffed inmates, and some empty. One of the men looks like he's barely eighteen, but his eyes are long-past dead as he stares with vacancy at the tearful woman across from him.

A chill slithers down my back.

And then that chill manifests into an ice storm in my veins when my eyes land on the man I once called my father.

Good 'ol Pops.

Now he's just a rodent who tried to burn my stepbrother and best friend alive.

I figured he'd be wearing an orange jumpsuit like they do in the movies, but he's dressed in a khaki-colored uniform instead, with buttons down the front and unhemmed sleeves. His usual shadowing of stubble has grown out to a full beard of gold and silver, and his bronzed complexion from days of golfing under the sun has faded to a chalky shade of gray.

What makes him look older, though, is the downturn of his shoulders and the haggard expression he wears as he gazes down at his handcuffs.

He used to emit confidence.

Composure.

A silent power I once confused with strength.

Now, he's nothing but a gangly, dried-up man with hollow eyes and sunken-in cheeks. The extent of his burns, from that same fire he set in motion, are far worse than mine, and the sight of him covered in puckered, blackened scar tissue casing the left side of his face and roping down his neck, offers me a small pocket of consolation.

He's a nobody now.

A waste of oxygen.

The correctional officer points me to his table, as if I didn't already recognize the shit-stain sitting slumped over in a metal chair, bound by silver chains.

Apparently, we have thirty minutes, which sounds like twenty-five minutes too long.

Travis stands slowly, his eyes flaring when he spots me. "Son," he says.

I freeze beside the table, my hands balling to stone at my sides. "Don't ever fucking call me that again."

Sighing with a touch of resignation, he sits back down. "It kills me that you're seeing me like this."

"It *kills* you?" I yank my own chair out from the table and plop down, a solid few feet away. Breathing the same air as him is making my stomach roll. "You have no idea how much I wish it would."

"You don't mean that," he dismisses me, eyes drifting to the left, as if he's already bored. "I'm atoning for my missteps. Just look at me." Chains jangle when he raises his arms.

I gawk at him, my brows lifting to my hairline. "Missteps? You hired someone to murder my stepbrother because he caught you molesting the neighbor girl. Decades later, he shows back up because—*surprise*, your plan backfired—and you tie him and his girlfriend to a fucking bedpost and set their bedroom on fire to try and cover up your depraved secrets."

"Hmm." He tilts his head to the side, eyeing the room like he has better things to do. "That's the rumor going around, I hear. I'm confident I'll be awarded a fair trial."

This is a fucking joke.

My legs itch to carry me right back out the door, but unfortunately, this meeting matters.

It matters because *she* matters.

When all I do is stare at him blankly, Travis leans back in his chair. "I assume you have questions."

"A few, yeah. Tell me why you have some prick breathing down my neck, demanding over a million dollars."

He clears his throat, lacing his fingers together atop the table. "Well, there's this loan," he explains. "My intentions were noble. There was a restaurant I'd been in the process of—"

"I don't give a shit about the restaurant. Tell me why you have him coming after *me*." I slap the palm of my hand against my chest. "One of his cronies gave me a concussion in my driveway and threatened my girlfriend."

"Girlfriend?" The barest smirk tilts the corner of his mouth. "This is a proud-father moment, Gabe. I never thought I'd see the day when you traded in your barbaric bachelor ways for a chance to settle down."

My eyes narrow. "Answer the question."

"There was no question, and you didn't say please."

I stand from the chair, prepared to bolt.

"All right, all right," he relents. "I'll explain everything. Sit."

I don't.

I glare at him and fold my arms.

Scratching at his graying whiskers with tethered hands, Travis exhales slowly and fumbles for an explanation that I'm certain will only be a partial truth.

"It was a private loan through a…*disreputable* source," he discloses, glancing down at the table, his jaw ticking. "I had every intention of paying it back, of course, but circumstances did not play out the way I'd intended." He holds out his cuffed wrists like visual evidence. "The man in charge wants his money back since the restaurant went under. He's not the friendliest."

"I couldn't tell."

"He has a frightening amount of power," he continues. "Connections with an Irish mafia family in Chicago called the O'Learys. I'm sure you've heard of them."

"Yeah, I have them all on speed dial."

"Anyway, he seems to be the one pulling the strings. He'll do whatever he needs to do to get paid, and he's proficient at making people disappear." Travis shrugs. "Since I'm in here, and you're out there, you're regrettably in the line of fire."

"Regrettably," I echo with disdain. "Interesting how you've been blowing up my phone recently. You must really have my best interest at hand, trying to warn me."

"Of course I do. This is my mess, and I'd hate for you to fall victim to these vultures."

"Such a doting dad," I sing-song, canting my head. "I mean, you're obviously protected in here. There's no way your ass is on the line, too. It would be illogical to think that this jackoff might have someone on the inside threatening your life if he doesn't get his money."

Travis's face falls, his eyes thinning as he stares at me. A few quiet beats pass between us. And then a knowing grin blooms on his lips as he squares his shoulders. "I see you're not as dense as I thought, Gabe. All those years of excessive marijuana use didn't seem to scramble your brains, after all." The smirk broadens. "A miscalculation on my part. Perhaps I have raised you well."

Everything inside of me wants to fly across the table and throttle him. Wrap my fingers around his throat until he turns purple. Watch him wheeze and choke on his own pathetic breath.

Pretty sure the only thing holding me back is the notion that I might have to share a jail cell with him because of it.

I keep my hatred in check by grinding my molars together

until they're close to chipping. "You and I both know I don't have that kind of money."

"You would if you managed to listen to even a shred of my advice growing up. Instead, you prioritized partying and hook-ups over making a prolific life for yourself. It's disappointing."

"Right," I bite out. "I'm deeply shamed that I failed to follow in your felonious footsteps. How silly of me to secure a morally acceptable job and use my money to pay bills and feed myself instead of hiring hitmen and borrowing millions of dollars from crooks. You should write a memoir or something."

"I'm considering it."

"Tell me where to get the money," I demand. "Tell me how to clean up another one of your fucking messes."

His cold eyes rake over the scar along my bicep that peeks out over the collar of my T-shirt, drinking in the consequences of his last "mess." A condescending hum skims his lips. "I heard you were a real hero that night." Travis snaps his eyes up to mine and leans forward, grazing his tongue along his teeth. "You marched right through those flames with little regard for yourself. Pulled your brother to safety, along with that burdensome Neville girl."

My chest tightens. That blustering Christmas night flashes through my mind like a movie reel of post-traumatic stress.

Smoke fills my lungs. Flames lick my skin.

Sydney's wails of desperation echo in my ears to this day as I yanked her off of Oliver and carried her down the staircase.

"I hate you! I hate you! Let me go!"

She didn't know it was me, at first. She didn't recognize the arms around her as she kicked and flailed and clawed at me.

If Oliver had perished in that fire, she *would* hate me...that much I know.

Syd had planned to die that day, curled up on top of her lover as he lay helpless on the bed—anchored to the headboard with rope—the unforgiving blaze more than eager to swallow them whole.

I could hardly breathe as I raced back up the stairs and into the yellow-orange wall of flames. It was 360 degrees of black smoke and terror. I used my pocketknife to cut Oliver loose, hauling him off the bed seconds before the ceiling caved in behind us.

He said one word to me as we stumbled down the stairs, coughing and choking.

"Brother."

I blink back to the visitation room.

I can almost taste the soot in my throat as I stare across the table at the man who nearly killed us, all in a sick attempt to save himself. My fingers dig into my kneecaps to keep myself from strangling him. "I'd do it all again if I had to," I murmur. "In a heartbeat."

He *tsks* his tongue as if the notion is deplorable. "Such empathy." Another sigh falls out, something patronizing. "Clearly, a weakness from your mother's side."

My fingernails nearly burrow through my jeans. "How do I get the money," I hiss out, less of a question and more of a chewed-off demand.

I'm done with this little rendezvous.

Travis shrugs, noncommittally, glancing at his dirty fingernails. "I was hoping we could put our heads together and figure something out. What do you have in your savings account?"

"Not enough."

"Stocks, investments?"

"I don't have shit, okay? I have my house. My car. A bit of money to get by if the furnace blows or my engine kicks it. That's it." The realization that my father doesn't seem to have a simple solution to this monumental problem has my nerves climbing, heart racing. "What about your house in Lake Geneva? That's got to be a cool mil's worth of blood money. Can't you sell it?"

"My third ex-wife has it. She divorced me, instantly. Took everything."

"Savings?"

"My accounts were frozen thanks to all these absurd charges."

Fuck.

His golden hair, peppered with silver, glints beneath the light fixtures. "What about that lovely mother of yours?" he tries. "She was always the responsible type. Surely, she can contribute something."

"I'm not bringing Mom into this. Not a chance."

"You need to work with me here, Son. I'm not a magician."

I lunge forward, slamming my hands down on the table.

"Don't call me *Son*." My tone drips with venom, each word punctuated.

A guard immediately grabs me by the arm and hauls me back. "Easy. Take a seat," he clips. "This is your one and only warning."

I fall into the metal chair, elbows to knees, head in my hands. Scrubbing my palms over my face, I steeple my fingers and glance up at my father, noting the twinkle in his eyes. The bastard is getting off on watching me sweat. "I'll never forgive you for this. If something happens to her, I'll…" Choking on the thought alone, I lower my voice so only he can hear me. "I'll fucking kill you."

"Bold claim. You're too soft to even hurt a fly."

"He threatened my fucking *girl*," I grind out, teeth bared. "You have no idea what I'm capable of doing if she gets hurt. You've never been in love. The only thing you've ever cared about is yourself." My pulse is throttling with fire and brimstone. "I *will* kill you."

"Guard." Travis lifts his gaze to the beast of a guy pacing our table. "My son is threatening my life. I don't feel safe."

"You're disgusting."

The correctional officer motions me to stand. "We're done here, kid." He signals another guard over to deal with Travis. "Let's go."

I stand from the chair with such force, it almost tips over. "I don't have the money," I say to my father. "Looks like your time is ticking."

"Unlikely." His ankle chains clank across the white-and-blue tiles as he's guided away from the table. "Sounds to me like you have just as much to lose here, *Son*. I'm convinced you'll figure something out."

I'm hauled away by the bicep, my stomach in knots.

"Oh," Travis calls out, glancing back over his shoulder. "Do me a favor and send my regards to Oliver. I certainly hope he's doing well." With a devilish smirk, he disappears around the corner.

A feeling of crippling defeat funnels through me as I'm dragged from the visitation room toward the prison exit. My mind is reeling, my skin itchy. Sweat lines my brow as I swipe the back of my hand across my forehead.

I have no idea how I'm getting myself out of this with only a few days left.

This is impossible.

Travis Wellington fooled a lot of people, but I'll never get over the way he fooled me.

And now?

I need to figure out a way to fool an army of bloodthirsty criminals before they come after the woman I love.

CHAPTER 29

TABITHA

I stand in Evan's driveway with my eyes on the sky.

An airplane flies overhead, and I think about that plane ride we never got to take. I can't help but wonder—if Matthew had made it out of the basement with me, would I have been brave enough to do it?

Would I have stepped on that airplane?

I don't know.

I think what hurts the most is the fact that I never got the chance to find out.

A woman walks by with her dog, sending me a happy wave when my attention pulls away from the condensation trail left behind by the aircraft. Her wave feels *too* happy. I realize it's probably just a normal wave, offered by a regularly happy woman who doesn't know that the person she's waving to is about to relive the unhappiest moment of her life.

So I wave back.

My hand lifts with halfhearted happiness, and I wonder if she notices.

"Hey!"

I jolt in place when Summer calls out to me from the foyer, her foot propping open the screen door. Fiddling with the tungsten ring around my necklace chain, I send her a small smile and step forward, greeting her in the entryway. "Hey, Summer. I haven't seen you in a while."

I set down my purse and swipe my clammy palms down my thighs.

Summer beams at me.

She beams because she doesn't know.

She beams because she has no idea I'm about to recount the single-worst moment of my life, just like the happy waver from the sidewalk. It's funny how life goes on, despite it all. The sun shines brightly when your mind is filled with rain and clouds, and music plays even when you can hardly recognize the melodies. Birds fly when you're collapsed and broken, and you don't understand how they can fly so high, so effortlessly, when you can't even find your own footing, let alone your wings.

People beam.

They wave, and they smile.

And all you want to do is cry.

Tugging on her ponytail, Summer chomps on her bubblegum, oblivious to my plight. "Yeah, my friend Raina and I have been spending the summer doing makeup tutorials online." She points to her dark-violet eyeshadow and inky, winged liner. "Not too bad, huh?"

I clear my throat and force away the bleak thoughts, attempting to beam right back at her. "Very impressive. You could probably teach me a thing or two."

"Tell that to my dad. He thinks I'm too young for makeup."

"You're eternally nine. We've talked about this." Evan appears from the edge of the hallway, pulling a baseball cap off his head and ruffling his hair. A gloom steals the gleam from his eyes when his attention pans from his daughter to me. "Hey, Tabitha. Everything is set up."

His words travel over to me, and I can't hold on to the beam, just as he can't hold on to the gleam.

Everything is set up.

Ready to go.

My heart has been prepped for mass destruction.

I give him a nod and inhale a big breath. "I'll be right there."

Nodding back, he forces a smile and heads back down the hallway while Summer watches him retreat.

She glances back toward me with a frown. "Are you getting to the third-act breakup in the story or something? The mood got weirdly tense."

"Third-act breakup?"

"Yeah, like, in my mom's historical romance books I sneak off to read when I visit her in Tennessee. There's always this tragic turn of events that shakes everything up. I hate that part."

My hands feel shaky, so I lace my fingers together in front of me. "Something like that," I say, clearing my throat. "I think your dad is wrong, by the way. You're far from eternally nine."

She grins, smacking her pink gum between her teeth. As her eyes dip lower, they pause on the star ring still circling my finger. "Oh, hey, you're wearing that ring I gave you." Her eyes sparkle bright blue. "I love it."

I hold it up, watch it glint in the sunlight pouring in through the front window. "I love it, too. Thank you again. It's grown to mean a lot to me."

"Yeah? What does it mean?"

A tickle of happiness skips across my chest as I think of Gabe. I fiddle with the ring, recalling the moment he slipped it over my finger in a gas station parking lot. "New beginnings, I think. Second chances," I murmur. "Hopefully…a little bit of good luck."

"Ooh. Is this about love?" she wonders. Then she gasps, noting which finger the ring resides on. "Wait, are you engaged?"

The idea warms me. I think it's always warmed me, even when he said it teasingly, jokingly, not thinking for a second I'd agree to play along. It warmed me last night, the same way his body did while we drifted off to sleep after making love for the first time. His arm was draped around me, one hand locked with mine, both of our palms tucked to my chest. He toyed with the little ring, circling it around my finger, and I think, in that moment, we both wished that it was real.

My gaze floats back to Summer as a smile crests. "Something like that," I echo softly.

After I wave a quick goodbye, I stroll down the hallway and make a pitstop in the bathroom before joining Evan in his office. I take a moment. I just need a few seconds to gather my thoughts, my strength, my energy. My reflection stares back at me as I splash cool water over my face and inhale a shaky breath. For a second, I'm in that bathroom again.

The other bathroom.

The one with ugly floral wallpaper that peeled from the

corners, the one that reeked of mold and mildew. Water-damaged walls. A dirty, cracked mirror. Every time I gulped down water from the faucet, I debated smashing the mirror with my fist and stabbing a shard of glass into my captor's jugular. I pictured his blood spurting out when I severed his artery. I envisioned the way he'd clutch his throat as horror and disbelief stole his expression and clouded his eyes. I imagined him falling at my feet as his life drained out, and I cheered and laughed and celebrated our victory.

We win.

Regret eats at me that I never did it.

Maybe I could have saved him.

Maybe I would have stepped on that airplane.

I dry off with a hand towel and smooth my hair back, glancing in the mirror one last time as I press forward on the edge of the sink. "I can do this," I mutter to myself. "I will do this."

No more regrets.

I make my way out of the bathroom and step into Evan's office, heaving in a deep breath and centering myself as I prepare for what I need to do.

It's time to relive the then, so I can finally live in the now.

I clutch the tungsten ring in my fist, squeezing gently, then glance down at the star ring circled around my finger.

My past.

My present.

I cling to them both, because they are each responsible for shaping my future.

Evan sends me a welcoming nod from his desk as I step forward.

And I close the door behind me.

CHAPTER 30

GABE

She's hunched over on her front porch when I saunter up her walkway with a hot cup of tea. It's already nighttime, the moon replacing all remnants of the summer sun, and darkness stealing the light in her eyes I saw less than twenty-four hours ago. "Tabs. Hey."

She lifts her head slowly, eyelids puffy and rimmed red.

Her lips part, but she doesn't say anything. She just stares at me with those lightless eyes as I pick at the cardboard sleeve on the cup.

Swallowing, I pause a few feet away from her and slip my free hand into my pocket. "You didn't come over after your interview. I thought…" I guess I thought she was going to come over, considering she usually does, and, also, we just had sex for the first time. Maybe I was being presumptuous in thinking things would be different now. "I waited for you."

A few seconds tick by.

She offers me a blink.

The tree branches shimmy above us, caught up in a breeze that blows through, a breeze that nearly swallows her words. "I'm sorry," she murmurs. There's a detachment in her voice that complements the shadows swirling around her.

I frown, taking a cautious step forward. "Are you okay?"

"No." Looking away, she hugs her knees to her chest and shakes her head. "No, I'm not. You should probably go."

"You want me to go?"

"You should," she says quietly.

"That's not what I asked." I take another step forward, then one more, until I'm toe to toe with her front stoop. She keeps her eyes locked on something across the yard. A squirrel, I think. Or maybe nothing. "Tell me what's wrong."

A word falls out with her wobbly breath. "Everything."

"Everything is wrong?"

She nods. "I feel like I should still be down there. In that basement. He never got to leave, so why was I so lucky? It doesn't seem fair that I'm the lucky one, and he's the dead one. It's not right."

Her tone is numb, almost deadened. I crouch down until I'm at eye level with her, even though her eyes are still aimed at the imaginary squirrel somewhere to the right. "Hey, look at me," I tell her gently. "Please."

She doesn't. Her lips quiver slightly, so I know she heard me. I know she's intentionally avoiding eye contact.

"You weren't lucky," I say. "You were brave. You were strong. You were smart."

This causes her head to snap toward me, our faces mere inches apart. Emotion flashes in copper-brown eyes that look a shade darker than midnight in the lack of porchlight. "He was braver. Stronger. Smarter," she hisses back. "And he's still dead."

She glances down at her knees, but I catch her chin with two fingers and pop her head back up. "Look at me, Tabs. Don't look down."

A tear slips from the corner of her eye, but she holds my gaze.

I hand her the tea. "Okay," I concur. "You were lucky. It wasn't bravery or strength or clever tricks. It was pure luck."

Chamomile wafts around us, mingling with the lilac breeze. Her eyes dip to the tea I'm holding out to her, and the sight of it has more tears pooling in her eyes, streaming down her cheeks. She accepts the cup, her hands trembling.

"The point is, it doesn't matter how you survived. All that matters is that you did. That's what counts." I'm still in a crouching position in front of her, eye to eye, as my hands reach out and graze along her floral-printed leggings. "Your daughter isn't going to look at you and question the how and why of your existence in her life. She's going to look at you and smile, because you're here, and you're her beautiful, perfect mother, holding her in two arms that fought for every second of being with her. Maybe it was luck, maybe it was cosmic design, maybe it was something we'll never fully understand—whatever it was, it doesn't fucking matter, Tabs." I inch closer, giving her thighs a squeeze. "You. Are. Here. Hope is here. And every life you've changed, every person you've touched *because* you're here? That's where you find your healing. It's not back there. It's not in that basement," I tell her. "It's right now. It's right here."

Her eyes flutter closed as tears trickle down her cheeks and lips, dangling from her jaw.

I slide my palm to the center of her chest and rest my forehead to her knees, inhaling a tapered breath, savoring the feel of her heartbeats vibrating through me.

Th-thump, th-thump, th-thump.

But then she's scrambling to her feet, croaking out a tortured sound.

Tabitha pulls herself up, unsteady and frantic, shaking her head as she stares down at me. "It *does* matter, Gabe. The why, the how…" Inching backward to her front door, she squeezes the cup of tea in her fist, liquid pooling out the top. "It matters."

She races inside, and I'm on my feet, following her into the house, the screen door slapping behind me. "Why didn't you come to me?" I call after her as she winds through the foyer, through the living room, placing the tea on her coffee table with her back to me. "You always come to me. Why didn't you let me comfort you?"

"Because it's not fair to you."

"What's not fair?" Her arms are wrapped around her middle like a protective shield. A barrier. I move in closer, desperate to break through. "You think I'll be forced against my will to hold you, to love you, to kiss away your tears while you break apart in my arms? Jesus, Tabitha, I would do that every minute of every day if it helped bring you one step closer to healing."

Shivers ripple through her, causing her body to tremor through her tears. "It's not fair that you love me that much," she whispers. "That you love me with your whole heart."

"You think this is easy for me?" I hedge, holding my arms out at my sides, my emotions climbing. "It kills me to know that you'll never love me back, that you'll never—"

"I *do* love you!" she shouts, severing my words as she whips around to face me, her chest heaving. "I love you. But not with my whole heart, because my heart is no longer whole. I love you with the chewed-up, tattered pieces of it. The shredded remains that have somehow kept me alive for this long. And you don't deserve that, Gabe. You don't deserve to be loved with scraps, with the bloody leftovers. *That's* not fair."

I stare at her, frozen in silence.

Thunderstruck.

Her words sink in, bleeding into my skin, my bones, my marrow, my essence.

Three little words.

My question falls out like a stunned whisper. "You love me?"

She blinks, lips parting as she registers and rejects the joyous disbelief in my eyes. "D-did you not hear me? I said I can't love you like you—"

"You love me." A smile blooms, pulling at my lips, pulling at my heartstrings. I'm smiling so hard, my jaw aches. "That's what I heard."

She steps away, swinging her head back and forth. "No…no, stop it. You're meant for so much more than what I can offer you. I'm a single mother with a dead-end job and a screwed-up past. No savings, no career, no future. You don't want this. You have so much to live—"

"Nothing. I have nothing," I cut in, stepping forward, closing the gap between us and taking her face between my hands. Our foreheads crash together as I tell her firmly, "I. Have. Nothing."

"Gabe, please…"

"Give me the sun and the moon." I press a kiss to her hairline. "Hand me the sea." A kiss to her forehead, to her tear-streaked cheek. "Steal every star from the fucking sky…and *I still have nothing*." Another kiss to her nose, to the perfect bow of her lips. She's still shaking her head like she doesn't believe me, but I *need* her to believe me. I place a final kiss to her mouth before inching back and whispering, "You're my everything, Tabs. Without you, I have nothing."

Her face crumples the moment our eyes lock.

A tsunami of grief, of mourning, of survivor's guilt.

She lets it all fall on me as she collapses against me and becomes dead weight in my arms.

I hold her tight, gathering her closer, accepting every weight she hands me as I sprinkle more kisses in her hair. "I'll take your leftover pieces. I'll cherish those pieces. And I'll spend my whole damn life doing everything in my power to make your heart whole again."

Sobs rip through her.

Heart-wrenching, bone-rattling sobs.

Her hands fist my T-shirt, her tears soaking through the fabric.

My hands cup the back of her head, fingers grazing her scalp. "I've got you, baby," I murmur. "Always."

As her cries fade to whimpers, Tabitha buries her face in my chest and drags her palms up and down my torso, her touch feather-light. Her breaths come in deep, heady inhales, morphing into sighs of longing as her fingers dance to the hem of my shirt and sneak underneath.

Nuzzling me with her nose, she parts her lips and scatters dozens of kisses across my chest. Her fingers skim along my bare skin, exploring every divot, every muscle, every slow-healing bruise. A moan escapes her, warming me through the fabric of my T-shirt. It feels like she's trying to burrow inside me and tie our hearts together with a tear-soaked ribbon.

My eyes fall closed, my footing unsteady as she touches me. The emotions between us shift into something else, something more. Despair is still despair, but it bleeds with passion, and I think somewhere between the two is where Heaven and Hell collide.

Fire and serenity.

Madness and magic.

Balance.

I drag my lips down her temple, then her cheek, and she lifts up on her toes at the same time with her nails digging into my skin and my hands in her hair. Our mouths meet hungrily. Tongues winding, moans tangling. She pulls my bottom lip between her teeth, then peppers open-mouthed kisses down my jaw to my neck, nicking the skin as her hands slide around to my back.

My dick jumps, straining against denim.

Fuck.

I fall to my knees and take her with me, lying her down on the plush white rug in her living room. We don't make it to the bedroom. Eager to be inside her, I wrench the shirt over my head and toss it behind me. My eyes don't leave hers as I unhook my belt buckle, tug at my zipper, and shove my jeans down my hips. Tabitha wriggles her way out of her leggings and underwear, kicking them across the room and spreading her legs for me. Lamplight casts her in a warm glow, brightening her damp cheeks and the desire glistening between her thighs.

I drape myself over her and dive back into her kiss as her hands fall across my shoulder blades, holding me close. She reaches lower and grips my bare ass, gouging me with her fingernails. The underside of my erection glides up and down her wetness, and I moan into her mouth, rocking against her. "Fuck," I grind out, pulling away and pressing my forehead to hers. "You're soaking wet." I keep rocking my hips, and the slippery slide of my cock against her pussy has my neck craning back, a deep groan rumbling in my throat.

As I rock forward, she moves her hips, and the head of my dick slips inside of her.

I almost lose it.

Only an inch inside, and my body tenses up.

Shit.

I still for a moment and manage to get it together before I blow my load in one-point five seconds like a pent-up teenager.

"Wait," I rasp, kissing the shell of her ear. "Condom."

I'm about to ease my way out of her, when she squeezes my ass and bucks her hips. "No…I want to feel you," she whimpers. "All of you. Bare."

"Christ." I bury my face against her shoulder, propping myself up on my forearms. "I always use a condom. Every time."

"So it's safe, then, right?" Her fingernails dig into my skin, tracing fiery lines along the ridges of my spine. With a firm grip, she pulls me closer, her arms wrapped tightly around me as if she's afraid to let go. "Gabe…fuck me."

And I'm toast.

The animal inside takes over and I sink into her all the way.

A guttural groan falls out of me as I push up on my hands, thrusting once, twice, again.

Slow but hard.

I shove her ivory blouse up past her breasts and yank down

her bra, sucking a nipple into my mouth as her back bows, her fingers fisting my hair in a needy grip.

"Gabe, Gabe…oh God."

"Fuck, Tabs." Her thighs are spread wide, knees pushed back toward her chest as I move inside her, my spine arching with each thrust. Both palms are splayed on either side of her head to hold myself up, and my ribs burn and hiss, but I'm too wound with pleasure to slow down. "Say it again," I husk, our skin slapping together as I plow into her on her living room rug. "Say it."

She moans, pushing her hair back from her eyes with one hand while the other clasps the nape of my neck. "I love you."

My hand slips between us, two fingers rubbing her clit as she whimpers, her breasts bouncing below me. "Again."

"I love you."

My grunts fuse with her mewls as I thrust into her, harder, faster. "Say my name as you come on my cock."

Her cheeks are flushed bright pink, her hairline damp with sweat. Mouth hanging open on a low moan, she tenses, her legs coiling around my lower back, ankles locking.

"*Gabe*…ohh, Jesus…" She comes hard, breaking apart, eyes squeezed shut.

I've been inside of her for a minute, tops, and we're already unraveling.

I pump into her a few more times and my head tips back as I groan through the onset of my release. Miraculously, I'm coherent enough to pull out of her as my orgasm peaks. Lifting to my knees, I latch onto her hip and lean over while fisting my cock with my opposite hand. I jerk myself off with a throaty groan, my cum pooling onto her stomach as waves of euphoria ripple through me.

She watches, eyes glazed over, her body limp from release.

A small, love-laced smile tips her lips as I collapse beside her on the rug with my jeans still caught around my knees.

We're both breathing heavily, sweaty and sticky.

My abdomen pulses with agony, pissed at me, but I can't help the smile I shoot her as I hike up my jeans and reach behind me toward the ottoman. I snatch up a knitted blanket and swipe it across Tabitha's stomach, cleaning her up.

She pulls up on her elbows. "My grandmother crocheted that."

"She'll be thrilled to know that her handiwork is being put to good use."

"Oh God." She cups a hand over her mouth to hold in the giggles and falls back down to the rug, her dark hair framing her head like an inky halo as she tugs her leggings back up.

I ball the blanket between my hands and toss it aside. Propping my head up on my palm, I gaze down at her as she stares at the ceiling with a fading smile, her cheeks still glinting with drying tears.

I brush the backs of my fingers along her cheekbone, and her lips quiver, a shadow of pain etched across her face. "Tabs, I want you to know…" I wait for her eyes to meet mine before I continue because this is important. When her gaze cuts back to me and holds steady, I tell her, "I'll never expect you to love him less, okay?"

She inhales sharply.

I can almost feel the way her chest constricts with emotion.

Something raw. Something potent.

"I'll never ask you to choose. I'll never tell you to let him go." I cup her cheek, hoping she feels my truth, because it *is* the truth. "Love's not a competition, and it's not always singular. I don't care what the books say, or what society tells us. Don't ever feel guilty for sharing your heart. You said it like it was a bad thing, but it's not, baby. It's not. It's a beautiful thing."

And then she deflates with a long sigh, with a breath she's been holding on to. Maybe for months.

Something like relief.

"I meant everything I said." Pressing a kiss to her forehead, I murmur, "There's nothing I wouldn't do for you."

Her gaze skims my face, throat working through a tight lump. "Just don't leave me," she says. "That's all I want."

"Impossible."

"Promise me," she whispers, rolling toward me, burrowing into the breadth of my arms. "Promise me you won't leave. Tell me you're immortal, superhuman. Death-defying. Your love is unshakeable." There's desperation in her eyes and in the way her hand reaches out to grip my bicep. She glances at my scar, taking in the fragile humanity staring back at her in the form of puckered flesh and discolored skin. "Promise me."

I tug her closer until my lips tickle the skin below her ear, and the mess with my father skips across my mind. Stoney's threats. My broken ribs, with promises of worse. A clock quickly counting down. Danger lingers at the forefront of my mind as I whisper the only promise I know how to keep:

"My love is unshakeable."

CHAPTER 31

GABE

Fresh off a jobsite, the last thing I expect to see when I stroll to my car the next night is Stoney.

My hackles rise, insides pitching with anxiety. I slowly pull the hard hat off my head as our eyes meet across the parking lot and he lifts up from the hood of my Challenger.

Chester Stonehocker.

After the prison visit with my father, I quickly learned that Jackson Walsh and his right-hand douche, Chester "Stoney" Stonehocker, are notorious for two things: being the lowliest human beings alive and managing to get away with it. Somehow, these cretins always find a way to escape any real penalty or prison time—must have something to do with the millions of dollars they acquire from extorting innocent citizens.

"What the fuck are you doing here?" I call out, picking up my pace after a brief hesitation. "This stalker act is getting creepy. Not that I'm not flattered by your newfound obsession with me." Pushing past him with a shoulder-bump, I reach for my car door handle. "I mean, I don't blame you if you need a friend. Your buddy Walsh seems to be as cuddly as a cactus."

Stoney reeks of menthol and smoky gunpowder as he parks his hip against the door, blocking me from opening it. "I see you've finally spoken with your father."

"I humored him, yeah. The old man isn't looking so great. I'm sure it's been tough sharing a cell with some dude with a rampant libido."

"You've come to a solution, I gather?"

"A solution to the bullshit between my father and your skeevy boss that I literally have nothing to do with?" My glare is icy. "I'm not sure. But let me know how that goes since I'm unwillingly invested now." I reach for the door handle again.

And then I wince when the barrel of a pistol slams into my ribcage. It's like he knows exactly where my bruises hide, where my brutalized ribs cower.

I grind my teeth together, breathing out through my nose and trying not to show that I'm weeping on the inside. "You're going to shoot me in a parking lot?" I bite out, glancing around at the idle cars. One of my coworkers is on his cell phone as he paces around his vehicle. "Rogers doesn't really like me, but I think he'd find it in him to be a good samaritan if you blow me away twenty feet from his Prius."

A grin curls on his scarred face as he burrows the barrel deeper. "No, Gabe, I'm not going to shoot you. I just wanted to watch you squirm for a moment." His arm rears back, and he returns the pistol to his waistband. "I tend to avoid getting my hands dirty. My tactics are more subtle."

My abdomen throbs as I step away and blink back the pain, refusing to give him the satisfaction of watching me *squirm*. "How honorable of you."

"I prefer morally flexible." He leans back against my Challenger and folds his arms, pale-blue eyes gleaming beneath the underside of his cap. "The real question is: how honorable are you?"

I tense my jaw and tilt my head. "I always return my library books on time. I ask my plants for permission before pruning them because I respect their autonomy." I shrug. "Oh, this one time, I ran into a burning building and pulled two people I love to safety. That counts, right?"

"Mhm. Well, then, perhaps this will trigger your righteous reflexes." Stoney bends over and reaches for a manilla folder propped up by the wheel of my car. "Take a look."

The folder is shoved at my chest, and a handful of photographs slip out, fluttering to the pavement.

One lands right-side-up, and my eyes dip down.

I blanch.

It's a photo of Tabitha.

At the grocery store.

"What is this," I breathe out, wondering how I'm even still breathing. My head snaps up, my eyes wide as I stare at him. I can't hide the terror in them. "What the fuck is this?"

"There's more. Please, take your time. I'll wait." He whistles, glancing at his Rolex before perusing the parking lot and getting comfortable against the side of my car.

I realize my hands are shaking as I crouch down and gather up a stack of loose photographs. Flipping through them, my chest seizes with every new image I uncover.

Tabitha at work, smiling as she distributes mugs of coffee to customers.

Tabitha at her house, bent over a garden bed with a little shovel in her hand.

Tabitha in her car at a stoplight.

Tabitha and Hope, sitting at the park with another woman, playing with a white-and-silver Husky.

Tabitha.

And Hope.

My fucking girls.

I'm shell-shocked as I glance back up at him, frozen.

Stunned.

He's been following her. He knows everything about her—her schedule, where she works, where she lives. My entire world has been placed in the hands of a corrupt criminal.

"Poor thing," he notes, still looking off to the side like he's only marginally engaged. "She's had such a hard life already, what with her abduction and witnessing the heinous murder of the man she loved. Truly tragic. I can only imagine what it would do to her if more tragedy fell into her lap. Especially with that adorable little girl she's single-handedly responsible for protecting."

I shake my head, swallowing down my horror. It feels like I'm underwater and he's talking to me just above the surface, his face murky and out of focus, his words garbled.

"Now," he states, attention drifting back to me. "Since you're the hero who rescues people he loves from burning buildings, imagine this." His hand waves between us like a grand unveiling. "Your lover and her child trapped inside that burning building. The roof collapses, the walls cave in. Flames, smoke, imminent death." *Tsking* his tongue, he feigns sympathy as he pulls out a pack of cigarettes from his pocket. "A dire scene, indeed. She's screaming for you. Both of them are screaming for you, begging for their lives." He grins, lights up the charcoal tip. "But…you can only save one."

My heart stops.

It peters out and shrivels up, ashes and decay slithering through my bloodstream.

I can't process what he's telling me.

Can't blink, can't move, can't breathe.

"Tell me, Gabe," he finishes, blowing a tapered plume of smoke toward the blue-gray sky. "Who would you save?" A glimmer brightens his eyes, a spark of depraved thrill. "Rhetorically speaking, of course."

Everything continues to blur as I gape at him, his words settling like tar-steeped bricks in the pit of my gut.

I shake my head back and forth, processing.

Unable to process.

"You…you wouldn't," I choke out. The pictures fall from my hands, scattering at my feet. Panic unfurls in the center of my chest, and I bend over, gripping my knees with white-knuckled hands as I try to keep myself from buckling. "You wouldn't do that."

"Mmm, I can see how much this scenario is upsetting you," he mutters. "Well, no worries. I'm certain you'll do everything you can to avoid it. There's no need for dramatics…as much as I do enjoy them."

"Please…please don't hurt them." I straighten back up and tug at my hair with both fists, still struggling for a full breath. "Don't you *fucking* touch them."

He squints at me. "You seem to be confused, Gabe. I'm not the one holding the cards here. That would be you."

"I don't know what to do," I confess, bile in my throat. "I-I don't know how to get that kind of money."

"Ah, we're back to that, then." He sighs. "Shame. My boss was gracious enough to extend your deadline, and all you seem to do is take advantage of his generosity."

"Do what you want to me," I grit through my teeth. "Just leave them out of this. For the love of fuck—*leave them out of this*."

Stoney lunges at me, gripping me by the work vest with

knobby fingers as the cigarette dangles between his lips. I'm limp, a ragdoll. My fight has been pilfered away by the imaginary screams of Tabitha and Hope perishing in a fiery blaze.

He'll make them disappear.

He'll take my whole life away from me.

"Leave them out of this? Now why would I do that?" His grip is firm, but his tone is devil-may-care. "They're a part of this little arrangement. You made them a part of this. *You.*"

Releasing me, he takes two unhurried steps back and plucks the cigarette from his lips.

My words are all dried up. I just stand there, speechless.

Blank.

"You have two days. Forty-eight hours to fulfill the requirements you've been given. My boss's patience is wearing thin, as is mine." His eyes sparkle as he issues a final salient threat, tilting his head ever so slightly. "Her bed sheets smell like lavender, you know."

My pulse stutters, heartbeats misfiring.

No.

I fist my hair again, fighting for clean air, swinging my head back and forth.

"They say the scent is calming. Soothing," he continues thoughtfully. "I wonder if it might bring her a touch of comfort when she awakes in the night to a stranger in her bed prying those pretty thighs wide open." Stretching a smirk, he does a one-footed spin and stalks away from me while muttering over his shoulder, "Perhaps we'll find out."

Whistling, he traipses out of the parking lot with a staggered limp and leaves me behind in shards and ruins.

The moment he's out of sight, I collapse, sinking to the asphalt and falling back on my haunches. When I was a junior in high school, I spent a summer as a lifeguard getting paid minimum wage at the community pool. There was a little girl flailing in the water below me while her mother sat in a chaise lounge with a book shielding her eyes. Panic rippled through me, catapulting me into action. I dove in, hero instincts firing, desperate to save the little girl…

And then my head hit the bottom of the pool.

Blood stained the water red. My vision blurred, my lungs water-clogged and heavy.

I thought I was dead.

I truly thought I was meant to die.

When my eyes opened, I was sprawled out on the concrete with worried faces looming over me as I coughed and spluttered up chlorine-bitter water. The little girl was there, staring at me with wide eyes, wrapped up in a beach towel. She was safe. Someone must have rescued her.

Someone must have rescued me.

I only suffered a minor concussion and a few stitches, but I often think about what a close call that was. I could have died, and maybe I almost did.

As I fall onto my back, I'm sprawled out on the concrete once again, but this time, no one is here to rescue me. Tabitha flashes across my mind; her beautiful porcelain face and broken smile. I picture a monster in her bed, defiling her, stealing that smile away for good.

Grief sucker-punches me, and I drape my hands over my face and choke down a sob.

Ever since that day at the pool, I always wondered what it would take to kill me.

Now I know.

HER TEXT STARES BACK at me as I sit in my driveway, the window cracked, music shut off.

Crickets chirp on the other side of the glass as a sticky breeze filters inside the car, doing nothing for my strangled lungs.

I've been sitting here for twenty minutes, just rereading her text. Tossing my phone onto the passenger's seat. Reaching for it.

Reading it again.

TABITHA:

I'm wearing that red lingerie. I feel like it's time you finally saw it in person? ;) Call me when you're off work. I'll be waiting, xoxo

I've been off work for over an hour now, but I haven't called her. Haven't texted her back.

I'm numb, scattered, completely gutted.

So I just reread her text.

I imagine her in that sexy red lingerie, sprawled out on her white sheets, waiting for my phone call. Waiting for me to saunter into her bedroom and tear the lingerie off her curves, right before I bury my face between her wet thighs and let my tongue bring her to ecstasy.

I imagine a lot of things.

But my imagination is compromised by visions of Tabitha and Hope tied to a headboard, locked in opposite rooms as thick smoke envelops them and flame-drenched walls bury them alive.

I hear them calling for me. Tabitha begging me to save her baby. Hope wailing for her mother, her tiny screams laced with terror. Both of them doomed to die in a fiery blaze because I don't know which door to run through first.

I just stand there, helpless.

Then I perish with them, dying a coward.

Nausea rolls in my gut as I chuck my phone into the backseat and pound my fists against the steering wheel, growling my agony into the night.

This would be easier to ignore if it were only just a vision. A nightmare I'll wake up from the moment the sun paints the sky in splashes of yellow and gold. But it's not. This will be my reality if I don't manage to come up with over a million fucking dollars in a couple of days.

This will be my fate.

This will be *their* fate.

Because of me. Because of my fucking asshole father.

My forehead falls to the wheel, my eyes closing as I try to keep myself from irreparably breaking down. When I lift back up, my gaze settles on the raised-ranch house sitting in front of me. Honey bricks and dark-mocha shutters. The old khaki-colored front door was recently painted over by Sydney, and is now a coastal shade of blue. The paint color was called Barbie Dreamhouse—an intentional decision, and a tidbit she was more than eager to share with me while she snorted through her laughter at my disgruntled reaction. I let her do it, though. And it looks good.

It reminds me of summers under a similar coastal-blue sky. Lemonade stands at the end of the driveway, forts in the trampoline out back, endless games of tag and red rover in the front yard. Childhood. Innocence. Days when all I had to worry about was making it through the front door before the streetlights turned on, and what pajamas I was going to wear to bed that night.

My heart pangs as I drink in the house I've called home since the day I was born.

"Gabe?"

I startle, blinking away the daydreams as my head pans left. Oliver stands a few feet away on his front lawn, watching me with a furrowed brow, illuminated by my headlights.

Clearing my throat, I pull the key from the ignition and kick open the door. "Hey."

"You seem distressed."

"Rough day at the jobsite. Misaligned framework." I sniff. "Are you busy?"

"Not particularly. Syd is working at the bar establishment tonight." His arms cross, that reflective expression he always wears tinted with worry as I approach. "Can I assist with something?"

Scratching the back of my head, I glance down at the grass as a cricket skips across the toe of my shoe. "Just an ear to lend, if that's cool."

"Certainly."

We make our way to his front stoop, right in front of a custom-made bird feeder shaped like a cottage that's been carved with Oliver and Sydney's initials. I stare at it for a few minutes while I gather my thoughts. Seeds and shells litter the wooden platform as the house swings gently in the night breeze, waiting for sunrise and black-capped chickadees to liven the sky.

Leaning forward on my knees, I think about Tabitha's mockingbirds, and about the one that succumbed to her father's firecrackers. It had no idea it was about to be struck down.

Then I think about my girl sitting at home in her lingerie, waiting for my text to come through.

Vulnerable and unsuspecting.

My heart hurts. It hurts so fucking much.

"That misaligned framework seems to have truly sucked the life out of you, Gabe," Oliver quips to my right, already knowing that something else is bothering me.

Luckily for him, he'll never know the true extent of my

despair. I refuse to involve the people I love in this mess. "Yeah, it's a bitch."

"We could commiserate over a bottle of Boujee Blancs de Blanc if you'd like. Sydney acquired it at her workplace. I hear it's quite distinctive."

I shake my head. I'm not in the mood to drink; it'll only heighten my anxiety and paranoia. "Nah. I'm good." Swallowing, I glance at him, taking in his firefly-yellow V-neck with navy pinstripes, his hair a mess of chestnut waves. There's a question in his gaze as he stares at me beneath the porch lantern. I heave in a breath. "Remember when I came back from the burn unit and said you owed me big time for saving your life?"

Oliver blinks slowly through a frown, then nods once. "Yes. I assumed it was in jest. You asked me to incorporate you into one of my comic books as a powerful demigod who radiates molten good looks and sexual mastery." A small smile crests. "I plan to."

I can't manage a smile back. Only pain skates across my face, triggering Oliver's smile to fade. He's always been perceptive— he knows I'm not joking around anymore.

"Gabe." Concern glimmers in his ruddy-brown eyes as he fully faces me. "Something tells me you need a favor, and I'm not going to like what this favor entails."

My eyes close, my pulse thrumming with resignation. It feels like there's an avalanche in my chest, a landslide of no-way-outs and impossible choices. I drop my head into my hands and link my fingers behind my neck as I fixate on the cement cracks.

"I'll do anything," Oliver continues, waiting for more context. "You know I will."

It takes a few more stifled heartbeats for me to pop my head back up and look him in the eyes. "I need you to keep an eye on Tabitha for me." I almost choke on the request, almost suffocate on my own air. "I need you to watch over her and Hope."

He swallows, allowing my words to process. He's registering my favor and everything it implies. Oliver glances away, blinking into the dark night, then looks back at me. "You can't possibly be saying what I think you're saying."

I tent my hands to my chin. "I know that sounds vague and bleak, but I need you to trust me."

"Gabe, what is going on? What makes you think you won't be here to watch over them yourself?"

There's a possibility I'll be here. There's a chance I'll make it out of this with my head still attached and my heart still beating, but that heart won't ever be the same.

And she'll never forgive me for what I'm about to do to her.

"It doesn't matter," I tell him. "I just need you to promise me you'll do it."

"I can't accept this." He shakes his head firmly, words shaded with denial. "I will not."

"Please. I've never asked you for anything serious. Not ever. This is my only request, my only wish. I *need* you to do this for me." My hands are still tented like a prayer as I plead with him.

Oliver releases a disbelieving breath, his face clouded with uncertainty. Crickets continue to sing my lament, their rhythmic melodies bleeding with the sound of my heart breaking.

This. Fucking. Hurts.

He looks away again, squaring his jaw as his attention snags on the dormant bird feeder. Elbows pressed to his thighs, he folds his hands between his legs and releases a long exhale. "This has to do with that so-called mugging, yes?" he murmurs, sparing me a quick glance.

I roll my lips and say nothing.

"Drugs?"

My head rears back at the assumption. "What? No. Fuck, no…nothing like that."

"What, then? Why are you getting beaten half to death in your driveway, receiving visits from suspicious strangers, and saying these ominous things to me? If your life is in danger, I won't stand by idle and uninformed. I refuse."

"The less you know, the better, okay? You have Syd to think about," I tell him, watching his eyes flare with apprehension. "I just need to get out of town for a little while. My life isn't in danger."

Still shaking his head, he rests his chin on his fists. "This isn't right," he says. "You've been there for me from the moment I returned home. You never once turned your back on me, so I am more than a little reluctant to turn my back on you."

"I know." I nod, swallowing down the rubble in my throat. "Trust me, I get it. I'll explain everything as soon as I can."

"And what if something happens to you? What if you're not around to offer that explanation?"

I glance skyward and blow out a breath. "Nothing is going to happen to me. I'm fine."

"I've been through my fair share of suffering, Gabe, but my circumstances were always out of my control. Regret isn't a burden I've had to carry with me. But this..." His voice is strained, tormented, as emotion fills his eyes. "This would forever be my greatest regret."

I close my eyes, a hopeless shiver snaking down my spine. All I want to do is confide in my stepbrother, but I can't put him in danger. He's worked too hard to build a new life for himself, for his future with Sydney.

I'm out of options, out of alternatives.

Out of hope.

Heavy silence simmers between us as I close my eyes and prepare for what I need to do. Then I turn to him, holding his gaze, praying he can see the apology staring back at him.

Praying, one day, he can forgive me.

"Keep her safe for me, brother."

I leave him with those words as I stand from his front stoop, trudge back home, and set my plan in motion with a knife in my heart.

CHAPTER 32

TABITHA

Two Years Earlier

A sharp breeze smacked me in the face, stealing my breath.

Gasp.

Wheeze.

Swallow.

My eyes popped open as my lungs inhaled giant gulps of fresh air for the first time in months—*months.* I was outdoors. I wasn't chained to a pole in a dank basement.

I knew I should have been grateful for the small miracle, but fear rattled my bones instead, because I couldn't see anything.

I couldn't see.

Darkness swallowed me whole.

I panicked at first, envisioning vacant eye sockets, my eyes gouged out with pliers. Only the pain didn't come. If my eyes had been removed, there would be pain.

"H-hello?" I rasped. I was shivering, but it wasn't cold outside. It was breezy and balmy.

Blinking several times, I deduced that there was some sort of blindfold secured around my eyes. The cool cotton fabric tickled my eyelashes, and the knot was tight and severe against the back of my skull.

God, where was I?

"Hello?" I repeated, lifting my head.

Another sharp breeze whipped through, and it felt like I was still wearing only a ratty T-shirt. My legs trembled, my senses returning one by one, sluggish and delayed. It took me a moment to realize that I was lying down, sprawled out on my side with my knees curled to my chest.

Dead leaves and twigs crunched beneath me as I tried to move and lift my body into an upright position, my sore, healing wrist bones hissing against the effort.

When I attempted to reach out and steady myself, it finally registered that my hands were bound behind my back, tethered with thick, coarse rope.

No, no, no.

Panic sunk into me again. "Help me!" I cried out, my voice broken and frayed.

Help.

I needed to find help. A road, a town.

Scrambling to my knees, I felt sticks and small stones dig into my kneecaps, causing me to wince. I managed to find my balance, pulling myself to bare feet. My chest heaved in and out as I drank in quick bursts of breath, canting my head in multiple directions, as if that would help me see something through the blindfold.

It was so dark.

I was so scared.

My lips quivered, chafed and dry. "Hello?" I croaked, hoping for a sign of life. Something, anything. "Somebody help me!"

The summery breeze was the only thing that answered me as it picked up speed and tried to knock me off my feet. Pine needles, damp moss and bark, and the distinct scent of honeysuckle tickled my nose, all familiar smells I recalled from camping trips with friends.

Nature.

I was in a forest.

The woods.

But...*why?*

The man must have set me free. He must have let me go.

The last thing I remembered was my captor trudging toward me with a syringe in his hand. I had thought it was over. My veins were going to be poisoned with something lethal, and I would never wake up. That basement would become my coffin.

Instead, he'd knocked me out with something. Dropped me off somewhere.

I itched to extend my arms to help guide me through this blind maze, but I was completely useless. My eyes couldn't see, my arms couldn't move, and even my legs were struggling to hold my weight. More panic unfurled in my chest, mingling with terror and nausea as I began to stalk forward.

One step, two steps.

I was practically holding my breath, expecting to bump into a tree or nosedive off the edge of a cliff. The thought had me pausing my feet, tiny whimpers catching in my throat. I was petrified. Lost, alone. Shaking and queasy.

I needed Matthew. I needed his comforting voice and kind words.

Trust me.

I'll always be with you.

Shivering uncontrollably, I collapsed back down to my knees and let out a guttural scream. "*Matthew!*" I bent over, my forehead pressing into a pile of leaves as tears dampened my blindfold and my hair flew all around me with the breeze. "Why did you *leave me here!*" There was no lift at the end, no question. The last word was clipped, like it had been bitten off and chewed.

Silent sobs poured out. I was hunched over in the middle of nowhere, my belly swollen and cramped, waiting to become dinner for a hungry bear.

That was when I heard it.

From far away, a muffled echo reached my ears.

"Hello?"

My head popped up. I stopped breathing, my senses going into overdrive.

I wasn't alone.

"Help!" I shouted, stumbling back to my feet and making a clumsy trek forward. "I'm over here!"

I picked up my pace and ran into a tree. The bark scraped my chin and the tip of my nose, but I bounced back, trying to regroup.

Someone was there. I wasn't alone.

"Hold tight, I see you!" a voice called back.

My heart was beating so fast it was about to vaporize between my ribs. I felt the soles of my feet cutting on branches and rock, but I kept going. I kept moving, instinctually jutting my shoulders out in hopes they would take the brunt of any more tree collisions.

"I'll come to you!" he shouted.

He was getting closer.

I moved faster, unable to stay still.

Bumping into another tree, I squeaked out a cry of pain, then kept going.

I kept going.

More tears spilled down my cheeks. I still had no hands to touch, no arms to reach.

No eyes to see.

But I was free, I was free, I was *free*.

My ankle caught around weeds or roots, and I flew forward, faceplanting into a pile of brushwood. God, I wanted to cry. I wanted to curl up in the thicket and surrender to my grisly fate as I lay there, bruised and helpless, my shoulder nearly dislocated after taking the majority of the impact.

"Where are you, girl? I can't see you!"

"I-I'm here," I said, hoping the stranger could hear me. With a mournful cry of both pain and weakness, I twisted my body until my knees were under me and I was able to stand. "I'm here."

I sounded feeble and broken, like the world's saddest song.

As I gathered my footing, my courage, and my wildly beating heart, I began to move again.

That's when I was stopped in my tracks by two hands grabbing my shoulders.

I screamed, terrified.

"Shh, it's all right, I got you."

The blindfold was yanked from around my eyes. I blinked, my vision adjusting. It wasn't quite nighttime, but the sun was low, the sky gold and dusky. Leafy trees were the first thing I saw, the branches swaying when a breeze blew through. A family of birds soared overhead in a V-shape, the only other witnesses to my liberation.

And to my right, there was a road.

A road!

Finally, my head whipped left, and I was eye to eye with a middle-aged man with a sandy beard, wearing red-and-black plaid and a worried expression. I blinked again, praying he was real. Begging for him to be more than a delusion, more than a hopeful dream.

I was standing just inside a tree line. There was a rusted white pick-up truck pulled off to the side of the road through the branches and leaves, its hazard lights blinking.

"Jesus Christ, what happened to you, girl?" The man began untethering my tied wrists. "I thought I saw something through the trees. Dark hair, a white shirt. Who did this to you?"

Part of me wondered if I could trust the man.

What if it was all a part of some sick game?

What if he was only there to play tricks on me?

I took a cautious step back the moment my hands were freed.

"Whoa, hey, I ain't gonna hurt you. Tell me your name. I'll take you to a hospital."

My head shook slightly, my eyes casing my surroundings. "I-I was kidnapped. He...he let me go, I think. I don't know where I am."

"You're in Bristol, Wisconsin."

I glanced back at him, blinking slowly. I wasn't sure where the man had kept us, but that was so far from my apartment in Chicago. Sixty miles north, at least. "You're...you're not working with him? My kidnapper?"

It was silly for me to think the man would openly admit it if he had been.

His face soured at the question. "'Course not, honey. I was just driving by," he said, his eyes soft and trustful. "Let's get you safe and warm. I've got a blanket in my truck."

The air was mellow, but I couldn't stop shivering.

My wrists were sore and barely healed. Chafed, too, the skin rubbed raw. My legs were wobbly, my knees scuffed and stained with dirt. There was a carving in the middle of my ribs, right below my breasts, that stung against the itchy cotton T-shirt.

And my heart...my heart was nothing like it used to be.

Not seeing any other options, I followed the man, holding onto his burly arm for support as we trudged through the sticks and shrubs. He glanced at me every so often as he guided me to his truck a few yards away.

My belly cramped.

It was a miracle my body hadn't bled out and purged the

fragile life from my womb, given the circumstances and months-worth of abuse, terror, and neglect.

The baby growing inside of me was a fighter, that much I knew.

As we made our way to the vehicle, the good Samaritan helped me up into the passenger's seat and fetched a ratty quilt from the bed of the truck. It was draped around me when he hopped into the driver's side, and it smelled like mothballs and bonfire smoke. I savored the scent. All I'd breathed in since the day I was taken had been basement mildew, death, and my own vomit.

And Matthew.

I missed the scent of his skin. Cedar, spices, and safety. Even sans a shower, he'd been a breath of fresh air to my clogged lungs.

"I'll take you to the nearest emergency room. It's about eight miles from here."

"Thank you," I whispered to the stranger as we pulled out onto the main drag. Trees blurred by as I stared out the window and drank in the dark-blue hue of the sky. Blue, just like his eyes. "Thank you for finding me."

His reply didn't register as I squinted toward the clouds. The fluffy streaks of white were still too far away to touch, but they were closer than they were before.

I was free.

I was free, and I was no longer alone.

Inhaling a shuddering breath, I clasped my hands over my swollen belly and closed my eyes.

If it was a boy, I would name him Matthew.

If it was a girl...

Maybe I would name her Hope.

Present Day

EVAN CLICKS off the tape recorder and stares at me, silently.

He has that look in his eyes.

That questioning, dubious look.

I'm already in a dejected mood. All I want to do is get this interview over with and go home, video call my baby, and burrow under my bed covers with a hot cup of tea.

Gabe ignored my text all night, leaving me sick with anxiety. The message showed Read, but he never replied.

Not until early this morning.

All he said was:

GABE:

> Sorry, got busy with work. Let me know when you're around so we can talk.

Talk.

He wants to talk.

There was no mention of my provocative invitation, no reference to the red lingerie I wore all night in hopes that he'd show up and rip it off of me. No flirtation, no playful emojis or silly quips. Zero hint of *my* Gabe.

My instincts tell me something is wrong, but our last encounter was perfectly, beautifully *right*. Nothing makes sense. Nothing explains his emotionless text, nor the uneasy lump that sits heavy in the pit of my stomach.

I cower back in my rolling chair, glancing down at the maple-brown desk as I chew on my fingernail. "What is it?" I mutter to Evan.

From the corner of my eye, I see the way he rubs a hand over his jaw and scratches at the dark stubble, a humming sound skimming his lips.

It's that questioning, dubious humming sound.

"Nothing, I just..." Pausing, he waits for me to look at him. When I do, he fills his cheeks with air and blows out a breath. "A few things are feeling a little 'off' to me."

My molars clack together. "I don't know what you want me to say. I told you everything." I swallow. "Everything up until the police station, anyway. I was about to get to that part. I was questioned by detectives, but all I could give them was a composite sketch. I never knew where I was...it was just a basement. I didn't even know what town I was in, and the man never gave us his name. There wasn't much to go on."

"Okay. That part makes sense." He squints at me like he's

trying to uncover hidden words and bitten-back secrets. "But some of the earlier details are a bit shaky. Earl Hubbard's motives for letting you go, specifically. And Matthew's...death."

"He was a madman. A psychopath. Some people are just sick, and their motives stem from that sickness."

"I get that." He nods, pulling his bottom lip between his teeth and sliding it left to right. "I've just done a lot of research on serial killers, sociopaths, et cetera. And I've done a hell of a lot of research on Hubbard."

I twist the hem of my blouse between my hands. "Okay."

Evan sweeps his fingers through his hair, weighing his words. "You're telling me he developed feelings for you. A bond. He couldn't kill you, so he let you go."

"He did let me go. Obviously, there was a bond, or he would have killed me, too."

"That's not the detail I'm stuck on," he says. "It's the *why*. The nature of the bond."

I remain silent, chewing on my cheek.

"Earl Hubbard wasn't capable of falling in love with you, Tabitha. He just wasn't, and Matthew knew that. He advised you to pivot in a new direction, to create a different kind of bond, and I think that's what you did. But there's a reason why you're holding something back...there's more to the story." A softness reaches his eyes, diluting the heaviness of his words. "Listen, you're not required to tell me everything. Well—anything, for that matter. Your mental health is more important than a book deal, please know that. But, if you're doing this to move on, to really move forward...it might be worth it to be completely truthful. Maybe that's what's keeping you from healing."

My legs cross, one over the other, as the sounds from the other rooms seep into the office. Summer's giggles. A television show laugh track. A car driving by outside the cracked window. I look down at the metallic ring laced through the chain around my neck before taking it in my hand, cupping it in my palm.

Evan leans over the desk to fetch the tape recorder and presses an assortment of buttons, starting it, stopping it, rewinding, again, again.

Eventually, he stops at a specific point and lifts his eyes to me. "Listen to this part."

He presses play.

My voice filters through the speaker, detailing Matthew's glossed-over death.

"*—The knife swung, and Matthew crumpled before me. The light left his eyes as he stared up at me, confessing his love while he bled out. It was over. He was gone. And then the man kept me down in that basement for six more weeks, having developed strong feelings for me. He couldn't let me go. I belonged to him now. I was terrified I would become his forever pet…*"

He stops it.

Now it's just the residual echo of my words mingling with the various external sounds.

I inhale a long breath.

"Hmm," Evan hums softly.

My throat feels like I swallowed a lump of coal. "Wh-what's wrong?" I stammer.

Rubbing his neck, he leans back in the chair with a sigh. "Well, considering all the details you've provided throughout these interviews, the nature of Matthew's murder felt oddly… ambiguous. Vague. You've been so thorough, but that whole bit was skimmed over, like it was just a minor bullet point in the narrative."

Glancing down at my clasped hands in my lap, I pull my lips between my teeth and swallow. "It was a difficult moment to recount."

"I know." Evan squints at me before scooting back and moving to open his desk drawer. He pulls out that news article again and sets it in front of me, pointing at the picture with his middle finger. "Fiona Leigh Hubbard. Your abductor's mother."

"I know who she is."

"Hubbard's father was abusive—he beat Fiona while she was seven months pregnant with Earl's sibling. The beating triggered premature labor. She suffered a subdural hemorrhage and passed away a few hours post-delivery, and the baby died two days later."

"I know," I repeat.

Evan levels me with a long stare. "When Earl Hubbard was six years old, he stabbed his father to death. It was calculated, premeditated. His father was passed-out drunk on the recliner, and Earl butchered him. Stabbed him close to two-hundred times until the man was hardly identifiable. Hubbard later said that it was punishment for killing his mother," he explains. "The cops found him sitting right in the middle of the carnage watching Captain Kangaroo with this photograph of Fiona clutched in his hands. He'd used his father's blood to draw a heart around her pregnant belly."

Uneasiness slithers through me as I imagine the grisly scene. "I'm familiar with his history. I saw bits and pieces of that Matchmaker documentary."

All I could stomach, anyway.

It hit too close to home.

Seeing photos of the victims flash across the screen had me switching the television off and crying myself to sleep with Hope curled around me.

Sunlight seeps in through the window behind Evan, backlighting the pensive expression I can barely make out through the shadowy cast. He pulls an ankle up to his opposite knee and leans back in the chair, studying me from across the desk. "You said you were vomiting regularly shortly before Matthew died."

"They were traumatic circumstances. There's nothing out of the ordinary about it."

"The last time I brought up Hubbard's mother, you got fidgety. I could tell the topic made you uncomfortable, so I let it go." His smile is sincere as he tilts his head. "I don't want to make you uncomfortable, Tabitha, but I do want to do your story justice. And that last interview has me scratching my head a little. It feels like I'm missing something."

My heart rate quickens, my hands clamming up as I continue to twist the hem of my blouse into a sweaty ball of linen.

He's right. I'm fidgety.

Evan picks up a pen and clicks it with his thumb, his foot bobbing atop his knee. "Why did you gloss over Matthew's death?" he wonders curiously. "What are you protecting?"

Instinct has my hands clasping over my stomach as my eyes close, my mind spiraling back in time, reliving those last two months.

Reliving the moment that triggered them.

It's time.

It's time to explain what really happened on Matthew's last day.

"I was protecting Matthew," I finally whisper, the words catching on a small sob.

Evan inches forward, steeples his hands.

Stares at me and waits.

I suck in a deep breath and finish, "I was protecting the truth about our baby."

CHAPTER 33

TABITHA

Two Years Earlier

Drip. Drip. Drip.
　　The drippy sounds echoed off the cement walls, the stars bringing little light to our barren quarters.

We hadn't eaten in two days.

We'd only been given brief bathroom breaks, after the man told us that he didn't want to breathe in any *mess* we might make down there. It wasn't because he cared; it wasn't because he felt anything other than pure evil.

With only handfuls of water in our bodies and hollowness seeping into our bones, it was getting harder to hold on to any semblance of hope.

Drip. Drip. Drip.

I was so thirsty.

My dreams had been filled with images of breaking free of my chains and guzzling down dirty water from the dripping pipe. It felt like my body was shriveling away to dust.

Matthew and I had spent the day telling stories, finding sweet memories and pockets of laughter within the hopelessness. There was a heaviness hanging between us, an ominous breath of finality, so we made the most of what little time we likely had left.

When the night sky twinkled at me through the narrow window, I squinted at the stars before glancing across the way at Matthew, who was borrowed by shadow. "The stars," I said softly. "You tell me to look at them when I'm scared. Why is that?"

I could tell he wasn't asleep by the way his shoulders stirred slightly and by the way his head gently tilted. "I've always had a fascination with stars. They are boundless, limitless. I could get lost in them." His voice trailed off for a handful of seconds. "Whenever I was at a crossroads, I would stare up at the constellations for a long time. They gave me peace and direction."

"Stars always made me nervous when I was a kid," I admitted. "They were so high up, and I was scared of heights. My friends would tell me that falling stars were a magical thing, but all I could do was imagine myself falling from that great height." I felt his eyes on me as I shook my head. "It was silly...but it's why I can't fly on an airplane."

"We'll have to change that one day."

I smiled with melancholy. "Do you believe stars are more than what they are? You know...like dreams?" I wasn't sure if that had made any sense, or what I was hoping to gain from his answer, so I just waited for him to laugh at the strange question.

There was no laughter or amusement, even though I pictured his mouth tipping with a little grin. Maybe it didn't do that at all, and maybe it only remained in a flat, hopeless line, but I pictured it anyway because the image had my own mouth tipping.

"Yes," he said. "I do."

"What do you think they are?"

"I don't know, but I think it does us a disservice to look at the stars and believe that they are only stars. There is too much we don't understand and too much we can't see to remain boxed into simplicities. That feels too...easy, I suppose. Human beings are complex creatures, and the world created for us is no different. Exactly like dreams."

His response fascinated me.

Matthew Gleason was a psychology professor with a brain steeped in sound logic and facts. It seemed odd that he'd believe in whimsy and mystical design. "No offense, but you strike me as a man too smart to believe in fantastical things like that."

And there it was.

A soft burst of laughter, telling me his mouth was tipped up with that smile my eyes longed to see.

"I believe that the sharpest minds find logic in the notion that logic cannot be found in everything. The smartest people know that they can't possibly know all," he told me, an air of fluidity in his tone. "The universe is too vast, too mysterious. Coincidence, fate, luck, dreams—those things can't be discredited. Those things add another layer to the human condition and are just as important as science."

My attention dipped to the old watch secured around his wrist. The way his body was perched against the pole allowed me to catch sight of the glass face whenever he shifted, and when a trickling of moonlight hit it just right. "Luck," I whispered. "You told me that you wear your wristwatch for good luck."

"Mhm," he acknowledged. "It's a Vulcain Cricket my grandfather acquired in the fifties. It's worth a pretty penny these days, but I could never part with it."

I swallowed, looking down at my bare legs that seemed to blend in with the gray floor. It was all a muddle of shadows. "I'm sorry to tell you this, but it doesn't seem to be bringing you much luck."

"No?" He went quiet for a few beats, my words hanging heavy in the air. "I disagree. I used to keep it in my nightstand, too afraid to wear something that was so valuable. I didn't want to break it or lose it," he explained. "Honestly, I'm not sure what compelled me to put it on that day...but I did."

I waited.

I waited in the shadows, hoping his next words brought me light.

"I put it on...and then you walked into my classroom."

My heart shriveled. I fisted the ring he gave me in my sweat-slicked hand, squeezing it tight. "Meeting me was the unluckiest thing of all," I croaked out. Tears blurred what little I could see of him. "Look at where that got you."

"That's one way of looking at it," he stated. "But I'm here with you, bringing you a little bit of joy and happiness when you could be entirely alone. Maybe that's my purpose. Maybe I was always meant to be here, to give you the strength to make it out of this alive."

No.

That was an awful purpose.

That was an absurd, twisted way of looking at his entire existence.

I shook my head adamantly, clenching my jaw. "If that's the case, then I don't believe in the stars. I don't believe in cosmic design or fate," I shot back. "It seems too cruel."

Silence infected us as my heart pounded. It pounded like every heartbeat was rejecting his every word.

And then he said, "Maybe you'll see it differently when you're lying in your warm bed one day with the man you love, with a child sleeping peacefully down the hall, with a thriving, beautiful life filled with beautiful things."

I gasped, and I choked on that gasp.

"No," I cried, still swinging my head back and forth. "No."

"Tell me, Tabitha," he continued, his voice fused with new emotion. "If I told you that my dying wish was for you to live that life, would you fight for it?"

"Matthew, don't..."

"Would you hold on to that wish and let it push you into survival mode, let it fuel you into escaping to the other side of these walls, no matter the cost, no matter the heartache or how hard that might seem...even if I'm gone?"

My head dropped back against the pole with a sob as my body shook and shivered, tears streaming down my cheeks in rivulets of pure grief.

I wanted to tell him *no*.

I wanted to tell him, no, no, no, I wouldn't do that at all, because promising him those things would make him complacent and willing to surrender all the more.

But a dying wish was a dying wish.

And that was really all a dying man had left.

So, I told him, with everything I had left, with every piece of my broken, broken heart: "Yes."

Matthew's sigh of relief carried over to me as he responded in a choked whisper, "Then I would consider myself a lucky man."

My sobs nearly buckled me over as I pulled my knees to my chest and trembled against the pole. I would like to say the moment was fractured by the sound of Matthew's laughter, or by another noble, hopeful word tumbling from his lips, but instead, it was shattered by the sound of that goddamn door bursting open and steely boots stomping down the stairsteps.

Our captor approached me first, his gaze trailing me up and down, drinking me in. He paused in front of me. The black look in his eyes faded slightly as he stared, something softer infecting the shadows. It was strange to see. It didn't fit into his cruel features. It didn't blend with his thin lips and angry jawline. But it did give me a jolt of hopefulness, a shot of prospect, because it wasn't a look I was familiar with.

He lumbered toward me, his eyes fixed on my own popeyed gaze.

And then he just…stared.

An uncomfortable amount of time passed as he zoned out, slightly teetering back and forth. Swaying; almost like something had taken possession of him.

I watched his face scrunch up. "What?" I whispered.

He shook his head, features contorting with distress. "You didn't deserve that, Fiona."

There was a fog around him. Rainclouds and gray mist.

My attention drifted to Matthew as he stood there, staring at me, before nodding with encouragement. Almost as if to say, *"Go with it, Tabitha. Go with it and pretend. This is the way out."*

I fisted the ring in my hand, my nerves on edge. "Y-you're right. I didn't deserve it."

"What he did to you…" He frowned. "That bastard should've been swallowed."

"Yes."

His dark eyes were still clouded, blackened with memories. "I did it for you, you know. Thought you'd be proud of me."

"I was," I rasped. "I was so proud."

He stared for another handful of beats, and then he blinked.

It was a blink and a headshake, and the haze dissipated. The cloud cover cleared, leaving him looking confused. He scrubbed both hands over his face, then swiped them across the top of his head. Pivoting back to Matthew, he stormed over to him. "What are you waiting for? Let's go, get up."

Disappointment filtered through me.

The moment had passed, and we were back in the basement.

I tuned out through the standard routine, making myself numb to it. Our captor unchained Matthew, sing-songing his sick motives as he forced him in my direction for what the man considered another assault.

It wasn't an assault; not by Matthew.

It was my only salvation.

Longing trumped the disappointment when Matthew reached for me, cupping my face between his palms. A look came over him the moment our faces were inches apart. It was that same look that sparkled in the blue of his eyes every time he was close enough to see me clearly.

"You can see me?" I asked softly.

He smiled, his index finger grazing down the curve of my jaw. "I see you."

Matthew's buckle unhooked, his jeans falling to the cement. As always, he kissed me instantly, and I fell forward, pulling toward him as much as my cuffs would allow.

And then, a pocket of restoration. As soon as he was inside me, I felt renewed.

It was magic, sweet relief.

It was a nagging tug of hope, and it felt too cruel to let myself get lost in it.

Matthew cradled my face and brushed away the tears stuck to my cheeks. "I'm getting you out of here," he whispered. "You know that, right?"

Mindlessly, I nodded.

I trusted him; I trusted him with everything I had left.

Everything felt so pure for a few heartbeats.

Everything felt like it would be okay.

Soon, soon, it would be okay.

He was kissing me again, twining his fingers through my crusty, matted tresses and peppering kisses to my cheek, throat, ear. A moan slipped out, laced with sorrow, while he held on to me like a trove of priceless treasure.

But, just like that, something in the air shifted, and a growl polluted the tenderness. I was vaguely aware of the man breaching our bubble.

I panicked. It couldn't be over, not yet, not now. "Keep kissing me," I whimpered. "Don't stop."

Matthew glanced to his right as our captor hauled his pants up his hips and started pacing in aimless circles, muttering gibberish under his breath. Swallowing, Matthew slammed his lips to mine. Our mouths collided, and for a moment, I forgot about everything.

The plan, the ruse.

The chains, the rats, the leaky pipe, the stars.

I even forgot about the man still growling and pacing, sounding closer than he was before and mumbling incoherently.

Matthew's lips caressed mine, warm and alive, seeking and needy.

I savored it.

It was a perfect moment.

A final perfect moment…

"No," the monster seethed. "Get the fuck away from her. No, this ain't right. Get back, stop fucking touching her."

Matthew stilled and pulled back, obeying the command. He tucked himself into his pants and stared at me with a look I couldn't decipher as he stepped away.

I glanced at the man, then back to Matthew, frazzled, unsure. "You're unchained," I whispered. "There's a chance. Maybe now's your chance—"

He shook his head, remaining silent. His navy eyes appeared black as they glistened, telling me things I didn't want to know, showing me things I didn't want to see.

"Matthew…"

He returned his attention to the unraveling man.

Our captor jabbed the pistol toward the ceiling a few times, pacing around. Then he smacked the butt against his forehead and chanted, "I killed him. He's dead. That fucker can't hurt her anymore. I killed him."

I watched something in Matthew's expression change as he studied him. A flicker. It was both a lightbulb moment and a dark shadow, fused as one.

Anxiety inched its way between my ribs.

My heart teetered.

The man continued to spout madness, waving his pistol around. "No, no, no," he rambled, sweat glistening on his partially bald head. "Fuck. This is wrong, this is wrong. I killed him. He's fucking dead. He can't touch her."

Matthew's eyes glassed over, his throat moving with a deep swallow as some sort of revelation washed over him.

He looked back at me, and it was brief, fleeting, the span of a single second…

But I saw it.

It was a look of finality.

He reached for me quickly, leaned in, and whispered against my ear, "Pretend to be Fiona."

I sucked in a sharp breath, feeling it stall in my throat.

My heartbeats quickened with rising panic.

"Do it," he said, dragging his lips down the side of my neck as he choked back what sounded like a sob. "Play along."

My eyes closed, lashes damp with grief. "Please, I don't—"

"That's enough, Fiona," Matthew said suddenly, tone stern.

I swung my head back and forth, inching away, tucking my lips between my teeth. "Matthew, don't." I was terrified he'd trigger the man. I was petrified he'd be beaten again, and with little hope of ever waking up. "Please don't."

Matthew buried his face in my shoulder and inhaled the scent of my skin. I probably smelled like dirty hair and weeks-old body odor, but he breathed me in like fresh air on a midsummer day. "Trust me," he whispered again, and it hit the air like a goodbye. "I love you."

The hairs on my arms stood straight up.

I squeaked out a little sound of despair and lurched forward, reaching for him the only way I could, desperate for more kisses. For one last kiss before he was shackled again, too far away for me to make out the blue of his eyes. "Matthew…"

"Stop, Fiona. Stop running your mouth." His voice cracked on the last syllable, face twisting with apology. "You never fucking listen to me."

The words punctured me like sharp tacks, but they punctured me with awareness, not pain. I was starting to understand.

Matthew was playing into a madman's delusions. Taking on a role.

But there was a problem with that…

The role he'd taken on would be his death sentence.

"No," I gritted out through bared teeth. "Don't you dare do this."

He grabbed me by the shoulders, shaking me. "Shut up. Just shut up."

"*Matthew*. This isn't the way. No, no, don't you—"

"Hey!" the man blasted, rushing toward us. "I said get the fuck away from her." His eyes flicked between us, wild and unhinged. "He can't hurt you. I killed him," he said to me before looking right at Matthew. "I killed *you*."

The two men locked eyes.

And then I gasped when Matthew raised his hand to me, his expression tortured, tears streaking down his cheeks.

He faltered, though.

He wavered, and I knew he couldn't do it. He couldn't hit me. *He couldn't pretend.*

But he didn't get the chance. His wrist was snatched midair when the man lunged at him, and I caught a glint of shiny metal whipping by in my periphery.

Thwomp.

Matthew grunted.

A wheeze.

With a sharp breath, his lips parted, mere inches from mine.

He stared at me, and the world stopped. Shock glazed his eyes and dilated his pupils as he pulled away, a frown wrinkling his brow. Delayed realization creased his forehead when he glanced down at the red stain blooming on his sweater.

He staggered and looked back up at me, clutching his abdomen. Blood trickled from the corner of his mouth.

"No," I murmured.

It was just a frayed whisper at first, because it couldn't be real.

This wasn't happening.

The knife sliced through the air again before I could process it. I watched the blade plunge into Matthew's gut, and my whisper became a wail, because it was happening, it was happening, it was happening.

"*No!*"

Another stab.

Another, and then another.

It was happening so fast, I could hardly register the swing of the knife, the sound of tearing flesh, the sensation of warm liquid dribbling onto the tops of my bare feet.

"You fucking piece of garbage," the man snarled, still swinging the blade. "You killed her, so I kill you. That's how this works, you worthless motherfucker. You killed that baby. You killed them both. You stole from me. Fuck you. *Fuck you.*"

Matthew wrenched forward with a piercing exhale, and a spattering of blood misted my face.

I flinched.

I held my breath as I blinked through the shock.

One of his hands landed on the pole above my head as his other arm draped across his stomach. He stared at me as the light drained from his eyes and he croaked out, "Tabitha."

And then he buckled at my feet in a slow-motion collapse. His knees hit first, one of his hands curling around the hem of my T-shirt like he was unwilling to let me go.

I gazed down at him, dumbstruck.

Numb.

When I was seven years old, I'd watched a car accident unfold before my eyes. My mother had been fiddling with the radio, preoccupied, missing that the light had turned green.

A car had honked from behind.

That was when metal collided into metal right in front of us, right in the middle of the intersection, just as her foot had pressed the accelerator. She'd slammed on the brakes, narrowly missing the collision that had ended up taking a young woman's life.

That same feeling pierced me now. The disbelief, the horror, the mind's refusal to comprehend what the eyes were seeing. It was a delay, a denial—as if we weren't capable of understanding something so heinous in mere seconds.

Life-altering moments took time to sink in.

"You monster. You baby killer. How does it feel, huh?" The man growled, kicking Matthew onto his side as he adjusted his waistband.

My mind caught up.

Reality sank its jagged teeth into my heart, and I blurted out, "I'm still pregnant! Stop! The baby didn't die. I'm still pregnant." I shook my chains, twisted and writhed, shrieked at the top of my lungs. "*Stop!*" A beastly, inhuman sound ripped through me, but it didn't rip me open. I wished it would. I wished it would incinerate me from the inside out until I was nothing but dust and confetti being carried over to the man I loved bleeding out on the cement.

We could be together that way.

"Please, stop, I'm pregnant, I'm *pregnant*," I wailed.

Our captor paused, sweat gleaming on his brow. He turned to me, eyes narrowed and glassed-over. "Liar. He killed the baby."

"No, I swear it, I promise. Let me take a test and you'll see that I'm pregnant. I was before. I was…before you took us," I confessed, and it was finally out there; it was finally real.

And it was too late.

Matthew groaned beside my feet, blood gushing from his stab wounds and sputtering from his lips. He gazed up at me, shell-shocked in every way.

I nodded with confirmation, tears spilling down my cheeks.

I'd suspected it; my period was late in the days leading up to our abduction.

I knew, I knew, I knew.

I should have told him.

I knew I should have, but I thought we were going to die down there. He didn't need to know there could have been one more life to lose, a life that was growing inside me. Everything would have become a thousand times more tragic.

The man blinked at me, his gaze trailing down to my belly. We had only been down there two weeks, far too soon for me to know I was pregnant, so dubiety clouded his expression.

"Ah, fuck it, he's a dead man anyway," our captor mumbled. Then, grunting and huffing, he bent over and gripped Matthew by the collar of his sweater and started dragging his bleeding body back to the pole, away from me.

The man I loved wasn't even allowed to die beside me.

"NO!"

I didn't recognize my own voice. There was nothing familiar in it. It belonged to the darkness now, where music forgot its melodies, and the sun forgot how to shine, and stars forgot that they were made for granting wishes.

"Don't touch him! Leave him alone!"

Matthew fought back with the little strength he had, his feet stumbling along the floor, sliding through the bloodstains left behind. He reached for the man's arms, scratching and twisting, wheezing through his meager attempts to break free.

It was no use.

There was never any hope for us.

I screamed and screamed, and I couldn't stop screaming. The bone-rattling cries depleted my lungs, shredded my throat raw, and it was all I could do.

There was nothing else I could do.

The man heaved and puffed as he tinkered with Matthew's

cuffs, securing him to the pipe. Positioning him in his final resting place. He kicked him one more time before he hobbled back toward the staircase, tugging at his hair, still rambling under his breath. "He's a dead man. He's a dead man, it's all right. I took care of it." He glanced at me one more time as he spun around. "You'll be all right. It's okay now. I saved you."

The door slammed shut.

He left us down there. He left me a screaming, hollering, hopeless mess, while Matthew choked and spluttered on his own blood.

"*Matthew!*" I shrieked, lunging forward. "No, no, *no!*"

He was riddled in holes. At least a dozen.

Blood pooled out from the stab wounds, leaving puddles of crimson beneath his body. They grew in size, a grisly stream traveling at a downward trajectory, right where the floor dipped.

"Tabitha..." he gasped, blood oozing from the corners of his mouth. His throat worked as he struggled to spit out more words.

A single question.

"Yes, yes, it's true," I cried, confirming. "It's true. I was going to take a test that night, after you drove me home. I was late, and I...oh God, please, stay with me, stay with me, please, *please.*"

I couldn't breathe. I couldn't even breathe.

I wanted to die with him and break my promise.

I just wanted it to be *over.*

"Our...b-baby," he stuttered, his breathing shallow.

"I didn't say anything because I didn't know for sure, and I thought we were going to die. I didn't want to give you another loss to grieve, another heartache to carry. I'm so sorry, Matthew, I should have told you sooner...because maybe you wouldn't have done that. God, why did you do that? Why did you *do that!*" I screeched, violently jerking my chains.

We'd only had one night together.

One reckless night that was never supposed to be more. It had been foolish, spontaneous. I'd run into him at a bar with Corbin and two other friends a few weeks before the abduction. A conversation over billiards turned into him offering to drive me home, which turned into making out in his car, which turned into a cheap motel room where we'd spent one passionate, blissful hour together before reality had set in.

We hadn't used protection.

He was my teacher.

It had been a mistake, a lapse in judgment, and we never spoke of it again.

But it happened.

It was real, it was everything, and now there was a life growing inside me; I was certain of it.

"Matthew, please, you *have* to fight. You have to," I plead. "Fight for me. Fight for our child."

He was sprawled out on his back, arms twisted behind him. His bent knee fell flat as he murmured, "Remember...your p-promise. Live. Fight. Tell her...about me."

All I could do was howl, beg, bleed with him.

I pulled on my chains so hard, my wrist bones broke. I felt them crumble, nothing but useless brittle inside of me. The pain didn't compare to what I was feeling, to what I was witnessing.

"I'll always...be with you." His breathing became shallower with every syllable. "I love..."

My vision blurred as a blanket of tears coated my eyes and my mind dizzied. I felt myself shutting down. Something in me died right along with him, and I fell to the cement, repeating his name through my awful, sobbing moans.

"Matthew, Matthew...*Matthew*," I cried. "Don't leave me here. Don't you *leave us*!" I slammed my chains against the pipe, ignoring the pain that shot through both broken arms. I relished in it. I welcomed it. "We're in this together. We're in this *together*. You can't leave. You can't go. Please, please, we need you. I love you. You're all I have. I can't do this without you."

He didn't say anything.

He was hardly breathing anymore.

"*MATTHEW!*" I shrieked.

Finally, he coughed. A splintered, frail cough. Matthew twitched, his eyes fluttering closed, and he whispered raggedly, "To rank the effort...above the prize...may be called..."

The words trailed off.

They just faded into nothingness as his chest heaved a final time then went still.

I stared at him in horror, in awful realization. "Matthew."

This couldn't be it. This couldn't be goodbye.

Two weeks ago, we'd been discussing cognitive psychology

and the study of attention and its role in perception and memory while Professor Gleason had paced the classroom, his dark-blue eyes trailing to me every so often through black-rimmed glasses.

I wanted to be that bright-eyed psychology student again. Just a college girl who'd been carrying around a scandalous secret.

"Matthew," I repeated.

No response.

Not a cough, not a wheeze.

Not even the barest breath.

"No," I whimpered. "Matthew, please…"

Panic jolted through me as I blinked, trying to clear the fog from my eyes. Trying to see something that wasn't there.

Nothing.

He didn't move.

"Matthew, Matthew, *Matthew*!"

I wasn't sure how many times I yelled his name. I shouted it, cried it, whispered it, an assortment of different pitches, lilts, and timbres. I said it a thousand times, a thousand different ways.

He never responded.

Those were his last words.

And then I flinched, jumped in place, when a grating sound rang out through the basement.

An alarm.

A shrieky, buzzing alarm bell.

It sounded like a dying symphony of cicadas. I yearned to slam my hands over my ears to block it out, but I couldn't, I couldn't do anything but sit there and listen to that high-pitched ringing while Matthew lay lifeless before me.

The sound was coming from his watch.

His lucky, lucky watch.

Tears racked my body, blending with the sound of the misfiring watch, until the noise eventually stopped. It stopped, just like his heart had stopped, just like my will to live had stopped along with the swing of a knife.

The monster left me alone with Matthew's body for two days.

Nearly forty-eight hours.

It wasn't enough to lose him. It wasn't even enough to watch him die in front of me.

No...I was forced to share my cell with his cold, lifeless body for two days while his blood still stained my skin.

The sun rose, and the sun set, telling me I was still alive. The stars twinkled on the other side of the glass window, immune to my suffering, and the moon served as a weak nightlight in my darkest hours when sleep failed to give me the smallest reprieve.

On the second day, insomnia spurred a bout of madness, and I'd convinced myself that Matthew was faking it; that it was part of the plan. I'd watched his chest fall up and down through the shadows, and counted his breaths out loud. I'd made it to seven hundred and thirty-two before losing track and starting all over again. When the rats had come sniffing around him, I'd cursed them away, shouting that he was still alive, he was still alive, he was still alive.

He was just pretending.

I'd told him stories and shared my secrets as I laid sideways on the cement, my legs tucked to my chest, my wrists painfully fractured. One of my secrets was that I talked to my houseplants like they were people. I'd never told anyone that before. I named them, too.

I talked to my plants like they were people, and I talked to a dead man like he was still alive.

I felt myself going mad.

I was wrought with delirium, just like my captor, as I told Matthew that he was going to be a wonderful father to our baby.

Her.

Matthew had thought it would be a girl.

Then, as the sun set that second night, I realized, for absolute certain, that Matthew was gone. He wasn't coming back. I was ripped from the hallucinations when the man returned with food and water. There was a brown paper bag of groceries under his armpit, and a bowl of noodles in one hand, a cup of water in the other. The cup was a muddy shade of brownish-red, the ramen most likely chicken. It was hard to say for sure because it tasted like ashes on my tongue as I let the noodles slide down my throat, unchewed.

The man jabbed a glass of water at my lips, forcing my teeth to unclench. Liquid dribbled down my chin as I gulped and sputtered. I choked on it, sobbing my grief and denial.

He continued to feed me, telling me it would be okay, and

that Matthew couldn't hurt us any longer. Whistling, he sauntered backward and emptied the paper bag. The contents spilled around my legs. Fruit, crackers, granola bars, and a box of pregnancy tests.

I swallowed, blinking slowly, feeling numb as my chains were untethered, and I was hauled up the stairs to the dingy bathroom.

When I stepped out, I had a used pregnancy test tucked inside my fist.

Positive.

The man grinned when I showed him the result. "I'll take care of you now," he said. "No need to be afraid."

He told me he'd protect us and keep us safe.

And I bent over and heaved, retching all over his disgusting boots.

"Ah, fuck," he cursed.

Minutes later, I was chained to the pole again, my broken wrists hissing with pain as they were cuffed behind my back.

The man finally left, taking Matthew's body with him. He wrapped it in a blue tarp and hauled it up the staircase with thick ropes, sweating and muttering "fuck" under his breath hundreds of times. At one point, he stumbled halfway up the steps and fell on his ass, grunting something about a "goddamn corpse" before kicking the human-shaped tarp and trying again.

It took him twelve minutes to make it through the door.

And then, he was gone.

They were both gone, and I was entirely alone, and it was so, so quiet.

It was just me.

Me and the rats.

Me and the useless stars.

Me and a fatherless baby who would be born inside the pits of Hell.

Me…

And that leaky fucking pipe.

Drip.

Drip.

Drip…

Present Day

EVAN CATCHES me as I collapse.

He's on his feet and around the desk in a flash, just as I crumble and my body slides from the chair, my knees hitting the floor. I slump against his chest with my face buried in my palms.

"Whoa, shh, it's okay," he tells me, patting my back. "You did good. Let it out, take a breath. You're okay. You're fine."

"I-I'm s-sorry," I croak out, quivering and breaking down. "I didn't mean to…hide anything from you…I just—"

"It doesn't matter. This isn't about me."

"I wanted…to protect him."

"I know."

"I was afraid people would think…less of him. And he was… so much. He saved me. He saved *us*." I'm choking on my sniffles and cries, purging and releasing. "I've never told anybody."

"It's okay. I'll leave that part out of the book, you have my word," Evan assures me, still patting my back like he's soothing his young daughter. "I won't say anything. Your secret is safe."

My face lifts from my hands as I drop back on my haunches, my eyes flaring. "Everything else was true, I swear. Every detail. I don't want you to think—"

"No, hey, don't worry. I believe you. I understand your reasoning for keeping that detail private, and the timing of the pregnancy was so close, nobody questioned it. They assumed you got pregnant in the basement, given the circumstances. I just happen to be obnoxiously thorough—it's a curse." A small grin lifts as he settles across from me on the floor, flicking a hand through his hair. "I hope I didn't back you into a corner. I just thought that maybe being completely forthcoming would give you some kind of breakthrough. Another step toward healing."

I nod, swallowing the burning knot in my throat.

He's right.

Even though I'm a broken-down mess right now, after

reliving the single-worst moment of my life, I feel like a weight has been lifted. A smothering boulder has been pushed off my heart.

My hair is stuck to the tear stains on my cheeks. I swipe the damp strands out of my eyes, inhaling a shuddery breath. "He was a good man, Evan. An incredible man. He had a moment of weakness that night we were together, but that didn't make him weak. I hope you believe that."

"Of course I do. The picture you painted was of a selfless, noble man. A hero. I never once questioned that."

I let a smile slip, wiping the heels of my hands along my cheekbones.

"He was brave and smart. He saw a crack in Hubbard, and then he saw a way in," he says. "That way in was a way out for you."

"And my way out was his demise." I shake my head, my eyes welling with more tears. "He knew that, and he did it anyway."

Evan scratches at his cheek. "Hubbard was mentally ill. That doesn't excuse anything he did, not by a longshot. But he suffered delusions, psychotic breaks. He was a very sick individual and eleven people lost their lives because of it. Matthew sensed that Hubbard was correlating you with his dead mother, so he took on the role of his abusive father who ended her life. He believed that if Hubbard felt like he was protecting you—or, in his mind, protecting Fiona—you stood a chance at getting out of there." Glancing over my shoulder, he rubs his jaw and sighs. "Turns out he was right."

My eyes feel dry and bloodshot as I scrub away more tears and rise to my feet. "It's been easier to tell people that my captor fell in love with me. No one really questioned it, you know? I was worried that if I gave away too many details, more details would spill out and people would start to connect the dots. Suspect things. I was scared they would learn the truth about my relationship with Matthew, and then the world would crucify him. Punish him, taint his beautiful memory. I couldn't stomach that. People can be…cruel."

Evan stands and leans back on the desk, his arms crossing. "Yeah. I get that."

"I was down there six more weeks," I continue, returning to the rolling chair. "The man…Hubbard…kept one of my wrists unchained, so I was free to eat and drink at will. He'd come down once a day to take me to the bathroom and he'd rub my belly, calling the baby Wilson." A shiver rolls through me. "I played into the illusion. I kept my promise to Matthew because it wasn't just me I was fighting for…it was Hope, too. So I played the part. He never raped me again, never raised his hand to me. Never called me 'Kitten' or degraded me. In his mind, I was his mother, and the baby was his sibling."

Evan cants his head, eyes squinting. "And then he let you go."

My throat stings as I bob my head. "Yes…I don't know why. I truly thought he'd keep me forever, and that my baby would be born in that basement."

"Yeah," he muses, nodding. "That surprises me. Given that you saw his face, and that he associated you with his mother, one would assume that he'd be unwilling to ever let you go. On the contrary, he wasn't playing with a full deck. We'll probably never know what triggered him to release you that day. He was careful about it, too. There was self-preservation there—drugging you, blindfolding you, and dropping you far enough away from his property." Evan's lips twist with thought. "It's bizarre, but I guess it doesn't matter in the end. You made it out. And Hubbard is dead, so he can't hurt anybody anymore."

"Yes," I mutter. "Matthew's sacrifice wasn't in vain."

Evan sends me a tender smile, laced with pride, like he's happy to have been a part of a really good thing. We say our goodbyes, and I stand from the chair, giving him a hug before I leave the interview room for the last time.

The click of the tape recorder shutting off sounds like a burden being cut loose. Chipped away. My traumatic past attached itself to me like a tumor, and while I'll never be fully free from it, it somehow feels less heavy.

Less terminal.

My story has been told, and the crippling weight of my secret has been shared.

I did it.

I'm finally in recovery.

CHAPTER 34
TABITHA

I reread his latest text message as I twist the key into the lock and push open my front door.

GABE:

> I'm working late, but I'll stop by your place around 8 if that's cool. Just want to talk.

My heart pounds.

All he wants to do is...*talk*?

No lovemaking, no candlelit dinner, no drifting off to sleep tangled in each other's arms?

Something doesn't feel right but I try not to overthink. I try to keep my thoughts from twisting into dark, heartbreaking premonitions, even though my intuition is stabbing at me like a dull dagger between my ribs.

After my breakthrough with Evan today, I'm feeling...

Free.

My secret has been purged and a weight has been lifted off me. I'm going to tell Gabe tonight—I realize it's not a groundbreaking confession, and it doesn't change anything between us, but it's a piece of me I haven't allowed him access to. And that feels wrong. Our relationship was built on trust, so keeping *anything* from him feels like a tiny betrayal to everything we are.

I glance at the grandfather clock in the corner of the room tick-tocking through the silent house. It's a little past seven and my heart is restless. Normally, I'd relish in the ticking minute hands because they sever the quiet I've grown to hate.

But tonight, they sound like a countdown to something ominous.

Shaking off the goosebumps, I busy myself in the kitchen by whipping together a salad, cleaning the countertops, and organizing my spice rack alphabetically, just to keep my thoughts from spiraling. The lettuce slides down my throat in slimy lumps. The cucumbers are bitter. The dressing tastes like acrid bile on my tongue.

I toss it in the trash and stare at the clock.

Tick, tick, tick.

Five minutes past eight, there's a soft knock at my front door, and the sound has me jolting in place.

It's fine, I tell myself. *Everything is fine.*

But when I whip open the door and meet Gabe's shadowy eyes and slumped posture, the knot in my belly tells me it's not fine. "Gabe."

"Hey." He swallows and looks away. "Can I come in?"

"Of course." I step aside and watch him enter. His gait is sluggish, his disposition closed off. He doesn't touch me, doesn't hug me, and just quickly moves past me and stares at the wall. "Is everything okay?"

"Yeah, I just…" Clearing his throat, he scratches at his shaggy, uncombed hair and shakes his head. "I think I'm coming down with something. The flu, maybe."

Relief sinks into me. I feel guilty for that because I don't want him to be sick, but at least it's an explanation. It's a reason for his sudden shift in mood.

"Oh, well…I'll make you soup. I have chicken noodle."

Another headshake. His back is still turned on me, chin dipped downward. "No thanks. Not hungry."

I force a smile and pace forward. "Okay. We can go lie down, then. You should rest." When I reach him in the center of the living room, I curl my hand around his bicep. "I wanted to tell you something. It's about my interview with Evan today. I confessed some things that…" My voice trails off when Gabe doesn't acknowledge me. He's like a stone wall. "Gabe."

A slight pause, then his head twists in my direction, his eyes still aimed at my white rug. "What did you confess?"

I blink, hating the nothingness in his tone.

It's just a mess of words with no meaning, no life.

I move in front of him, facing him, my hand still latched around his arm as the other reaches for his palm. It's stiff and clammy. My fingers lace with this, but he doesn't hold me back. Doesn't squeeze. "Let's go to my room," I suggest, my nerves heightening. I force the little smile back onto my face and sprinkle flirtation into my voice. "We can have a repeat of the other night, somewhere more comfortable than my living room floor. I can help you wind down...if you know what I mean."

He slams his eyes shut, jaw clenched tight, looking like what I just said was tragic.

My cheeky grin fades.

He *does* look sick; he looks positively ill.

I keep trying, desperation clawing through me. "Gabe, please...touch me. Hold my hand, will you?" I squeeze his fingers, but his grip is loose and limp. He won't even look at me. "What's wrong? Did something happen?"

Silence.

It's like he's shut down, somewhere else, unreachable.

"Hey...please, talk to me." I raise both hands to cup his face, forcing eye contact. "You're freaking me out."

He shrugs me off him, his body vibrating with tension. "Don't."

Rejection burns me. My cheeks feel hot, my chest tight. "Gabe..." Anguish climbs my throat as I lift up on my toes. I try to kiss him, but the moment before our lips meet, he turns his head away.

He dodges my kiss.

And then he utters two words that slaughter the remaining tatters of my heart:

"Tabula Rasa."

I freeze on my tiptoes, my nails digging into his arms to keep me from buckling.

"Say it and we stop. Say it and it's over."

It's a slow-motion collapse to the soles of my feet. My hands fall from his arms, and I inch backward, farther, farther, putting more distance between me and the bloody remnants of my heart that plunged to the living room rug.

Gabe stands there, statue-still, his eyes on the floor.

I stare at him in shock, shaking from head to toe, because I can't believe he just said that.

I can't believe he used my safe-word against me.

And I suppose it's as they say: what goes up must come down.

But it's a shame they don't tell you about the crash.

They don't mention how hard you'll hit, or how much it will hurt. There's no talk of the bones cracking, the lungs wheezing, the heart bleeding and bruised.

Even worse, the look in your lover's eyes when he watches you plummet to the pavement and rupture into a thousand grisly pieces at his feet.

It's a bloodbath, a massacre, a catastrophe.

It's inevitable, though; there's always a crash.

And I think if I'd have known…

I never would have tried to fly.

CHAPTER 35

GABE

My father always used to tell me, "Never look those fuckers in the eyes before you kill them."

Not exactly the sage wisdom a child would expect from a parent. While other kids my age were being told to never go swimming on a full stomach and to stay away from strangers in white vans, I was being taught how to kill without hesitation.

Hesitation was a gateway to empathy, he'd tell me, and empathy made a man weak.

He was talking about hunting, of course.

Deer, rabbits, and even turkeys in late fall when we'd bundle up before the sun crested and chase longbeards through the grass. Funny enough, I never cared much for hunting. There was nothing rewarding or satisfying about watching an animal bleed out in the dirt.

My father told me I was pathetic one day while a twelve-gauge shotgun trembled in my grip and my shoes sunk into spongy earth. I begged the ground to turn into quicksand, just so I wouldn't have to pull that trigger.

"You're pathetic, Gabe. An embarrassment to the Wellington name," he spat, hocking a mouthful of tobacco near my shoes. "Shoot the damn thing, Son."

A stunning deer stood frozen a few feet away, looking right at me.

I stared into its eyes as my gut rolled with dread and my heart raced with indecision.

"Christ, give me that."

My father yanked the weapon from my hands and put a bullet in the deer's head without even blinking.

I didn't eat the venison that night. All I could think about was that look in the animal's eyes when I'd pointed my gun at it, marking it for death.

As I stand here now, those words swim through me, settling in my chest like bricks.

Never look your kill in the eyes before you pull the trigger.

I took his advice this time. I kept my eyes on the floor as the ashes of my words sprinkled around us like black confetti, and the lingering smoke made her choke.

Only then, I looked up.

And here's the thing: my father told me about the *before*.

But he never once warned me about the *after*.

He didn't tell me about the look I'd see staring back at me after that bullet had met its target.

Stunned shock. Glazed-over disbelief.

Annihilation.

He failed to mention that it would feel like I had just turned the gun on myself.

My heart shatters while I do everything in my power to keep the wretched torment out of my eyes, to keep my limbs from trembling, to keep my arms from reaching for her and telling her how much I don't want to do this.

But I *have* to do this.

It's the only way to keep her safe.

It's the only way to keep her alive.

Tabitha's hands ball at her sides, her legs wobbling beneath her. "What?" She whispers the word like she didn't hear me.

My throat burns with shame. "I'm sorry. I wanted to make this quick and painless."

"Quick and painless?" Her neck tilts back, emotions bubbling, roiling. "What are you saying?"

"I'm saying it's over."

Confusion and incredulity shine back at me as she swings her head from side to side. "You're…ending things?"

I grind my teeth together. "Yeah, I am."

She barks a laugh, and it's a humorless, disbelieving laugh. Then she goes dead silent, as if she's waiting for the punchline. "You're lying."

"I don't want to hurt you," I mutter, forcing my tone to stay level. Impassive. "But this isn't working for me anymore."

"I don't believe you."

She *has* to believe me.

If she doesn't believe me, she'll fight for this. She'll peel back every lie-drenched layer until she uncovers the truth, and then she'll fight some more. She'll fight, because that's what she does —she *fights*. She'll fight until it kills her. Until *they* kill her.

I need Tabitha far, far away from me while I take care of this mess. And for that to happen, she needs to hate me.

Every muscle twitches, tightens, as I fold my arms across my chest to keep them from trembling at my sides. "I'm sorry, but I'm telling you it's over."

"Why?" Her features harden with outrage, with denial. "Tell me why."

"Because it's too much. I can't do these ups and downs with you, this emotional fucking rollercoaster." My brows bend, a sickly coil of guilt curling its way inside. "I can't do it."

There's a crack in my voice, and she notices.

She stomps toward me, cheeks red, eyes furious. "I hear your words, but I don't believe a single one of them. I believe what you've *shown* me, and it's not this. It's not even close."

I spin around, turning my back to her while I attempt to scrub away the evidence of my heartbreak. Heaving in a breath, I cup a hand over my jaw and exhale slowly. "That's because I was trying, okay? I was really fucking trying to make this work, but it's pointless. We were doomed from the start because you're still in love with another man. You're living in your past, and I'm living in his shadow. It's hopeless, Tabitha. You were right—I deserve more than that." My heart bleeds. Everything bleeds. "I deserve better."

"Liar," she hisses at my back. "At least have the goddamn decency to look me in the eyes while you lie to me."

I don't move. I can't.

"Look at me!"

Angry fingers snatch my elbow, whipping me back around, and I stare at her, my bottom lip quivering. It's impossible to keep my expression indifferent as I watch the tears stream down her face. I'm causing her pain when all I've ever wanted to do was take it away.

"You're barely holding it together," she croaks out, taking a step toward me as she assesses the unmistakable misery in my eyes. "Why are you saying this? You don't mean it. I know you don't."

"Tabitha, goddammit, it's over," I grit through my teeth. "Let it go. It's done."

"No…no, this is crazy. Something is wrong, something happened." She closes the gap between us and reaches for me again. Her warm palms frame my face as she begs for the truth. "Please. *Please.* Explain to me what is going on because I refuse to believe that the man who made love to me two nights ago, who held me in his arms until dawn, who told me his love was *unshakeable*, is capable of saying these awful things to me. It doesn't make any sense."

I lower her hands from my face and step back, barely containing the strangled cry in the back of my throat. "Believe it. Accept it."

She gapes at me, wide-eyed and wounded. Fury flashes across her face again, the little jade flecks in her irises fusing with copper and igniting into green flames. "I watched a man I loved die in front of me and I couldn't fight for him," she seethes, teeth bared, cheeks wet. "I was shackled to a pole with his blood on my skin, and I watched him take his last breath. I couldn't fight. I couldn't do a damn thing." Her words breathe fire as she relives the horror. "How *dare* you not let me fight for you."

Fuck.

All I can do is shake my head, my nostrils flaring. "Some fights aren't worth it."

There's a hole in my chest, and it hurts, it hurts so fucking bad.

Some fights are worth it all.

Tabitha lets out another huff of disbelief and crosses her arms, looking dazed, looking lost.

And then she hesitates.

She falters, and there's almost joking in her tone as she mutters, "It's not like there's someone else…"

Her words trail off when I don't respond.

She blinks up at me, waiting. Waiting for me to say no, no, of course not.

Of. Course. Not.

But I don't say that.

I swallow as a new wave of pain floods me, and I latch onto the implication with more silence.

The notion hits her like a sledgehammer, and her pupils dilate to giant inkblots. "No. There's not…" Her voice breaks under the weight of everything I'm not saying. "There's no one else…" When I just stand there, frozen and mute, she lets out a breathless gasp, her face crumpling. "Oh, my God."

My world spins, tilts, implodes, as my heart dismantles, piece by piece.

I still don't reply.

"Is there another woman?" she demands, her breathing growing more erratic, more unhinged. She looks like she's about to be sick. "Did you sleep with someone? Answer me, Gabe, or I swear—"

"Yes," I blurt out, the word escaping before I can stop it. "I fucked someone."

I know I can't hide the horror that sweeps across my face when the insidious lie falls out of me, just like she can't hide her own horror that extinguishes the light from her eyes.

Nausea churns in my stomach and my legs shake as they fight to keep me upright. "Last night," I continue, voice splintering. "That's why I didn't reply to your text. I went out to the bar after work. Had too much to drink. Ran into a girl I used to date, and we went back to her place…then we had sex." The false admission pours out of me like jagged bullet points. Sweat slicks my skin, and I run a hand over my face. "I'm sorry. I've just been overwhelmed with this back and forth with you, and I needed something easy."

She buys it.

I watch it wash over her like a bucket of ice water.

She buys it; she fucking *buys* it—she believes that I could actually do something like that to her.

As if she wasn't my whole goddamn world.

My *everything*.

"I hate you so much." She utters the words like little paper cuts, hardly noticeable but enough to sting. "I can't believe you would do that to me…after everything…" Panicked whimpers crawl up her throat as she drags her fingers through her hair and pushes it off her face. "I hate you. I *hate* you."

I blink rapidly, forcing the tears from leaking from my eyes. "Good. It's easier if you do."

A sob tears through her, and she lunges forward, shoving at my chest with both hands. "You asshole. You *asshole*," she growls. "You're disgusting. A coward, a cheater. A *joke*."

I stumble back. Panic seizes me, poisoning my blood with regret as I fully grasp the gravity of what I've made her believe. "Fuck, baby," I whisper. "I'm sorry."

"I'm not your baby! I'm not your anything. Just go. Get out. Get out of my house." She pushes me again, then again, and again. "*Go!*"

"I'm sorry." I reach for her shoulders, my hands refusing to believe that she is no longer mine to hold. This hurts too much. This is killing me. "Tabs…"

"Don't *touch* me!" she shrieks, twisting out of my grasp. "Go, go, *go*. I hate you. Never speak to me again. I wish I never met you." She keeps shoving me, pushing me, driving me backward, until my shoulder blades slam against her front door. "Stay the hell away from me, Gabe. You make me *sick*," she spits out. "I should've known you were no better than your father."

Her words gut me.

They hollow me out.

I nod slowly, knowing I deserve it, knowing this is what I set in motion.

My fingers rake through my hair, tears biting at my eyes and slipping down my cheeks. I want to tell her the truth. I want to confess everything—that no, there's no one else, there's only her.

I'm doing this *for* her, for her daughter.

My girls.

But I can't, because then she'll pry. She'll poke. She'll march right out onto the battlefield with no weapon, no armor, no protection, and those monsters will strike her down.

It's better this way.

I whip around and wrench open the front door, not bothering to close it behind me as I flee from the devastation left in my wake. My legs stumble and my feet trip as I stagger through her lawn and throw myself into the driver's seat of my car.

Shoving the key in the ignition, I waver, choking on a sob, and I make the grave mistake of glancing up.

She's there, watching me run away from her.

On her knees.

Collapsed on the front stoop.

Clutching her chest and crying her heart out.

With a guttural wail, she rips the star ring off her finger and flings it across the front yard. It dings as it bounces off the side of my car. "I hate you, I hate you, I *hate* you!" she howls before buckling forward and burying her face in her hands, her body shaking with betrayal.

Fuck, fuck, fuck.

FUCK!

My foot slams on the accelerator. I fly out of her driveway, my fists pounding the steering wheel, tears pouring down my face, and growls of regret shredding my throat as I disintegrate.

As I plummet.

Break.

Fucking die.

I only make it a mile before I pull off to the side of the road, lean out of my car, and vomit onto the highway.

CHAPTER 36

TABITHA

"You look tired, Tabitha. Are you getting enough sleep?"

I blink dazedly, my head lifting in slow motion. Martha Gleason studies me with worried eyes as the graphite sky prepares for imminent storms. My chin tips higher, gaze squinting skyward. "It looks like rain," I murmur.

"Yes, I think a thunderstorm is about to come through." She sighs. "The sky was crystal clear only moments ago. Funny how quickly the weather can change."

Yeah.

Funny.

Hope tugs at the skirt of my dress, her fist sticky with remnants of a strawberry ice cream cone. "Swing," she says.

The playground begins to empty as parents and children flee to their vehicles, the forbidding sky acting as a ticking time bomb. Forcing a smile, I bend over on the bench and scoop my baby into my arms, plopping her on my lap. "We need to get going, Pumpkin. It's about to rain."

She smooshes her thumbs and fingers together, then wiggles them around. "Spider song."

We sing the Itsy Bitsy Spider song while Martha watches from her place beside us, warmth glimmering in dark-blue eyes. There's a leather leash coiled around her hand as Echo sprawls contentedly near her feet, licking at the grass blades where dollops of ice cream had fallen.

It's the second time she's come to visit me. Last week we

found ourselves at the same park, watching Hope play on the swings and in the sandbox after a visit to the nearby ice cream parlor.

It was a good day.

It was a better day than today, with a storm brewing overhead and this hurricane in my chest.

Hope giggles when I tickle her and pretend that my fingers are squirmy little spiders crawling under her armpits. Her laughter keeps my heart from pinwheeling out of control.

"You avoided my question," Martha states, a soft smile tipping her muted-berry lips. "How are you feeling?"

I freeze, my throat lodging with debris.

How am I feeling?

I'd tell her I have nothing to compare this hollow, heart-sinking feeling to, but that would be a lie. It feels like I've been knocked out, my veins poisoned, then tossed into the woods with my hands tied behind my back and a blindfold over my eyes. I can't see anything in front of me. I'm panicked, bruised, dizzy. Everything is muddled as I crawl my way through dirt and splintered branches, my skin scraping, my stomach in knots. I'm screaming for help, hoping someone will find me and rip this blindfold off my eyes while carrying me to safety and telling me everything will be okay.

Yes, I'm more than familiar with this feeling.

Only, this time there is no good Samaritan coming to my rescue.

It's just me.

Alone, broken, and painfully lost.

Wandering through the woods with a knife in my back.

But I don't want to erase the smile from her lips, so I offer her a shrug as I bounce Hope up and down on my knees. "You're right, I haven't been sleeping well. My work schedule has been crazy, and I've been picking up extra shifts."

"You're such a hard worker," she muses, reaching over to squeeze my forearm. "A wonderful role model for Hope. She's truly blessed."

"I miss her."

My eyes mist.

I miss her so much, especially now. I have no more anchors, no arms around me holding my fractured pieces together, no one there to puncture the awful quiet with a joke or a kind word.

"You don't have to save yourself this time. You're not alone anymore."

So many lies; so many broken promises.

I'm always alone.

I'm forever, hopelessly alone.

I heave in a rattled breath and look away.

"Oh, Tabitha," she says gently, rubbing her palm up and down my arm. "You have no idea how grateful we are that you've allowed us this special time with our granddaughter. I know it hasn't been easy for you. I know you miss her terribly."

A tear slips. I nod, my lashes fluttering. "I do, but I understand. You needed this time with her. I can't imagine how hard the distance has been."

"We plan to move closer. The summer home we bought in Galena will eventually become our primary residence. The transition is just taking more time than we had hoped."

"It will be so nice having you closer." I pick absently at the frayed fringe of my coral-hued dress, the one I wore to the boardwalk. The one that snagged on a bolt when I stepped off the roller coaster. I hadn't noticed at the time, too caught up in being indelibly happy. "I appreciate all the text updates and video chats. And these visits. They really help."

The sky cracks with thunder.

I fist the metallic ring in my hand as it dangles between my breasts while ignoring the greenish stain on my finger where another ring once resided. That finger is empty now, the ring long gone. Likely buried in my driveway cracks with the rubble and dirt, where it belongs.

Rain starts to fall and a light drizzle dampens our hair and clothes.

"All right, we should get going," Martha says to me, hauling Hope into her arms. "We'll bring her back home in two weeks. Let me know what days you have off, and we can meet up for lunch. Pat and I head back to B.C. the first week of September."

"Okay. I'll take a look at my work schedule."

It feels wrong to hand over my child. To give her away to a practical stranger.

To trust.

My heart pounds with doubt and worry as I watch them stand from the bench, drizzle morphing into steady rainfall. Echo rises beside them, her fur soggy and soaked. When she shakes, the droplets go flying.

I lean in to kiss Hope's chubby cheek before they depart. "Mama loves you, Pumpkin. I miss you so much."

"Bye-bye, Mama," she babbles, slapping a sweet kiss on my lips.

We both giggle and I run my fingers through her dark tufts of hair that are curling and frizzing from the rainwater.

Just as I see them off with tears in my eyes and a lump in my throat, Hope calls out, "Gab?"

The lump grows tenfold, morphing into a boulder. I choke out a response. "He...he says hi, baby. Have fun with Gramma and Grampa. I'll see you next week."

"Bye!" Her hand flaps with a clunky wave as Martha throws me a beaming smile. They race for cover, hopping into a rental car and pulling out of the playground parking lot.

I just stand there, staring at the empty lot with empty eyes and empty arms.

The rain pours down in buckets, sluicing me in shivers. My teeth chatter. My hair mats across my forehead.

I should head home but my legs remain idle as my sandals sink into the mud.

All I do is stand there and tilt my chin up to the sky, blinking through the raindrops as they splash across my face.

My months of rebuilding have collapsed into rubble and ruin after trying so hard to build a new home for myself.

Four walls, a roof, a yard to run free. Tall windows to let the sunshine in. A fireplace to keep me warm.

And it kills me because I don't understand.

Nothing makes sense.

I don't know *why*.

I'll never know why he couldn't live here, too.

WHEN DEVASTATION SINKS its teeth into you, you either hide yourself away and tend to the bite marks alone, or you surround yourself with laughter and good people, and let them help you bandage the wounds.

Normally, I'm the hiding kind, but tonight?

I need my friends.

Dean steals a handful of popcorn from Cora's lap as she swipes the bowl away, trying to keep it out of his reach. She giggles. "Greedy."

"You're greedy, Corabelle. Holding popcorn hostage is cruel, and probably illegal."

She stuffs a handful into her mouth. "Your face is illegal."

An eyebrow arcs before a smirk stretches. "Nice." He lunges for the bowl again, then freezes when it tips over, the popcorn sprinkling onto the couch in a mess of greasy, yellow kernels. "Whoops."

A smile lifts on my mouth as I lean back and shake my head. I watch as they pluck stray popcorn pieces out of my sofa cushions, occasionally tossing one at each other then leaning in for a buttery kiss. The image is both adorable and heartrending.

Cora sets the half-eaten bowl between them and addresses me as she chews. "Okay, so this is clearly one of those emergency-friendship get-togethers. Tell me what's going on." She pivots toward me on the couch, drawing her feet up and picking at her sock that's patterned in Yorkshire terriers wearing pink nightcaps. "It's Gabe, isn't it?"

My heartbeats flounder, skidding erratically at the mention of his name. "How did you know?"

"I'm kind of an expert on relationship-specific heartache." She throws Dean an apologetic glance. "No offense."

He winces a little.

I clear my throat and settle back into the cushions. "Yes. It's about Gabe." I'm not sure how to get the words out. They're jumbled in my throat like twisted, overgrown roots. "He, um… slept with someone," I admit as another vital organ shrivels up inside me. "Someone who wasn't me."

Dean leans forward, looking at me around Cora with a stunned expression. "Whoa. Are you serious?"

Yes.

I think so.

I don't know.

I've always been good at reading people. My instincts are

strong and well-taught. Something about that night hasn't added up, hasn't sat right with me, but no other scenario makes an ounce of sense. I didn't believe him when he told me it was over between us after listening to his flimsy "reasoning." And then it was almost like he was piggy-backing off my lethal train of thought as I tried to work through what it *could* have been. It's like I handed him a make-believe scenario on a silver platter, and he slammed that platter right in my face.

The look in his eyes, though. That look has haunted me, day in and day out. He was crying, heartbroken. Hardly holding himself together. What could have easily been explained away as guilt for sleeping with another woman, for betraying me in the worst way, felt like…something else.

It felt like something else because I *know* him.

I thought I knew him.

Swallowing the ashes in my throat, I shrug lightly. "I guess. That's what he told me."

"You don't believe him?" Cora wonders, her expression aghast. "Holy crap, Tabitha. I'm so sorry. Why would he lie about something like that?"

"I-I don't know. Maybe he wasn't lying. Maybe I'm just drowning in denial."

Leaning forward on his thighs, Dean rubs a hand over his jaw. "How were things in the days leading up to it? Was he acting weird or suspicious?"

My mind explodes with sweet, perfect memories.

The way he touched me, the way he held me. The words he said—*God*, those beautiful words. They're the only words that have managed to ring louder than the bomb he dropped at my feet that night, the blast I can't unhear: *"Yes. I fucked someone."*

Hot pressure burns behind my eyes. "Things were incredible. I don't trust easily, but I never once doubted my trust in him. Never. It was just effortless. He was my rock, my anchor. I *felt* his love, deep in my bones…you know?"

They share a glance with each other.

Of course they know. They know better than anyone else.

Cora's hand slides over to Dean's lap and cups his knee, and he places his hand atop hers. She returns her attention to me, nibbling her bottom lip. "That's strange. Has he made any contact with you since? Any attempts to apologize, grovel?"

"No, nothing. It's been radio silence."

A frown creases between Dean's eyes as he squeezes Cora's hand. "I'm not going to pretend like I know the guy, or that I fully understand what kind of dynamic you two shared...but I do know a thing or two about being a martyr." He looks down at his feet. "About doing something hard for the greater good."

I watch Cora tense, her chin dropping to her chest as she continues to pick at a string on her sock while her other hand moves to tinker with the heart pendant around her neck.

My breath falls out shaky.

Ruffling his dark hair, Dean shifts on the couch. "I don't know. Maybe there's something going on behind the scenes, something he was trying to protect you from. Maybe he's going through some kind of crisis and he doesn't want you involved. You've been through a lot, Tabitha. He knows that. It's possible he doesn't want to put you through any more trauma."

I swallow. "I can't imagine anything being worse than what he just put me through."

And then I falter, my skin itching. I think about the mugging, about the way he was acting that night, about how I was convinced he was hiding something from me.

"Were you honest with the police?"

"I was mugged."

He wouldn't look me in the eyes, just like he wouldn't look at me that night in my living room when he used my safe-word against me.

My thoughts continue to reel back in time.

"I thought I was going to lose you."

"I won't let anything happen to you."

Me.

He was concerned about *me*.

My heart kicks up speed as I try to shove the pieces together, but too many pieces are missing. Nothing makes sense, nothing fits.

I pull out my cell phone and open up my social media app, scrolling through his feed, looking for any indication of what could be going on. There's nothing. He hasn't posted in weeks. The last activity on his timeline is the live video I tagged him in from the roller coaster in Atlantic City.

My stomach pitches at the still photo attached to the video.

It's an image of the precise second following when our lips brushed together. The unshakeable love in his eyes. The tortured, suppressed love in mine. The barest smile on his lips, like he couldn't believe our mouths had just touched, even for the tiniest moment.

I can hardly catch my breath as tears threaten to spill.

Cora peers over my shoulder while the phone quakes in my grip. "I watched that video," she murmurs. "You were so brave."

I *was* brave.

I was proud of myself. So proud, so happy, on the precipice of falling headfirst into soul-shattering love.

"Yes," I croak out.

Heavy silence settles in for a few beats before Cora straightens beside me. "I have an idea. Let's do a video together."

I blink. "What?"

"A live video. We all have a ton of followers. It could be fun," she suggests, glancing at Dean for confirmation. He shrugs, nodding. "I mean, maybe it will distract you for a little while. Take your mind off things."

The notion is mildly tempting. I'm not sure I'm prepared to be seen by thousands of viewers with my rain-limp hair and blood-shot eyes, but I wouldn't be doing it alone. Cora and Dean are here.

Rolling my lips together, I nod lightly. "Okay. We can do that."

Cora scoots closer to me, smoothing down her waves of golden hair and adjusting her ivory blouse. She snatches my phone and fiddles with the buttons, typing in a caption that reads, *"Survivor Chronicles, Part One: shenanigans and popcorn fights likely. Bring your questions!"*

A grin brightens her mouth. "Ready?" Ready or not, she presses the Live button and holds the phone out in front of her until all three of us are visible.

Viewers pour into the stream by the hundreds as I attempt to cower out of frame. Dean looks like a deer in headlights, while Cora radiates courage and enthusiasm.

"Hey, guys! We just wanted to pop in and say hello. Dean and I have never done this before and generally try to avoid inter-views and media attention, but Tabitha had me seeing this opportunity to connect with you all in a different light. Maybe we can bring a smile to someone who needs it. I think there's healing and growth to be found in watching other people overcome their own suffering." The viewers reach five-thousand in less than a minute. Cora gulps, then gouges Dean with her elbow.

"Uh, hey." His smile is strained.

Questions start rolling in, faster than my eyes can keep up.

The first question I notice has my face heating, and I wrinkle my nose.

You guys look great! Dean, why were you with Cora's sister for so many years when Cora is clearly your one true love?

Yikes.

Cora lets out a trembly laugh and clears her throat. Dean averts his eyes and shovels a handful of popcorn into his mouth.

I love that you three are friends. Who made the first effort?

Cora speaks up. "I did, actually. I wasn't sure it was the right move at the time because I didn't want to intrude on her privacy, but something compelled me to reach out. And I'm so glad I did. Tabitha is truly the most resilient person I've ever met. She's an angel."

My heart flutters with affection as I bop her with my shoulder, smiling into the screen. "I thought about reaching out to Cora after her news story broke, but I wanted to give her space. Time to heal and process."

What was it like in that basement?

A moment of harrowing silence sweeps between us.

I answer first, the response falling out freely. "Eye-opening," I reply. "It's easy to say it was terrifying, awful, painful, horrific. It was all of those things, definitely, but mostly…it was eye-opening. It makes you appreciate the tiny blessings in day-to-day life. Dew on the grass at dawn. Every unique color of the sunset. The bridge of a song you love that had always been outshined by the chorus. Butterflies, hot tea, the smell of fresh lavender in the summertime." My eyes water, and I blink away the sentiment. "People, too," I add. "People, especially. You don't take anybody for granted anymore. You cherish your friendships, your connections. Life is so beautifully fragile."

Cora tips her head to the side, resting her temple on my shoulder. "That was a perfect answer."

More questions fly in, too many to cover. Our favorite foods, a vivid memory, a book recommendation. Some questions are too personal, too raw, and a lot of them pertain to our abductor. We avoid those. We pretend like he never existed, because existing was more than he deserved.

Eventually, the mood turns silly, and a new popcorn fight commences, and there is laughter and joy, and so much love. Cora shrieks a giggle through her final send-off to the camera when Dean tickles her ribs, and she clicks off the video, all of us waving goodbye as the phone topples to the floor. He pulls her in for a kiss, but he's still tickling her, and she's still laughing, and I want that.

I want that.

But I don't have that, so I laugh with them, living vicariously through their love, and when Cora accidentally kicks me with her ridiculous Yorkie socks, more laughter pours out of me in back-bending, tear-inducing giggles.

I laugh, and I laugh, and I laugh.

My belly aches. My cheeks are wet, streaked with glee.

Then, slowly, progressively, that laughter takes on a different sound. The pitch changes with an unmistakable crack, and the cadence swings left, taking a sharp turn into devastation.

I buckle.

Both arms drape across my stomach as if to keep my insides from spilling out of me, and I lurch forward, my universe tilting, its axis askew. The sobs take on a life of their own like a vicious possession, and my body slides off the edge of the couch and onto the floor with a bruising plunk.

I tip sideways, arms still curled around my middle, knees tucked to my chest. I'm vaguely aware of Cora and Dean joining me on the floor as I cry my heart out. The slow-beating tatters of the organ wither like a dying rose, the petals slipping to the dirt one by one, until there's nothing left but a thorn-studded stem.

Dragging me into her lap, Cora strokes my hair off my cheeks as she shushes my tears, whispering words of solace against my forehead. Dean sits back on his haunches, rubbing Cora's back, comforting her while she comforts me.

And there is comfort in that.

There is beauty in knowing that, sometimes, love does prevail. Trust, though fragile, exists. Loyalty, though hard-fought, is out there.

It's funny how quickly the weather can change.

But I know, deep down, that rain doesn't last forever.

CHAPTER 37
GABE

I t's fascinating how the nonexistence of something can feel like the most prominent thing of all.

The hum of nothingness rings the loudest, echoing in every room.

A gaping hole is a back-breaking weight.

That missing piece is the heaviest piece.

All I can see, feel, and breathe is the fucking loss of her as I watch the playback dozens of times.

So many times, I've lost count.

"Life is so beautifully fragile," she says into the camera, her eyes unblinking as if her mind were somewhere else. Maybe she was in that basement again, watching her lover bleed out before her eyes. Maybe she was in her living room again as *I* bled *her* out.

Tied and hung, upside down, a slash to her jugular vein.

Still alive to feel every drop drain out.

Rewind, rewind, rewind.

I wish I could rewind. I'm not sure what I'd do differently or which moment I'd rewind back to, but anywhere is better than here, trudging through this post-apocalyptic emotional Hell. I'd probably go back to our trip to Delaware, to the music-infused car ride with the wind in her hair, a smile on her rosy lips, and a little star ring on her finger. Or the boardwalk where we slow-danced amid tourists and street performers. Maybe the guest bedroom, while lavender-scented candles watered her eyes and cool sheets tangled with her nightdress. Stolen kisses, rhubarb pie, and sunburned cheeks.

Life is so beautifully fragile.

It is; it really is—but love? No, love is not fragile at all. It's long-lasting, bone-burrowing, and unshakeable. Real love doesn't snap or fizzle out because of circumstances and tough decisions. It doesn't just dissolve because you want it to, because you *beg* it to. Those things only make it hurt. Those things only make it sink deeper, until you're choking on that love. Suffocating. Bleeding out while still breathing. Love latches on to you, consumes, and then it haunts you. Forever.

Love isn't fragile.

It's fucking shatterproof.

Unfortunately, our hearts are not.

I lean back against the moving truck in my driveway, checking the time as the late-summer sun heats my skin. Like clockwork, Stoney strolls up to me from the sidewalk like he materialized out of the shadows. My lips purse with disdain.

"I expect good news," he drawls, a cigarette between his fingers. He scratches at his cheek, gaze briefly landing on the moving truck stuffed full of boxes and furniture. "Did my buyer come through?"

Pushing up from the side of the truck, I saunter over to him, feeling numb. He could gut me right here in my driveway and I wouldn't feel a thing. "Yeah, he took the house," I tell him. "He'll have the cash in ten days. I sold my car, too, so I'll have your fucking money. I just need until then."

"Show me the contract."

Jaw clenched tight, I pull up the contract on my phone and tilt the screen toward him.

His eyes narrow as he snaps a photo of the evidence. "This shows a sale price of 450,000 dollars. A drop in the bucket."

My stare is cold and dead as I shove the phone back into my pocket. "I'll have the money."

I won't have the money, but I'll have something.

And I'm going to negotiate the rest.

Turns out, banks aren't too keen on allowing giant six-figure cash withdrawals. Even if I did find a non-shady buyer for my house, there's no telling when we would officially close, and it would be next to impossible to get my hands on that cash. A wire transfer was off the table because criminals prefer their thievery to be untraceable.

Stoney hooked me up with one of his dodgy comrades who snatches up houses and flips them for a profit. Luckily for me, my house is a solid fixer-upper in a prime location, so we locked in an under-the-table deal.

If that avenue had fallen through, I have no idea what I would have done.

Probably forced Tabitha into witness protection.

Stoney clicks his tongue. "I'm supposed to believe that you'll magically come up with over a half-million dollars in two weeks? Oh, Gabe, you underestimate my intelligence. That is never wise."

"I don't give a fuck what you believe," I bite back. "Feel free to kill me, but then you won't get paid. I sold everything, drained my bank accounts. I have nothing to my name now, so congratulations. I'm penniless, homeless, and heartbroken."

His head cocks to the side, arms crossing as he slips a sly grin. "I wouldn't say you have nothing, no? After all, you still have her."

I bark out a derisive laugh. "No, I don't. She's no longer in the picture. She fucking hates me."

Another head tilt, another grin. "How tragic."

He has no goddamn idea.

My teeth clack together as I glare at him and say nothing.

Stoney rolls his lips, studying me. He's mentally assessing my terms, weighing his options. When his phone dings, he spares it a quick glance and straightens with an airy sigh. "Very well, then." He tucks his phone away. "Ten days. Bring the full payment to the address I'll provide you. Show up promptly and unarmed. No tricks, no stunts." The sun brightens the joyless gleam in his eyes. "While I'm apt to believe that your lovely lady friend holds little affection for you these days, I'm confident your feelings for her have not changed. I encourage you to not be stupid, considering the consequences have not changed, either."

That's all he says before whistling as he walks away, half-limping down the sidewalk and disappearing around the corner.

The threat doesn't rattle me this time because I'm confident Jackson Walsh will accept my terms. For as cold and callous as these cockroaches are, they're businessmen, first and foremost.

As I bend over to pick up a box of meager belongings, I catch Sydney's Jeep careening into her driveway with a Smashmouth song blaring through the open window.

Great. Time for more lies and deception.

"What the hell is going on?" She leaps out of the Jeep and storms over to me wearing a messy bun and a paint-splattered T-shirt of a Nirvana album cover. "Why is there a moving truck in your driveway?"

I deflate, dropping the box at my feet. "I'm shacking up with Darius for a while," I say, keeping my tone void, expression blank. "It's nothing."

She stares at me, unblinking, waiting for the rest of the story while squeezing her car keys.

Too bad she'll be waiting forever. "What?" I turn away from her and hop into the back of the truck, pushing my dresser to the far end until it smashes up against a bookcase.

"I asked you what the hell was going on, and you haven't answered me yet."

"I answered you. You just didn't like my answer."

"Gabe."

"Syd."

Both fists slam against her hips and her stare turns deadly.

"You're being a nosy neighbor."

"Lorna is a nosy neighbor. I'm the concerned best friend," she snaps. "I swear to God, I'll sic my raccoon on you if you don't tell me what the fuck is happening right now."

Pretending to be absorbed in shuffling boxes around, I make a humming sound and avoid eye contact. "Athena would never betray me like that. She remembers that time when I let her live in my spare bedroom and she managed to escape her cage. She had free reign of the house for hours. Ate through multiple sofas, a dining room set, and five bananas. We have an unbreakable bond now."

"I'll make her eat *you*."

"You can try."

A huff leaves her as she continues to stare up at me and wait. There's no way she's walking away without some kind of explanation.

Sighing my surrender, I finally face her and drop to a sitting position, my legs dangling over the ledge of the truck. "I needed the money to start up a new business."

"What business?"

"Music recording. Darius has a soundproof studio in his basement. We're going for it." Darius lives in a two-bedroom condo with his on-again-off-again girlfriend and five African Grey parrots and couldn't tell an amp from a speaker. But she doesn't need to know that. "Don't worry, I'll still be coming around so long as Oliver keeps making that lasagna with the white sauce."

"Bechamel," she mutters faintly. Her lips vibrate as she blows out another breath and crosses her arms across her chest. "This seems fishy. Why didn't you mention you were thinking about selling your house? Does Oliver know?"

I shake my head.

"You've been here your whole life, Gabe. We have so many memories in this place." Crystal-blue eyes glaze over as she stares at the brick raised ranch just beyond the moving truck. "I thought we'd always be neighbors."

Me too, Syd. Me fucking too.

I also thought I'd be engaged by the end of the year—*actually* engaged. Maybe even a father soon, or at the very least, a father figure to Hope. Knowing that my dreams have been viciously ripped away from me has bile crawling up my throat. Tamping it down, I roll my jaw. "I don't know, it was kind of a spur-of-the-moment decision. You know me...I've always been reckless and spontaneous. Honestly, I didn't think it would sell this fast."

Lies, lies, lies.

I've gotten so fucking good at lying I'm starting to scare myself.

"What about Tabitha?"

Both of my legs jerk like she just tapped my kneecaps with a reflex hammer. My muscles lock up, and I duck my chin to my chest. "What about her?"

"Why didn't you just move in with her?"

"Because I fucked somebody else and broke her heart." The practiced piece of fiction falls out way too easily.

Sydney's eyes bulge through her cat-eye glasses as her head whips toward me. "You *what*?"

"I cheated on her. It's over." Heart palpitations have my

breathing quickening and my skin sweating, but I try to hide my inner turmoil. "I'm an asshole."

She gawks at me as her jaw unhinges, blinking a million times in a row like she has some sort of tic.

And then she bursts out laughing.

I frown at her. "Why is that funny?"

"Because you're joking, and I laugh at jokes."

"I'm not joking. I went to the bar the other night and got shit-faced, then went home with some blond chick. I'm a prick and a cheater. Tabitha hates me."

She's laughing so hard she's practically wheezing.

My eyes narrow.

"You're the worst liar I've ever seen. I have secondhand embarrassment right now. C'mon, dude, do you really think I'm going to believe that?" Holding up four fingers on her right hand, she starts to count them down. "One, you go for brunettes."

"Your sister is not a brunette."

"That was temporary insanity and a whole mess of psychological issues coming to a head, so I'm not counting it."

I scoff at her, scrubbing both hands over my face as I prop my elbows on my knees and wait for more of her pointless logic.

"Two, I've known you since you were in your potty-training era and pissing your Super Mario undies. I know you would never cheat on anybody."

"Luigi," I correct.

"Three, no. And four—just *no*," she finishes, slamming her index finger to her pinkie. "Tell me the truth."

"That is the truth. Let it go, Syd."

A legitimate growl leaves her as she charges at me, and I swear there are tears in her eyes. My armor slides out of place for a minute. I blink at her, knowing I can't hide the flash of despair that infects me, that washes over me like a bone-chilling rain. She knows me too well. She sees right through the bullshit.

But I can't bring her into this.

I can't.

"Look, I need to finish up here," I say, voice hitching as I hop down from the bed of the truck. "Let's grab Mexican food later this week. Text me when you're free."

"Gabe."

I ignore her. I have to ignore her before she whittles me down and I confess everything, and there is another person I care about caught in the crossfire. Turning my back to her, I send her a half-hearted wave and flee toward the front of my house as her words follow.

"The man I know runs into burning buildings," she calls after me. There's an awful fracture in her voice, a breakage that has my gait slowing.

I come to a full stop, listening, waiting, dying inside.

"He would never, *ever* run back out without the one thing he loves most."

The sound of her sandals slapping against the asphalt tells me she's walking away. The way my heart twists painfully in my chest tells me she's right.

And the way the sky dims, darkening to gray, tells me a storm is coming.

I collapse onto my front stoop while the rain untethers, and I watch the clouds break with me.

CHAPTER 38

TABITHA

Ten whole days pass me by.

Ten days of gray clouds and long work shifts. The only music floating to my ears has come from Hope's sweet giggles during our twice-a-day video chats.

Four more days.

Four more days and my baby will be home. My arms will be fuller, my home will be louder, and my heart will have one less gaping hole in it.

I pad across my bedroom floor, sweeping and organizing, fluffing my duvet cover that still smells like him. Nautical and clean. I should probably wash it, but I haven't even been sleeping in my bed since the last time we were in it together. Right now, there's a pile of blankets and a single pillow bunched up on my living room couch, telling anyone who comes over that the sofa has become my sleeping quarters for the time being.

I can't sleep in my bed.

Not now; not when the wounds are still so fresh and raw. All I can think about is the last time Gabe was mine, curled around me like a perfect lover, spinning the star ring on my finger, and whispering promises into my ear as I drifted off to sleep with a smile on my face.

"Maybe you'll see it differently when you're lying in your warm bed one day with the man you love, with a child sleeping peacefully down the hall, with a thriving, beautiful life filled with beautiful things."

He died for this.

He died for my hollow, lonely existence, and I wish so badly I could take it all back. I'd never promise him what I promised. I'd tell him that, *'No, no, we are getting out of here together. You and me, Matthew; you and me and the baby you so desperately wanted.'*

Maybe then, he would have fought a little bit harder to live.

Tears cloud my eyes as I move around the bedroom, sniffling when the emotion swells. I dust off my dresser and wipe down the mirror. But before I turn away, I pause for a moment, my eyes dipping to the cracked-open dresser drawer. The clutter drawer.

The drawer that holds both nothingness and everything.

I swallow.

Slowly, carefully, I pull the drawer open all the way and peer down inside until the vintage watch stares up at me, the glass face full of tiny scratches and scuffs.

A ring for love, and a watch for luck.

Matthew believed in luck. He believed in luck and stars and cosmic design.

His death had me believing in none of those things.

And still, for some reason, I reach inside the dresser drawer for the first time and my fingers graze over the white face. I'm not sure why I pluck the wristwatch from the pile of knick-knacks. I'll never know why I unbuckle the dark leather and fasten it around my wrist.

I just do. I just want to.

Maybe it's because I miss him, or maybe it's because I miss them both.

Maybe some buried part of me *wants* to believe in luck.

Sighing, I tilt my arm from side to side, admiring the trinket he adored. Even at the tightest notch, it still hangs loose, dangling at the edge of my hand.

I've had it since his funeral. I've had it tucked away in this drawer ever since the day Pat Gleason placed it in my shaking palm, moments after Matthew's body was lowered into the ground. His body had been recovered from Earl Hubbard's property, and this Vulcain Cricket watch was found with his remains. Scratched, tarnished, and covered in dirt. It doesn't work anymore, but it meant something to him—it meant *so much* to him.

That's why his father wanted me to have it. As a token, a memory. I don't think he knew that I already held on to

Matthew's tungsten ring and, on some nights, when the stars shined far too brightly, I'd tuck it underneath my pillow to will the nightmares away.

A little piece of me wanted to reject the offering. The wristwatch belonged to Matthew's grandfather, so it made sense that his father held on to it instead of me.

Instead of the woman who could do nothing for his son but watch him die.

But he refused. "He'd want you to have it," Pat told me as the sun blazed overhead. It was so sunny that day. Painfully sunny, cruelly warm. "Please, Tabitha, take it. It's something to remember him by."

As if my mind were capable of forgetting anything about him, from the upturn of his lips, to the deep blue of his eyes, to the way his voice cracked on his dying words.

As if I didn't already have something far more precious to remember him by, bundled inside of a baby stroller, fast asleep, unaware that her father was now buried in soil soaked with her mother's tears.

Still, I took it.

I took it through my shaking sobs and ran as fast as I could away from the burial grounds before stuffing it in my dresser drawer, so I didn't have to look at such an unlucky thing ever again. I didn't want to look at it and remember that awful, shrieking alarm sound it made as Matthew took his final breath. The noise still haunts me.

He still haunts me.

The knot in my throat tightens as I hold out my arm, the watch heavy on my wrist and weighing it down. Then I swallow and get back to cleaning.

I suppose that as long as he haunts me, it means he's still here.

And I'll take any part of him I can get.

Even his ghost.

SYDNEY SITS beside me in a lounge chair, her skin bronzed and shimmery underneath the late-August sky as my skin makes a valiant effort to not turn lobster red. She's engrossed in her cell phone, singing along to a Better Than Ezra song blaring from a poolside speaker. The music plays, but I hardly hear it. It's a muddle of chords and notes that hold no harmony.

The midday sun reflects off the blue pool water, making it glitter. I think about the last time I was here, the time I almost drowned. Not in the water, of course, but in the residual trauma eating away at me like a parasite. Gabe had followed me out of the pool and comforted me, holding me in his arms as he chased away the bloodsucking memories with just his voice and soft touch.

"You're flying. You're free. You're safe. Don't look down, okay? Don't look down."

I fold my arms across my chest as a chill creeps across my skin, despite the eighty-degree heat. My eyes land on the wristwatch as a sunbeam reflects off the scuffed face and makes it light up.

Sydney invited me over for a swim this afternoon. Today was my day off, and my empty, quiet house was driving me mad, so I agreed to come by for a little while. She brought out a platter of store-bought snacks and two glasses of iced tea.

Hers is the Long Island variety.

"So," she mutters, flipping her sunglasses up to the top of her head, eyes still narrowed at her cell phone screen. "'Operation: Save Gabe' is officially underway."

I blink. "What?"

She glances at me, turning the volume down on the music through her phone app. "I have good news and bad news."

"Okay…"

"The bad news is, he found the AirTag tracker I slipped into his shoe." Her lips purse to the side. "He was pissed. Told me that my best-friend status had been decreased to subpar acquaintance."

"You're tracking him?"

"Yep. Want to hear the good news?"

"Sure?"

"I'm happy to report that he did *not* find the AirTag I hid underneath the front seat of his rental car." Snapping her bubble gum, she pulses her eyebrows at me.

My heart revs. "Wait, you…you really think he's in trouble?"

"It's the only thing that makes sense," she says, lifting one knee as she opens the tracker app on her phone. "He sold his house, sold his car, and dumped his girlfriend all within a week. That, plus the 'mugging' and weird secrecy? Something is going on."

Anxiety stabs at my chest because her theory rings true.

I texted him a few days ago, unable to sleep, hardly able to breathe.

ME:

> At least let me know that you're okay and that you're not in any real danger. Please...you owe me that much.

My message went unanswered. He never even opened it.

"Oliver and I tried to stage an intervention today, but he ghosted me. I wonder if he has a gambling addiction. It can happen." Taking a sip of her cocktail, she glances down at the tracker app, though Gabe's location remains idle. "Why else would he need that kind of cash? It doesn't add up."

Gambling.

I guess it's possible, but I hadn't suspected such a thing. He's never once mentioned gambling, and he's been responsible with his money since I've known him.

It doesn't sound right, but then again, nothing sounds right.

"You guys went to Atlantic City, right?" Sydney wonders. "The boardwalk is notorious for its casinos."

I frown. "Yes, but we didn't go gambling. Not even the penny slots."

"Did he ever go anywhere without you?"

Chewing on my cheek, I think back to that last day in Delaware.

And then I remember that, yes...he did.

After the white-hot kiss I managed to bungle, and after I threw myself at him and made him believe I was only using him, he told me he was going to visit his grandmother. I stayed behind, wallowing in my poor choices and nursing my battered heart with too many helpings of Janie's rhubarb pie, a fiction novel, and songbird melodies that serenaded me from the deck.

I wring my hands together and lower my eyes. "He did, actually. I hardly saw him that last day." My fingers pluck at the fringe along my jean shorts. "But, we'd had a small fight, so I didn't question it. He told me he was visiting his grandmother in hospice."

Her eyes flare as she straightens on the chaise. "Bingo. He was at the casinos," she chimes, pointing a finger at me. "Gamblers are good at being sneaky and covering their tracks. You never would have suspected anything."

Blinking rapidly, I nod, processing her words.

She could be right. It makes sense, I think.

But…something still seems off.

My skin feels itchy, and my instincts are dinging with uncertainty.

"Tabitha, I know this is bad, but…" Sydney extends her hand to squeeze my forearm. "But he's not cheating on you—and that, I am one-thousand percent sure of. He's a good person who just lost his way. We're going to help him, okay? We'll dig him out of this mess because that's what friends do. He has a lot of people who care about him." A melancholic smile touches her lips. "Trust me, he loves you. So much. You guys will come back from this."

I continue to nod slowly, working through Sydney's speculations, knowing, *knowing* that it's not the right angle. We're missing something.

I just don't know what.

Pulling her hand away, she guzzles down the rest of her drink and scoots off the chair. "I have to pee real quick," she proclaims. "When I get back, we'll start brainstorming. Oliver is working at the library, but he should be home in an hour or so. Did you need anything?"

I shake my head, my focus foggy.

Sydney sets her phone down on the little patio table between us and I eye it as my stomach pitches and churns. I slide my bottom lip between my teeth when she saunters away from the pool and swerves toward the front of her house.

No. I shouldn't.

I need to let this go. I need to let *him* go.

Whatever he's involved in, it didn't include me. Regardless of his reasons, regardless of whether or not those reasons were fused with lies and deception, it doesn't matter. He ended it.

He ended *us*.

And yet…I can't shake this feeling. I can't rid myself of the awful intuition that Gabe is in serious trouble, and if I sit around idle, wallowing in my indignation, something is going to happen to him. Then, it will be too late.

Then, I will never forgive myself.

I glance at the house as Sydney slips inside before shifting my attention back to the phone.

My throat tightens. My chest squeezes.

I have to.

Heart racing, I snatch it up from the table and slide it into my back pocket before rising from the patio chair. I pace beside the edge of the pool for a few minutes before traipsing through the grass and making my way to Sydney's front door.

Poking my head inside, I call out, "Um, I need to go. An emergency came up."

The toilet flushes and Sydney appears from down the hallway a few seconds later. "Really? Everything okay?"

"Yep…it's nothing major."

"A non-emergency emergency?" She squints at me and wrinkles her nose. "Is it Gabe?"

"No, it's just…" I clear my throat, picking at the hemming of my tunic as her cell phone weighs heavily in the pocket of my shorts. "Well, the Gleasons are in town with Hope. They wanted to meet up for ice cream."

She suspects nothing.

Her head bobs through an easy smile. "Gotcha. Go love your baby, I get it. I'll text you later and we can figure out this Gabe thing."

"Great." I swallow hard. "Thanks for inviting me over today. I think I needed it."

"Any time." Giving me a salute, she adjusts her bikini and waves me off. "See ya."

I smile back.

And then I book it.

My hair whips across my face as I race through her front lawn to my car and jump inside, pulling out her cell phone as I start the engine. I stare at the tracker app, noting that Gabe's location bubble is still inactive. It says he's currently five miles away at what looks to be a jobsite.

So that's where I go.

That's where I sit, parked in front of the construction site for an hour, feeling like a total creeper.

I could march over to him, talk to him, demand that he give me answers. *Real* answers—not those halfhearted, force-fed lies he threw at me.

But, deep down, I know that he won't.

When he stood in my living room that night and broke my heart, he had no intention of ever piecing it back together with the truth. Whatever is going on with him, it's big.

It's big enough that he was willing to destroy me in the process. He was willing to walk away from the one thing he promised he'd wait forever for.

But here's the thing about forever: forever is a measure of time, and time, I've learned, is painfully fickle.

It's fleeting.

Unpredictable.

I don't believe in forever; I believe in right now.

And right now, I'm going to save the man who saved me.

CHAPTER 39

TABITHA

As raindrops break free of the clouds and day turns to dusk, I find myself at an abandoned parking lot fifteen miles north of Gabe's jobsite.

I've been following him since he left work. He pulled the hard hat off his flattened head of hair, shook the sheetrock and sawdust from his clothes, and strolled to his rental car while slipping out of his neon vest. There was a falter in his gait as he approached an older-model Kia sedan, a car I could only imagine he loathed. He paused with his hand on the door latch, then pressed his forehead to the metal, as if needing to catch his breath after a long, arduous day.

But I knew it wasn't the day itself.

It was the days past, all catching up to him. Whatever he's doing, whatever it is, I intend to find out. I'm no longer tied to a pole with my wrists locked behind my back. I'm not helpless anymore.

I refuse to watch another man I love wither away to nothing before my eyes.

I'd parked my car across the street from his jobsite where a new-build subdivision came to life with custom houses. He didn't notice me when I slunk lower in my seat as he pulled out onto the main road, or as I started up the engine and followed him, trailing a few car lengths back.

Guilt gnaws at my bones, but no greater than the anxiety I feel as I've watched Gabe go about his day. He made a pitstop at a condominium complex I didn't recognize, jogging inside, then returning to his car a few minutes later with a black duffel bag.

My instincts piqued.

And so I continued to follow him to his next stop, fifteen miles away, to a town I'd never been to before. The splashes of color left the sky during my trek over, consumed by shades of gray. Rainclouds rolled in along with dusk, darkening my route.

With a lump in my throat, I sit idle for a moment and watch him, moments after driving past where he pulled in and then turning around, just so he didn't think anything was amiss.

Gabe parks his rental car in the empty industrial lot, hopping out of the driver's side and slinging the strap of the duffel bag over his shoulder. He moves farther into the shadows, glancing behind him two separate times as I kill the engine. I'm watching from a part of the street that's shrouded by a lush tree line, so he doesn't notice me.

Heaving in a breath, I decide to follow, slipping both cell phones into my back pockets as I traipse through the gravel with quiet footfalls.

I follow him, and I trail him, and I feel like a crazed stalker, but I follow and trail until his duffel bag swings out of sight as he curves around a beat-up building at the far end of the lot.

I glance around, left to right, still shielded from his view as I creep up along the tree line. Rain drizzles down, wetting my loose hair. I step on a branch, but he doesn't seem to hear the snap of it. There's hardly any illumination thanks to the gray sky and unlit lot, but I still see him, I can still see the way he paces around in circles, tapping his cell phone against his thigh.

What is he doing here?

Part of me wondered if I'd find him meeting up with a woman—but, the bigger part of me knew I wouldn't find that at all.

The bigger part of me feared it would be much worse.

The air is an anxious swirl of raindrops, mimicking the knot in my belly. My hair mats to my forehead and cheeks as I peer around the trunk of a tree and watch as Gabe fidgets, checks the time on his phone, pockets his phone, then repeats the steps.

A bubbling of hysteria blooms inside of me.

I need to know what's going on. I need answers.

I don't allow myself to think before I stomp forward through the damp leaves and branches, making my presence known. I charge at Gabe, my eyes locked on his profile, questions and need-to-knows fueling my quickening gait.

His head pops up briefly, and he does a double-take when his mind catches up to what his eyes are seeing.

And then those eyes flare with a glaze of fear I've never quite seen before.

The color drains from his face. Even in the dim lighting, I see it, I see the way he pales before me. After all, my eyes adjusted to the darkness a long time ago.

His mouth hitches, words stuck like glue on his tongue.

Then I ambush him. "Tell me what's going on. Tell me *right now* what the hell is going on with you. And don't lie to me, Gabe. Don't you *dare* lie to me again." My demands rush out as quickly as I rush toward him, my arms swinging in opposite time, front to back, my sneakers slapping the parking lot pavement.

The clenching of his jaw looks painful, but not nearly as painful as the bone-deep fear dimming the emerald of his eyes. "Tabs." He chokes out my name like that was painful, too.

I haven't even reached him when he drops the duffel bag and storms at me. There's a crazed, desperate look in his eyes mingling with the fear. He looks wild, terrified.

When we meet, he doesn't hold me or hug me or pull me into the arms I miss so much. Instead, he grabs me by the shoulders and starts walking me backward, back toward the tree line that I appeared from. "You need to go," he says through gritted teeth. "Now. Right now."

"No, no, stop." I try to shove him away, but his grip is unyielding. "Gabe, please, stop this. You're scaring me."

"You can't be here."

"Well, here I am, and I'm not leaving until you talk to me." I manage to twist myself free, watching his ashen expression morph into a mask of frenzy. When he reaches for me again, I dodge him, flipping my ropes of wet hair off my face as my body shivers. "Tell me what's going on. And don't say you're cheating on me because we both know that's bullshit."

His gaze skips over my shoulder, then back to me, then back to the entrance of the lot. Both palms scrub across his face, fore-head to chin, as he whips his head back and forth and meets my eyes with a look of pure distress. "Tabitha, you need to get the fuck out of here. I'm meeting a woman. You don't need to see that."

"Stop lying."

He tilts his head up, staring up at the sky as a long exhale leaves him. A jittery hand sweeps through his waves of hair and he closes his eyes, the lump in his throat bobbing when he swallows. "Please, just go. I'm begging you to go. Right now. Don't look back, don't follow me again, and just…pretend you never fucking met me."

"Impossible." I lurch forward, my fingers curling around the damp fabric of his T-shirt. My grip is tight, my knuckles bleaching white to match his shirt. "You know I can't do that. I love you. You love me. You need to explain what's going on because I will *never* stop fighting for the truth."

A tortured sound slips past his lips as his hands fly out to cup my face. He pulls our foreheads together and squeezes his eyes shut, his fingers digging into me. "Tabs…"

The sound of an engine rumbles in the distance and his eyes pop. More color leaves him, turning him bloodless. Practically choking, he drags me off to the left as my feet trip over themselves and headlights illuminate the lot.

"Gabe, what is—"

"*Go.*" It's a growl, a desperate, ragged growl. "You need to hide. Right now." He shoves me behind a stone retaining wall where the ground dips, just as the headlights beam brighter, and he jogs away, pulling out his cell phone and attempting to look nonchalant as his rushed movements morph into an unhurried pacing.

I clamp my hand over my mouth to hold in the strangled cry as I curl my body behind the half wall. My heart dizzies out of control, my legs shaky when they crouch to half-sitting, and I twist around the edge of the wall, hoping to see whoever is pulling in. Desperate to catch sight of whoever it is that has made Gabe believe I am better off without him.

A black SUV rolls up to Gabe and my heart skips. He doesn't look at me. He pretends I'm not here. But his eyes still look tortured and clouded with fear as two well-dressed men exit the vehicle, their faces obscured by shadows when the headlights die out. I stretch my ear, the voices barely audible over the sound of rain pounding against the old building's metal roof.

One man moves toward Gabe with a newsboy cap hiding his eyes from me.

Only…

I've seen him before; I recognize him.

And so I know that his eyes are ice blue, and that the left side of his face is scarred and puckered.

It's the stranger from the restaurant, the day Gabe got mugged.

What is this?

What is happening?

Holding my hand over my mouth, I lift up until only my eyes are peeking over the wall. As long as I can keep this cry in my throat, and as long as I can keep my heart from fleeing from my chest, they won't know I'm here. I squeeze my eyes shut, trying to get my breathing under control.

The parking lot is dark and dank, with only a sliver of lowlight seeping out from the sky. Memories of the basement whirl through my mind as the air thickens with the smell of musty concrete, and the sound of dripping rainwater echoes in my ears.

Drip. Drip. Drip.

Panic threatens to sink me, but I hold it together.

I *have* to hold it together.

Beside the scarred stranger, a brick wall of a man marches forward wearing a black duster, his expression flat and indifferent.

On instinct, my hand clenches tighter around my mouth to keep the cry from spilling out, to keep my broken, confused heart from climbing up my chest and making a daring escape.

My legs want to run to Gabe, uncaring of the guns on display tucked into both of their waistbands as their backs face me.

Oh God.

Shivers race down my spine like a cluster of spiders. Cobwebs catch in my throat.

"Mr. Wellington," a voice says, a voice that spills from the man in the hat. "Always a pleasure. You're prompt, at least."

Gabe swipes a hand down his face and bends over to retrieve the duffel. "Here." He tosses it at them.

The driver of the SUV catches it and hands it to the man in the newsboy cap. Then he pats Gabe down from shoulders to shoes, searching for a weapon.

Shaking his head, Gabe extends both arms at his sides and glances up at the falling rain, his jaw ticking. "I'm not that stupid," he clips.

"All clear, Stoney."

Stoney is the man in the newsboy cap.

He moves to unzip the duffel bag. Money fills the inside of it, and both men glance at the crisp stacks of bills before they are pulled out and counted by quick fingers.

What the hell?

My heart races. Sickness rolls through me as my wet hair drapes across my eyes in tangles.

I need to do something.

I need to stop this, distract them, *do something.*

Mind spinning, I dig into my pocket for my cell phone as I sit crouched behind the retaining wall. I should call the police.

But they'll hear me.

They'll hear my shaking, petrified voice, and the police will never get here in time before I'm riddled with bullets, or before Gabe is shot down in front of me and I'm forced to watch another man I love die as he chokes on his own blood.

Oh God, oh God.

I have no weapons.

I have nothing.

My eyes lift, landing on Gabe as my cell phone trembles in both hands. His gaze cuts to me, just for a moment, just for the quickest, briefest moment before his attention slides back to the two men. I watch the way his throat works as the money is counted, the way his skin glistens with sweat and rain.

I have to help him.

No weapons, no time, no hope.

And then I pause.

Words from years-past skip across my memory, and I heave in a sharp breath.

"We do have a weapon," Matthew said to me, slumped against his pole with chained wrists and hollow eyes.

An idea unfurls, springing to life between my ribs. My stomach pitches with action, with the only weapon I have. It's the weapon that saved me once before. It couldn't save Matthew, but maybe it can save Gabe.

Thinking fast, I swipe open my social media app. My fingers are shaking so badly, I tap numerous wrong buttons before I type a caption that reads, "*SOS!!! Abandoned parking lot off Adams Ave in Melrose*" and click the Live video prompt. The camera is angled at the grass before I tilt it up, holding it just beyond the wall until the scene is visible through my phone screen.

I type more words into the comment box as the viewers pour in.

"*Send police to the abandoned lot off Adams Ave in Melrose. Guns. Man in danger. Hurry!!*"

My hand slaps across my mouth again, holding in my cries, suppressing my ragged breathing. I don't have an exact address. I'm lucky I even noticed the street name.

At the thought of my luck, I glance down at the rain-laden watch hanging off my wrist.

"All there?" From the black SUV, a window rolls down halfway and an unfamiliar voice echoes through the lot. There's another man in the car.

I try to pop my head up far enough to identify him through tinted windows, but all I see is a human-shaped shadow in the backseat.

Stoney continues to flip through the stacks of bills.

Then he offers a quick headshake as if telling him *no*, it's not all there. Zipping the duffel closed, he drops it to the pavement and eyes Gabe with a look of irritation. "This is barely six-hundred thousand. Do you think I'm a fool? Were my instructions unclear?" He lets out a long sigh, then tips his head at the driver.

It's only a quick tilt of his chin before a gun is pulled from the driver's waistband.

I freeze, I crumble, I stop breathing.

The man with the gun grabs Gabe by the back of the neck.

Gabe's hands fly up, palms forward, as he struggles out of the man's grip. "Listen," he says quickly, inching backward. "I tried, but you'd be amazed by how challenging it is to come up with one-point two million dollars on the fly. Sold my house, sold my car, sold my soul. Still came up short."

Stoney's jaw tightens. "This is disappointing, Gabe."

The driver with the gun remains silent, awaiting instruction.

My breath lodges in my throat, and I glance at the video stream, the screen speckled in raindrops. Thousands of viewers are watching. I don't have time to read through the endless comments flashing across the screen, but my eyes skim over a few of them.

Holy shit! Is this for real?
OMG
I called the cops, hope this is legit!
Police have been called. Stay safe.
This is WILD!!

Urgency slams into me with every heartbeat as tears slide down my cheeks. I lean forward on my knees, peeking around the wall.

The muscleman reaches for Gabe again with his unarmed hand, hauling him toward the SUV.

I'm about to scream.

I'm about to leap out from behind the wall.

But then...

But then...

The wristwatch starts shrieking its grating alarm sound, the same alarm that started ringing the moment Matthew died in front of me.

My eyes bug out as my body turns to stone.

I stuff the phone into my back pocket and smack the watch with the heel of my palm, begging it to shut up.

No, no, no.

The alarm rings out as an awful, grating echo...

And then it stops.

My hand is over my mouth again as I drop down to my butt and squeeze my eyes shut. There's no way they didn't hear that.

Stoney barks an order to his associate. "Check that."

Gabe cuts in, sounding frantic. "Wait, wait, wait. I have a proposal for you. For your boss," he rushes out. His voice pitches higher, as if speaking directly to the boss, who is presumably in the back seat of the SUV. "Let me work for you. I'll work off the rest of the debt. Every penny of it. I'll do whatever you want, whatever you ask me."

Heavy footfalls thump nearer, so I begin to crawl my way

down the ledge of the wall as fast as I can, begging for police officers to storm the lot before Gabe gets hurt.

Sweat trickles down my temple.

My legs won't stop shaking.

Before I can take another breath, still scampering away on my hands and knees, a meaty hand flies out and rips me up by my hair.

I scream.

I'm yanked to my feet. My phone slips out of my pocket, my shoes skidding and slipping across the wet grass as the man in the leather duster drags me out from behind the wall. I struggle against the sting of my hair being pulled from the roots, wishing I could grab my phone and record this. "No!"

My gaze pans to Gabe's horrified expression as he stands there, hands still raised in surrender. Eyes wide, skin slick and sallow, he shakes his head back and forth. "Wait, wait...I'll go with you. Do whatever you want to me. Kill me, I don't fucking care."

Stoney's gun is aimed at Gabe's chest. "What do we have here?" he sneers, sparing me a glance. "A stowaway."

"No," Gabe croaks.

The man drags me up over the small hill as I fight and try to kick myself free.

Taking one step back, Stoney cocks his gun and points it directly between Gabe's eyes. "I don't appreciate plot twists." He grins. "Unless I'm the cause of them."

A meaty hand slams over my mouth to hold in my scream.

Stoney looks over his shoulder at the SUV. "How would you like me to handle this, boss?"

My eyes pan to the backdoor of the vehicle as it starts to open, and a leg tapered with a gray pantsuit steps out.

"Take care of him," the voice orders.

A shriek of despair bursts out of me, stifled by the thick hand over my mouth.

And then the watch goes off again.

The alarm screeches loud over the terror lodged in my throat.

Stoney's attention is stolen by the sound, and he glances at me, distracted, a look of confusion marring his brow.

Gabe lunges at him.

It happens so fast, just a flash of motion and quick feet, as

Gabe grapples for the gun and Stoney's balance teeters, and his arm flies back.

A shot rings out.

A shot rings out through the night, followed by a shattering of glass from the back window of the SUV.

The alarm silences.

Oh, my God.

Stoney stares at the broken window, his normally impassive expression twisted with rage. He pauses, lowering the pistol before nodding his chin at the other man to do the same. "Grab her phone," he says. "Destroy it."

The man's hold on me tightens as he snatches Sydney's phone from my back pocket, then drops it to the cement and smashes it under his heavy boot. In an instant, I'm shoved forward, collapsing onto my hands and knees as the barrel of a pistol slams between my shoulder blades.

"Get her in the fucking car," Stoney blares. "She probably called the cops. We're not doing this here."

My tears fall freely.

Gabe tries to rush at me, uncaring of the loaded gun that has returned to his head, uncaring he could be executed with a single flick of Stoney's finger. "Don't, don't…fuck, please, leave her alone. Take me with you, kill me, bury me where no one will find me, fucking please, just leave her out of this. I have nothing. I have nothing else to give you."

His prior words sink into me.

"Without you, I have nothing."

I sob, hunched over on the pavement with a gun to my back.

It's over.

The police will be too late.

These monsters are going to kill us.

I cry out when a thick hand fists my hair again, and the gun bruises my spine, and I'm lifted off the ground and hauled to my feet like I weigh nothing. "No, *no!*"

Gabe is dragged toward the vehicle by Stoney, who jabs the pistol against his temple, but he still resists, he tries to get to me, to reach for me, to hold me one last time as I'm hauled away with an angry hand in my hair and another locked around both of my wrists.

Our eyes meet.

"I'm sorry, baby," he rasps. His eyes fill with sorrow, with desperation, with love. "I'm so sorry. None of it was true. I love you. I love you so much."

"I know," I cry out. "I know."

These are his last words.

I'm chained to a pole again, hands tied, bones breaking, as I listen to a man's final words.

I love you.

I'll always be with you.

Tell her about me.

They were words to me, words *for* me.

Except…

I'm not cuffed and shackled this time. I'm not trapped and helpless. There's a gun pressed to my back, yes, but the trigger hasn't been pulled.

Before I'm wrenched around the trunk of the vehicle, I lean over and dig my teeth into the man's hand as it uncurls from my wrists. He lets out a snarl of pain and releases me long enough for me to yank myself free and scamper away to the retaining wall where the still-recording phone had fallen, the screen facing the sky.

I grab it, raise it up, and brandish it between the two men, back and forth, trembling terribly. I tilt the camera toward them and shout, "Stop! I'm live recording you. Everyone is watching."

Terror races through me, but it's trumped by power.

I have the power now.

Still struggling with Gabe, Stoney glances at the man who stalls mid-reach for me. My video recording glimmers on full display.

I approach cautiously.

"You're bluffing." Stoney's throat moves with a trace of nerves.

"I'm not bluffing." Swallowing my own fear, I hold it up to his face, standing just out of reach. "It's been livestreaming since you pulled up. I have a large following, so tens of thousands of people are watching you right now." I look over at Gabe, my chest heaving, my limbs shaking. "I'm documenting a crime for a live audience. If you shoot us or force us into that vehicle, you'll never be able to talk your way out of the consequences. You'll rot in a jail cell, hopefully for life. Even if you delete it, it'll be too late. Screenshots and screen recordings have already been made."

My heart pounds, almost painfully. I turn the camera to the shattered window of the SUV, my gut rolling with nausea when I finally capture what's behind the partially opened door.

Carnage.

The man in the backseat is dead, his head half blown off, his dress suit smattered in blood and brain matter. My free hand flies to my mouth, holding back the bile that crawls up my throat.

Stoney's jaw clenches as he releases Gabe.

I lower my hand, still shaking, still on the verge of vomiting. "This—" I point the camera toward the backseat "—was an accident." I swerve it back to Stoney's narrowed eyes and ticking jaw. "Whatever you do next will not be an accident."

I hold my breath, the tension in the air palpable. Our fate rests in their hands, and the world is watching.

The driver moves first, knowing it's too risky to call my bluff. He shoves the lifeless leg back inside the vehicle, then darts toward the driver's side, rips open the door and revs the engine. I almost think he's about to pull out without Stoney, but Stoney levels me with a hard glare.

"Fuck," he mutters with reluctant surrender. He glances at the duffel bag full of money resting a few feet away, and then moves around to the passenger's side of the SUV.

The door slams shut.

Tires screech as they reverse out of the lot.

The moment the headlights fade into the mist, the cell phone slips from my shaking fingers. It clatters to the pavement amid a splattering of bloodshed, and a panic attack squeezes my chest as my eyes meet with Gabe's.

My throat burns. My legs quake, nearly giving out.

We both move at the same time.

I let out a cry of soul-shattering relief and race toward Gabe just as he races toward me, and I fling myself at him, my arms encircling his neck.

We collapse to our knees, holding each other. My face is buried in his collar, his hands fisting my rain-soaked hair, and we're both crying, both shaking, both squeezing each other tight.

He kisses me, then kisses me again, over and over, my hair,

my forehead, my cheeks, my lips. "So brave," he murmurs, tears dampening his cheeks. "So *stupid*, baby. But so fucking brave."

Shivering and trembling, I nuzzle my face into his neck and breathe him in, sobbing and boneless in his arms.

He's alive.

He's not bleeding out in front of me, croaking my name on his last breath.

My hands are in his hair, cupping his face, and I pepper his throat with kisses, whispering through my tears. "I love you. Don't you *ever* do that again," I beg. "Don't you dare."

He pulls our foreheads together, blowing out a long breath. "I'll explain everything. I'm so fucking sorry. I never wanted you involved in this."

"Involve me," I murmur back. "Always, forever. I'm with you. We're in this together now."

Sirens ring out in the distance as we sit collapsed in the vacant lot, rain falling down and mingling with tears. Gabe pulls back and stares at me for a long while, his thumbs dusting over the skin beneath my ears.

Swallowing, he glances at the watch along my wrist as my fingers curl around the front of his shirt. "What is this?" he asks me, taking my hand in his and studying the piece as it glitters with raindrops.

My heart clenches, another little sob breaking free, and I whisper softly, "A good luck charm."

Half of his mouth quirks up with a smile, and he pulls me back to his chest.

I glance up over his shoulder.

I glance up, and up, and up, wishing I could see through the clouds.

Wishing I could fly right through them.

Wishing I could thank the stars.

CHAPTER 40

GABE

F orty-eight hours after one of the worst days of my life, I'm standing on Tabitha's doorstep, much like I did two weeks ago when I thrust a dagger through her heart. I recall exactly how I felt that night, idling on her front stoop, wishing I could delay the inevitable. The sound of her footfalls padding through the foyer sounded like lead bullets tearing through my chest.

Might as well have been.

She opens the door with a similar expression, akin to cautious hope. The last time I stood on the other side of it, I shredded her trust with a handful of words. A trust I'd built from the ground up, a trust that was precious to me.

It's sprinkled at our feet now, and all I can do is pray it doesn't get carried away with the wind before I can start reassembling the pieces.

"Come in," she tells me, dressed in white denim shorts and a peachy blouse. The barrette in her hair is shaped like a dinosaur, which is strange and quirky, and doesn't match the ordinary outfit she dons, but feels perfectly paired, nonetheless.

The door cracks wider.

My heart pounds like I've been smacked with some sort of post-traumatic stress trigger. Still, my feet manage to move, finding the courage to push forward through the threshold. "Thanks."

Thanks.

Thanks for letting me into your home again after I burned it to the ground the last time I was here. I swallow, shoving my hands into my pockets as I stare down at the olive-green tiles in her foyer.

"I, um…made us dinner."

Blinking, I raise my chin slowly. She made us dinner. She's feeding me after I fed her bullshit and watched her choke on it.

A single word slips out. "Why?"

Two heartbeats pass before her eyes narrow through the dim lighting. There's a burned-out lightbulb in her dated chandelier, and she tried to make up for it by scattering flameless candles throughout the space. The home smells like lavender, and I can't help but wonder if she's grown to enjoy the scent after our sleep-over in Mom's guestroom, or if she just gravitates toward things that made her sad.

Things like me.

"I…thought we could talk over a meal. I don't know, after everything that happened I just thought…" Her arms lift and fold across her chest, like she's putting up a defensive shield, newly uncertain of my intentions. "Maybe I was being presumptuous."

"That's not…" I shake my head quickly. "I didn't mean it like that. I want to have dinner with you. I'm just surprised you want to have dinner with me."

She throws my one word back at me. "Why?"

"Because the last time I was standing in your living room, I broke your heart, and you told me you hated me."

It smells like lavender, but it also smells like something savory. Some sort of garlicky marinade. My gaze shifts to the small table sitting in the middle of her kitchen that's plated with chicken, biscuits, and a bowl filled with tongs and lettuce.

I blink back to her.

"A lot has happened since then," she murmurs. "We can talk about it."

Her eyes look glazed, as if she's moments away from tears. I nod once, then toe off my sneakers. We spent the better part of the last forty-eight hours at the police station, giving our statements to detectives. It's no surprise her video went viral. Instantly. Millions of viewers tuned into the live streaming of events that, when I watched it back, looked like some kind of low-budget action movie made for social media clout.

It's hard to believe it was real.

And if the cops hadn't tracked down Stoney and his henchman and arrested them on the spot, moments after the SUV careened out of that parking lot, I wonder if the authorities would have questioned the legitimacy, too.

But there was a dead guy in the backseat. It was hard to write that off as make-believe.

Tabitha gnaws on her lip as she leads me toward the kitchen. "The guy that was shot," she begins, pulling out one of the dining chairs. "He was their boss, apparently. It was all over the news. He was a prominent business guru known for sketchy transactions and mafia ties."

I stop just short of the table and run a hand through my hair. "Yeah."

While we waited at the police station that night, soaked to the bone and shivering with our respective post-adrenaline spikes, I told her everything. My father, the threats, the pictures they had of her and Hope. It felt like I didn't have a choice. There was nothing I wouldn't do to keep her safe.

She'd broken down with her head in her hands as I held her and apologized over and over again.

And then we were whisked away to separate rooms.

This is the first alone time we've had together since it happened, and I'm so far out of my element, so torn on how to make this right, that all I can do is press forward on the back of the chair with my jaw ticking and my chest tight.

Do I hug her? Touch her? Hold her?

I want to. I want to so fucking badly.

But what I did to her still hovers over me like a black cloud. I hear the sharp ding of her star ring smacking against the side of my car. A little clank of betrayal. That thread of trust snapping in two. I'm not even sure if I should sit down, or if I should run back out the door like I did that night.

It's the image of her collapsed on her front stoop again that has me collapsing into the chair.

Tabitha takes a seat across from me, the chair legs squeaking against the old tile floor. Candlelight flickers around us, and all of this feels romantic.

A romantic tragedy.

"Gabe," she whispers. I'm zoned out, staring at the plate of chicken breast. "Gabe, look at me."

My chin lifts, my eyes meeting hers over the table.

Can she see how sorry I am?

Does it matter?

My throat lodges with a burning ball of shame. "Tabs, you don't have to pretend like everything is okay. You don't have to cook for me and act like I'm just waltzing in after a long day at work. I fucking hurt you."

She's tense, her features pinched, shoulders squared. "Why do you assume I'm pretending? Why can't everything just be okay?"

"Because it's not. I wrecked you. I ruined everything I fought so hard to build."

"And I'm telling you it's not ruined."

Swallowing, I glance back down at the tablecloth. It's ivory and lace, patterned with a simple cherry design. A few seconds pass in silence, and I'm vaguely aware of her rising from the chair and moving over to me, the scent of her skin matching the cherries on the tablecloth. She's standing so close that her blouse grazes my shoulder, and even that small contact has my heart doing cartwheels.

My teeth grind together, but I can't look at her. I keep my eyes trained on the tablecloth like a coward.

"I almost watched you die," she says softly.

I slam my eyes shut.

"There was a pistol aimed at your head. I thought you were going to be shot right in front of me. I thought I was going to lose you before I ever truly had you."

"Tabitha—"

"*Look* at me."

I blow out a breath through my nose because my jaw is locked, my molars close to chipping. Finally, I look up at her, and she's staring down at me with such tortured desperation, I'm on my feet in an instant. Our chests graze as my hands ball to fists at my sides.

"Did you cheat on me?" she asks. She asks it with little emotion because she already knows the answer. There's no terror or trepidation in her tone.

Closing my eyes again, I shake my head. "No."

"Then what are we doing?" This time, there's a small crack in her voice. A hitch. "Why are you standing there not touching me? Why are you acting like it's over when, just two days ago, it could have been?" Somehow, she steps closer. Her arms are at her sides, and mine are at my sides, but the tip of her nose skims the front of my shirt. "You don't need to grovel. You don't need to beg for my forgiveness. This isn't that. You just need to love me, to promise me you'll never put yourself in that kind of danger again. You just need to hold me, Gabe, please hold me, because the thought of you never holding me again was the only thing that truly wrecked me."

A groan catches in my throat, a mix between torment and yearning.

I'm not sure if it's too soon to touch her, too soon to hold her or kiss her like I used to. All I know is that it's been too long since I've done any of those things.

I reach out with one hand and cup her jaw, tugging her to me. *Hungry.*

I'm starving for her as I pull her face to mine and feel her soft, full lips open without hesitation, only with longing. My tongue thrusts inside like her mouth is a fundamental need.

She falls against me, weightless, boneless, moaning through our tangle of tongues.

Urgent, aching. Fucking dire.

I walk her backward toward the counter, and my hand raises to sift through her hair, moving it over her shoulder as I bend down and press a light kiss to her collarbone. She stills, lets out a soft gasp. Goosebumps prickle her skin. My other arm reaches around her to grip the edge of the countertop, caging her in as I pepper more kisses up along the column of her throat.

Her breathing grows unsteady as she sways, leaning into me.

"If this is too much, I understand," I whisper near her ear, my lips grazing the shell as my eyes flutter closed. Cherry blossoms fuse with jasmine as I breathe her in. "I can stop. I can stay with Darius tonight." Tabitha doesn't pull away, only presses closer. I sigh, the breath falling out shaky. "I want to earn your trust again. I know it'll take time. I can—"

Inching back, she reaches down and curls her fingers around

the hem of her blouse, then tugs it up over her head until her hair falls back down in dark waves.

Pearly skin, black lace bra, slender curves.

The swell of her breasts heave up and down as my eyes rake down her body.

"I trust you," she murmurs.

My throat works. My heart thunders, my dick hardening as her words heat me up just as much as the image of her silky skin bare before me. She glitters against the ambient kitchen light and flameless candles, her eyes flickering brown and green.

My free hand trails up her flat belly and palms her breast sheathed in lace, while my other hand cradles her cheek, my fingers braiding in her hair. "I'm sorry."

"I know."

"I love you."

"I know."

Blinding relief sweeps through me. Maybe I don't deserve it, maybe it's too soon, but I fall to my knees in front of her, my lips trailing down her skin as I drop. Everything becomes a flurry of movement, a fast-paced tumble toward ecstasy. Her hands grip my shoulders as I unbutton her shorts and tug the denim down her hips. She arches into me, her back bowing against the countertop, her fingernails digging into my skin.

I inch her matching lace panties down her legs until they spill at her ankles, then I hook one leg over my shoulder before burying my face between her thighs.

Fuck.

She's perfect. So goddamn perfect.

Something between a cry and moan rips past her lips as one hand latches onto my hair and squeezes. Trembling, she bucks forward against my mouth when my tongue plunges inside of her.

She whimpers, thrusting her hips against me. "Gabe…"

The last time I ate her out, she came on my face within seconds.

It was the hottest fucking thing.

One hand continues to palm her breast, yanking down the lace and pinching her nipple, while the other holds her to me by the hip. She's soaking wet, musky and sweet. Rocking against my mouth, she pulls at my hair as my tongue slides in and out of her, hard and fast. I feel her trembling, hardly able to stay upright, only making her hold on me tighten while her nails burrow into my scalp. She rides my face and I work her clit with perfect pressure and rapid sucks, sensing she's close, knowing she's going to come fast again.

My erection strains and throbs as I carry her to the pinnacle with my tongue, mouth, teeth, nipping and sucking, growling while I eat her out, desperate for her to break apart.

"Gabe, Gabe...I'm close, keep doing that..." She thrusts against me as I suck on her clit and use my tongue to take her over the edge.

A sharp cry falls out of her as she tenses up and arches her back. Her body tremors with shuddery waves, squeaky little mewls meeting my ears while she comes, her thighs clamped around my face. She collapses, breathless, her grip loosening on me.

"That's it, baby," I murmur against her. "That's it."

Then I inch away with a smile I can't contain and glance up at her, reveling in the warm flush of her cheeks and messy hair.

Unhooking her leg from my shoulder, she tugs at my hair, coaxing me back to my feet. There's still dark hunger in her eyes. As I straighten in front of her, she leaps at me, her arms slinging around my neck and her leg raising again to coil around my hip.

Our mouths meet, tongues sliding together, hands everywhere.

I lift her up and carry her a few feet away into the living room until her spine hits the back of the couch. Her legs uncurl from my waist as she falls back down and my mouth smashes against hers. The kiss is only broken when she yanks my shirt over my head and tosses it across the room.

"You want my cock, don't you?" I husk into her ear, flipping her around until her stomach is pressed to the back of the couch and she's half-hunched over the edge. "That's what you need." I'm already fumbling with my belt buckle, desperation sinking into my bones. "You want me to fuck you hard. Rough, like you asked me to."

She juts her ass backward, offering herself to me through a low moan.

I tear off my belt and shove my jeans and boxers down my legs until my cock is fisted in my hand, the head pressing between her thighs from behind. Groaning, I grab her by the hair and tug her to me until her back is flush with my bare chest, my teeth nicking her ear, nibbling her neck.

I thrust into her, my grip on her hair tightening, my mouth latched around the soft skin of her throat. "Oh, fuck, baby."

Part of me truly believed I'd never feel this again—our bodies twisted and joined, her wet warmth bringing me to my knees.

I still for a moment, savoring the feel of her clenching around me, before I pull out halfway and shove back in. When I let go of her hair, she bends forward and grips the edge of the couch as I grab her by the hips with both hands and ram back into her.

Our bodies slap together.

She whimpers, then moans, then whimpers again.

My hand crawls up her spine and curls around the front of her throat with a loose hold while I slam into her. The slippery sounds of our bodies fusing together echo through the room as I pull out and push back in.

Unlatching her bra, it slips forward down her arms, and I palm her breasts as they bounce beneath her. "So sweet, so tight," I grit out, my eyes glassy and half-lidded as I gaze down between us where my cock disappears inside her. "You're going to come again."

I drag my hand down her body until I'm rubbing her clit, this-close to losing it as I watch my dick move in and out of her while I get her off. My hips pump hard and fast, my movements turning jerky as I feel the orgasm crest. "Fuck, Tabs, I'm already close."

Her knuckles go white as she clutches the back of the sofa, red fingernails digging into the orange-flowery print. "Ohh, I'm coming," she moans, dropping her forehead to the couch and crumbling, her internal walls fluttering around me.

Three more pumps, and the third has me buried to the hilt, bent over her back with my hand squeezing her breast and my cock jerking and emptying inside her. My face twists with a tapered groan as my release tops out and my body shudders, my lips pressed to her tangled mess of hair.

We float back to reality together, both breathing heavily, slicked in sweat. I lift my weight off of her as my cocks slides out, still hard, still wanting her.

I blink down at the slickness between her legs, where my release coats her thighs.

Fuck.

I came inside her.

Tabitha pulls herself up and turns to face me, her cheekbones tinged with a blush-pink glow and her hair in disarray. "I just started on the pill," she says, reading the look in my eyes. "We're okay."

Bending for my jeans, I can't help but wonder if she would have stopped me if she wasn't on the pill. The thought of putting a baby in her and starting a family one day warms my chest.

Not yet...not right away.

Someday.

Someday, I want that.

I want that so fucking much.

Tabitha cleans herself up in the hall bathroom, then strolls back out to the living room wearing one of those see-through nightgowns I've seen her in more times than I probably should have. My jeans tighten at the image of her dusky nipples poking through the satin as I lean back against the couch and watch her move toward me. Her cheeks are still rosy, but her hair is freshly combed. A smile paints her mouth, soft and sweet. A little shy.

"Come here," I tell her, holding out my hand.

She crawls into my lap and straddles me, just like she did less than two months ago in my living room when she told me not to wait for her.

As if I had a choice in the matter.

As if the stars hadn't already aligned in a way that wrote our names out side by side, the letters twinkling against a midnight sky.

Her gown inches up to her hips as her thighs cage me in. My hands glide up to her waist and hang on tight, our eyes meeting through the dim candlelight.

She sighs, pressing her forehead to mine. "You should have gone to the police," she murmurs. "That was so dangerous."

I shake my head. "Too risky. He threatened your life if I involved the cops." Maybe a smarter man would have done it differently, but I was a man deeply in love, so it was my heart calling the shots.

I wouldn't do a thing differently.

"I almost lost you. I thought he was going to shoot you," she whispers, the words frayed and brimming with tragedy.

My eyes close.

If I'm being honest, I thought that day was going to be my *last* day.

And I'd thought about Tabitha's words to me at my mother's house, her fears about her last day not being perfect and memorable. But I knew, with absolute certainty, that any last day without her in it was doomed from the start.

So I did nothing spectacular on that day. My mind was blank as I woke up, showered, clocked in a long shift at work, ate a mediocre sack lunch, and thought about never seeing her beautiful eyes again. There was no point in doing anything else. I thought I'd lost the one thing worth living for.

I wrap my arms around her and pull her to me, trailing my fingers through her hair as her face burrows into the crook of my neck. "I'm here, Tabs. I'm right here."

A shaky breath skims her lips, warming my skin. "You could have been killed."

"Nah," I murmur, a smile hinting. "I'm immortal, superhuman. Death-defying."

She sighs, shaking her head.

"Besides, I definitely would have killed him first. I had a plan."

I had no plan.

My only plan was believing in the fact that Oliver would keep Tabitha and Hope safe once I was gone.

A shiver rolls through me as she sniffles against my shoulder. "By the way," I whisper, smoothing back her hair. "I would, you know."

She lifts up. Her gaze darts across my face before she blinks down at me. "You would what?"

"Die for you."

Something flashes in her eyes. A thin line between epiphany and horror.

She knows I'm not lying.

Her face crumbles a little, her eyes glossing over with tears, her bottom lip shaky. "Gabe," she says, hardly keeping the sob in her throat. "I don't want someone who kills for me. I don't want someone who dies for me." Swallowing the emotion, she raises both palms and clasps my face. "I just want someone who will *live* for me."

My heart stutters.

I squeeze her so goddamn tight, peppering kisses into her sweet-smelling hair.

And then I realize…

That's really what it's all about, isn't it?

Living.

Truly living.

That's what love is.

It's finding that perfectly imperfect person that complements your heart, that brightens your shadows, that sees your broken, mismatched parts and wants to spend the rest of their life piecing them into place. And even if those pieces never fully fit, they love you anyway. They love you more.

And I think we forget sometimes, the whole point of it all. We forget the beauty of living while we're still alive.

And there is no better way to live than to love.

Silence settles in as I hold on to her, both of us entangled and content. Then my lips dip to her ear and a single question falls out. "Music?"

I can almost feel her smile.

"Sure."

CHAPTER 41

TABITHA

September rolls into October, and I stand outside on my tiny back deck, watching the birds while Hope pulls blades of grass from the lawn.

"Tabitha, did you want to help me make this pie?"

I turn, glancing at the cracked patio door as Janie pokes her head out with a smile.

Gabe's mother is here. She flew in shortly after his grandmother passed away and is staying at a nearby hotel since my house is hardly big enough for the three of us, let alone a guest.

"I'd love to," I tell her, eager to assist with the baking and cooking. I've never had a chance to do those things while growing up, or during adulthood. It's always just been...me.

I've never had a real relationship with my own mother, so I'm grateful the universe made up for it by giving me Janie Kent and Martha Gleason. Now, I have two incredible women in my life, two maternal figures who are filling that hole tenfold. Two women I can bake with, cook with. Go on shopping dates with, and maybe, someday, pick out a wedding dress with. The future feels just as bright as the early-October sunshine painting the sky in an orange glow.

I traipse through the lawn and gather Hope, holding her hand as we head back inside the kitchen. Gabe is munching on a celery stick from the veggie board spread out on the table. His green eyes light up when we enter, as if he didn't just have his arms around me ten minutes ago with his lips pressed to my temple.

My grin stretches at the same time his does.

He moved his belongings over from Darius's condo the week after I invited him over for that dinner we never got around to eating, far too preoccupied with lovemaking and heart-mending. His furniture is in my garage while we figure out our next step.

Gabe inches toward me, cupping his hand behind my head and pulling me in for a forehead kiss. "I missed you."

"We were only outside for a few minutes," I tease, leaning up on my tiptoes to find his lips.

"I still missed you." He reaches for my hand, lifting it up and twirling the star ring around my finger. It glints against the sunshine streaming in through the patio door.

I've been wearing it since the morning I saw Gabe off after our emotional night together. It was sitting there on the cream-colored pavement, twinkling under the sun, right among the weeds that were sprouting from the driveway cracks. I didn't think twice before slipping it back over my ring finger.

It hasn't left my hand since, and I hope it never will.

Gabe tugs my hand to his lips and presses a kiss to my knuckles, then to the ring.

"Gab!" Hope bounces beside us, pulling at his pantleg. "Tickles."

"Tickles, huh?" The smile doesn't leave him as he turns to Hope and bends down, scooping her up like she weighs as much as a flower petal in the wind. He situates her on his shoulders and waggles his eyebrows at me. "I've been summoned for a tickle fight. If you don't hear from me in roughly ten minutes, send the troops. It's possible I've been defeated."

Hope's tiny fingers dance along his neck as she tries to tickle him.

Giggling, I watch them go.

Janie chuckles beside me, turning her attention to the dough she's laid out and prepped for the pie. Her hair is pulled back into a short ponytail as her bangs fall loose and float into her eyes. "It's finally persimmon season," she says to me before tipping over a brown paper bag and letting the fruits tumble onto the counter. "You'll have to let me know what you think. It's Gabe's favorite pie."

I'm distracted as my eyes track Gabe carrying Hope into the

living room on his shoulders. They collapse onto the couch, a heap of happiness.

Her words hardly register.

"Tabitha?"

I'm still zoned out as I murmur aloud, "He forgot the money."

Janie pauses right before she leans in to knead the dough. She glances at me, frowning with confusion.

My eyes mist as I stare into the living room, watching as Gabe bounces Hope on his lap and blows raspberries against her chubby neck. She giggles, hardly able to catch her breath. The genuine smile he wears tugs at my heart to the point where my chest physically aches.

"In the parking lot," I continue, still staring at them, still watching through the beautiful ache. "He had his whole life in that duffel bag. His house, his car, every penny from his savings account. And he just left it there. It didn't even cross his mind to take it." I blink back the tears before they spill. "He held me in his arms as the cops drove us to the station, as if I were the only thing that mattered. A police officer gave the money back to him that night, and I saw the look that flashed across his face. It was like he'd completely forgotten that it existed."

When I finally pull my eyes away from the living room, I see that Janie is now leaning back against the counter with a similar misty-eyed expression.

"That doesn't surprise me," she says. "His life isn't defined by anything that can fit into a duffel bag. And he's always been like that. Gabe is the exact opposite of his father in every way." She looks into the other room just as Hope smacks both hands to Gabe's face and squeals with delight when he blows another raspberry. "You know that saying, 'they would give the shirt off their back for anyone?'"

Blinking at her, I nod.

"He did one time. During one of my visitations with him when he was young, maybe seven or eight, there was a dog chained to a street post, shivering in the rain. He pulled off his T-shirt and draped it over the dog, worried that the animal was too cold." She laughs lightly, shaking her head. "When we met back up with his father, Travis scolded him. Told him he was foolish, and that now he was going to be freezing all night. Gabe just shrugged and shot back, '*Yeah, but the dog isn't.*'"

I've tried to hold the tears in, but the story makes me break.

It makes me cry.

It makes me so, so excited for a future with this man, a future I never thought was meant for me.

It makes me feel like the stars have finally aligned, and that thought only makes me cry harder.

"Oh, Tabitha," Janie says, stepping toward me and running a warm hand up and down my spine. "You both are so very lucky. And that makes me feel lucky, too."

I sniffle, swiping at my cheeks. "Do you…believe in luck?"

Gabe told me once that his mother was always the logical one. A no-nonsense type. I stare at her, curious for her answer. I never used to believe in luck, but everything changed in that parking lot.

Everything changed when Matthew's watch went off, twice, both times right before Gabe was about to be shot. It could have been coincidence. It could have been a broken watch with a broken alarm mechanism, doing what broken things do.

But it could have been something else.

My heart pounds.

Janie glances down at the floor for a moment before looking back up at me. "I don't think it matters what I believe, Tabitha. All that matters is what *you* believe." Twisting back toward the counter, she reaches for a persimmon and tosses it my way.

I catch it, fisting the ripe fruit as Matthew's words sweep through me.

"I think it does us a disservice to look at the stars and believe that they are only stars. There is too much we don't understand and too much we can't see to remain boxed into simplicities."

Do I believe in luck?

Fate?

Cosmic design?

Do I believe that the people we love, the ones we lose along the way, are never really lost?

I don't know.

All I really know is that it does me a disservice to reject the possibility. I want to believe in them because the idea of those things brings me peace. It brings me hope that, perhaps, in some way, the stars are more than just stars, and that maybe, *maybe…* those stars really are on our side.

Strolling back to the counter, I place the fruit on a cutting board and reach for a knife while the sound of Gabe reading Hope a board book echoes from behind me and pulls a smile to my lips.

My ring twinkles in the window light as I cut into the persimmon.

And when I pull the two pieces apart, my heart skips.

My eyes water.

I gasp.

There, etched into the fleshy side of the fruit, a little star design shines back at me.

TWO DAYS after Janie heads back to Delaware, and while Gabe is at work, I clock out of my shift at the restaurant to meet up with Cora and Mandy at a nearby park. Hope is in her stroller, fresh from daycare, eating an ice cream cone as the pink treat dribbles down her hand.

Mandy throws me a Mandy smile, her teeth flashing white as she swallows down the rest of her own cone. "You have no idea how deprived I've been without this little munchkin in my life," she says. She reaches into the stroller and ruffles Hope's dark curls as they flutter in the breeze. "I know you have Gabe these days, but you better not promote him to Lead Babysitter. I'll never forgive you."

I smirk. "He works full time. In fact, I'll probably be calling you more often, considering I have a dating life now."

"Gah. Look at us," Mandy beams, glancing up at the shimmying treetops. "We've been through some real shit, you know? And here we are, on the other side of it, happy and in love."

We slow to stop in front of the playground, and Cora and I watch as Mandy reaches into Hope's stroller and hauls her out with promises of swings and slides.

"She's so good with her," Cora muses, her eyes trailing her sister as Mandy plops Hope into the toddler swing. "She's always saying she's too busy to be a mom, now that she's managing the hair salon she works at, but…I think that's what she really wants. I know that's what Reid wants."

I smile thoughtfully. "She'll make a great mother."

"There was a time when I didn't think that because Mandy was always all about Mandy, and it was hard for me to picture her with those nurturing instincts. That sounds terrible, but it's true." Nibbling her lip, she sighs. "Just goes to show you that people are always changing, always growing. Who we are at one point in time isn't necessarily who we'll always be. It's just a starting point, and it's up to us to pick a direction."

Taking a seat on a park bench, I move the stroller to the side as Cora sits next to me. Her dark-blonde hair shimmers two shades lighter when the sun beats down on her. "You and I know that better than anyone, don't we?"

"Yeah," she murmurs, floating away for a moment. Just for a moment. "We do."

"Something tells me we're both heading in the right direction." I turn to face her, watching her eyes sparkle as she ducks her chin.

"Dean got the job transfer," she says, unable to tamp down the beaming grin that tips her lips. "He's finally moving back." She glances at Mandy a few feet away, almost like she's worried about her sister overhearing her, but Mandy is completely engrossed in pushing Hope on the swing.

"Oh, my God, that's amazing. Finally."

"I know, it felt like it was never going to happen. I was even considering quitting my teaching job and moving to Bloomington just to be with him. It didn't feel right being apart for so long. The weekends kept feeling shorter, the weekdays longer."

I understand that all too well.

Those ten days in Gabe's absence felt like a tortuous eternity.

Cora glances my way, her eyes dipping to the star ring on my finger. "What about you? Things seem pretty serious with Gabe?"

Now it's my turn to beam. I fiddle with the ring, knowing there is no official engagement, while still feeling like there is; like this little ring on my finger is a promise of forever. "Yes…it's serious. He moved in with me last month. We're going to look for a bigger place soon." My attention turns to Hope, who laughs as the wind carries her back and forth on the swing with Mandy pushing her gleefully from behind. "He's so good with her, Cora. Hope just adores him."

Smiling wide, she reaches for my hand and laces our fingers together. "We found our heroes," she whispers. "Our lifelines."

As her words settle into my heart, a flock of birds swoop overhead, chirping and singing, flying free across the clouds. A sense of peace washes over me, a feeling of purpose.

I'm making it to the other side, one baby step at a time.

Don't look back.

Keep going.

Don't look down.

Keep flying.

With my head tipped toward the sky and the sun on my face, I squeeze Cora's hand and smile.

CHAPTER 42

GABE

We are being terribly irresponsible.

Tabitha's wrists are tied above her head with a pair of pantyhose, and her eyes are blindfolded with a silk tie. My swim trunks are pooled at my ankles as I stand at the edge of the bed and thrust into her, her legs hooked over my shoulders.

Music and laughter from the backyard barbecue across the street mingles with her moans through the cracked window.

"Oh, ohh, Gabe," she cries out as she comes, back bowing off the bed, her bikini strings untied, breasts bouncing as I slam in and out of her.

"Fuck, yes," I groan, bucking my hips two more times until I spill into her, my release causing my legs to nearly buckle from under me.

Breathing hard, I untangle her legs from around my shoulders as drowsy smiles claim both of our faces. I lean over, freeing her wrists and pulling the blindfold off her eyes.

She's grinning wide, her cheeks pink with sunburn and a post-quickie flush. Sitting up on the bed, Tabitha tugs her bikini top back up and ties it into place. "That was…"

"Hot as fuck."

"Kind of rude of us."

"But hot as fuck."

We booked it from Sydney and Oliver's backyard ten minutes ago, claiming Tabitha's chili was burning.

It wasn't.

But now it probably is.

Giggling, she scoots off the mattress and pulls her bikini bottoms up her legs until they're secured around her hips.

She's wearing a bikini.

She never used to wear bikinis or crop tops, too self-conscious of the initials carved into her skin leaving little jagged scars behind. The sight of her traipsing around the pool area in that itty-bitty two-piece had me embarrassingly hard, and everyone knows that swim trunks paired with a raging erection is never a good look.

There were no other options.

I glance at the pantyhose strewn across the sheets as I adjust my trunks into place. When Tabitha asked me to tie her up one night a few weeks ago, I felt unsure about it, considering her history. But she told me she wanted to try it, thinking it could be therapeutic. A way for her to take back control and replay her past trauma in a safe, consensual way.

It's added another dynamic to our relationship, another layer of trust.

Tabitha glances in the mirror, smoothing down her hair and swiping away a few mascara smudges under her eyes. I can't help but stare at her reflection for a beat, drinking in the smile she wears, a smile that seems to brighten more and more as every day goes by.

One week ago, we moved into a house across the street from Sydney and Oliver that went up for rent. It's a three-bedroom colonial with far more space for us to grow, and I still get to be neighbors with my two best friends. A win-win. Whoever that shady dude was that bought my previous house managed to renovate it within a month and put it back on the market.

The big surprise?

My mother bought it.

My grandma passed away in late September, succumbing to cancer. After the funeral, Mom put her house up for sale and submitted an offer on the raised ranch next door to Oliver and Syd. I was content not buying it back. Not only would it have been painful purchasing it for one-hundred thousand dollars over what I sold it for, it just didn't feel right. It was where my life began, but it's not where it's going to end. Memories grew there, but it's not where they'll continue to bloom. Tabitha and I are going to plant new roots, make new memories. We're saving the money I got back from the police station to purchase a forever home one day, and in the meantime, we'll be putting some of those funds toward Tabitha's college education.

She wants to be a teacher.

A psychology professor.

She told me one day, not long ago, that there was a theory in psychology that suggests human needs can be organized into a hierarchical order. Number five is self-actualization—one's ultimate, true sense of purpose. Tabitha always knew her future career would be rooted in psychology somehow, but that purpose blossomed, taking on a new direction after her experience in the basement with Matthew.

I couldn't be more fucking proud of her.

"I'm still debating if I should keep this, or give it back to Matthew's father," Tabitha muses, her attention dipped to a trinket in her hands.

I blink out of my daze and step forward, coming up beside her in front of the dresser. She's holding the old vintage watch, the leather band dancing along her fingers as she stares at the scuffed face. "Maybe you should pass it down to Hope one day."

"I don't know." She rubs her lips together, considering the idea. "It seems like every time the alarm fritzes out, somebody dies."

"That's one way of looking at it," I murmur, smiling softly. "On the other hand...maybe every time the alarm goes off, somebody lives."

Her eyes flare with awareness. She glances up at me, blinking as her pupils dilate.

"Perspective," I tell her. "It's whatever you make of it. Good luck, bad luck. Or maybe it's just a watch that belonged to Hope's father, and it's something she'd love to carry with her as she grows up. A little piece of the man she never got to meet. Maybe that's its true purpose."

Tears glaze her eyes as she bobs her head. "Yeah," she whispers. "You're right." Giving it a squeeze, she slips it back into the dresser drawer and shuts it into place. Then she turns to me, sighing deeply, shaking away the memories. "I guess we should—"

"Marry me."

Her lips part with a sharp breath. She stares at me with wide brown eyes, almost like she didn't quite hear me.

I drop to one knee in front of her, my hands grazing up her thighs and curling around her hips. I press a kiss to the scar above her belly. "Marry me, Tabs. Be my wife. For real…forever."

A squeaky, breathless sound falls out of her as her fingers slide into my hair. "Yes."

"Yeah?" My heart gallops as I glance up, a smile spreading across my face.

"Yes. Of course, yes. Gabe…*yes*."

I fly to my feet and cup her cheeks with both palms, drawing her lips to mine. I kiss her hard through our mutual grins, through our laughter, the future laid out before me in bright lights and a canvas of every color. "I love you, baby. So much. I'll get you a real ring, a better ring, I promise. I just needed to know, right this fucking minute, that you're never going away. You're here, you're mine. I need you by my side, in my arms, until I take my last breath."

"I'm here. I'm yours. You have me." The tears pooling in her eyes trickle down her face as she pulls back and cradles my jaw. "And this *is* a real ring, Gabe. This is the ring I want." She holds up the dingy star ring still circled around her finger. "It's perfect."

She's perfect.

We fit into every role together.

Sweet and tender moments bleed with silliness and laughter. Long, hard talks are often followed by mind-blowing sex.

This life, this woman…

Perfection.

"Let's go back to the party. I want to tell everyone," she says, giddiness lacing her words. "Mandy is bringing Hope by any minute."

I press a kiss to her hairline, then her nose, then her sweet lips. "After you, Wifey."

"Cannonball!"

It's late-October, but the Midwest has been kind, giving us a few consecutive eighty-degree days and prompting one last pool party before the weather officially gives in to crisp breezes and red-brown leaves. I push my sunglasses over my head as music pours out from the speaker. I managed to fuse some of my own favorite bands with Sydney's nineties playlist, so I turn the volume up when a Bad Omens song starts playing.

As I stand over the grill flipping burgers and hotdogs, my gaze skips between our group of friends who are swimming, munching on chips and fruit skewers, and laughing over beers and cocktails.

Darius strolls over to me as his on-again girlfriend sunbathes in an adjacent lounge chair next to Sydney's sister, Clem. Clem's daughter plays in the grassy area with the writer's daughter, Summer, tossing a beach ball back and forth, and Hope amuses herself in a makeshift playpen with two inflatables tucked around both arms.

I smile and nod at Darius when he approaches.

"Thanks for inviting me, Mason." He grins, giving me a fist bump on the shoulder. "Please tell me you want a bird."

My eyebrows arch. "What?"

"Lexi adopted a lovebird right after she dumped me. She gets a new bird whenever she's feeling emotional. It's a thing. That's why I have a thousand fucking parrots in my condo."

I flash back to the earplug-ridden weeks spent in Darius's condo that doubled as an aviary, before barking a laugh. "Jesus, I don't know. I'll ask Tabitha."

"I already asked her. She said '*immediately yes*,' but wanted me to check with you."

"Shit." This all feels so sudden, but I guess it could be worse. It could be a raccoon. "Okay, then. I guess we'll take a random bird. Why the hell not?"

"You're the man. Consider it an engagement gift." He slaps me on the shoulder again. "I'll bring her by later this week. Let's grab a drink after work tomorrow, yeah?"

"Absolutely."

Sydney charges at me then, her wet hair bouncing over her shoulders, her feet slapping the pavement. Oliver trails behind her, shaking his head back and forth with a look of bewilderment.

She's been immersed in Reddit threads with Oliver and Mandy for the past twenty minutes, scrolling through sheer absurdity on the new phone I bought for her since her old phone met an untimely demise. "Look at this. It's a wearable robot that feeds you tomatoes." She shoves the phone screen in my face. "Gabe, look. It's *specifically* tomatoes."

I blink. "What a time to be alive."

"You should get one for your wedding. It would be hilarious."

"Why would I do that?" I squint at her before glancing back down at the sizzling burger patties. "Never mind. The answer is: you're insane."

Mandy shouts at us from the side of the pool, her feet dangling in the water while she sits beside her fiancé, Reid. "Syd, look!" They only just met today but have become instant besties. "Check this out. It's a weird kissing machine for lovers in a long-distance relationship. This is crazy."

Sydney's eyes bulge with intrigue as she bolts in the other direction.

Oliver watches her go, head tilting to the side, brows furrowed thoughtfully. "Why only tomatoes?" he muses.

"Why did I just inherit a bird?"

We share a grin as Oliver reaches for a grill spatula and helps me flip the patties. "Congratulations, by the way. I'm immensely happy for you."

"Don't be too happy yet. I have no idea what to do with a bird. You might be gaining a new pet to add to your zoo in the upcoming weeks."

"Not the bird." He chuckles, sparing me a glance. "The engagement announcement. It appears your love story has been worth all of the harrowing moments along the way. I knew it would be."

My eyes lift to Tabitha chatting with the writer, Evan, at one of the patio tables, sipping her iced tea, while Cora sits on Dean's lap beside them. There's a flutter in my chest watching her smile, watching her laugh, remembering a time not long ago when I wondered if those things would ever be mine. I swallow, nodding. "It's wild, right? It feels like yesterday when the cops showed up at my door, telling me you were alive. I was just a lonely bachelor with no direction in life, and now we're brothers again, both of us engaged to the loves of our lives." I pause for a moment to process the journey. "It blows my mind when I think about it."

"Mm," he says agreeably, grabbing a serving platter and piling it with burgers. "Life is a curious thing. Only a fraction of it lies within what it throws at us, while the greater part is determined by our responses to those things. It's in how we react, cope, and ultimately, how we rise above." He looks across the way at Sydney who sets her phone aside and dives back into the water, squealing with laughter when she resurfaces. "We've risen quite effectively, don't you think?"

I can't help but look at Tabitha again, and those heart flutters gain wings when she glances over at me at the same time. The glittering smile she sends me has my skin heating, my stomach flooding with butterflies. "Yeah," I murmur. "I think we're doing a damn good job." When I return my attention to Oliver, I add, "By the way, I can't wait for your best man speech. I'm anticipating profound greatness."

"I'll admit, I've been preparing it since you made the announcement earlier. I'm looking forward to yours as well."

"Mine will be profound disappointment. My public speaking skills are about as polished as a gravel road."

"In that case, we can commiserate afterward at the open bar." Oliver reaches into the nearby cooler and pulls out two beers. "Cheers, brother."

The bottles clink. "Cheers."

We pile more burgers and hotdogs onto plates and carry them over to a large glass table, already strewn with a pot of chili, potato salad, veggies and dips, and an assortment of finger foods. I whip up a plate for Tabitha and carry it across the patio after handing Hope a strawberry to num on.

"You look like you worked up an appetite," I tell her, waggling my eyebrows and handing her the meal.

She blushes.

I pivot to Evan, and we do that bro-type handshake that every male on the planet was somehow born knowing how to do.

"Hey, man," he says, nodding with a smile.

Tabitha is perched on the chair beside him, fiddling with a straw. She peers up at me over her sunglasses. "I was just talking to Evan about our book."

"Yeah? What's the status?"

She bites her lip. "I want to hold off on publishing it for now."

Somehow, this doesn't surprise me. Tabitha was never one for being the center of media attention, and I always knew these interviews were more for her own personal healing than for exposure.

"Everything is just so crazy right now," she continues. "Especially with that video that went viral. I'm kind of burnt out on the attention." Laughing lightly, she looks down at her tea. "I'm excited to revisit it in the future, though. I had a lot of breakthroughs. No regrets."

Tabitha ended up telling me about her biggest breakthrough: the truth about Hope. The fact that she was conceived *before* the abduction took place, and that Tabitha kept that secret hidden to protect the professor's name and reputation.

She was worried I'd be upset by the revelation, but on the contrary, it only made me understand her better. The bond she shared with Matthew was established long before they were thrown into that basement, making the loss of him ten times more difficult to bear.

My heart broke for her. It still breaks, thinking about what she endured.

Evan chimes in, leaning back in his chair. "I'm knee-deep in another book right now, trying to wake this coma patient up after a twenty-year long nap, so I'm good with tabling it for now. Honestly, the experience alone was eye-opening and evocative. I learned a lot about the human condition and survival. I'm glad we did this." He turns, sending Tabitha a smile. "I'm glad you trusted me enough with your story, and I plan to do it justice when the timing is right."

Tabitha smiles back, then bumps her shoulder with Cora's. "Hey, if you're ever looking for someone to write your story, I know just the guy."

Cora is still nestled in her boyfriend's lap. Dean's arms tighten around her as he presses a kiss to her collarbone, and she leans into him with a charmed grin. Then she reaches for the heart locket around her neck and says, "If I ever decide to go that route, I have the perfect title for the book."

Conversation rolls on for a few more minutes before I reach for Tabitha's hand. "Dance with me."

She doesn't hesitate, rising to her feet and discarding her tea and half-eaten hotdog. We stroll along the side of the pool to the grass, and I watch as she plucks Hope out from the playpen and sets her down beside us. Then she reaches for my cell phone and scrolls through the music app, settling on a song. Within seconds, the opening chords to *With or Without You* echo around us. She grins. "I'd love to share this dance with you."

I immediately pull her into my arms just as Hope toddles over to us in the lawn while newly golden leaves float down to our feet from a nearby tree. "Will this be our wedding song?"

"Mhm," she murmurs. "I can't wait to become Mrs. Kent."

A grin stretches at the thought. I changed my last name at the beginning of the month—the name Wellington is officially dead to me, just like the sorry excuse for a man who passed that name down. With no other children, Travis's diabolical legacy dies with him.

If we're lucky, his life will end in a prison cell.

And if luck is really on our side, Stoney and his band of cretins will be right there with him.

Hope latches on to my leg and sways with us to the music, giggling as we move and spin. One of my hands presses to the small of Tabitha's back, while the other links with Hope's tiny palm.

Tabitha's cheek is pressed to my chest, her arms wrapped tightly around me. Party sounds fade out behind us, and all I hear is music and the beats of her heart vibrating with mine.

"I would have waited forever for you," I say, pressing a kiss to her temple. "Even if you never loved me back, I would have waited, and I never would have regretted a single second of it."

She looks up at me, sunlight glimmering in her eyes, erasing every shadow. Then she leans in, kisses my jaw, and whispers back, "To rank the effort above the prize may be called love."

EPILOGUE
TABITHA

Two Years Later

"**M**y *father has a private jet. I'd like to take you on it one day.*"
My muscles lock as I stare at the propellers from inside the cabin.

It's not a private jet, but Matthew's father is a licensed and certified skydiving instructor, and he agreed to fly with me as I plummet ten-thousand feet through the air.

Gabe is seated beside me in the small aircraft, both of us secured with helmets, jumpsuits, and harnesses. "You're really doing this," he says, his voice pitching over the roar of the engine.

I'm really doing this.

There's a knot unfurling inside my belly, and my heart is trying to make a clean break, but I'm doing this.

He would *want* me to do this.

"I'm doing it," I say back, though all the color has left my face and I'm shaking like a leaf in the wind. "You don't look even a little bit petrified."

His crooked smile shines back at me through the helmet. "Are you kidding? This is the coolest thing I've ever done. Especially since we're doing it at night." Turning, he looks out the window, staring at the stretch of inky sky twinkling with starlight. "It's incredible."

There's an illuminated altimeter wrapped around my wrist to monitor altitude. I pretend it's my good luck charm, just like Matthew's watch.

All of our friends and family are waiting for us down below; even our sweet lovebird that Hope named Sunny. Hope is excited to watch us land while she waits eagerly along with her baby sister—our eight-month-old daughter, Faith.

Faith Hadley Kent.

The name was chosen to match the initials carved into my skin, transforming the ugliest part of me into my favorite part of me.

I turned a flaw into something beautiful.

And now, I'm turning my greatest fear into a life-changing experience with my husband by my side.

"I think, sometimes, the things that frighten us become more bearable when you don't have to face them alone."

Matthew's words have been on my mind all day, giving me strength.

Making me brave.

It was important we did a night jump, even though they are rarer and generally reserved for more experienced skydivers. There was a lot of training involved, additional equipment, and an extensive amount of courage…but I knew it was right.

I wanted to fly among the stars.

Gabe reaches for my trembling hand, giving it a squeeze. "I'm so damn proud of you."

Heaving in a breath, I nod.

I'm proud of me, too.

The star ring glimmers through our laced fingers, newly polished and studded with tiny diamonds. While I didn't want any other ring, Gabe insisted on cleaning it up and making it shine. He surprised me with it the night before our wedding last year, where we danced to music, shed more than a few tears, and toasted to a future I never truly believed in until the day I met him.

As I bring our clasped palms to my lips, I press a kiss to his knuckles. "Gabe?"

He smiles. "Tabs."

"Thanks for flying with me today."

He wraps a strong arm around me and pulls me close. "Always."

Pat Gleason signals for me then, telling me we've reached the designated altitude. I'll be jumping with Pat, while Gabe jumps with another instructor.

And I'm going first.

Closing my eyes, I try not to faint as Pat goes over the jump plan once again and connects our harnesses.

"Are you ready?" Pat asks me, his eyes shimmering a familiar shade of dark blue.

I swallow. "I'm ready."

I look over at Gabe and send him a beaming smile with my whole, pieced-back-together heart, before letting go of his hand. My chest is tight but infinitely full as we share a final, love-laced glance, and I spring forward.

With the stars by my side, I let out a gallant cry of joy as I jump.

I soar.

I fly.

And I don't look down.

The End

ALSO BY JENNIFER HARTMANN

Did you enjoy getting to know Tabitha's interviewer, the **hot writer**, Evan? His gritty, messy, revenge-fueled romance is now available in *The Thorns Remain*.

And if by chance you did NOT read *Still Beating* or *Lotus* prior to picking up this book, learn more about the other couples—Cora & Dean and Sydney & Oliver—in their own harrowing love stories.

The Thorns Remain

I used to be someone: an up-and-coming writer, a doting father, a husband who believed he was the center of his wife's universe.

Then everything crumbled.

Thanks to Benjamin Grant, I became a joke. A divorced man. A shell. Thirsty for revenge, I needed him to feel the weight of loss like I did.

Enter Josie—Benjamin's wife and the key to my vendetta. My aim was to infiltrate her life, seduce her, and use that to hit my enemy where it hurt most. It was supposed to be straightforward. But as any writer knows, stories rarely stick to the script. Now I'm caught in a plot twist I never intended to write.

Vengeance was the goal, and Josie Grant was my way in.

I never meant to fall in love with her.

Now?

There's no way out.

Still Beating

When Cora Lawson attends her sister's birthday party, she expects at most a hangover or a walk of shame by the end of it. She doesn't anticipate a stolen wallet, leaving her stranded and dependent on her sister's fiancé, Dean Asher—her archnemesis and perpetual thorn in her side.

And she really doesn't anticipate getting knocked out and waking up chained in a madman's basement, Dean in his own shackles beside her.

After fifteen years of teasing, insults, and never-ending pranks, the ultimate joke seems to be on them. The two people who always thought they'd end up killing each other must now work together if they want to survive long enough to escape.

But Cora and Dean don't know that their abductor has a plan for them. A plan that will alter the course of their relationship, blur the line between hate and love, and shackle them to each other long after they are freed from their chains. They're in this together—no matter what their unexpected bond might cost them.

Lotus

To the rest of the world, he was the little boy who went missing on the Fourth of July. But to Sydney Neville, he was everything. Her heart hasn't been the same since her best friend disappeared, but she's learned to build her life around that missing piece.

Twenty-two years later, the last thing Sydney expects is for Oliver Lynch to return. Having been captive underground for decades, he's unfamiliar with the strange new world that awaits him—but he's alive. He's here. And no matter how he's changed, he and Sydney both still feel the connection that runs between them.

But as their reborn friendship begins to feel like something more, Sydney and Oliver realize there are still jagged, painful truths creating space between them. The walls Sydney's built don't want to come down, and as Oliver hunts for his missing memories and lost time, he realizes his nightmare is not yet over.

With nothing as it seems, is there space for love to bloom in this dark place?

More from Jennifer:

ACKNOWLEDGMENTS

If you've been in my acknowledgement section before, you probably know what's coming.

Yep: I LOVE YOU, JAKE HARTMANN.

I think, more than with any other book, my husband was there to hold my hand through the ugly dregs of insecurity, self-doubt, and sleepless nights. This was the hardest book I've ever written. Bar none. Thank you, dear husband, for helping me piece this complicated beast of a story together, for giving me inspiration (Matthew's watch!), and for always being my wings when it's hard to fly.

You probably know what else is coming.

Yep: I LOVE YOU, CHELLEY ST CLAIR.

Chelley is my ride-or-die and the best developmental editor a gal could ask for. Thank you for taking on Matthew as your pet project and for helping me through the psychological elements of this story. Your insight is top tier and your friendship is invaluable. Only we could turn Earl into a laugh-out-loud caterpillar GIF war at midnight.

Thank you to my amazing beta readers: Paramita, Kate, and Shabby. Paramita, you convinced me to rewrite my prologue and I am forever grateful that I took you up on that. I so appreciate your honesty. I have the very best tribe.

All the thanks in the world to my line editor, Lori Wray White, and proofreader, David Michael. This book was almost titled: *The Comma Book*. Adore you both.

Thank you to my PA, Jen Mirabelli, and to my incredible PR team at Valentine. Your services keep me connected with my amazing readers and that's what it's all about.

And, of course—thank you, amazing readers. Where would I be without you all? Probably still writing Spuffy fanfiction, that's where. I love you. Thank you for allowing me to live this life filled with fairy tales, imagination, and endless love stories.

Until the next tale unfolds! Cheers.

FOLLOW

Give me a follow!
Reader Group: Queen of Harts: Jennifer Hartmann's Reader
Group
Instagram: @author.jenniferhartmann
Facebook: @jenhartmannauthor
Twitter: @authorjhartmann
TikTok: @jenniferhartmannauthor

♡

Merch, Newsletter, and More:
www.jenniferhartmannauthor.com

PLAYLIST

Listen to the playlist *HERE*

Falling Apart – Neverending White Lights

Karma Police – Radiohead

We Are Mice – Azure Ray

Red Right Hand – Nick Cave & The Bad Seeds

Lonely Ghosts – O+S

Tonight and the Rest of My Life – Nina Gordon

Precious – Depeche Mode

Undisclosed Desires – Muse

Just Pretend – Bad Omens

Collapse The Light Into Earth – Porcupine Tree

Losing My Religion – The Rescues

Ten Million Years – Black Lab

The Killing Moon – Echo & the Bunnymen

Look Right Through Me – Revis

Through Glass – Stone Sour

Night Drive – Jimmy Eat World

If I Fall – Tara MacLean

Gravity – Black Lab

Temple of Thought – Poets of the Fall

Falling For You – Jem

In the Blood – Better Than Ezra

I Want All Of You – The Verve Pipe

Blurry – Puddle of Mudd

Give Me Strength – Over the Rhine

Good Night Sweet Girl – Ghost of the Robot

Weapon – Matthew Good

Hanging By A Moment – Lifehouse

Love Her – Paul Durham

Don't Look Down – Superheart

With Or Without You – U2

Lay It All on Me – Rudimental, Ed Sheeran

Breathless – Better Than Ezra

Stars – Sixx:A.M.

ABOUT THE AUTHOR

Jennifer Hartmann resides in northern Illinois with her own personal romance hero and three children. When she is not writing angsty love stories, she is likely pondering all the ways she can break your heart and piece it back together again. She enjoys sunsets (because mornings are hard), bike riding, traveling, bingeing *Buffy the Vampire Slayer* reruns, and that time of day when coffee gets replaced by wine. She loves tacos. She also really, really wants to pet your dog. XOXO.

Made in the USA
Monee, IL
28 September 2023

43633500R00273